Under A Dark Moon

Brandon Brothers - ADAM

STELLA RILEY

ISBN: 9798715607379

Cover by Ana Grigoriu-Voicu, books-design.com

CONTENTS

Chapter One	1
Chapter Two	14
Chapter Three	25
Chapter Four	37
Chapter Five	48
Chapter Six	59
Chapter Seven	72
Chapter Eight	82
Chapter Nine	93
Chapter Ten	104
Chapter Eleven	116
Chapter Twelve	130
Chapter Thirteen	143
Chapter Fourteen	154
Chapter Fifteen	166
Chapter Sixteen	180
Chapter Seventeen	193
Chapter Eighteen	208
Chapter Nineteen	221

	Page
Chapter Twenty	231
Chapter Twenty-One	243
Chapter Twenty-Two	256
Chapter Twenty-Three	272
Chapter Twenty-Four	285
Chapter Twenty-Five	299
Chapter Twenty-Six	311
Chapter Twenty-Seven	321
Chapter Twenty-Eight	332
Chapter Twenty-Nine	346
Chapter Thirty	357
Chapter Thirty-One	369
Chapter Thirty-Two	379
Chapter Thirty-Three	392
Chapter Thirty-Four	404
Chapter Thirty-Five	413
Chapter Thirty-Six	424
Chapter Thirty-Seven	435

CHAPTER ONE

Within twenty minutes of bidding his friends good night and leaving the tavern, Adam Brandon became aware that he was being followed. This was annoying on several counts. He had no idea who would go to the trouble of setting a tail on him or *why* they would since, just at the moment, he didn't imagine he could be of any particular interest to anyone. Admittedly, that wasn't *always* true … but right now it was. Then there was the possibility that this wasn't the first time someone had dogged his steps; that it had happened before and he hadn't noticed. That pricked his pride. He'd thought himself better than that.

He continued on his way without altering his pace. He considered luring the tail into a dark alley where he could be grabbed, pinned to a wall and questioned. It wouldn't be very difficult. On the other hand, it might be premature. There was a chance, however small, that he was merely being followed by the only footpad in Paris stupid enough to tackle an armed man for the sake of a few coins. And that being so, the sensible course was to simply stroll onwards, taking a few sudden detours, to see if the fellow stuck with him.

He did … and was still there when Adam reached his lodgings on the Rue des Minimes. With a brief nod for the concierge, he ran swiftly upstairs to the nearest window and was just in time to see his follower raise a hand as if signalling to someone before melting into the shadows on the far side of the street.

Not a footpad, thought Adam with a sort of amused grimness. *And not alone. What, then? And why? What possible reason could anyone have for wanting to know my every move? But whoever it is, they're making a mistake because now I'll have to do something about it. And that's just tiresome.*

* * *

On the following day, in between giving a private lesson in swordsmanship to a youthful vicomte and overseeing a lively group fencing session, Adam sought out Emile-Henri Peverell to say, 'Is there any reason why I would be of interest to someone? Repercussions from the d'Orsay affair, for example?'

'Not that I've heard. What makes you think there might be?'

'I was followed home last night ... and not by a footpad.'

'A professional?'

'Possibly. Probably. Look out of the window.'

Emile did so. 'The fellow with the newspaper sitting outside Café Violette?'

'He's been there all morning.'

'Maybe he's a slow reader.'

'And an even slower drinker?' returned Adam, acerbically. 'I doubt it.'

'So do I. Shall I send Jacques to watch him?'

'No. If somebody wants to pay him to sit there all day, let them.'

'In other words, you will deal with him yourself when you're ready.'

'Yes.'

Neither of them bothered to say what they both knew. If Adam wanted to leave unseen, there were ways to do it. Although it no longer looked like one, the *Salle d'Armes* had been a theatre until royal decree had ordered its company to combine with that of the Comédie Française. A century of modifications had resulted in numerous peculiarities and more than one discreet exit.

The day wore on. At around three in the afternoon, the man with the newspaper was replaced by another dressed like a lawyer's clerk and carrying an armful of documents which he settled down to peruse in detail. Adam rolled his eyes. You couldn't fault their tenacity but watching from the same spot for hours didn't exactly help them to remain unnoticed. Whoever was paying them needed to find sharper tools.

He enjoyed an hour's swordplay with Armand Laroche, one of only a handful of the *Salle's* clients who shared his passion for the heavier style of military blade and was also skilled enough to present a challenge. Then he spent the last hour of the afternoon performing the series of exercises he had been taught years ago by a uniquely talented swordsman from Rouen; exercises designed to maintain a peak level of speed, flexibility, strength and grace. And finally, drenched in sweat, he sat down to give his blade the loving care it deserved.

He owned numerous swords. He collected them. Some he had bought and others had been made to his specific requirements. Most, of course, were in his rooms at Brandon Lacey ... but he had brought three with him, of which the one currently in his hands was his favourite. Its engraved gilt brass scabbard deceived one into thinking that the weapon inside it would be equally pretty. In fact, the sword was plain to the point of austerity. A Mameluke-style hilt with an ebony grip, a flat cross-guard held by brass studs and a thirty-two inch blade with a killing edge. But in weight and balance it was a thing of perfect beauty.

Adam left the *Salle d'Armes* just as dusk was falling and set off at a brisk pace for his lodgings three streets away. He was aware that the 'clerk' had been forced to snatch up his so-called documents in a hurry and was struggling not to drop them whilst scurrying along behind him. Once in his rooms, Adam watched through a chink in the curtains as the fellow disappeared into the building opposite. He continued watching until he saw light at an upper floor window ... and then, lighting his own lamp, began readying himself for the evening whilst reflecting that knowing where to find at least *one* of the spies at any given time might be useful.

He was spending the evening at the Comédie Française. Adam wasn't especially fond of the theatre but there was no escaping it when visiting the Peverells. Theatre, like swordplay, was in their blood and had been for generations; and tonight the entire family – complete with in-laws and cousins to the fourth remove – was turning out to see Emile-Henri's younger sister play her first leading role. So Adam dutifully washed, shaved and donned his best coat of gun-metal grey brocade, all the time wondering if the spy across the street would follow him to the Tuileries.

He did – with the result that only half of Adam's attention was on *Tartuffe*. The rest of his mind was busy sifting through the various alternatives of what to do *after* it. He'd had enough of being secretly watched and intended to put a stop to it.

When the play finally ended, he said all the properly appreciative things to Emile-Henri and asked him to pass on his compliments to Veronique who had been quite splendid. (In truth, Adam didn't know whether she had or not ... but she seemed to have remembered her lines and was sufficiently easy on the eye for half the audience not to care if she hadn't.) He politely excused himself from joining everyone for supper and made a leisurely way out of the auditorium, lingering for a few moments in the light of the flambeaux as if merely enjoying the cleaner air outside. Then, secure in the knowledge that the tail was following, he strolled past the Louvre in the general direction of the Tour St. Jacques ... and the network of narrow, twisting alleyways surrounding it.

He was just approaching the Pont Neuf when a large fellow blocked his path. Adam watched him tossing a cudgel from hand to hand ... and in the same moment, heard footsteps. A brief glance revealed that his faithful tail had arrived three steps behind him.

What now? he thought. And then, *Doesn't the fool realise I've watched him nearly as much as he's watched me?*

The cudgel bearer edged closer and in truly atrocious French demanded his purse.

Adam sighed. He didn't want a fight. He was wearing his only decent coat, for God's sake. On the other hand, he wasn't about to empty his pockets even if this *had* been about simple robbery – which, of course, it wasn't. Flatly and in English, he said, 'No. And you'd be well-advised to get out of my way.'

'You reckon?'

'I *know*.' His hand was on his sword-hilt though he had no intention of drawing it against a pair of idiots who didn't know they'd need more than a cudgel. 'Move.'

They moved – but not in the wisest direction. Aware that the tail was the closer of the two, Adam whirled around and slammed an elbow into his throat. The man gave a strangled gurgle and dropped to his knees, clutching his gullet and gasping for air. Adam, meanwhile, spun back to find the cudgel-bearer preparing to whack him across the shoulders. Pulling his sword part-way out of its sheath, he used the hilt to clip the fellow hard under the jaw. He, too, dropped like a stone.

'Next time,' he said to the tail who, though still looking sick, was struggling to regain his feet, 'perhaps you'll heed a piece of good advice when you're given it.'

Then letting his blade slide back into the scabbard and straightening his cuffs, he sauntered calmly on his way.

He didn't go far. At the first opportunity, he slid into the concealing shadows of a gateway and waited. He could hear a rasping voice urging his unconscious comrade to wake up; and in due course, a series of groans as the man seemed to be doing so. Then, the first voice again. 'You gotta get up, Cooper. We was to report to His Nibs right after.'

More groans and a muffled curse, followed by, 'Alright, alright. Just gimme a minute.'

And finally sounds of Cooper heaving himself to his feet.

Good, thought Adam. *I'd like a word with His Nibs myself.*

He remained motionless until, hearing unsteady footsteps moving away, he judged it possible to quit the gateway unseen. Apparently holding each other up, the pair were taking the Rue Pont Neuf towards Les Halles. Adam waited a little longer and then, silent as a ghost, set off after them. Progress, slow at first, grew a little brisker after they turned in the direction of the Place Vendôme. Too busy grumbling to each other, neither of them bothered to look over their shoulders. Adam shook his head over such carelessness and continued following at a discreet distance.

At the corner of the Rue Royale, the pair disappeared into an elegant building which he guessed housed a number of equally elegant apartments. He gave his would-be attackers time to get inside before entering the building himself. As he'd expected, a concierge asked – somewhat long-sufferingly – whom he wished to visit. Adam held up two *louis d'or* and said, 'The same one as the men who just arrived.'

The concierge eyed the coins for a long moment as if debating turning him away or asking for more money. Finally, however, he held out his hand and said, 'Second floor.'

Nodding his thanks, Adam let the coins fall, set his foot to the stairs and ran lightly upwards. Since there must be at least three men in the second floor apartment – possibly more – he supposed he ought to be plunging into the unknown with a little more caution. Instead, he found himself looking forward to seeing their faces. Reaching the door he wanted, he paused for a moment to listen to the rumble of voices within. Three? Or perhaps four? He couldn't tell. He considered knocking ... then wondered how likely it was that the door had been locked behind the recent arrivals. Not very, he decided.

Wrapping his fingers about the handle, he pushed slightly. The door gave. With a fatalistic shrug, Adam shoved it wide. Four men; two of them well-dressed, the older one seated, the younger coming hurriedly from his chair; and his former attackers wheeling to meet him, fists raised.

'*What the hell* --?' began the man who had risen to meet him.

And in the same moment, 'Cooper, Black – stand *down*!' ordered the other.

There was a moment's silence as everyone looked at everyone else. Adam closed the door behind him and leaned against it, his eyebrows raised. 'Well, gentlemen?'

The man who was clearly in charge gave a small appreciative nod and stood up.

'Good evening, Mr Brandon ... and my congratulations. You've surprised me.'

Adam inclined his head in polite acknowledgement.

'Thank you. But you have the advantage of me, sir.'

'My name is Goddard and my colleague here is Martin Fletcher. Cooper and Black you have already met. They were just describing their ... slight fracas ... with you.'

'That can't have taken long. But I don't appreciate being watched, followed and attacked in the street – however unsuccessfully. An explanation wouldn't go amiss.'

'And you shall have one,' promised Goddard. 'But first I think we may dispense with Messrs Cooper and Black. Show them out, Martin ... and please find out exactly *how* Mr Brandon was allowed to follow them right to my door.'

'Sir.' Fletcher nodded and gestured for the two men to precede him.

Adam moved unhurriedly aside to let them pass. He was aware that, while Black merely looked surly, Cooper's expression suggested he'd like to go another round. Adam raised a provocative brow as they passed.

'Will you sit and take a glass of wine?' asked Goddard. And when Adam did not immediately reply, 'The explanation you want may take some time. But perhaps it will help if I start by confessing that tonight's attack was in the nature of a small test.'

'A test of what? Whether I'd allow myself to be robbed or beaten to a pulp?'

'Of how far you would go to defend yourself,' corrected Goddard gently. He turned away to pour wine, having apparently no qualms in offering his unprotected back. 'The sword you wear is not a toy and I am aware that you are exceptionally skilled at using it. I wanted to know if, when provoked, drawing it would be your first instinct.'

Adam stared at him. 'You risked two men's lives to test my *instincts*?'

'Yes. What I already knew of you suggested it wasn't so great a gamble.' He turned back, holding out a glass. 'I don't work with men who wound or kill unnecessarily, you see.'

'I've never killed anyone,' snapped Adam. 'If you'd asked, I could have told you that. As for any possibility of my working for you --'

'Sit down, Mr Brandon. And please hear what I have to say before you refuse. I guarantee you'll find it interesting. You may even find it tempting.' The door opened on Mr Fletcher, 'Ah. Excellent timing, Martin. What did Cooper and Black have to say for themselves?'

'Excuses, mostly. But they eventually admitted that our friend here took them down in one move apiece.' He looked at Adam. 'Did you?'

'Yes.'

'Despite which it never occurred to them that you might follow,' growled Fletcher disgustedly. Then, to his superior, 'I'm sorry, sir. I knew Black was a blockhead but I thought Cooper knew his business. If anyone else had been available --'

'But they were not,' said Goddard. 'Look on the bright side, Martin. Mr Brandon has ably demonstrated that I was not mistaken in him.'

'Mr Brandon,' said Adam crisply, 'is waiting to hear why he's been dogged by a pair of incompetents since yesterday. And he'd rather it didn't take all night.'

'Take the wine, sit down, employ a little patience – and it won't.'

Goddard spoke pleasantly but with unmistakable authority. Adam took in the powdered hair, the unostentatious but obviously expensive tailoring and the steely glint in the otherwise unremarkable grey eyes. Whoever this fellow was, he was accustomed to being obeyed without question. Adam found he could respect that though, at present, he didn't particularly like it. So he accepted the glass and took the nearest chair, saying, 'Very well. I'm listening.'

'Thank you.' Goddard resumed his own seat. 'I am the head of a lesser-known government department – the purpose of which I will explain to you presently. *You* were brought to my attention by my old friend, the Chevalier d'Orsay. When he became a victim of blackmail, he informed me that you resolved the situation with great efficiency and discretion ... two qualities I prize above all others and which suggested that you might be a suitable addition to my small but multi-talented team.'

'If the two I met tonight are anything to go by,' remarked Adam, setting his untouched glass aside, 'that is scarcely flattering.'

'Oh for God's sake!' muttered Fletcher. 'Cooper and his ilk are merely paid to do as they're told without asking why. They aren't agents.'

'Quite so,' agreed Goddard. 'But to resume ... *might* be suitable was not good enough to justify my meeting you.'

'Meaning what, precisely?'

'Meaning that I first needed to know a great deal about you.'

Adam felt his temper starting to rise. 'Such as what?'

'Such as your background and personal habits. Enquiries have been made and, as you are aware, I have recently been having you watched. The results of all this are encouraging. Your older brother, the baron, remains largely in Yorkshire tending the family estates with some assistance from your younger one. Your mother is a widow and your sister is married to the gentleman commonly known as the Virtuoso Earl and who was very recently the darling of Paris. As for yourself ... you appear to have no skeletons in the closet or any of the usual vices. You don't drink to excess; you don't gamble; and if you have a mistress, I congratulate you on conducting your liaison so discreetly that I have been unable to discover it. There is, in fact, only one thing that counts against you.'

A pulse was beating in Adam's jaw – the only sign of the outrage that was bubbling inside him. He said, 'Only one? That's a relief. But you'll have to enlighten me.'

Ignoring the icily sarcastic tone, Goddard said, 'The connection between your family and the Duke of Rockliffe is a point of concern.'

This was unexpected. 'Why?'

'His Grace has a habit of learning things one would rather he didn't,' replied Goddard wryly. And seeing a shift in Adam's expression, 'Ah. You didn't know that.'

'No. I'm barely acquainted with him. Can you get to the point?'

Mr Goddard took his time considering the matter. Finally he said, 'That rather depends on whether or not you are prepared to listen with an open mind. If you are not, I will waste no more of either your time or mine – nor will I give you information you do not need to have.' He leaned back, his smile faint and glacial. 'Well, Mr Brandon? What is it to be?'

Some of Adam's anger converted itself into curiosity. Grudgingly, he supposed that men with loose mouths didn't become section chiefs in government departments; he was also beginning to suspect that this particular department was "lesser-known" for a reason ... which suggested that all this cloak-and-dagger stuff might actually be necessary.

He said slowly, 'All right. I'll hear you out and give what you say due consideration.'

'And keep it to yourself afterwards – regardless of the outcome?'

'Yes. That, too.'

'Good. I should begin by admitting that my department has no official title and is generally referred to as M Section – M standing for miscellaneous, which leads to the assumption that my people deal with unimportant loose ends. This isn't entirely untrue but neither is it by any means the whole story. Some of what we do – such as the business which has brought me to Paris on this occasion – can loosely be described as diplomacy. But our primary function is dealing with situations which have the potential to cause embarrassment in high places – namely, the Crown, the government, the military or any other prominent organisation.' Goddard paused briefly and then said, 'Questions?'

'Yes. It sounds as if it ought to be called *The Gentleman's Secret Protection Society*,' said Adam frankly. 'If it *is* that, I have no interest in it.'

'If it was that, neither would I,' agreed Goddard. 'We don't mop up the indiscriminate messes of the aristocracy. We deal with serious issues and our instructions come from top-ranking officials. Absolute discretion is vital – as I hope you can appreciate.'

Adam nodded but reflected that he couldn't see himself making a career of something that sounded like a cross between spying and the Bow Street runners. He said so.

'There *are* similarities, of course. But matters requiring espionage are the province of the Intelligence Service. As an agent of M Section you would most likely find yourself resolving situations not unlike the one affecting the Chevalier d'Orsay. And you would not have to make a career of it – which brings us to the part you may find tempting.'

'Try me.'

'Much of our work is, by its very nature, spasmodic. There are sometimes weeks or even months when our particular skills are not required which means that, with the exception of myself and Mr Fletcher – he being my second-in-command – all other operatives are kept on retainer. When called upon, they are expected to serve and are paid generously for their time and efforts. For the rest, they are free to live as they choose. Two of my current agents hold titles and the responsibilities that go with them. One sits in the House of Commons and another is a professor at Oxford University. *You*, if you were to join us, would be free to combine any personal ambitions you may have with fulfilling the occasional commission. For example, if you are considering matrimony in the near future --'

'I'm not.'

'Ah. Well ... I am merely pointing out that your life could proceed largely as normal.'

'I had rather supposed,' remarked Fletcher thoughtfully, 'that your ambition was to establish a *Salle d'Armes* offering serious swordplay as well as fencing. Is it?'

It had been. Certainly he and his friend, Felix Jordan, had talked of little else at university. They'd planned their partnership and every detail of the imaginary future *Salle* down to the last floorboard. So yes, that *had* been his ambition and he supposed it still was; just ... not yet. He'd enjoyed helping out in Emile's salon but had recently become aware that he wasn't ready to settle into the role of tutor; for a time, at least, he wanted something more. So perhaps *this* – which sounded as if it might be stimulating and even offer an occasional *frisson* of risk – might be it.

Goddard had been regarding him steadily and with patience. Finally, he said, 'You are considering it, I see. Good. Since it is unlikely that I will return to London before the turn of the month you may continue doing so.' He held out his card and, when Adam took it, added, 'That is the address of my office. If I do not hear from you by the middle of June, I will assume you have decided against joining us.'

Adam drew in a long breath and prepared to throw his future into the melting pot of chance. 'I'll say yes now if we can agree terms.'

Fletcher's eyes widened slightly. Goddard looked faintly amused.

'Terms, Mr Brandon?' he queried gently. 'Whose? Yours or mine?'

'Both. Provide clearer information about what might be required of me and what I'd be paid for doing it ... and I'll agree to a trial period of six months. I think that is reasonable.'

'Do you indeed?' Goddard came to his feet, indicating that the meeting was coming to a close. 'Unfortunately, however, that is not how this works. Come to me in London, Mr Brandon ... and we will have further discussions then.'

* * *

When the door closed behind their unexpected guest, Martin Fletcher rose to pour more wine and said, 'Stern-looking fellow, isn't he?'

'Very.' Goddard accepted the glass and nodded his thanks. 'But what one notices most about him is that he doesn't waste words.'

'He certainly has no problem coming directly to the point. Am I right in thinking that you've something specific in mind for him?'

'Yes. When I can persuade her to stop hiding in the country and return to London, I believe he might work well with Millie.'

'*Millie*?' Fletcher stared at him. 'You can't mean it! Since the Staplehurst debacle, the only men she can stomach have been you, her brother and Rory Farthing.'

'Farthing has withdrawn his services due to impending fatherhood and will probably retire permanently. If and when Millie resumes her position, she will need a replacement.'

'And you think that Brandon will suit?'

'Don't you?'

'No. She'll chew him up and spit out the pieces.'

'She will try. But I suspect that young man will give as good as he gets ... and without ever losing one iota of that chilly courtesy. When Millie comes to terms with that, I believe they could make a very effective team.'

CHAPTER TWO

As May became June and still living with her grandmother in Oxfordshire, Camilla Edgerton-Foxe put her uncle's latest letter aside and unanswered, along with all the others. She wished Grandmama was as easy to ignore. But she had long ago stopped answering Lady Martindale's systematic campaign to get her to London except in her head.

'It's been a year, Millie.'

Not quite. There are still twenty-six days to go.

'And there have been dozens of juicier topics for gossip since then.'

What difference will that make if he and I come face to face in public?

'Come with me for a few weeks – even if just to have some new clothes made.'

I don't need new clothes. I have a whole damned trousseau *of them.*

'You're only twenty-three. There's still time for the right gentleman to come along.'

I thought he had – and look how that turned out.

'You can't let what happened turn you into a recluse for the rest of your life.'

I'm not a recluse. I wouldn't give him that satisfaction.

'So won't you come to London? Just for a couple of weeks? No more than that. And if it doesn't go well, we'll come home and say no more of it.'

This time Camilla decided it was worth unlocking her jaws.

'Is that a promise?'

'Yes.'

'Two weeks and not another word on the subject?'

'Absolutely.'

'Then I'll come ... but not until next month.'

'*July*?' wailed her grandmother. 'Most people will have left town and those who haven't will be preparing to go."

'I know. But those are my terms.'

Hearing that curt, intractable tone, Lady Martindale knew she was beaten. Casting up her hands in exasperation, she said, 'Very well, then. July it is – for all the use *that* is likely to be.' And more gently, covering Camilla's hands with her own, 'It will all be perfectly fine, Millie. You'll see.'

That's what you said last time, thought Camilla drearily.

And it nearly – so *very* nearly – had been better than fine. It had almost been perfect. A dream come true … until it had turned, without warning, into ashes.

* * *

London, eleven months ago …

She hadn't wanted a third Season because it would probably be exactly the same as the first two, during which she had refused four offers of marriage from gentlemen with whom she hadn't wanted to spend a weekend, let alone a lifetime. But Grandmama had been so eager, so sure that this *time would be better, that she'd let herself be persuaded.*

'Just once more, Millie – to make up for the Season you missed last year after we lost your dear parents. And one never knows what may happen, does one? I'm convinced the perfect gentleman is out there somewhere. And wouldn't it be worth a few weeks in London for the chance of having your own home and family?'

So Camilla had resigned herself to the usual faces at the usual balls, assemblies and soirées … but not expected anything to be different this time around. She had certainly not expected something so extraordinary that it resembled a miracle.

It came in the form of Stuart Vallance, the new Earl of Staplehurst; tall, athletic and handsome enough to have stepped out of a fantasy. The kind of man who could have any lady he chose by merely crooking his finger. And, incredibly, he seemed to be crooking it towards her. He singled her out for the first time at the Cavendish ball, danced with her twice and called on her the next day, bringing roses and an invitation to drive with him.

Camilla was stunned, flattered and confused. Grandmama was ecstatic.

'He's looking for a wife. He must be turned thirty and he inherited the title just over a year ago. He's looking for a wife, Millie … and he's looking at you.'

In addition to the fairy-tale hero good looks, Lord Staplehurst was also charming, impeccably mannered and intelligent. He invited Grandmama and herself to share his box at the Opera. He escorted them to Montagu House to see the latest exhibits in the museum. He encouraged Camilla to share her opinions on art and music. Being the centre of his attention was heady stuff. Within a week, she was fathoms deep in love; at the end of three, his lordship went down on one knee; and a month later, they were mere days away from exchanging their vows. It hadn't seemed quite real. Sometimes she'd had to pinch herself.

And then, five days before the wedding, the world had come crashing down around her ears. She'd been at Phanie's, having a final fitting for the all-important gown and staring, entranced, at the image looking back from the mirror. The blush pink figured silk with its almost-but-not-quite-daring décolletage was so beautiful that it made her *look beautiful even though she knew she wasn't. She had felt happy and excited and as unlike her usual sensible, clear-headed self as it was possible to be … until voices drifted from the room beyond; voices she recognised.*

They'd begun by talking about what they intended to wear for the wedding. Since one of the ladies was Lord Staplehurst's sister, Sara, and the other, his Cousin Emma, there was no need to ask which *wedding. Camilla smiled to herself and paid closer attention. Later, when every word she'd heard was engraved on her brain, she would wish she hadn't.*

*'You could have knocked me down with a feather when we received the invitation,' said Emma. '*Val? *Getting* married? *I could scarcely believe it!'*

'He hasn't any choice. It was one thing putting it off while Papa was alive. But now … well, he's had the last year in which to come to terms with the fact that he can no longer shirk his responsibilities.'

'True.' There was a pause. Then, 'Does she know, do you think?'

'Harriet? She must do. Even if Val hasn't --'

'No. Not Harriet. Millie.'

There was a long silence while Camilla, suddenly oddly breathless, strained her ears.

'I doubt it. After all, who's going to tell her? Not me.'

'And not Val either, I should think. But surely he can't intend continuing as before?'

'I don't know. He doesn't talk about it and makes it impossible to ask. But it's been eight years, *Em – and with Harriet married for most of them! As for Fordingly, his health may be notoriously poor but he could last another decade for all anyone knows to the contrary. And as I've said, Val can't wait forever.'*

Camilla's heart was thumping and she began to feel a little faint.

What were they saying? Like Stuart's friends, Sara and Emma never called him by his given name – always Val, as in Vallance. So this was about Stuart and ... and Harriet Fordingly? No. Surely that couldn't be right.

Emma was saying something, her voice much softer and less distinct. The only words that Camilla caught past the buzzing in her ears were, 'a rumour ... her children ... true?'

'What difference ...?' replied Sara equally softly. '... Fordingly acknowledged ... legally his ... Val has no claim ...' And more loudly, accompanied by a rustle of taffeta skirts, 'But here is Lucy at last. Shall we take tea before we go to Bond Street?'

Camilla was no longer listening. Numb with shock, she pieced it together. Stuart and Harriet Fordingly were lovers. Stuart had been waiting for her to be widowed so that he could marry her. And her children ... Camilla had seen them. A girl and a boy; both of them angelically blond and blue-eyed. Like their mother. Like Stuart.

Her stomach heaved at the thought. No. No, no, no! It isn't true. How can it be? I love him. I *know* him. He wouldn't do this. He couldn't.

One of the girls fussing with her hem was speaking to her, while across the room, her maid prepared to help her change back into her ordinary clothes. Had any of them heard? But no. They couldn't have – and wouldn't have understood if they had.

It took an age to get dressed and all the time her mind was scrambling about like mice in a cage, searching for something solid to cling to. She told herself it couldn't be true. Then she tried to face the fact that it could. A bit of her brain wondered how many people knew ... another part said that was irrelevant. What mattered was whether or not what she'd heard was true. And there was only one sure way of finding out.

The coachman blinked when she'd demanded to be taken to Hanover Square but he didn't demur. Her maid, on the other hand, said urgently, 'You can't go to his lordship's house, Miss Millie! If anyone was to see --'

'They will see me calling on my fiancé, accompanied by my maid.'

'Yes. But --'

'It is not open for discussion, Martha.'

Taking her place in the carriage, the maid had muttered darkly, 'Well, goodness only knows what Lord Staplehurst will think. He's not going to be pleased and that's a fact.'

Camilla said nothing but thought, No. He's really not. But I can't help that.

The earl's butler didn't exhibit even a glimmer of surprise at his lordship's intended turning up on the doorstep with only her maid for company. He merely bowed, ordered a footman to conduct Miss Edgerton-Foxe to the drawing-room and said he would see if Lord Staplehurst was at home. Since it was the butler's job to know whether his noble employer was in the house or not, Camilla took this to mean that he was. She told herself that it was fortunate because if she had to wait until tomorrow to do this she would probably lose her nerve. Even now, her knees were turning to jelly and she wanted to be sick.

She stood at the window, staring unseeingly into the square. She heard Stuart enter the room but couldn't bring herself to look at him.

Concern threading his voice, he said, 'Camilla? Is something wrong? My dear, you really ought not to be here, you know.'

Swallowing, she told Martha to await her in the hall … and was grateful that her voice emerged cool and steady as ever.

'But Miss --'

'Just go. Now. And close the door behind you.'

There was a second or two of silence and then the door clicked shut. Stuart said her name again and, hearing him move closer, she made herself turn around. And there he was … her sinfully beautiful fiancé … all tawny-gold hair and forget-me-not eyes. Adonis with the physical proportions of Achilles. Perfect in every way. Or so she had thought an hour ago.

Something twisted painfully in her chest and must have shown on her face because he came to a halt four steps away from her and said gently, 'Sit down, my dear. You are clearly upset … so sit down and tell me what I can do to help.'

In the carriage between Maison Phanie and here, she had thought of a dozen ways to begin this conversation. She could even remember some of them. But all contained an accusation.

What is your relationship with Harriet Fordingly?

Is it true that you and she are lovers?

Are you the father of her children?

Was the whirlwind courtship so I didn't find out before it was too late?

Why did you walk into the Cavendish ballroom and cross the floor with eyes for no one but me? It was so romantic I never questioned it. But now I wonder if I wasn't so much *your* choice as Harriet's suggestion. Is that how it was?

And yet, looking at him in this moment, she no longer wanted to accuse. She wanted to trust – to believe. *So she said carefully, 'We are to be married on Saturday. If … if there is anything that you have not told me and which I ought to know … tell me now.'*

Wariness flickered briefly in the blue eyes and his shoulders tensed. He said, 'That is an odd request. Do you have a particular reason for making it?'

'I wouldn't ask if I didn't.'

For perhaps half a minute the only sound was the ticking of the clock. Then, his expression growing remote, he said, 'What have you been told?'

And that was when Camilla knew. Dread threatened to overwhelm her. She felt as if she was sinking into a deep hole. For a handful of seconds, even breathing was an effort and she only managed to remain upright by holding tight to a chair-back. Then, because pride and dignity were all she had, she said expressionlessly, 'Nothing. I've been told *nothing. But I have... overheard ... something. Something concerning you and – and Lady Fordingly.'*

'Heard from whom?' he asked, quickly. Too *quickly.*

'That hardly matters, does it?'

He didn't reply to that and when he spoke again, his voice was toneless.

'Very well. But I can't confirm or deny what you heard unless you tell me what it was.'

'You already know *what it was. You admitted as much when you weren't surprised that there was something to tell. So I'd like the truth. All of it ... from your own lips.'*

His mouth twisted and he looked back at her.

'Are you quite sure about that?'

No, *screamed her heart.* I want this not to be happening. I want to go back to before I heard anything at all. *But she said, 'Yes. I think I deserve that much.'*

He nodded and, gesturing to the chair she had in a death-grip, suggested again that she sit down. 'Please. It may take a little while and you look ... unwell.'

Unwell? *Camilla gave a short, hollow laugh, slid into the chair and waited.*

Stuart didn't sit. He frowned down at his hands for a moment and finally, with a complete lack of expression, said, 'Harriet and I fell in love eight years ago ... but neither my father nor hers would permit us to marry; mine, because he deemed me too young and hers, because he was aware my family coffers were still suffering from the excesses of my grandfather. I was sent abroad for a year. Harriet had her first London Season and received several offers of marriage from amongst which her family encouraged her to accept the one from James Fordingly.' He paused and, with a slightly crooked smile, added, 'To be fair, it wasn't just about money – of which Fordingly had, and still has, a great deal. Although he was a decade older than Harriet, he wasn't yet thirty … and at that time, his health appeared perfectly robust. But whatever the reasoning, by the time I returned to England, they'd been married for four months … and it was a further six before Harriet and I met again.'

This time when he stopped he showed no sign of going on. So after a moment, Camilla made herself say, 'And when you did?'

'Nothing had changed. One look was all it took.' He hauled in a breath. 'But she was married … so we avoided each other. I spent more time on one or other of the family estates. When in London, I stopped attending society events and stuck to my clubs and bachelor parties. A year went by. I expected to hear news of a child. I even hoped for it because I thought she'd be happier if she had one. But after they'd been married almost two years and there was still no sign … Harriet wrote to me. And everything changed.' He shut his eyes briefly and then, opening them on her face, said, 'Do you really need me to say it?'

'You began an affair.'

'Yes.'

'And it's still going on?'

'Intermittently. And before you ask – yes. Fordingly knows and has done so almost from the beginning. He … condones it.'

Camilla wondered if it was possible to feel any more nauseous and not vomit. It wasn't hard to guess why *Lord Fordingly condoned his wife's infidelity.*

'The children are yours? Both of them?'

Stuart had no more colour to lose. 'In one sense only. In all the ways that matter, they are his. I am not permitted any contact with them.'

That was hardly surprising either. 'You never see them?'

'Only from a distance sometimes … in the park with their nursemaid.' He made an abrupt gesture with one hand. 'You asked for the whole story and now you have it. I am fully aware how sordid it sounds and I'm not proud of my part in it. But it's how things are.'

She stared down into her lap, dreading his answers to the only two remaining questions that mattered. 'If I hadn't found out, would you ever have told me?'

It was a long moment before he replied. 'I don't know. Eventually, perhaps.'

'But not before the wedding.'

This time he said nothing at all.

'I see.' With enormous difficulty, she summoned the crucial words. 'And after it ... what then? Do you intend to end the affair?'

He drew an unsteady breath.

'I will try. But ... I can't in all honesty promise it.'

She had suspected as much but still the truth hit her like a punch in the chest.

'Then there really isn't any more to be said, is there?'

It was taking every ounce of control she had not to cry and her fingers had been so tightly clasped that they were numb. She fumbled with her gloves, eventually managing to pull one off so she could begin tugging at her betrothal ring. It was a Vallance family heirloom and had always been a bit too tight

Seeing what she was doing, Stuart took a step towards her saying, 'Don't, Camilla. Please don't decide now. I know you're shocked and hurt but --'

'Stop!' Shocked and hurt? *He'd sliced her heart in two. There was the part that wanted him at any price and the part that knew there could be worse pain than this and that it wouldn't go away. The ring came free and she held it out. 'Take it.'*

He shook his head. 'No. Just wait until tomorrow --'

'Then I'll leave it.' She dropped the ring on the table at her side and, though standing up seemed inordinately difficult, she somehow managed it. 'I can't marry you knowing that your heart belongs elsewhere and so, intermittently, *does your body. Neither will I spend the rest of my life in a – a ménage à trois.'*

'It wouldn't be like that.'

'What else could *it be like? And what if we marry and six months later Lord Fordingly obliges you by dying ... what* then?'

'Fordingly isn't going to die any time soon.'

'But if he does? If you can't promise to give Harriet up, you can't promise you wouldn't do whatever you had to in order to be with her, can you?' She turned to go and then, looking back at him, said, 'You should have chosen one of the young girls who would have been satisfied with becoming a countess. I want more than that – and I thought I had it. Goodbye, my lord.'

* * *

Since cancelling the wedding, Camilla had spent the intervening months at her grandmother's home in Oxfordshire, refusing to explain her reasons for jilting the Season's most eligible bachelor to anyone but Lady Martindale. When pressed to share them with her brother and uncle, she had said, 'No. Guy is young enough to do something stupid and Uncle Hugh is powerful enough to do something worse. Neither would make this any better.'

As days and then weeks crawled by she tried not to think of what she had lost but caught herself doing it anyway. Sometimes she wished she had never found out ... and at others, that she'd married him regardless, worked at making him turn from Harriet whilst taking the risk that he might never do so. Then, angry with her own weakness, she told herself not to be a fool and be grateful that she'd learned the truth when she had. But the reality was that she didn't quite believe it and wasn't sure she ever would.

Through her grandmother's correspondents, she discovered that Lord Staplehurst had given *'a profound and irreconcilable difference of opinion'* as the reason for their broken betrothal. Camilla supposed that was as good an excuse as any. No matter what lie either one of them had told, speculation was always going to be rife ... except for those who, like his sister and cousin, were already privy to the secret.

For six months she heard nothing of him. Then she saw the announcement of his betrothal to Lord Heston's eldest daughter and a month later, notice of their wedding. Poor Patricia, she'd thought; plump, bespectacled and shy. Another of Harriet's choices just as Camilla suspected she herself had been? Probably.

But what that said about Stuart, she preferred not to contemplate.

And now, almost a year since it had all happened, she had agreed to spend two weeks in the last place on earth she wanted to be ... and knew that when she got there, Grandmama would be on a mission to push her out into whatever society remained in town.

Truly, it didn't bear thinking about.

CHAPTER THREE

'You're going to sign up to something without knowing precisely what it is?' Max asked incredulously. 'Have you lost your mind?'

It was just over a week since Adam had arrived in time to walk Frances down the aisle of Brandon Lacey's chapel and Max was well aware why he hadn't mentioned his plans until now. It was so that, if they didn't go down well, he could escape extended objection and argument by leaving immediately for London. And now, irritatingly, he wasn't taking the trouble to answer.

'Well?' demanded Max. '*Have* you?'

'No.'

'Then explain to me what you think you're doing.'

'I already have,' replied Adam with a long-suffering sigh.

'No. You haven't. For example ... let's start with this fellow, Goddard. Do you even know that he is who he says he is? That he really *does* head a government department? Do you know anything about him at *all* other than the yarn he spun you?'

Adam silently flicked Goddard's card across the table.

Max glanced at it, then sardonically up at him. 'M Section? Seriously?'

'Yes. Why not?'

'Are you really that credulous? No – don't answer that. Just tell me this. Has he given any real indication of the type of ... let's call them missions, for want of a better word ... he'll be asking you to perform?'

'Not as such, no.'

'Then what *has* he said?'

'Just that his department makes potential embarrassments disappear,' shrugged Adam. 'And that usually the work isn't so very different from favours I've done for a couple of Emile's clients.'

He realised, just a second too late, that it was the first time he'd mentioned that.

'And what,' asked Max grimly, 'might those have been?'

'Nothing very difficult. One gentleman was being blackmailed. Another's daughter had run off with a footman and he wanted her found. That sort of thing. Nothing I had to fight my way out of – if that's what you're thinking.'

'And this is how you spent your time in Paris, is it?'

'Not all of it.' Tired of feeling as if he had his back against a wall, Adam got up and paced over to the window. 'I'm not a complete idiot, Max. I know what I'm doing. And in case you've forgotten, I haven't agreed to anything yet.'

'That is the only thing preventing me from chaining you up somewhere.'

Adam looked back at him over folded arms. 'Try it.'

'You think I couldn't?' Since the only answer he got was a faint, annoying smile, Max leaned back in his chair and said deviously, 'Not that I need to do anything so drastic.'

The smile evaporated.

'You won't tell Mother. Not after all the things you've had *me* keep from her.'

Max shrugged. 'I don't recall secrets of any particular note.'

'No? That time at the races with Lottie and Ginny Skilbeck, when --'

'I was twenty, for God's sake!'

'And I was eighteen.'

'So? You don't come out of it any better than I do.'

'*I'm* not married.'

'Neither was I at the time.' Max stopped and drew an irritable breath, aware that he was being lured into juvenile argument. 'If that was a threat to reveal my youthful indiscretions to Frances, all I can say is go ahead. She'll laugh.'

'Maybe,' shrugged Adam. 'But I'll keep your secrets if you keep mine.'

There was a moment of uneasy silence.

'As you're perfectly well aware,' said Max at length, 'that didn't need saying. Of course I won't tell Mother – but that's for her sake, not yours. Now, can we get back to the point?'

'Must we?'

'Yes. Turn Goddard down and find something else to occupy you. What happened to your plans to open a fencing academy with Felix Jordan? Have they been tossed overboard?'

'No. Just ... shelved for a time. I'm not ready to spend my life teaching.'

'If you think that's *all* it would be, you can't have the faintest notion of the time and effort required for running a business,' observed Max caustically. And then, more thoughtfully, 'Are you and Felix short of capital?'

'For the moment. Felix is doing some private tutoring and if I join Goddard, I --'

'Forget Goddard. Let me give the pair of you the money you need.'

'No.' Belatedly catching his brother's lifted eyebrow, Adam added awkwardly, 'I mean, it's good of you, of course – but no.'

Sighing, Max tried again. 'At least give it some thought, will you? We can call it a loan if you prefer.'

'No.'

'Why not?'

'Felix's father could easily afford to help but he won't. And if the academy is largely funded by Brandon money, it would make Felix feel more like my employee than my partner. Neither of us wants that.'

'I must be missing something. How is you earning money by working for Goddard any different from you taking a loan from me?'

Adam hunched one shoulder, stared through the window and muttered, 'We'll both be earning what we need. And ... Felix thinks he'll be able to help me.'

'Help with tasks which – if I've understood you correctly – rely on total discretion and may be highly classified?'

'Yes. I know it's unlikely but --'

'Unlikely? Don't be so bloody naïve!' Max shoved a hand through his hair and drew in a calming breath. 'All right. If you insist on doing this, you'll take Harry Finch with you. He has ambitions to become a valet – though I imagine you'll find his

skills in that department less useful than his ability to watch your back. And that, brother mine, is non-negotiable.'

* * *

Adam and Finch arrived in London during a mid-June heat-wave. They stayed at the Belsavage on Ludgate Hill for three days until suitable rooms were found on Bury Street, off St James's. The city was stifling and their lodgings felt like an oven. Finch said there was a storm coming. Adam, dressing formally to pay a call on Goddard and already sweating, remarked that it couldn't come soon enough.

Although he could have walked, he took a hackney to Goddard's office in the frail hope of not arriving with perspiration trickling down his back. The address turned out to be a very ordinary-looking house in an unremarkable and slightly shabby street on the fringes of Westminster. Adam rapped the knocker and waited. The door was eventually opened by a fellow who *might* have passed for a butler if he hadn't been in his shirt-sleeves and sporting a black eye.

'Yes?' he asked curtly.

'Adam Brandon to see Mr Goddard.'

'Got an appointment?'

'No.' He'd considered sending a note to ask for one but decided arriving on the doorstep without prior warning might be more informative. Now, he took out Goddard's card and held it up, saying, 'I have this.'

'Oh. One of those, is it? Right.' He opened the door just wide enough to allow Adam to enter, then slammed it behind him. 'Wait here.'

Left alone in the dismal hall, Adam came to the conclusion that M Section was either a governmental poor relation or cloaking itself in nondescript anonymity. From above, he could hear male voices engaged in what sounded like good-natured, if boisterous, argument. Then the doorkeeper reappeared at the far end of the passage and, without bothering to walk back, called, 'Come on, then. He'll see you.'

Is this whole place completely ramshackle? wondered Adam.

As he approached the open door, he heard Goddard say mildly, 'Have you mislaid your manners today, Rainham?'

In an accent and tone totally unlike his previous one, Rainham drawled, 'No, sir. I was merely staying in the character required by my current assignment. Also, of course, answering the door is not my job – but as usual young Geordie is nowhere to be found.'

'I sent him on an errand.' Goddard emerged in the doorway, minus his coat but otherwise neat as wax. 'Mr Brandon ... welcome.'

Adam accepted the hand he was offered. 'Thank you.'

'Come in and take a seat. Rainham ... what are they arguing about upstairs?'

'About who will take over from Farthing.'

'Dear me. I had no idea there would be so much competition.'

'There isn't. Everyone is busy nominating somebody else.' And over his shoulder as he sauntered away, 'But all pointless under the circumstances, wouldn't you say?'

Goddard sighed, closed the door and sat down behind his desk, saying wryly, 'Half of my team is currently without employment.'

'So why are they here?' asked Adam.

'Being part of a small, elite unit promotes a particular sort of camaraderie. And this is the only place where they can safely gather together to discuss mutual interests.'

'They aren't required to keep their various activities separate?'

'No. Sharing is helpful. But enough of that. I assume, since you are here, that you are interested in discussing my proposition further?'

'Yes.'

'Good. Then let me begin by outlining the nature of our work. The first thing to say is that no two assignments are ever identical. Fraud and blackmail are probably the most commonplace and our help is sometimes sought by other government departments. But Mr Fletcher is currently disentangling a rare case of bigamy whilst trying to keep it out of the newspapers. And Rainham whom you have just met is working as a doorman at a new and currently popular gaming house where a member of the Prime Minister's family recently lost a spectacular amount of money. Normally, I would not be asked to take an interest in this sort of thing. But since it is not the first such occurrence there are suspicions of foul play. Rainham is there to provide assistance, should it be needed, to the colleague who is playing at the tables in an attempt to discover precisely what is going on.'

'Wouldn't a Captain Sharp suit your purposes best for that?' asked Adam.

'Yes. And fortunately sharping is Mr Archer's speciality. If he can determine what irregularities are taking place, the house can be closed and its owner prosecuted.'

'I see. And do all your agents possess a particular talent?'

'Not all –but most. Mr Charlesworth, for example, is fluent in five languages and Vincent Clive is our cryptography expert. Another member of my team – currently unavailable – has an exceptional memory.' Goddard smiled faintly. 'We are an eclectic group, Mr Brandon. If you were to join us I believe you would find the company both stimulating and enjoyable.'

Oddly enough, Adam was beginning to think so too, but he said coolly, 'Perhaps. May I first ask about the remuneration you mentioned?'

'Of course. I should explain that not all of my people are paid. Several gentlemen are wealthy enough to serve for love – which means that the Section's budget is available for those less fortunately placed. You would receive twenty pounds a month on retainer and twice that when on assignment. And in addition to this, there are occasional bonuses from cases that fall into the category of private work – such as bigamy, for example. The gentleman at the centre of *that* will pay handsomely for the privilege of keeping his name and that of his unsuspecting family out of the scandal sheets. So ... are the sums I've mentioned acceptable to you?'

'Yes. But I hold by what I said to you before. I want a six month trial period – to be cemented or dissolved by mutual consent.'

'I believe I can agree to that.' Goddard pushed a document across the desk. 'That is our standard contract. You will wish to read and digest it before signing. If the clause referring to your possible demise whilst serving causes you concern, allow me to point out that I haven't lost an agent yet.'

'I'm happy to hear it. Am I right in suspecting you have a specific role in mind for me?'

'Possibly. It will depend on your aptitude during training.'

Adam's brows soared. 'Pardon me?'

'Why are you surprised? Did you imagine I would give you an assignment without first ensuring you have all the skills you might need to complete it successfully?'

'What sort of skills?'

'The nefarious sort – of which I doubt you have any experience.' Goddard's eyes held a distinct twinkle. 'We generally begin with lock-picking and then move on to burglary.'

Silence. And then, 'Is that a joke?'

'Far from it. I am not saying you *will* have to use either of those – or indeed any of the other things you'll be taught. But if the occasion arises when you might need to, it would be useful to already know *how*.' He paused and then added, 'This is our standard practice. All your colleagues have received the same education.'

Adam wasn't sure how he felt about joining a team of lock-picking burglars or whether he was ready to hear what else he might be required to learn. Deciding he'd think about that later, he said, 'Who teaches these so-called skills?'

'One or other of your fellow agents. In the beginning, we had to bring in ... let's call them specialists from outside ... but now everyone is fully adept and capable of passing on their knowledge. The process takes roughly a month – sometimes more, sometimes less. But our experience is that it's time well spent.'

'I'll have to take your word for that. Exactly how many agents do you have?'

'Usually twelve. But at present we have a vacancy.'

'Because Mr Farthing has retired,' agreed Adam dryly. 'Why is it that none of the gentlemen upstairs are eager to take over from him?'

'That is a subject for another day, Mr Brandon.' Goddard rose and offered his hand. 'Take the contract and read it at your leisure. If you decide to sign, bring it back tomorrow ... and come prepared to work.'

* * *

As Camilla had insisted, she and her grandmother arrived in London in the middle of July and took up residence in Lady Martindale's house in Mount Street. No sooner was the knocker back on the door than the first cards were left and followed by a handful of gilt-edged invitations, all of which her ladyship accepted on behalf of both herself and her granddaughter – thus provoking a continuous argument.

After four days of it, Camilla said flatly, 'No, Grandmama. You wanted me to come to London and I'm here. But I will not pay calls or receive visitors; and I will not accompany you to any parties.'

'Why not? Staplehurst is not in town and hasn't been for months.'

'And Harriet Fordingly?'

'Ah ... well, yes. She and her husband are still here. But it's unlikely the two of you would ever be in the same room, let alone meet. And surely she has more reason to avoid you than the other way around? Both she and Staplehurst are aware you could put them at the centre of a very nasty scandal and should be on their knees in gratitude that you haven't. Fordingly as well, come to that – spineless fellow.'

'What good would harming anyone – especially those unfortunate children – do? None at all. As for why I won't go out in society, Lord Staplehurst put it about that we'd parted due to a disagreement. Consequently, everyone I meet will want to know what it was and will find a way of asking. That's not a position I want to be in.'

Lady Martindale looked at her for a long moment and sighed.

'Then what *are* you going to do, my dear? You can't go on like this.'

'I don't intend to. Guy leaves Oxford in a fortnight or so and, though he'll undoubtedly want to kick up a dust here in London with his friends for a few weeks, at some point soon he ought to take up residence at Dragon Hall. As should I.'

Her grandmother looked frankly horrified.

'Live in that godforsaken spot? You can't mean it!'

Smiling a little, Camilla shook her head. 'Romney Marsh isn't godforsaken – it's actually rather beautiful in a strange way. And although I've been content living with you these last two years while Guy was at university, Dragon Hall is *home*. It's where we belong.'

'Well, yes. Perhaps. But --'

'We can't go on being periodic visitors whilst leaving its care in the hands of the lawyers, steward and household staff – excellent though they all are. Also, the house hasn't been refurbished for a decade or more. If Guy is to be tempted to live there, it has to be made more inviting ... a place where he won't be ashamed to bring friends.'

Lady Martindale's expression grew suspicious.

'You're planning to go soon, aren't you?'

'Yes. Directly from here – since that makes more sense than travelling to Kent by way of Oxfordshire.'

'You can't live at Dragon Hall without a chaperone. It's unthinkable!'

'Why? I'll have my maid and Mrs Poole, the housekeeper, as well as Coombes, the butler, and the rest of the staff. Also, it isn't as if I shall be entertaining.'

'It will still look very odd, Millie. In fact, I will be surprised if your uncle allows it.'

Camilla was fully aware that she might have to work hard at persuading Uncle Hugh. He was her mother's brother and, since the tragic demise of their parents, Hugh had been both her own and her brother's guardian. He still was, in fact – because Guy wasn't quite twenty-one yet and she herself wouldn't come of age until her twenty-fifth birthday.

She said stubbornly, 'I don't see why he would refuse. I've a right to live in my own home, after all. And as you've said yourself, the handful of families still remaining in London will soon be gone – so what would be the point of me staying here?'

'I don't know. Doubtless we'll find out this afternoon. Heaven only knows why it's taken Hugh four days to call on us. After all the letters he sent – none of which you answered – I expected him to be on the doorstep before we'd unpacked.'

Camilla shrugged. 'He'll have had other fish to fry. He always does. But if he's only coming to repeat what he's said three times already, he might spare himself the trouble.'

'I trust you are not going to tell him that?'

'Not in those exact words, perhaps.' She sighed. 'Grandmama ... I'm not saying I'll *never* re-enter London society ... just that I don't want to do it *yet*. And for the next few months, Dragon Hall will suit me very well. It's hardly the wilds of Outer Mongolia or infested with tribes of bloodthirsty savages, is it? I'll be as safe there as I've been at Elmwood with you. And if Uncle Hugh has doubts on that score, he'll always be welcome to visit.'

* * *

Uncle Hugh, otherwise known as the Earl of Alveston, arrived promptly at three o'clock and bowed to Lady Martindale saying, 'You're looking well, Ursula. Not found another husband yet?'

Lady Martindale's first husband had been Malcolm Edgerton-Foxe. Since his death, she'd buried two other spouses and the betting at White's said she'd probably manage one more before turning up her toes. Now, not batting an eyelid, she said composedly, 'Dear me, Hugh. Are you offering?'

He smiled. 'You know better than to ask that. I still miss Maggie.'

'Yes.' She patted his hand. His wife had died in childbed six years ago giving birth to their son. 'I know you do – and I know you have your heir. But you're not in your dotage yet. And Maggie wouldn't want you to spend the rest of your life alone.'

'Perhaps not ... but that is my choice.' He turned smoothly to take Camilla's hands. 'How are you, my dear?'

'I'm well, Uncle. And you?'

'I'm happy that your grandmother has managed to prise you away from Oxfordshire. And will be happier still when I am assured that you've relegated the events of last year to the past where they belong and are ready to re-join the world. *Is* that the case?'

'No. At least, not just yet. Perhaps next year.'

Frowning a little, he waited until both ladies were seated before taking a chair himself and saying mildly, 'You know, Millie ... I never pressed you for an explanation about what happened between you and Staplehurst. But the fact that you clearly held him in great affection, leaves in me in no doubt that the *'profound difference of opinion'* was very serious indeed.'

'Yes.' *Having two children by a woman he can't marry but refuses to give up is a bit of a stumbling block*, thought Camilla. But said only, 'I'm sorry, Uncle Hugh. I can't speak of it. I can only repeat what I said before. I did not break my betrothal lightly.'

'Since it sent you into something resembling mourning for the best part of a year, I never imagined you did.' He accepted the cup of tea her ladyship passed to him, dropped in two lumps of sugar and stirred with an air of remote concentration. Then, raising his eyes to fix Camilla with a very direct stare, he said, 'But enough is enough, my dear. I want your word that you *will* come to London in April next year and remain throughout the Season. If you don't wish to look for a husband, I will not press you to do so. But --'

'Good – because I won't,' she muttered.

'But I cannot allow you to become a hermit. Do I make myself clear?'

She sighed. 'Yes. And I'm not a hermit.'

'If you won't accept invitations or even step through the door, what *else* can you call it?' asked Lady Martindale roundly. 'You're in a prison of your own making, Millie, and Hugh is right. It has to stop. You have nothing to be ashamed of and no reason to hide.'

'I know that.' Camilla was beginning to feel her patience fraying. 'But I reserve the right to live my own life as I see fit.'

'And that means isolating yourself on Romney Marsh, does it?'

'What's this?' asked her uncle. 'You're going to Dragon Hall?'

'Yes.' She held his gaze with a resolute one of her own. 'It's time, don't you think? Guy will be down from Oxford soon and it's his twenty-first birthday in October. It would be fitting if he celebrated it at home.'

The earl appeared to contemplate this. He said, 'As my ward, it would be equally fitting if he celebrated it at Alveston House. But I will not press the point, Millie. I won't even try to persuade you to remain in Oxfordshire with Ursula – though I can't deny I think it would be preferable. Dragon Hall is somewhat remote, after all ... and the Marsh not the most hospitable of places. But if a few months there will help you to find yourself again I won't stand in your way.'

'Thank you, Uncle.'

'However, I want something in return.'

'Oh?' Camilla realised that she should have expected this. 'What?'

'I shall be holding a small dinner party on Friday. You will attend it.' He sent a fleeting glance at Lady Martindale. 'I'd be obliged if you would act as hostess, Ursula.'

Her ladyship beamed at him. 'I would be delighted.'

'Yes. I thought you might be. Camilla?' And before she could demur, 'The other guests will be people you know and like, none of whom will mention Staplehurst's name. You need to get back on the horse, my dear – and this is how you begin. So you'll come?'

She wanted to say no but recognised that, if she wished to go home, it wasn't an option. Sighing, she said, 'Since I doubt you'll take no for an answer, it seems that I'll have to.'

CHAPTER FOUR

At around the time Miss Edgerton-Foxe arrived in London, Mr Brandon was approaching the end of his training period.

He had learned lock-picking from Fergus O'Malley – an Irishman with alarmingly clever fingers and a fund of terrible jokes. Rainham taught him to identify the best means of entering a building, then took him to an empty property in Kensington for hair-raisingly practical lessons on getting in and out unseen without breaking his neck. Oliver Bamford had drilled him in the art of searching a room without leaving any sign of ever having been there; and Russell Lawford took him out on surveillance and tailing exercises in daylight as well as darkness and come rain or shine.

Adam had found all of it more enjoyable than he had expected and also oddly satisfying. The ten colleagues he had met – all but the fellow Goddard had described as being currently unavailable – were good company and the gentlemen who'd tutored him in this skill or that had done so with patience, humour and efficiency. Everyone shared an 'office' with someone else. Adam had been allocated space in the room occupied by Roger, Baron Falconer who, since his expertise was law and research, left Wilfred Street as rarely as Adam remained in it. It was noticeable that like Falconer, no one ever used their titles – although Vincent Clive was a baronet and Rainham a viscount – and that Goddard was spoken of with affectionate respect. In short, everyone made Adam welcome and shared the benefit of their experience in a string of sometimes hilarious anecdotes and with much cheerful bickering. In short, they talked about anything and everything ... except the one thing he most wanted to know.

What had Rory Farthing's role been? And why did none of the other fellows want to inherit it? That there had so far been no word of replacing Farthing struck Adam as ominous and made him suspect that he himself had already drawn the short straw. Shrugging, he reflected that there was always a fly in the ointment ... and if this was it, so be it.

On a morning when, for once left to his own devices, he'd planned to go through his personal exercise routine in the small yard behind the house, he was startled by the sight of an expensive-looking sealed missive lying on his desk. Inside was a gilt-edged invitation to a dinner-party at the Earl of Alveston's home in Berkeley Square on the following evening.

Adam stared at it blankly for a moment and then looked across at Falconer who as usual was half-buried behind a pile of books. 'This must be a mistake.'

'What must?' asked his lordship, busy scribbling a note about something.

'This. An invitation to dine with Lord Alveston – a man I've never met.'

'Ah.' Falconer looked up and removed the spectacles behind which lurked an exceptionally good-looking man and arguably the sharpest brain in M Section. 'Has no one mentioned that? Or no. I suppose they haven't. Most of the time, we forget about it.'

'About what?'

'Goddard. When he's here, he's just ... well, Goddard. But outside he's --'

'The Earl of Alveston?' cut in Adam.

'Yes.' Falconer grinned. 'There's no need for his title to shock you. It's only the same as Rainham – or me, come to that.'

It wasn't so much the title that startled Adam as the fact that it explained a remark Goddard had made at their first meeting about the Duke of Rockliffe's habit of "*learning things one would rather he didn't.*" At the time, Adam hadn't known that the identity of M Section's agents was restricted to as few people as possible. Now he did and could understand the concern. Because though *Goddard* might not know the duke, the Earl of Alveston almost certainly *did* – which put a whole new slant on things.

Realising that Falconer was still waiting for him to reply, he said absently, 'It's not Rainham or you who have invited me to dinner.'

'Oh don't worry about that. Goddard does this from time to time and he's almost certainly invited one or more of the others.'

'But not you.'

'Not this time, no.' Falconer replaced his spectacles and prepared to get back to work, saying, 'Cheer up, Adam. It will be a small party and he'll have a reason for holding it because he always does. But at least you'll get an excellent dinner – and give your valet an occasion worth rising to.'

Adam didn't know whether to shudder or laugh. He thought, *I don't have a valet. I have Finch ... who has incinerated two of my shirts with the iron and made me fear for my life on the occasion I was rash enough to let him shave me. And he'll want to* help.

* * *

With painstaking care, Finch laid out Mr Brandon's best suit of sapphire brocade and the most opulent of his vests. Adam, who had tactfully refused an offer to shave him and was doing the job himself, caught sight of this garment through the mirror and sighed. He said gently, 'Harry ... perhaps the embroidered grey silk might be better?'

Finch looked at the scarlet and gold striped one he'd chosen.

'You don't like this one, sir?'

'I like it. Just not with that suit.'

'Oh.' Disappointed but undeterred, Finch exchanged his choice for the other. For a moment or two, he watched Adam finish shaving and then, imbued with another idea, said hopefully, 'Your hair's getting a bit long, sir. Maybe I could give it a trim?'

'*No*!' The word came out as a sort of strangled yelp along with an image of what Finch might accomplish with a pair of scissors. Adam made himself take a calming breath. 'That is ... no, thank you, Harry. That won't be necessary. Just pass my shirt, will you?'

Finch shook out the shirt and handed it over proudly.

'I reckon I've got the hang of the iron now, sir. See? Only this one little bit of scorching down the bottom.'

'Yes, indeed. So slight it's hardly worth mentioning, really. Well done.'

'Thank you, sir.' He handed over the vest and when Adam had buttoned it, held out the cravat. 'Shall I --?'

'No.' Adam whisked it away before it could be crumpled. 'There's a sapphire cravat pin somewhere. Perhaps you could find it?'

The pin was produced. Finch waited until it was in place and then held out Adam's coat, saying, 'What about your sword, sir?'

Regretfully, Adam shook his head. At Wilfred Street, he was under orders to leave it with Geordie, the doorkeeper, and in Berkeley Square he'd doubtless have to surrender it to the butler ... so he might as well leave it behind and go out feeling naked.

'Shall I call a hackney, then?'

'It's no distance. I'll walk. And no. Before you ask, I do *not* need you trailing four steps behind me. Take the evening for yourself and don't wait up.'

Finch eyed him uneasily. 'But his lordship said --'

'I know what my brother said,' growled Adam, snatching up his hat. 'He's an idiot. And if you want to stay with me, you'll follow my orders, not his.'

* * *

The façade of Alveston House was one of pale stone and white columns. Inside, the lofty hall and wide staircase was even more impressive. Adam gave his hat and gloves to a liveried footman and followed the butler up to the drawing-room – a vast space decorated in sage and cream. Rainham and Clive stood before the fireplace with Goddard – *no, better to think of him as Alveston this evening*; and four ladies were clustered about an inlaid and intricately-painted harpsichord. All seven heads turned in Adam's direction as the butler announced him. Mentally girding his loins, he summoned a smile and bowed.

Lord Alveston strolled towards him, hand outstretched and simultaneously signalling to the footman bearing a tray of glasses.

'Good evening, Brandon. You're just in time to join us in a glass of sherry. But first – since Rainham and Clive need no introduction – allow me to present you to the ladies.'

Well, that solved one problem. Adam hadn't been sure whether he was meant to know his colleagues from Wilfred Street or not. Taking the glass he was offered, he exchanged nods with them and carefully ignored the gleam of wicked laughter in Vincent Clive's eyes.

Hanging back a little while the newcomer was introduced to her grandmother, Lady Rainham and Lady Clive, Camilla surveyed him clinically. He was tall, leanly-muscled and moved with the lithe grace of a cat. But she supposed the first thing most people noticed about him was his hair. She didn't think she'd ever seen that particular shade on anyone's head; blond, yes – but so pale in colour that the candlelight turned it to silver-gilt. As for his face ... the high cheekbones, perfectly straight nose and severely sculpted jaw rendered him striking rather than handsome. The slight cleft in his chin and the set of an otherwise well-shaped mouth spoke of a man who didn't compromise; and the dark, smoky-blue eyes under those narrow dark brows reminded her of rain-washed slate.

His looks aside, the fact that he was already acquainted with Rainham and Clive spoke volumes ... while the fact that Uncle Hugh had virtually twisted her arm to come this evening, told her other things entirely, all of them equally unwelcome.

Well, she thought clinically. *If Uncle got me here to meet his newest recruit it's because he thinks Rory will resign from the Section. Whether or not Mr Brandon knows that yet is debatable. But, just in case he does, a little discouragement won't hurt.*

'And finally, my niece, Miss Edgerton-Foxe,' said the earl. 'Millie ... allow me to present Mr Brandon. Perhaps you met his sister last year? She is married to the Virtuoso Earl.'

Adam bowed, wondering if he was doomed to being introduced as Julian Langham's brother-in-law for the rest of his life. Miss Edgerton Foxe curtsied and said, 'No, I didn't have that pleasure. But I'm told you have your own claim to fame, Mr Brandon – though I see no evidence of it this evening.'

Alveston gave a small laugh and moved away, taking Lady Martindale with him.

Encountering Miss Edgerton-Foxe's extremely direct gaze and finding it disconcertingly reminiscent of her uncle, Adam said, 'I'm not sure what --'

'Sir Vincent assured us that you always wear a sword. Was he teasing – or did you forget it this evening?'

'Neither. My mother insists that weapons don't belong in the drawing-room.'

Lady Rainham laughed. 'Well, one can't argue with that!'

'And clearly Mr Brandon doesn't,' agreed Camilla sweetly. 'How refreshing to meet a gentleman who always does as his mother tells him – even in her absence.'

There was a second of silence before Lucy Clive said hastily, 'Well, I admit that I'm disappointed. Vivian and I are agreed that there is something very dashing – even *romantic* – about a gentleman with a sword. It's a pity that wearing one is no longer fashionable.'

Glimpsing a slight shift in Mr Brandon's impassive expression, Camilla thought, *He doesn't like being called dashing and romantic, does he? Excellent.* And opened her mouth to embarrass him a bit more.

However, before she could get a word out, Mr Brandon said, 'Forgive me, my lady – but it isn't a pity at all. If it was fashionable, men would be walking around with blades half of them don't know how to use adequately.'

'And I suppose you *do* know?' queried Camilla innocently.

Adam looked at her. What was she trying to do? Discompose him? Provoke him? Get his attention? Or was she always this annoying?

He said simply, 'Yes. My swords aren't fashion accessories.'

'Swords? Plural? You have a collection of them?'

He found he was beginning to grit his teeth. 'Yes.'

'Dear me. Everyone is entitled to a hobby, of course. But how ... eccentric ... of you. Or do I mean thrilling? Yes. That might be it. I'm sure it's what Lucy would say. What do *you* think, Vivian?'

'I think you should stop teasing the poor man,' returned Lady Rainham with a hint of amusement. And to Adam, 'Millie enjoys baiting people purely to see if they bite back, Mr Brandon. It's a habit with her – and not to be taken personally.'

'I'm sure Mr Brandon is more than equal to any small challenge I might offer,' retorted Camilla, smiling evilly into those cobalt eyes. 'Are you not, sir?'

By now, Adam was fairly sure that she was going out of her way to make him notice her. Rainham's wife was a stunning redhead and Clive's, a vivacious, diminutive blonde. Miss Edgerton-Foxe, with her dark brown hair, greenish-grey eyes and somewhat pointed – and right now, pugnaciously lifted – chin probably felt out-classed. On the other hand, he couldn't help noticing that she *did* appear to have a rather nice pair of –

Abruptly shutting down that thought before it could be completed, he said, 'In the event of you issuing one, I'm confident that I would be, yes.'

Lady Clive gave a peal of laughter, Lady Rainham hid a smile behind her fan and Miss Edgerton-Foxe's eyes narrowed dangerously. Adam made a slight bow, murmured an excuse and walked away to join the gentlemen.

'Millie routed you already?' murmured Sir Vincent with spurious sympathy. 'Or are you making a tactical retreat?'

'Neither. All I was losing was patience.'

Rainham nodded. 'Yes. She has that effect. But she'll hold her fire over dinner.'

'Why?'

'Because it's a small party and Uncle and Grandmama will be listening.'

This, as it turned out, appeared to be true. Adam found himself seated between Vivian Rainham and Lady Martindale with the irritating chit two places away on the other side of the table. He relaxed. The food was as good as Roger Falconer had said it would be; talk eddied and flowed around the table on myriad topics; and at some point over moist lamb cutlets in red wine, Lady Martindale nearly caused him to jump out of his skin by exclaiming suddenly, 'Brandon! Of *course*. Why didn't I realise it immediately?'

'Realise what, my lady?' Adam asked warily.

'I know your mother. She came out the Season before my eldest girl – Millie's aunt Antonia. Louisa Fancott, she was then –

and quite a beauty. If I remember rightly, the Marquis of Repton offered for her but she wouldn't have him and chose Lord Brandon's son instead. Well, fancy that – after all these years. I trust she is well?'

'Very well indeed, ma'am. My older brother married recently and Mama is enjoying having another daughter.'

'I saw the notice in the *Morning Chronicle*,' offered Lucy Clive from the other side of the table. 'He married Frances Pendleton, didn't he?'

'He did.'

'I was in St George's the day she left Lord Malpas at the altar, gaping like a fish,' she replied on a gurgle of laughter. 'Served him right, dreadful man.'

There was a short, abrupt silence. Miss Edgerton-Foxe kept her attention on her plate but a number of eyes slid briefly towards her, then away again. Lucy coloured and took refuge in her wine-glass; and Lady Rainham said quickly, 'Will your brother bring his bride to London, Mr Brandon?'

'Not at this time of year – though they may pay a short visit in the autumn.'

Lord Rainham remarked that he would doubtless bump into Max at White's ... and the odd moment passed. Adam wondered what had caused it.

But when Lady Martindale gave the signal for the ladies to leave and the port started its circuit of the table, Sir Vincent said, 'Lucy didn't mean any harm, sir – she merely forgot.'

'I know that,' replied Alveston a shade testily. 'And if everyone else had behaved normally instead of instantly looking at Millie, it would have gone unnoticed.'

'It's still a sore point, then?' asked Rainham, pushing the decanter in Adam's direction.

'Sore enough to make her eschew society – but more of that presently. My apologies, Brandon. I imagine you've no idea what we're talking about.'

'No. But it's hardly my business, is it?'

'I wouldn't be too sure of that,' said Vincent, only half under his breath.

Alveston shot him a look then turned back to Adam.

'A little under a year ago, Millie was happily betrothed to a gentleman who was widely regarded as the catch of the Season. Five days before the wedding she called it off and fled. This is her first visit to London since then and she's here under duress.' He glanced at the other gentlemen. 'She plans to spend the coming months on the family estate in west Kent.'

Rainham's brows rose. 'Romney Marsh, isn't it?'

'Yes.'

'Is that wise? The Marsh has a reputation as being a hot-bed of smuggling.'

'It does. But that is equally true of the entire Kent coast and, despite it, murder and mayhem are rare these days. Millie should be safe enough. She's not a fool; and most of her people have been at Dragon Hall for decades so they're unswervingly loyal. But to be on the safe side, I intend to take an extra precaution.' The shrewd grey gaze turned to Adam. 'How much do you know about smuggling?'

'Not a great deal. It isn't much of a problem in the middle of Yorkshire.'

'Then come to my office in the morning and I'll educate you. I'm told you're ready to go into the field so I'm giving you your first assignment – the precise nature of which I shall explain tomorrow.'

Vincent Clive started to laugh. 'You're sending him to Kent with Millie?'

'Yes.'

'Is he being punished for something?'

'Don't be ridiculous.'

Sir Vincent shook his head. 'My sympathies, Brandon. She'll have you grinding your teeth into dust.'

'She certainly made a good start in that direction earlier,' muttered Adam.

'And will doubtless improve on it,' grinned Clive.

Frowning slightly, Rainham said, 'Forgive me, sir ... but isn't it time Adam was told who Millie is – aside from being your niece, I mean?'

'In this particular instance, that is irrelevant,' replied Alveston dryly.

Adam waited and, seeing Rainham and Clive exchange glances, said, 'I don't mind being kept in the dark about things that are not my concern. *Is* this one such matter?'

'Not ... entirely,' sighed the earl. And added simply, 'Millie is M Section. She is the twelfth agent; the one you'll have heard referred to as being unavailable. And a few minutes ago you learned *why* she was.'

Adam nodded, distantly wondering why he was surprised. After all, why *wouldn't* there be a female on the team? If nothing else, she'd hear things that the men didn't. But that wasn't what Goddard had said about her, was it?

He said slowly, 'Miss Edgerton-Foxe is the agent with the extraordinary memory?'

Alveston nodded. 'Yes. On rare occasions when we need information to which we cannot gain access through the proper channels – and from documents which mustn't be absent long enough to be missed – her skill is invaluable.'

'How, exactly?'

'Mr Farthing ... liberates ... the papers in question and takes them to Millie who is stationed nearby. When she's assimilated the information, she shares it with me while Farthing puts the documents back where they came from with no one the wiser.'

Adam struggled to prevent his reaction becoming visible. Was *this* why he'd been taught to pick locks and get in and out of houses unseen? So he could take the place of a fellow who was damned lucky not to have been caught a dozen times over, slithering around places he had no business being? *Hell.* Goddard made it sound so simple a child could do it. But it wasn't simple at all, was it? Farthing had been breaking into somebody's private office not just once, but *twice* in one evening. And they thought *he* was going to continue the good work? *Seriously*?

'As I said, such operations are required rarely and only in extreme circumstances,' added the earl. 'You may wish to cross that bridge when you come to it. For now, I am merely asking you to deliver my niece safely to Kent and then spend a few days assessing the mood of the area and looking for signs of anything suspicious or even merely odd.' He rose from his seat. 'We will discuss all that thoroughly tomorrow in the office ... but for now, we have lingered long enough and should join the ladies.'

CHAPTER FIVE

They set out for Kent a week later by which time Goddard had furnished Adam with a purse for expenses, directions to New Romney and advice about where to make overnight stops along the way.

'It's a little over seventy miles. Just about possible in two days with dry weather and good horses but you'd better bargain for three. Stay at the *White Hart* in Sevenoaks and the *Chequers* in Tenterden – mention my name in both. I imagine you'll want to ride?'

'Yes.'

'Then my stables can furnish you with a horse.'

Good, thought Adam. If there was a worse fate than spending three days trapped in a carriage with Miss Edgerton-Foxe, he couldn't imagine it.

They had met twice since the dinner party; once in Goddard's office and again when he had called in Mount Street to check that none of the arrangements he'd set in place had been changed. On the first occasion, she had spoken as little as possible and behaved as if he was invisible. On the second, she looked down her impertinent nose and argued. Within ten minutes, Adam's jaw was aching from the effort of keeping his tongue in check.

'I do not require your escort – nor do I want it,' had been her opening sally.

'But your uncle does – so you'll have it anyway.'

She scowled at him in silence for a moment. Then, 'Very well – if I must. But under *no* circumstances will you travel in the carriage with me.'

'Well, there's one thing we can agree upon. Next?'

'Pardon me?'

'Have you any other stipulations? No? My turn, then.'

Her mouth opened in surprise but she rallied quickly.

'As my uncle's employee, I don't believe you have any right to set conditions.'

'Incorrect – but you're entitled to your opinion. What servants travel with you?'

'Just my personal maid. I do *trust,*' she added in a tone dripping with sarcasm, 'that you have no objection to that?'

'None. No liveried footmen on the back of the carriage? Nothing like that?'

Apparently deciding it was time to intervene, Lady Martindale said, 'Millie will be using my travelling chaise, Mr Brandon – complete with my coachman and groom.'

Adam nodded but said, 'We won't need the groom. My own man will replace him.'

'Oh. But ... is that really necessary?'

'Yes.'

'Bring your valet, by all means,' snapped Miss Edgerton-Foxe, 'but make alternative arrangements for him. I prefer to travel with my grandmother's trusted groom.'

'I dare say. But not on this occasion.' Deciding to take Harry Finch with him hadn't been difficult. The poor fellow was never, with the best will in the world, going to make a satisfactory gentleman's gentleman but there was no better man to have at one's back. 'And you're mistaken. I'm bringing someone of much more use than a valet. So if there's nothing else ...?'

He rose to take his leave but she surged up to meet him, saying hotly, 'You overstep yourself by a mile, sir! It isn't your place to dictate how I travel or with whom. Your job is --'

'I think *I* am best-placed to know what is or isn't my job, Miss Edgerton-Foxe. I was ordered to see you safely to your home and make a brief survey of the area around it. With or without your cooperation, I intend to do both. Good day.'

* * *

As was only to be expected, this conversation set the tone for the following day. He sent Finch to Mount Street with two valises containing their gear. When he arrived himself on horseback, it was to find the carriage already pulled up, fully-laden, and Finch sitting gloomily on the steps of the house with their own luggage still at his feet.

Not bothering to ask the obvious question because the answer to it was equally self-evident, Adam dropped from the saddle and tossed the reins to Finch, saying, 'Wait there.' Then, swinging around on the coachman, 'You. Strap those bags on the back.'

'I'm sorry, sir, but Miss Millie said --'

'What she said is immaterial. It is I who am ordering this journey. Load my bags.'

Recognising the tone of command, the coachman nodded unhappily. 'Yes, sir.'

Adam continued up the steps and through the open door into the hall where the Edgerton-Foxe chit and Lady Martindale were taking leave of each other. He said, 'Forgive my interruption, ladies ... but I'd like to be in Sevenoaks before dark.'

Inevitably it was the younger of the two who wheeled round on him.

'We shall leave when I am ready, sir. And I don't know what colossal nerve made you think you could send your own luggage --'

'Oh for heaven's sake!' The frail thread of Adam's patience finally snapped. 'I know you don't want me here. You have made the fact abundantly clear. But do you have to make *everything* into an issue? I can assure you that it will be my pleasure to stay out of your way as much as is humanly possible. So with that point established – may we please just *go*?'

For the first time ever, she said nothing but merely stared at him with intense dislike. Finally, she gave a curt nod, told her maid to go and wait in the carriage and turned back to give her grandmother a last hug.

'Don't worry about me. I shall be perfectly safe and I'll write, I promise.'

'Make sure you do – or I shall descend on you in person.'

'That wouldn't be so very terrible. But now I'd better go before that wretched man drags me out by my hair. Goodbye, Grandmama – and thank you for everything.'

Adam watched her sweep majestically down the steps only to pause, frowning, when she saw Finch seated beside the coachman. Then she continued on her way and, wearing an expression that said she would rather touch a snake, accepted his hand to climb into the carriage. He slammed the door shut, told the coachman to start his horses and swung into the saddle, thinking, *That's one hurdle behind us. But how many more, I wonder?*

* * *

Inside the carriage and still quietly seething, Camilla thought, *Rude, overbearing man! Of all the people Uncle Hugh might have chosen to accompany me, why did it have to be* him? *Why couldn't he have sent Sir Vincent ... or better yet, Roger Falconer? If I* must *have a damned escort, why couldn't it have been a man I find remotely tolerable?*

But gradually, as the streets of London fell away behind them, her anger began to evaporate. If she was honest with herself, the root of the problem wasn't Adam Brandon personally. He was M Section's newest recruit and was merely following orders, just as all of them did ... and she couldn't reasonably blame him for that. But he'd been right when he said she didn't want him with her, except that it wasn't *just* him. She didn't want anyone at all – particularly a *man*. And, in addition to his unfailing ability to bring out the worst in her, the gentleman currently riding alongside the chaise was more than an escort; he was almost certainly also Uncle Hugh's spy. It was bad enough that she'd needed Uncle's permission to go and live in her own home ... but downright infuriating that, even after he'd given it, he was still keeping her under his eye.

And then there was Guy. She had hoped – however briefly – to see him in London before she left for Kent. But no. In a typical, hastily-scribbled note, he had informed her that he'd gone directly from Oxford to High Wycombe and a house-party at the home of one of his university friends. And after that, he intended to spend a few weeks in London, visiting his tailor, persuading Uncle to put him up for membership at White's ... and presumably indulging in numerous other pursuits he wouldn't tell his sister about.

Camilla sighed. It had been petty of her to order Noakes not to load Mr Brandon's valises. Petty ... and pointless because it was becoming increasingly plain that Mr Brandon ground opposition into dust like a well-oiled mill wheel. She told herself that she'd find him marginally less objectionable if he ever *discussed* anything instead of issuing orders and expecting everyone – including her – to jump.

She looked around for the novel she had asked her maid to put in the carriage but couldn't see it. 'Martha, did you remember my book?'

No reply. The girl was staring at something on the other side of the window.

'*Martha*!'

Startled and a little flushed, the maid said, 'Sorry, Miss. Did you want something?'

'Yes. *Evelina* ... the book I asked you to bring.'

Martha rummaged in the bag at her feet. 'Here, Miss Millie.'

'Thank you.'

'Was there anything else, Miss?

'Not at the moment.'

Camilla opened the book and found her place, fully aware that Martha was once more gazing dreamily through the window. Curiosity stirred. What was so fascinating out there? Turning, she leaned forward to find out ... and was rewarded with the sight of a muscular male thigh and the scabbard hanging cross-wise beside it. Her eyes widened. Mr Brandon was indeed wearing a sword. She recollected that he hadn't been in Uncle Hugh's office or in Grandmama's parlour; if he had, she couldn't have failed to notice since the weapon in question wasn't a decorative small-sword but a larger and very business-like looking one.

How ... medieval, she thought. And with extreme reluctance, *But Lucy wasn't entirely wrong. A sword* does *lend a certain panache that isn't ... unattractive.*

'That Mr Brandon cuts a fine figure, don't he, Miss?' asked Martha slyly.

Embarrassed and thoroughly annoyed with herself for having been caught looking, Camilla shrugged and turned back to her book, saying coolly, 'I daresay he does. If one likes that sort of thing.'

* * *

They halted for a change of horses and Mr Brandon gave orders for the stabling of Lady Martindale's team until it should be required for the return journey. Camilla and Martha partook of a light luncheon. Through the window, Mr Brandon could be seen watering and rubbing down his own horse whilst joining Noakes, the coachman and the fellow who was not a valet in a pot of ale. He did not come inside the inn and the only dealings Camilla had with him came when he once more offered his hand to help her back into the carriage.

The afternoon wore on. By the time they trundled into Sevenoaks in the late afternoon, Adam was heartily sick of keeping to the pace of the carriage but grudgingly glad that doing so meant the earl's horse – a big, chestnut gelding called Hector – had been good for the entire day's journey. The *White Hart* was very busy but mention of Lord Alveston's name quickly produced the promise of a bedchamber with a private parlour for his lordship's niece and a large chamber overlooking the yard for himself and Finch.

Needless to say, Miss Edgerton-Foxe merely announced that she and her maid would take their dinner upstairs and asked for the smaller of her trunks to be brought up. Adam bowed, told Finch to see to it … and said that he would like to be away before ten o'clock the following morning, if possible. Then he bade her a good evening and walked away wondering if she was as disappointed by not having the chance to say it would be a cold day in hell before she invited him to dine with her, as he was at being unable to reply that it would be an even colder one before he accepted. At that point, it occurred to him that there was something faintly worrying about having imaginary conversations with her … but since he didn't know why that was he pushed the thought aside.

* * *

The following day was another fine one. Hector was feeling frisky after his night's rest and made it plain that he wanted a gallop. Adam waited until they reached an open stretch of country and then, calling up to Finch and Noakes that he'd re-join them in a little while, turned off the road and gave the horse his head.

'Lawks!' exclaimed Martha, watching them go. 'Did you ever see the like, Miss?'

Head bent over her book, Camilla pretended she hadn't heard. But, careful not to be caught out a second time, she watched cautiously from beneath her lashes and was conscious of envy. Given the chance, she too would prefer to be flying over the turf on horseback instead of being cooped up in the carriage.

The rest of the day followed the same pattern as the one before; a change of horses and luncheon, then onwards to Tenterden and the *Chequers*. This time fortune favoured Adam in that a separate chamber was available for Finch. Sharing a room the previous night had been a trial. But there was no private parlour for Miss High-and-Mighty – which meant she would have to dine in either the coffee room or her bedchamber. Shrugging, he left her to her own devices and followed his nose to the scent of steak and kidney pudding in the tap where Finch had found an empty table and already ordered two pots of ale.

Camilla, meanwhile, eyed the busy coffee room doubtfully. With a male escort, she might have been comfortable dining there; without one, she wouldn't. Sighing, she followed the chambermaid upstairs and asked the girl to send up trays for herself and Martha. It was only this one night, after all … and tomorrow, she would be home.

* * *

Adam arose the next morning equally eager to reach journey's end and aware that a small amount of forward planning was necessary. He would deliver Miss Edgerton-Foxe to her door and hopefully, if she didn't throw a tantrum over it, manage a discreet word with her senior staff. But he needed to find lodgings elsewhere and Goddard had suggested New Romney – so Adam instructed Noakes to pull in there in order to deposit Finch and their bags at whatever inn he might find. Since the town couldn't be more than a couple of miles from Dragon Hall, it occurred to him that he could have sought the lady's advice on this – did he not suspect she'd direct them to some flea-infested hovel.

They drew up at the *Cinque Port Arms* at a little before three and ascertained that there were rooms available. Adam wasn't surprised. The town appeared to be of reasonable size and possessed an imposing Norman church but what he'd seen of the area around it – endlessly flat marshland, intersected by water channels and inhabited mostly by sheep – was less than inviting. Even the sun, which had been with them nearly all the way from London, had disappeared behind rolls of low grey cloud. All in all, he didn't imagine the place got a lot of visitors. He also wondered how it still qualified as a Cinque Port since it wasn't on the coast. He was still pondering that when Miss Edgerton-Foxe leaned out of the carriage window to greet the inn-keeper who, until that moment and wearing an expression of curiosity verging on suspicion, had been watching Finch unload their bags.

'Good day to you, Mr Hadlow. I hope Mrs Hadlow and the children are well?'

He beamed at her. 'That they are, Miss Millie, that they are, and I thank you for asking. Mrs Poole said you was expected – and coming to stay for a good long while.'

'For some months, certainly.'

'And young Mr Guy? He'll have finished his studies by now, I'm thinking.'

'He has and he will be joining me here presently.'

Under cover of this exchange, Adam took the opportunity to say softly, 'Be careful, Harry. We're escorting the lady home and may stay on for a few days – that's all you know.'

Finch nodded. 'Reckon they don't see many strangers – and like it that way.'

'I think so too. Settle in and order dinner. I'll be back in a couple of hours.' He turned back to address Miss Edgerton-Foxe. 'Which is our best way from here?'

'Continue on this road and at the end of the town, take the left-hand fork,' she replied. 'Two miles further on you'll see the turning to Dragon Hall on the left.'

Adam nodded and climbed back into the saddle. He imagined that once out of town you could probably see every building in a three mile radius, the landscape in every direction being utterly flat. And sure enough, a mile further on a long, L-shaped house came into view, standing alone amidst the sheep-dotted acres. For the life of him, Adam couldn't understand why anyone would choose to live in such a benighted place. However, he was beginning to see all too clearly why Goddard had concerns about a lady living here alone but for servants. The nearest neighbours were either in New Romney or perhaps the handful of cottages surrounding another church tower he could see in the distance.

As he got closer, he saw that Dragon Hall was a half-timbered, three-storey construction to which a brick-built wing had been added at some later date. In the original, medieval part of the house was an arch-way that presumably led to the stables and other out-buildings. It looked solid and comfortable rather than grand and it sat its ground with an air of superior defiance.

By the time they arrived on the gravel sweep at the front of the house, what looked like the entire household staff had poured outside. And when Adam opened the carriage door to offer Miss Edgerton-Foxe his hand, he saw her smiling for the first time. It was a wide, uninhibited smile, dazzling in its warmth; a smile which completely transformed her. And although he knew it wasn't for him, Adam found himself smiling stupidly back.

Thankfully, he realised that she hadn't noticed. She had eyes only for the folk here to welcome her home. She brushed past him in a flurry of dimity petticoats and virtually flew into the arms of a middle-aged woman, wearing the lace cap and chatelaine of a housekeeper while younger maids and footmen broke into ragged applause. Every face expressed honest pleasure at seeing her. Clearly, thought Adam, the 'Miss Millie' they knew was not the one he'd been travelling with for the last three days.

That lady had forgotten he was there. After hugging the housekeeper and offering her hand to an elderly man Adam supposed was the butler, she beamed at the crowd of maids and footmen and told them how happy she was to be home at last.

Her maid, still hovering in the carriage behind him said, 'It'll calm down in a minute, sir.'

'Will it?' Turning, the smile still lingering around his mouth, Adam offered his hand so she could alight. 'I take it Miss Edgerton-Foxe hasn't been here for some time.'

'No.' Martha descended but kept hold of his hand. 'Not for more'n six months.'

'That explains the furore of excitement, then.' He gently disentangled himself. 'Doubtless someone will help with the trunks in due course.'

'I could ask Mr Coombes, sir.'

'Thank you.' And when she showed no sign of moving but continued to gaze admiringly up at him, 'Now, perhaps?'

Sighing, Martha moved away. Adam folded his arms and leaned against the carriage. Noakes, having finished untying the straps holding the luggage, emerged beside him and said, 'Think they'll remember us any time soon?'

'One can but hope.'

A few yards away on the terrace, Camilla was about to go into the house when the butler halted her saying, 'Pardon me, Miss Millie ... I'll send Thomas and Ned to bring in your trunks. But what about the gentleman? Will he be staying with us?'

'Oh – no. No, he won't.' A sudden surge of guilt heated her face. How could she have left him standing there unacknowledged? Mama would have been appalled! Worse still, she'd given him a stick to beat her with. 'I'll speak with him myself, Coombes.'

'Very good, Miss.'

Camilla approached her unwanted escort with a degree of reluctance and fully expecting some sardonic remark. Deciding to tackle the issue head-on before he could say anything at all and addressing both him and the coachman she said crisply, 'I apologise. The pleasure of being home again temporarily drove everything else out of my head. Noakes ... my people will see to the horses and unload the carriage while you find food and ale in the kitchen. And Mr Brandon ... perhaps you would care to join me for tea?'

She didn't sound as if she wanted him to but Adam knew why she had felt impelled to issue the invitation so he smiled in a way guaranteed to make her grind her teeth and said, 'I would be delighted, Miss Edgerton-Foxe. But perhaps I might first wash off a little of the dirt from the road?'

'Of course.' She stalked back towards the house before he could offer his arm and thus force her to either take it or appear even more impolite than she already had. 'Coombes will show you to one of the guest rooms and Mrs Poole will have water sent up. When you are ready, please join me in the yellow parlour.'

'Thank you, ma'am. I will endeavour not to keep you waiting.'

'Oh, don't give it a thought, sir,' Camilla replied grittily, determined not to be out-done. 'I am happy to await your convenience.'

He bowed. She curtsied.

Then he followed the butler up the stairs, subduing an impulse to whistle.

CHAPTER SIX

Shown into a small but pleasant bedchamber overlooking the stables, Adam decided to snatch a word with the butler while he had the chance.

'Have you been with the family a long time ... Mr Coombes, isn't it?'

'Thirty years, sir. And butler for the last twenty.'

Adam nodded, approvingly. 'Are most of the other staff similarly long-serving? Not as long as yourself, of course ... but a decade or more?'

Coombes managed a small smile.

'Mrs Poole, the housekeeper, has been here as long as I have and Cook, nearly as long. Then there's the steward and the head groom – both of them have worked at Dragon Hall for fifteen years or more.' He eyed Adam blandly. 'May I ask why you're interested, sir?'

'Yes. Lord Alveston asked me to escort Miss Edgerton-Foxe here from London and to evaluate her safety once she arrived. Needless to say, my first concern was the loyalty of her household ... but you have laid that to rest.'

The butler's shoulders relaxed. He said, 'Please assure his lordship that everyone at Dragon Hall is devoted to the family. Both Miss Millie's safety and her reputation are safe in our hands.'

'I'm sure they are.' Adam set down his hat and began stripping off his gloves. 'I shall probably remain in the district for a few days in order to give Lord Alveston a full report ... so, if Miss Edgerton-Foxe permits, I may call again. Or then again, not, if I see no reason to trouble her.'

'Very good, Mr Brandon.' He stepped aside to allow a footman to come in. 'Here is your hot water, sir. When you are ready, you will find the yellow parlour by taking the stairs at the end of this corridor.' And with a very correct bow, he withdrew.

Ten minutes later, having washed his face and hands and tidied his hair, Adam followed the butler's directions and found himself entering a large, airy room with numerous small, leaded windows along both sides and a vaulted truss-beamed ceiling. He looked around, guessing that this was the original part of the house. It had probably once been a great hall until someone had put in this upper floor to make the space more usable, not to mention less draughty. The walls were painted a very pale yellow, the floor islanded with colourful carpets and the furniture looked comfortable. It felt instantly welcoming ... which was more than could be said of its mistress.

Miss Edgerton-Foxe – and what a mouthful *that* was becoming – stood before the empty fireplace, hands folded at her waist and back ramrod straight. Briefly, he wondered what he'd done to make her take such an instant dislike to him. He might not be as effortlessly flirtatious as Max or as charming as Leo but he didn't usually have this much trouble with women. So why was she behaving as if he had leprosy or was about to put his hand up her skirt?

Sighing inwardly and deciding to keep up the good work he'd begun downstairs, he laid his hat and gloves on a nearby chair and bowed. 'Miss Edgerton-Foxe.'

She dipped a miniature curtsy. 'Mr Brandon. Please sit.'

'Thank you.' He took the chair she indicated and glanced around again. 'This is a very pleasant room.'

'Thank you. Tea?'

'A little milk and no sugar, if you please.'

Silence fell while she fussed with the tea things. Adam waited until she had handed him his cup and then said, 'Why Dragon Hall?'

'Pardon me?'

'I wondered why the house is called Dragon Hall. I wouldn't have thought dragons flourished in these parts.'

Her expression became positively scathing.

'They don't flourish *anywhere*, Mr Brandon. They never did.'

'My point exactly. So why name the house after them?'

Another silence. He watched her debating whether or not to answer. Finally she said, 'While the foundations of the house were being dug, the head of a Viking longship was found. My ancestor thought it lucky.'

'The Vikings were here?' asked Adam, surprised

'Here and in many other places along the Kent coast.'

'When?'

'At some point during the ninth century,' she replied impatiently. 'Cake?'

'Thank you.' He accepted the small plate she offered, placed an apricot tart on it and picked it up again as if intending to take a bite. Instead, he said chattily, 'We had the Romans.'

Caught unawares, Camilla narrowly avoided choking on a mouthful of tea. Swallowing hard, she managed to say, 'What are you talking about?'

'North Yorkshire. We had Vikings as well, of course – but mostly Romans. Or perhaps it just seems that way because they stayed longer. At any rate, there are Roman remains all over York.'

'Really? How interesting.'

'Isn't it?'

This time he did take a bite of the tart and waited to see it she would pick up the conversational gauntlet before he ran out of innocuous topics. Or any topics at all, come to that. Small-talk wasn't something he was good at. Leo maintained that he rarely uttered more than ten words at a time, which wasn't so far from the truth. But he was going to drag some civility out of Miss Edgerton-Foxe if it killed him. And on present showing, it might.

Having let the silence linger long enough to become awkward, he said idly, 'What happened to the sea?'

This time she stared at him as if he was insane. '*What*?'

'The sea at New Romney. If the name of the inn where I'll be staying is to be believed, it's one of the Cinque Ports, isn't it?'

'Yes.' She thought for a moment and eventually, with just a touch of acid incredulity, said 'You *know* about the Cinque Ports?'

'Yes – though no one has ever explained why it's pronounced sink not sank.'

'Because this is England, Mr Brandon – not France.'

'I believe I knew that. But presumably there's more to it?'

Since he was clearly going to pursue it, she sighed and said, 'Yes. Anyone who pronounces it as 'sank' is obviously a foreigner to these parts – and probably also a spy.'

He inclined his head and said gravely, 'I'd better be careful then.'

'It would be advisable.' She hesitated and relenting slightly said, 'Most people have never heard of the Cinque Ports.'

'And neither had I until my sister and brother-in-law spent Christmas with Lord and Lady Sarre at Sandwich. Another Port that actually *isn't* any more – although I'm told that the problem *there* was with the river. Here it's the sea. So where is it?'

'About a mile away.'

'As much as that?'

'Yes.'

Despite feeling that the conversation was like pulling teeth, Adam refused to let her win by giving up now. 'Did it withdraw gradually over time?'

'No. A massive storm brought in silt and other debris. It altered the coastline and the course of the River Rother.'

'Really? That must have been a spectacular event. When did it happen?'

'Centuries ago.' She eyed him narrowly. 'Is history a passion of yours, Mr Brandon?'

'Not especially. But it seems a fitting subject for the kind of polite conversation one is required to make whilst taking tea.'

She smiled sweetly at him and pounced. 'Something *else* your mother taught you?'

'Yes.' Adam's brows rose. 'Didn't yours?'

Smiling inwardly, he thought, *Well, Miss Millie – you walked straight into that one, didn't you?* And sat back, openly enjoying the tide of hot colour rising up her neck and into her cheeks whilst waiting for the sparks in those greenish eyes to translate into retaliation. Eventually, however, when she continued to merely glare at him, he added helpfully, 'But if the topic doesn't suit, why not choose one you like better?'

There was only one thing Camilla wanted to talk about and it consisted of two questions. *How long do you intend to stay here? And are you thinking of snooping about, interrogating my servants?* But there was no point in asking something that was unlikely to bring forth a truthful answer. Moreover, she wanted to irritate him as much as he'd been irritating her … and so, recalling a fleeting expression she'd glimpsed on his face during Uncle Hugh's dinner party, she said, 'Very well. A moment or two ago, you mentioned your brother-in-law, the Virtuoso Earl. Let's talk about him.'

Under normal circumstances, Adam would have groaned. In the months following Arabella's wedding, he and his brothers had grown heartily tired of Julian Langham being everybody's favourite topic of conversation. But Miss Edgerton-Foxe didn't need to know that so he said, 'By all means. What do you want to know?'

Since she actually wasn't remotely interested in the gentleman, Camilla fell back on the question most people probably asked. 'Does he play as well as everyone says?'

'Yes.'

'I suppose your sister met him at one of his concerts?'

'No. But for Belle, there wouldn't have *been* any concerts.'

This, she decided, sounded marginally more promising. 'How come?'

'Our Cousin Lizzie accepted a post as Julian's housekeeper but Belle took her place.'

Camilla blinked. 'Why?'

'I have no idea. But she and Julian fell in love … which, for reasons too complicated to go into, led to the Duke of Rockliffe arranging a debut performance in London. And the rest, as they say, is history.' He shrugged slightly. 'The next question is usually do I like him – and the answer is that it's quite difficult *not* to.' He smiled at her, mostly to see if she would smile back. She didn't, so he said, 'There. A few minutes of civil conversation. That wasn't so hard, was it? And now I should take my leave.' He stood up, reached for his hat and gloves and bowed slightly. 'Thank you for tea, Miss Edgerton-Foxe. It was most enjoyable.'

'Wait a moment.' Camilla rose and pulled the bell. Although she wasn't quite sure why, it seemed important not to let him loose in the house unattended. 'Do you intend to stay in the district for very long?'

'My plans remain flexible. But if you're wondering whether you'll have the pleasure of seeing me again ... the good news is that it's quite possible.'

She opened her mouth to tell him not to flatter himself but the appearance of the butler forced her to change it to, 'Mr Brandon is leaving, Coombes.'

'Very good, Miss Millie. Allow me to show you out, sir.'

Adam knew the way but he had one more question to ask so he merely bowed again to his reluctant hostess and followed the butler from the room. When he was sure he couldn't be overheard, he said, 'Mr Coombes ... if I asked the question I'm about to ask you of my family's butler I know exactly what he would say and the scathing tone in which he would say it, so please don't take offence.'

'I shall endeavour not to, sir.'

'Is there *anything* that goes on in or around this house that you don't know about?'

Coombes looked at him with what he could only call pitying indulgence.

'No, sir. Nothing at all.'

'Yes. That's what I thought.'

* * *

In the stables, a young groom had unsaddled Hector, watered him and just finished rubbing him down. When Adam appeared, he said hastily, 'I'm sorry, sir. I wasn't sure how long you'd be and the coachman said as you'd ridden from Tenterden this morning so I thought ... well, anyway I can have him saddled again in no time if'n you'll --'

'It's all right. I'm in no hurry and I'm sure Hector has appreciated the attention.' Adam strolled along the stalls, inspecting the stables' other inhabitants.

A nice dapple-grey mare ... presumably Miss Millie's own mount.

Four chestnut carriage horses.

And a disdainful-looking sable stallion.

'Whose is the black?' he asked idly.

'That's Vulcan – Mr Guy's horse. But he's mostly not here so it's usually me who exercises him. Got the strength of the devil, he has.'

'I can imagine.' He reached the last four stalls and looked thoughtfully at their occupants. 'And the ponies?'

'Two of 'em pulls the gig when the chief shepherd goes out around the Marsh.'

'And the other two?'

'They aren't usually here, sir.' The groom was busy tightening the saddle girth. 'But old Medley over at North Farthing's got a problem with his barn.'

Adam nodded and wandered back the way he had come. 'If I re-join the main road, is there a way to the sea?'

'Yes. There's places you can cross the Wall.'

'Pardon me?'

'The Dymchurch Wall, sir. Runs for miles. You can't miss it.'

'I daresay. But what is it?'

'It's there to keep the sea out. If it weren't, there'd be flooding and the sea'd take back what it gave – leastways, that's how parson puts it.' The young man thought for a moment. 'Tide'll be out at St Mary's. You'd get a good gallop along the beach.'

'Hector would enjoy that. He got very tired of following the carriage.'

'I'll bet he did. There you go, sir. All done.'

'Thank you.' Adam climbed into the saddle and tossed him a coin. 'And you are?'

'Brewster, sir – and thank *you*, sir!'

'Thank Hector. He'll doubtless look forward to seeing you again, Brewster.'

* * *

He rode away from Dragon Hall at a leisurely pace. Sheep, placidly cropping the grass near to the road, ignored him. Adam found himself studying them because it wasn't possible to be a Brandon of Brandon Lacey and not know something about sheep. These, he observed, were different to the ones he was used to. For one thing, the sheep at home all had curled horns, the ewes as well as the rams. But none of these had horns at all and some of them didn't have the same off-white fleece of their Yorkshire kin but were a sort of pinkish, sandy colour. Presumably they were a special breed. He'd have to ask someone.

Reaching the main road, he turned back towards New Romney ... and immediately found the Wall. Brewster had been right about that. One really *couldn't* miss it. The stone and lashed pilings structure which separated the land from the sea was some twenty feet high and ran as far as the eye could see. At last, Adam began to understand how the centuries-old storm Miss Edgerton-Foxe had mentioned and this massive flood defence related to each other. The Marsh was partly land given up by the sea and partly land reclaimed by man. But for the Wall, as Brewster had said, the sea would repossess it.

The beach was also a surprise. Broad, sandy and long. Adam laughed and said, 'What do you think, boy? Are we ready for a bit of fun?'

Hector's reply of a seemingly impatient snort suggested that he was ... and the merest touch of a heel sent him flying across the sand. Adam decided there might be something to be said for Romney Marsh after all.

* * *

From a window, Camilla had watched him ride away and found that, despite everything, she couldn't help but admire the easy way he sat in the saddle ... his back straight, reins in his right hand while the left one rested on the hilt of his sword. Clothe him in buff leather and body armour and he might have been a Cavalier off to join his regiment. She shoved that thought aside, telling herself not to be fanciful. On the other hand, it was impossible to deny that when he'd entered her parlour with a thirty-two inch blade at his hip she'd expected at least *one* collision with the furniture and some awkwardness when he sat down to drink tea – neither of which had happened.

She continued to stare unseeingly through the window while she went back over their conversation. It was dispiriting. Without appearing to try, he'd fractured her composure at least twice before watching her fall into a pit of her own making.

'Something else your mother taught you?'

'Yes. Didn't yours?'

Just recalling it made her shudder. What was the *matter* with her? She had invited him to take tea because it was the correct thing to do and she'd owed him some small show of courtesy. But as soon as he was sitting on the other side of the tea-tray something inexplicable had happened to both her brain and her tongue and instead of taking control of the conversation and being coolly polite, she'd let him rattle her from the onset.

Never mind what's the matter with me, she thought grimly. *What is it about* him *that enables him to get under my skin every time we exchange more than two words with each other? I'll tell Coombes to say I'm not at home if he should call. And with a bit of luck, he'll take himself back to London without me ever having to lay eyes on him again.*

* * *

Back at the *Port Arms*, Adam found his gear neatly stacked away in a spartan but scrupulously clean bedchamber and enticing smells coming from the kitchen. Running Finch to earth in the garden at the back of the inn enjoying a tankard of ale, he said, 'Any problems, Harry?'

'No, sir.'

'Is anyone else staying here?'

'Not as I've seen. But they probably get a few in the taproom of an evening.'

'Which may be useful,' Adam nodded. Then, 'How's the ale?'

'Champion, sir. Want me to fetch you some?'

'In a moment. I was thinking I might take a stroll around the town.'

'Already did that while I was waiting, sir,' said Finch. 'There ain't much to see. And the few folks I met weren't exactly the chatty sort. How did it go up at the lady's house?'

'She got a royal welcome. There's no problem there that I can see.' *Aside from those ponies*, whispered a little voice in his head. *Are they* really *there as a favour for a neighbour?* 'Since we may be here for a little while, we'll spend tomorrow familiarising ourselves with the town ... and finding out how many folk are inclined to pass the time of day with us.'

'Not many, I'll be bound.'

'Probably. But it won't hurt to let the locals get used to us. Then, the next day, we'll explore the surrounding area, paying particular attention to the coast. You'll need a horse for that, Harry, so ask the innkeeper if he has one for hire. You can fetch me that ale while you're about it – and find out how soon they can serve dinner.'

Five minutes later, Finch returned with the promised ale, news that dinner would be served in an hour and that, though the *Cinque Port Arms* didn't have a horse for hire, the blacksmith at the far end of the High Street did.

'So I thought I'd go and see about it now,' finished Finch, draining his own tankard. 'How long shall I say we want it for?'

'I don't know but tell them a week.' Adam handed over a couple of guineas. 'It shouldn't be more than that.'

After Finch had gone, Adam remained outside. The sun had finally put in a late-afternoon appearance and the garden was a pleasant place to sip his ale and consider some of the information given to him by Goddard.

'You may not have realised it,' he'd said, 'but England has been almost constantly at war since the turn of the century. At present, we're sending troops to the Colonies; before that it was the Seven Years War; and before *that*, the Jacobites – twice. Wars are expensive; the money to pay for them comes largely from taxation; and taxation is the root cause of smuggling. Put simply, it works like this. English wool is much sought after in France and the Low Countries so exported wool is heavily taxed, resulting in farmers trading through the smugglers. French brandy and silk, Belgian lace, Dutch gin and tobacco are all subject to high import duties, so smugglers provide affordable alternatives. Basically, the Trade works both ways. It's been going on for centuries – and no government has ever managed to stamp it out.'

'Why not?'

'Three reasons. Those engaged in it know every trick in the book. There are few arrests because there are never enough Revenue cutters to patrol off-shore or dragoons to back up the Preventive Officers on land – thanks, once again, to those wars I mentioned. And on Romney Marsh, as elsewhere, you can be fairly sure that *everyone* is involved to some degree or other. Fishermen take their boats out to meet French and Dutch ships mid-channel and sail back fully laden. Farm labourers are paid to unload contraband and carry it inland to temporary hiding places until --'

'Such as?' cut in Adam. 'Caves? Tunnels? Where?'

Goddard shook his head, smiling faintly.

'Romney Marsh is what its name suggests. A marsh ... so no caves or tunnels. My own suspicion is that the local churches are used. There are a surprising number in a relatively small area – all of them with belfries or crypts, spaces suitable for overnight storage. But to resume ... as soon as possible after coming ashore, the goods are moved on – mostly to London. After that, as you'll realise, merchants get cut-price silk and lace which are subsequently bought by otherwise respectable members of society; cheap brandy and tobacco are widely available ... and it's estimated that four-fifths of the tea drunk in England is smuggled because the legally imported tea brought in by the East India Company is taxed at seventy percent over cost.'

'No wonder my mother complains,' murmured Adam. 'But if, as you say, so many people are involved, why isn't information easily obtained?'

'Because no one talks. Ever. The code of silence is absolute. It's fuelled by loyalty or fear ... and by money. Those who do the actual leg-work are well paid for both their efforts and their silence.' Goddard paused and then, coming to the point, said, 'The current situation is this. There has recently been a marked increase of smuggling on Romney Marsh which suggests the existence of a large-scale, efficient and well-funded operation, controlled by someone in the local area but with a chain of command that stretches much higher up. We need a way into that chain in order to follow it upwards ... and for that, we need someone on the inside who can be persuaded to talk.'

'I see. And is that my brief? To find you an informer?'

'Yes – but not for the reason you are thinking. I've told you a lot about smuggling because it is your route to uncovering something darker and far more dangerous which goes on hand in hand with it.'

Hoping that Goddard was finally getting to the point, Adam said, 'Go on.'

'The Trade doesn't just stick to brandy and tea. It also carries letters to and from foreign agents ... and sometimes even the spies themselves. The Intelligence Service has arrested two such in the last three months, both of whom were ... persuaded ... to admit having arrived via Romney Marsh.'

'In which case, presumably the Intelligence Service has taken measures of its own.'

'It has. Two agents were sent to investigate. One barely escaped with his life; the other never returned. Sir Oswald Rayburn, currently Head of Intelligence, has concluded that sending strangers into the area without supplying them with a motive for being there is asking for trouble.' Goddard fixed him with an acute grey stare. 'I believe I told you that M Section is sometimes asked to assist other departments. This is one of them. And fortunately, Millie's sudden desire to go home and my natural concerns about her safety make a plausible excuse for sending you with her.'

Adam thought that, as cover stories went, this one was paper-thin. But he said bluntly, 'From what you've said so far, I'm surprised you're letting Miss Edgerton-Foxe go there at all.'

'If I thought she'd be in any danger, I wouldn't be. But the violence that characterised the Hawkhurst gang and others like it forty years ago has stopped; and since Millie will have no dealings with the smugglers, they will have no reason to take any interest in her. She will be safe enough. *You*, on the other hand, will need to be extremely careful. I can't stress that too strongly. For example, there will be Preventive Officers at Rye or Hythe – perhaps both – but *under no circumstances* must you be seen talking to them. And do not ask questions that might lead folk to guess what you are looking for. The Marsh is a place where men can vanish overnight with no questions asked ... so take every precaution and watch your back at all times.'

'Lovely,' murmured Adam. 'Is there anyone that I *can* talk to?'

'Six months ago, I'd have advised you to call on Viscount Wingham – his estate lies near Rye. But he passed away two months ago which means that the family will be in mourning, so ...' Goddard stopped abruptly, as a thought apparently struck him. 'Wingham's heir is one of Rockliffe's friends so you may have met him at your sister's wedding. Sebastian Audley?'

'Audley? Yes. Very briefly – but yes. He and my older brother became friendly.' He paused as another name came to mind. 'I also met Lord Sarre and he --'

'Lives near Sandwich,' interrupted Goddard. 'Yes. Further away from the Marsh than Rye ... but still ... I believe a note to both gentlemen might be politic. I will see to it.'

'Thank you, sir. Is there anything else I should know?'

'Only that I'd prefer Millie to remain ignorant of your activities if at all possible.'

Adam nodded absently. 'You don't think Miss Edgerton-Foxe must know about the smuggling and be able to guess why I'm there without being told?'

'Probably – in which case you may have no choice but to admit it. But without mention of spies or vanished agents, if you please.' Goddard rose and stretched. 'And one last thing. Keep me informed of developments – in particular, any increase in violence, civil unrest or visiting Frenchmen. If *that* happens, you may expect to be either recalled or reinforced.'

CHAPTER SEVEN

On her first full day back at home, Camilla took a very early ride along St. Mary's Bay, enjoying both the solitude and the freedom to gallop across firm, wet sand. Then she spent the rest of the morning speaking to each of the servants in turn and hearing all the latest news. Among other things, she learned that Ruth and Tom Bradley's baby was another girl; that old Mr Fairclough had broken his leg; and young Ben Randall had gone as apprentice to the stonemason at Burmarsh. She, in turn, was asked about her brother and grandmother and her uncle, the earl ... and whether she was really here to stay after more than two years of merely visiting. It felt good, she discovered, to be able to tell them that she was.

The single, catastrophic event that changed everything had taken place in the spring of 1777. Guy had been in his second term at Oxford and Camilla was preparing for her third London Season. Papa was looking forward to seeing old friends at his club; Mama cheerfully predicted that *this* was the year Millie would make the perfect match. Everyone was happy and optimistic. And then tragedy had struck. Returning from a dinner party in Hythe, Mama and Papa had been caught in a sudden storm. With the road turning swiftly to mud, the coachman had lost control of his horses and the carriage had careered from the road into a freak high tide. In the rain and the dark and with no help for miles, the result had been inevitable. Anyone who might have survived the carnage drowned.

After the funeral, Uncle Hugh – their maternal uncle and now their guardian – had insisted that Guy return to university to complete his education. And Lady Martindale, their paternal grandmother, swept Camilla away to her own home in Oxfordshire where, aside from periodic visits to Dragon Hall, she had remained through her year of mourning and then her final, catastrophic Season.

During her absence, the house had been well cared for but nothing had been done in the way of refurbishment and Camilla was determined to remedy that. Consequently, she and Mrs

Poole inspected every room, making lists of which ones needed fresh paint and which curtains and hangings ought to be replaced. Then they sat down and discussed where to begin and how best to set the work in hand.

Throughout it all, Camilla found herself prey to conflicting emotions. While it was comforting to be once again sleeping in her own bedchamber, she was constantly aware of an eerie feeling that, if she opened the library door quickly enough, she would find Papa sitting in his favourite chair or that the faint scent of lilac in the parlour was because Mama had only just left the room. She told herself that these fancies were natural and would fade with time. Then she asked herself if she wanted them to. But in the meantime, the best antidote was to keep busy … and fortunately there was a great deal to be done.

Equally fortunately, money was not a problem. The Dragon Hall flocks of Romney sheep were extremely well-tended and their fleeces fetched superior prices. In addition, Papa had made a number of very shrewd investments which yielded excellent quarterly returns. Consequently, when Guy reached his majority, he would inherit a comfortable fortune.

It was in response to this thought as she sat with Mrs Poole amidst the litter of pattern books and fabric samples she had ordered during her last visit that Camilla said slowly, 'I think perhaps it's time my brother moved into the master suite … and since I doubt he'll be home for another few weeks, we could have it refurbished before he gets here. If the room looks different – new curtains and bed hangings and perhaps some fresh paint – Guy will view the idea more kindly.'

The housekeeper nodded but said tentatively, 'And your Mama's room?'

'No. I'd like that kept as it is for now … possibly even until Guy chooses a bride.'

'Well, that won't be any time soon, Miss Millie.'

'No. I imagine not.' She picked up the swatch of bronze and blue brocade and let it slide against her fingers. 'Papa's room gets plenty of sun so this might be nice. Completely different from the red velvet that's there now but sufficiently masculine, wouldn't you say? And I believe I will purchase this dark green damask for the library as well so we're ready to attack that next.' She stood up and stretched. 'Can I leave you to work out the quantities for each?'

'Yes. I'll set the maids to measuring up first thing tomorrow.' Mrs Poole also rose. 'But what about *your* rooms? The curtains are badly faded.'

'I know, but they can wait. I want to refresh the reception rooms and spare bedchambers first so that if Guy wants to invite friends to stay, he needn't fear them thinking his home looks shabby.'

'Young gentlemen don't notice shabby, Miss Millie – not so long as they can go out shooting things, then come back to a good dinner and a bottle or two of wine.'

Camilla laughed. 'I daresay you're right. But still ... the house and I have our pride.'

'As is right and proper.' Pausing in the act of gathering up the samples and as if at random, the housekeeper asked, 'That gentleman who escorted you from London ... does he *always* wear a sword?'

All vestiges of amusement vanished. 'So I'm told.'

'My goodness! That's not a thing you see every day, is it?'

'No. He's quite the eccentric.'

'Yes, indeed. But can I ask ...' She stopped, looking troubled.

Camilla repressed a sigh. 'Ask what, Mrs Poole?'

'Well, Mr Coombes says you told him to deny you if the young man calls again. So I wondered ... Miss Millie, has he been over-familiar with you?'

'Certainly not.'

'Never?'

'No.'

'Well, that's a relief. Mr Coombes said he wasn't the sort to take advantage – but *I* say a man can be well-mannered and still be a rogue.'

He wasn't too polite to point out my own deficiencies on that score, was he? thought Camilla irritably. But said sardonically, 'One of those rare gentlemen who do as their mothers tell them, I believe. Now … if there's nothing else, Mrs Poole, I will take a turn in the garden before it starts to rain.'

* * *

Adam and Finch, meanwhile, had taken a dawdling stroll around New Romney. With extreme reluctance, Adam had left his sword at the inn. Men who rode about armed received odd looks at the best of times and there was no point in making the local populace any more suspicious of him than they would be of any stranger.

It being market day, the High Street was busy with stalls and traders hawking their wares so Adam decided to begin with a slight detour to the church of St. Nicholas. It was an imposing edifice with a square, Norman tower … but what Adam found most interesting was that the main door lay some four feet below ground level, suggesting that at some point in the past, it had been partially buried. Strolling over to a fellow busily trimming the verges, Adam gestured to it and said, 'Unusual. What happened?'

'The great storm happened,' grunted the man without stopping work.

'Really? And when was that?'

A shrug and, 'When Noah was a lad for all I know.'

'Was the church on the coast at one time?'

'So they say.'

'Is it possible to go inside?'

'Try the door. If it's open you can. If it's not, you can't.' And he turned his back on them.

'That's helpful,' remarked Adam. 'We might never have worked it out on our own.'

Finch gave a snort of laughter. 'Do we *want* to go in?' he asked.

'If we can, we might as well.'

The door wasn't locked. They went inside and killed half an hour wandering down the central nave between dark wood box pews and side chapels separated by sturdy pillars, the lower parts of which were stained from long ago flooding. Emerging once more into the fitful sunlight, they continued along the road flanked by cottages and little else until a turning led them back on to the High Street. Another diversion took them past a Priory and the Hospital of St John. Adam was beginning to suspect that New Romney was perhaps a town of greater importance than he'd previously thought. The only thing he couldn't work out was where the coastline had originally been. He wondered if anyone had an old map.

Their arrival back at the *Cinque Port Arms* coincided with that of the afternoon Mail Coach. Two men got off, no one got on and a sack of mail was carried inside. It was a scene that could have been taking place at any coaching inn anywhere. It looked comfortingly normal ... and yet there was an uneasy prickling at the back of Adam's neck that he couldn't account for.

* * *

On the following morning, he and Finch rode most of the four miles from New Romney to Dymchurch along the beach where, as it had been yesterday afternoon, the tide was out. Six or seven fishing smacks were visible out at sea and the only marks in the sand were a solitary track of hoof-prints.

'Looks like somebody's been riding fast along here,' observed Finch when he ran out of questions about the Dymchurch Wall, most of which Adam couldn't answer.

Adam nodded but said nothing. If he had to guess, the spacing and depth suggested a smaller horse than Hector and a lighter rider than himself. Miss Edgerton-Foxe, perhaps? If so, she rode well. And early.

At this point, he found himself thinking that anyone less like a *Millie* he couldn't imagine. The only one he'd ever met was a parlour maid at home – and she was a plump little thing with rosy cheeks and dimples. He could only suppose that, in Miss Edgerton-Foxe's case, Millie must be short for something worse ... Mildred or Millicent, perhaps ... because if it wasn't he doubted she'd put up with it.

They reached Dymchurch and crossed the Wall onto the High Street at the *City of London* tavern. It was quiet with very few folk about and those they did meet, replied to Adam's polite 'good morning' with little more than a nod before going on their way.

'Don't exactly make you feel welcome, do they?' grunted Finch.

'No. But judging by the number of faces at windows, a lot of people want to know who we are, what we want and where we're going.'

'And where *are* we going, sir?'

'To take a tankard of ale somewhere as if we've no particular goal in view and are merely thirsty. After that … well, we'll see. It's either onwards to Hythe or back across the Marsh to find out if there's anything there except sheep.'

Finch nodded. 'Funny looking things, aren't they? Not like the ones at home.'

'No. But there are a lot more of them per acre and they look remarkably healthy. Ah – there's an inn by the church. Let's see if they'll serve a couple of shady-looking characters like us.'

The inn was a small one, its sign so weathered as to be indecipherable. A man stood in the open doorway, his expression equally inscrutable. He said, 'Ale, sirs?' And when Adam nodded his agreement, he somewhat reluctantly stepped aside to let them enter.

One glance into the dark and grubby interior was as much as Adam wanted to see of it. Spotting a bench against the outside wall he gestured to it saying, 'I think we'll take it out here. It's a pleasant day, after all.'

'Won't last,' grunted the innkeeper and disappeared into the gloom.

Finch rolled his eyes but said nothing. Pitching his voice to be heard inside, Adam remarked that the church looked interesting and might be worth a visit. The landlord reappeared with two foaming tankards and tersely informed them that the church was kept locked outside service times.

'Really? Why?'

A surly shrug and, 'Vicar's orders. Will you be wanting anything else?'

'Thank you, no.' Adam handed over some coins. 'How far is it to Hythe?'

'Five mile, give or take. If you're heading that way, best be quick. Rain's coming.'

Waiting until the fellow had stamped back inside, Adam murmured, 'Keen to see the back of us, isn't he?'

'Looks that way. So ... are we going to Hythe?'

Adam glanced at the sky. 'Not if it's going to rain – and it looks as if it might. I think we'll take a leisurely ride back through the Marsh.'

'Wouldn't do that if I was you,' cautioned the innkeeper sourly from the doorway. 'Tisn't easy for them as don't know the paths.'

'But there *are* paths?' queried Adam.

'Some.'

'Then we'll bid you good day and take our chances.'

Five minutes later and having finished their ale, they left the town by way of a narrow lane leading inland which gradually dwindled into an even narrower track, forcing them to ride in single file. For a little while, there was nothing but marsh and the bleating of sheep ... and then they came upon the ruins of a church and the tumbled remains of a handful of the cottages that had once been dotted about it.

Adam drew Hector to a halt, frowning. 'What happened here, I wonder?'

'Dunno, sir. But whatever it was happened a good while ago.'

'Yes. At least a century – perhaps more.' He set Hector in motion again thinking, *If I ask about this, will it be met with a wall of silence? As yet, I can't decide if people here just don't like strangers or are close-mouthed because there's something to hide.*

They rode on towards a church tower – this one seemingly intact – that was visible in the distance. Unfortunately, although it had looked little more than a mile, it took them the best part of an hour to reach it because they were forced to alter their route three times by water channels some eight or nine feet wide which snaked their way through the Marsh.

Damn it, thought Adam irritably. *A map would help – as would knowing how deep these drainage ditches are because I'm not about to try riding through one in case Hector ends up to his hocks in mud.*

The church, when they eventually reached it, was a massive stone structure looming over a well-kept inn with colourful window-boxes and a freshly painted sign of a bell. The surrounding village, by contrast, was little more than a huddle of cottages. Adam drew Hector to a halt outside the graveyard and dismounted murmuring, 'It seems disproportionately large for the size of the village, doesn't it? However … let's see if anyone stops us going in.'

No one did. The door of the porch stood wide and the inner one opened at a touch. The vast space was cool and faintly scented. With Finch at his heels, Adam strolled a little way down the nave and paused to study a large cartouche, brightly painted with the Royal Coat of Arms and dated 1775, which adorned the north wall. From that, his gaze drifted downwards to a small external door, on either side of which were sturdy brackets of the kind designed to hold a stout bar.

This struck him as odd and he continued to dwell on it whilst sauntering on between grey-painted box pews. Then, just as he had reached the intersection leading to the side chapels, a cheerful voice said, 'Welcome to St George's in the parish of Ivychurch, gentlemen. If you would like the sixpenny tour, I'll be happy to give it.'

Turning, Adam found himself facing a small, rotund cleric wearing wire-rimmed spectacles and a jolly smile. This was so unlike his experience of Romney Marsh thus far that he took a second to reply. Then, 'Thank you, sir. It's a fine church you have here.'

'It is indeed.' The little fellow bustled forward, hand outstretched. 'I am Reverend Downing, the incumbent of it these five years. And you, sir?'

Adam shook the vicar's hand, supplied his name and added, 'You'll have to forgive my surprise, sir. We were in Dymchurch earlier and were told that the church there is kept locked except when there are services.'

'Locked?' Reverend Downing frowned briefly and then shook his head, laughing a little. 'The children will have been running in and out, playing hide and seek, I'll be bound. It happens here, too – but the sexton or I chase them out again quickly enough. We don't lock the doors. No need for that. Now ... come and admire our splendid tower. It is a later addition, of course, built around 1450, roughly a century after the nave was completed. The majority of the church is composed of Kentish stone but ...'

Adam followed where he was led, letting the Reverend's enthusiastic discourse drift over him. But as soon as he had the opportunity, he said, 'On our way here we came upon the ruins of a church and its village. What happened to it?'

'That would be Blackmanstone. It is one of a handful of such lost villages.'

'By lost, I take it you mean abandoned?

'In most cases, yes – though the oldest ones were wiped out by the Black Death.'

'And the newer ones?'

The vicar sighed. 'Marsh fever. It is prevalent in the area – although mercifully less so in the last forty-odd years. But some villages were abandoned when the death rate soared.'

Adam didn't much like the sound of that. He said, 'Why is it less severe now?'

'The fever is caused by insect bites and it was eventually – one might say, belatedly – recognised that the insects seemed to breed close to still or stagnant water,' explained Reverend Downing. 'So a Drainage Committee was formed to begin clearing out any such channels ... and over time the number of fever cases and deaths fell noticeably.' He smiled at Adam. 'The fever still exists, of course, but you need not worry unduly, sir. Town dwellers rarely catch it ... and since the insects are busiest from dusk to dawn, avoiding the marsh at night is the best precaution.'

Adam smiled back and said blandly, 'I shall bear that in mind. But I interrupted your history of the church, didn't I?'

Twenty minutes later, the vicar walked with them to the church gate expounding the best route back to New Romney before bidding them a cordial farewell. Adam could feel the oh-so-friendly and helpful cleric's eyes boring into his back all the way down the street but quelled the impulse to turn his head.

Avoid the marsh at night, he thought. *Honest advice ... or a warning?* Either way, he suspected that prowling the marsh under cover of darkness was going to be inescapable. Unfortunately, the damned innkeeper seemed always to be up and about and when *he* wasn't, his wife or oldest boy or stableman were ... so getting in and out of the inn without being seen wasn't going to be easy.

Adam spent the ride back mentally cataloguing the things he needed to learn – starting with the pattern of both tides and moon. The first might reveal evidence of night-time activity if he was able to visit the beach early in the morning before the tide washed it away; the second, he reasoned, could suggest the timing of a smuggling run since it was logical to suppose that cargoes were landed in the dark of the moon. And while he was establishing those things, he would see what could be done about making his comings and goings less visible to Innkeeper Hadlow and anyone else in New Romney who was taking an interest.

He said, 'Harry ... tomorrow, I'll want you to deliver a letter for me.'

'Yes, sir. Where am I to take it?'

'To Viscount Wingham of Audley Court, near Rye.'

CHAPTER EIGHT

While Finch was riding to East Sussex and back, Adam decided to return to Dragon Hall in the hope that Miss Edgerton-Foxe's land agent could furnish him with a map of Romney Marsh. He didn't hold out much hope for this but decided it was worth a try.

In the stables, several things were not as they'd been on his last visit. Hector was taken in charge by the head stableman, a grey-haired wrinkled fellow who introduced himself as Dawson. Brewster, the young groom, and Vulcan, the black stallion were both missing. Adam supposed that the reason for that was self-explanatory. He did, however, wonder why three of the ponies had vanished.

Coombes, the butler, admitted him with a bow and an expression of slight discomfort but when Adam asked if he might speak to the steward he relaxed and said, 'Not today, sir. It is Mr Robson's quarterly meeting with the wool merchants in Tenterden. Is it possible that I can help in his stead?'

'Not unless you have a map showing the pathways and water channels on the marsh. Do you?'

'I do not. And I very much doubt that Mr Robson has one either, sir. As I believe I mentioned to you, he has tended the Dragon Hall estate for nigh on two decades and knows every inch of it by heart.'

Adam sighed. 'I suspected as much. Actually, I wouldn't be surprised to learn that no such map exists.'

'I fear that may be so. However, the office of the Lord of the Level can probably supply one which charts the parish boundaries. Would that be of any use?'

'It would be better than nothing. But who is the --?'

'Thomas?' The voice of the mistress of the house drifted down from an upper landing. 'Come up here, please. We need of a pair of strong arms.'

'Thomas isn't back from Dymchurch yet, Miss Millie,' replied the butler.

'He isn't? Then who were you --?' She ran down to the turn of the stair, came to an abrupt stop and said flatly, 'Oh. It's you.'

'Indeed,' agreed Adam; and couldn't resist supplying the word implicit in her tone, 'Again.'

'Quite. Why?'

'I'm pursuing a forlorn hope.'

He surveyed her with lazy interest. Her hair, though covered in a headscarf, showed imminent signs of escaping its pins; she wore a voluminous apron over a gown of faded green cotton; and there was a generous smear of something that looked very like paint on one cheek. But she seemed oblivious of all those things and looked more like a busy little housewife than the stiff-necked creature he'd known previously. He wondered how deep the changes went and whether they might survive ten minutes in his company.

She said, 'I don't know what you mean. Is there something we can help you with?'

'Sadly, no. But perhaps *I* can help *you*.'

She blinked and pushed back an errant lock of hair. 'I'm sorry?'

'You wanted a pair of strong arms. Might mine do?'

'*Yours*?'

'Yes.' Smiling a little, he held them out. 'Adequate to deputise for the absent Thomas, do you think?'

What Camilla thought was that he was impeccably dressed and better-looking than she'd previously thought him. The slightly over-long silver-gilt hair gleamed; the dark red coat, though not new, was of a cut that emphasised a pair of excellent shoulders; and the half smile lurking in those smoky-blue eyes contained an invitation to smile back. All she could think of was that if she let him upstairs, the maids would go into a complete tizzy.

Clearing her throat, she said, 'Yes. I mean, I don't doubt your ability and I appreciate the offer but it wouldn't be ... that is, I couldn't possibly ask --'

'You didn't. I offered.' He strolled to the foot of the stairs, head tilted to look up at her. 'Of course, if we chat about this much longer Thomas may return. Or then again, not. So why not just show me what you want doing?'

Pulling herself together, she gave a brisk nod and turned to retrace her steps.

'Very well. Thank you.' Acutely aware of him approaching behind her, she added, 'It's a pair of oak chests. We need them away from the wall but they're too heavy to lift and we can't drag them because of the carpet.'

'Have you thought of emptying them?'

'Oddly enough, we did – but they're locked and we can't find the keys. Oh!' Struck by a sudden idea, she whirled round to face him so fast that he nearly cannoned into her. 'But you don't need keys, do you? Fergus O'Malley has taught you to open locks without them.'

'He did. But surely he taught you the same skill?'

'Me? Oh no.' Her mouth curled derisively and she continued climbing. 'I'm a mere female, Mr Brandon. It's only the *men* who are allowed any *fun*.'

'And that rankles, does it?'

'What do you think?'

He fell silent for a moment and then said, 'Would it help if I admitted that there's nothing amusing about hanging from a window-ledge by one's fingernails?'

Camilla was startled into a small choke of laughter.

'If that's so, you're the only one I've ever heard admit it.'

Thrown a little off-balance by that seductive, throaty gurgle, Adam said, 'Men don't admit weaknesses because we're supposed to appear impervious to them.'

Reaching the top of the stairs, she glanced back at him. 'But not you?'

He shrugged. 'To a degree, I suppose. But I'm not ruled by it.'

That makes a change, she thought ... but didn't say it. Instead, arriving at an open door beyond which lay a hive of activity, 'Here we are. As you can see, we're in the throes of an extensive refurbishment in advance of my brother's homecoming.'

It was a generously proportioned chamber and dominated by the large bed from which all the hangings had been stripped. Two chattering housemaids were rolling up the only carpet that didn't have furniture standing on it while a third was busy taking down curtains. All three stopped work to gaze, open-mouthed, at Adam.

Camilla sighed. 'Thomas isn't here so Mr Brandon has volunteered to help instead. Perhaps you might all stop staring and carry on with what you were doing?'

They giggled but did as she asked, whispering to one another in between covert glances across the room. Ignoring them, Adam eyed the padlocked chests thoughtfully. 'Since I don't commonly carry lock-picks around with me, opening them will have to wait. Do you know what is inside?'

'Diaries and other ancient documents or ledgers. Papa had them brought from the attics because he thought he might write a history of the house one day. But he never got around to it and the chests just stayed here. They ought to go back where they came from but they're too heavy to move as they are.'

'Well, I can help with that. But for now, where do you want them?'

'Far enough from the wall for us to get behind them. But if you can lift them just a little, we could pull the carpet free so they can be dragged over the floor.'

He nodded, reached down to grasp the handle on one side of the chest nearest to him and tested the weight before setting it down again. 'No wonder you couldn't budge it.'

'Is it too heavy to move?' she asked doubtfully.

'No.' Adam hauled off his coat and tossed it on to the bed. The three maids promptly stopped work again and stared. 'Ladies … I'd be obliged if you could be ready to tug the carpet free the instant I've lifted it clear.'

'You heard him, girls,' said Camilla. 'Molly and Jill take that side; Susan, you can help me with this one. Good. Whenever you're ready, sir.'

'On three, then. One, two, *three*.' He heaved the thing a few inches clear of the floor and held it, muscles screaming, for the moments it took them to shift the carpet. Then because, regardless of anything he might *say*, a man had his pride, he lowered it gently back to the floor and dragged it towards the centre of the room.

The maids sighed admiringly and in triplicate. Camilla couldn't blame them. The sight of his shirt pulled tight over compact muscles was ... impressive. She told herself that the heat in her face was due to annoyance at finding it so.

Adam compounded the problem by smiling. 'And the second one?'

'Over there.' She whirled away to point. 'Same thing again, if you please.'

'Yes, ma'am.'

The tone was meek enough to set the maids giggling again. And inevitably, as soon as the second chest had been repositioned they broke into enthusiastic applause. Adam thanked them gravely and then asked Camilla if there was anything else he could do.

'Nothing, thank you.' She waved the maids back to work. 'That was very helpful ... but I think things will progress faster if you are not here. Perhaps you would care to --'

'Miss Millie!' The housekeeper bustled in, immediately and disapprovingly taking in both the presence of a gentleman and her mistress's unkempt appearance. 'Wouldn't you like to go and – and wash your face?'

'My face? What's wrong with it?'

Before Mrs Poole could reply, Adam gestured to the patch of light blue paint on one of the walls. 'You've been painting, I think.'

'Testing the colour. Yes. How did you – oh.' She raised her hand to her cheek and shrugged dismissively. 'I forgot about that. I was about to offer you tea but I daresay Mrs Poole is right and I should tidy myself first.'

'Don't bother on my account.' He replaced his coat. 'And don't feel obliged to sit drinking tea with me if you're busy.'

It was at this point that Camilla realised she hadn't been acting out of obligation. She actually *wanted* him to stay a little longer. He seemed different today. Or was it she who had changed? Yes. She suspected that was nearer to the truth ... but she couldn't think about that now. She said decisively, 'I'm not – too busy, that is. Mrs Poole will show you to the family parlour and bring tea. I will join you in a few minutes.'

Hiding his surprise, Adam bowed and followed the housekeeper.

Camilla turned to the maids and said, 'Finish stripping the room as best you can, girls. If you need help, Thomas should be back soon. And meanwhile, if you think you've done all you can in here, take the carpets outside for beating.'

They curtsied and smiled at her in a way that was half-envious, half-knowing and which caused her to add, 'And stop that this instant.'

'Stop what, Miss?' asked Molly innocently.

'Letting your imaginations run riot. It's tea – not a tryst.' And walked out to the sound of yet more giggles.

In her bedchamber, one glance in the mirror was sufficient to show her the worst of the damage. Having washed her hands and face and shed the apron, she rejected the notion of changing her gown because of the time it would take and the possibility that it might be misinterpreted. Then, sitting before the dressing table while Martha attempted to restore her hair to some semblance of neatness, she investigated her earlier thoughts regarding her reaction towards Adam Brandon.

In London and throughout the journey here, she had been seething with resentment – partly at having to spend time in London to please Grandmama but mostly due to Uncle Hugh's high-handedness in the matter of her homecoming. And unfairly, she now realised, she had taken that resentment out on the only person available to her; Adam Brandon. Now, back in her own home, free to do as she pleased and able to see things more objectively, she wondered why she had been so determined to dislike him and to be as difficult as possible. She'd always known, hadn't she, that he was only following orders? And that brought her to the crux of the matter and forced her to recognise something that, deep down, she had known all along. He wasn't here purely on her account. The head of M Section didn't send agents out to play nurse-maid or spy on his relatives. So if Adam

Brandon was remaining in the district it was for other reasons entirely.

He wasn't unlikeable, she admitted. Giving credit where it was due, he had been under no obligation to help. And their brief exchange on the stairs had been interesting. He'd assumed she had been taught the same nefarious skills he had and been surprised that she hadn't. She rather liked that – if, of course, he actually *meant* it.

Not a hint *of treating me differently because of my sex – which is more than can be said of Rainham and the rest of them,* she mused. *And no masculine posturing either. Quite the reverse, in fact. Why did he let me see that? After the way I behaved towards him, he probably thinks I'm a witch.*

When she entered the parlour, the gentleman in question was leaning negligently against the window embrasure and gazing down into the garden but he straightened as soon as she walked in and said, 'How old was your brother when your father died?' And then with a frown, added quickly, 'Forgive me. I've no business asking.'

Camilla sat and began pouring the tea. His question was unexpected but neither as intrusive nor as upsetting as it might have been. Also, she was learning that Mr Brandon didn't talk for the sake of talking and that when he *did* speak, there was always a point. She said composedly, 'Father died when Guy was in his second term at Oxford.'

'So ... eighteen or nineteen?'

She nodded and passed him his tea. 'Why do you ask?'

'I was that age when my father died. Max – my older brother – was twenty. It took him until earlier this year to move into the master suite and then only because he'd married.'

'I see. But your mother is still alive, isn't she? I imagine that would make a difference. Our Mama is not. She and Papa died in the same accident.'

Adam stared at her for a long moment. Finally he said, 'My apologies. I hadn't realised. That must have been hard.'

'Yes. It was.' She offered a plate of small sandwiches and waited while he took one. 'I'm aware that Guy may be reluctant to take Father's place – hence the refurbishment. But the choice shall be his.' And then, deciding a change of subject was called for, 'No sword today, sir?'

He shook his head. 'Nor any day while I'm here. The local people are suspicious of strangers and my walking around armed won't make them less so.'

'You sound regretful.'

'I am.' Silence fell while he ate his sandwich. But finally he said, 'I came to ask if your land agent had a map of the marsh but, in addition to mistiming my visit, Mr Coombes tells me that it's unlikely. However, he said I might perhaps acquire one from the Lord of the Level – except that I don't know who that is or even what the title signifies.'

'The Lord of the Level is a sort of county sheriff, responsible for law and order on Romney Marsh and you'll find him at the New Hall in Dymchurch,' replied Camilla. 'But if you go in there asking for a map, be prepared for an inquisition. Sir Cuthbert will try to do everything but count your teeth. I don't suppose you want that.'

Adam shot her a wary glance. 'What makes you think so?'

'Do you really need to ask that?' And when he didn't answer immediately, 'You aren't here because of me, Mr Brandon. Escorting me from London was just a convenient excuse to get you here. You've been sent on some M Section business that my uncle has probably ordered you not to tell me about. And if *I'm* to be kept in the dark, I don't see you confiding in anyone else.' She sat back and regarded him steadily. 'Well? Am I right?'

She was, of course – and she clearly knew it. For perhaps the fifth time since he'd entered the house he was tempted to ask her about the ponies in case the innocent explanation he'd been given was true. But he couldn't in case it wasn't. So he settled for, 'If you are, I'm hardly going to admit it, am I?'

'Goodness. Uncle Hugh must be absolutely *thrilled* with you. He loves discretion. Any of your fellow agents would just have said yes. But then, I suppose that they know me and you don't.' She thought for a moment and finally said, 'All right. We didn't get off to the best start, did we? My fault, I know. At the time, I was ... angry. Angry about a good many things that were not your fault but for which I let you bear the brunt.'

Adam raised one eyebrow. 'Is that an apology?'

'The nearest thing to it. And you don't need an apology, do you? You need to be able to negotiate your way about the marsh.' She met his eyes squarely. 'I can help you with that. I know it as well as anyone and can show you the most reliable paths. But I'll want something in return.'

'What?'

Her smile was sudden and blinding. 'Teach me to pick a lock.'

He gave a brief laugh. 'If that's what you want. But much as I'd like to accept your offer, we can't be seen riding about together.'

'Why on earth not?'

'People will talk about you and—'

'I don't give a fig for that.'

'—and take far too great an interest in *me* as a consequence,' he finished imperturbably. 'The best solution is for you to simply draw me a map.'

'I can't.'

'Why not? You know the terrain and I was told that your memory for detail is faultless.'

Her eyes narrowed and her chin lifted. 'It is.'

'Then what's the problem?'

'The *problem* is that I only know it from the *ground*. Odd as it may seem, I've never floated above it on a magic carpet to see it as a whole pattern.'

'Oh.'

'Exactly.' Realising she'd been rather sharp, she offered him another sandwich as a peace-offering and said, 'Is a map really essential?'

'It was yesterday. It took nearly an hour to get from Dymchurch to Ivychurch because I had to retrace my steps three times to get around water channels.'

'Didn't anyone warn you to turn left at the Blackmanstone ruins?'

'I was warned twice – but not about that,' he said aridly. 'An innkeeper said the paths were hazardous for strangers. And a vicar told me to keep off the marsh at night if I wanted to stay healthy.'

'Subtle,' she remarked sardonically.

'Wasn't it?'

Camilla eyed him meditatively while she tried to decide whether to speak her mind or not. Finally, she said, 'You side-stepped the question earlier and you can do it again now. But it isn't exactly difficult to guess why you're here. There are only two things on Romney Marsh in which anyone from outside it is remotely interested. One is our wool ... and I doubt you're here to study the sheep.'

'And the other?' he asked, suspecting he already knew the answer.

'Owling.'

Not the answer he'd been expecting. '*Owling*?'

She nodded. 'Smuggling, to you. Here, it's called owling.'

'Why? No. Don't tell me. Because they do it at night?'

'Oh it's better than that,' she assured him. 'Years ago they apparently signalled to each other by hooting like an owl. Nowadays, of course, they're much more sophisticated.'

Adam wasn't surprised that she knew about the smuggling. Born and bred here, how could she not? But he did wonder just how *much* she knew. He said carefully, 'You speak as if what goes on is common knowledge.'

'The fact that smuggling *happens* is common knowledge. How and when it's *done* is known only to those involved in it. And they don't talk.'

'I suppose not.' Deciding that this conversation had already gone further than it should have done, Adam rose and reached for his hat. 'I've taken up far too much of your time and ought to let you get back to marshalling your troops.'

Camilla also came to her feet saying pleasantly, 'Retreating, Mr Brandon?'

'In good order,' he agreed. 'If you want those chests opening, I'll come back and see to it for you – but probably not tomorrow.

I'm hoping a gentleman I need to speak with will allow me to call on him.'

'Whenever it's convenient – on condition I get the lesson you promised.'

'*Did* I promise? I don't recall it.' And when the stubborn glint with which he was all too familiar appeared, added, 'But we won't argue. If you really want to pick a lock, I'll show you how to do it.'

CHAPTER NINE

Since Finch brought a cordial invitation from the new Lord Wingham to call on him the following day, Adam set off for East Sussex directly after breakfast. It was a pleasant day and an even more pleasant ride. It was also a relief to leave the marsh behind him.

Rye, when he passed through it, was a pretty place of cobbled streets winding up above the river and half-timbered houses with colourful plants tumbling from boxes on nearly every windowsill. Pausing at the *Hope Anchor* for a small mug of ale and a chance to tidy his appearance before presenting himself at the viscount's home, Adam learned that like New Romney and Sandwich, Rye no longer had the sea on its doorstep due to centuries of silt and a change in the path of the river.

Audley Court lay five miles further on and inland. The fields around it looked well-tended and prosperous. The house, approached by a short avenue of elm trees, was a neat, flint-walled manor, prettily situated amidst gardens but unostentatious. Adam tried to recall what he knew of Sebastian Audley but could come up with little beyond red hair and an irrepressible sense of humour; not that he imagined the fellow would be cracking jokes now, having buried his father a bare two months ago.

The butler was outside the door the instant Adam brought Hector to a halt and already ordering a footman to take their visitor's horse to the stables. He said, 'Good morning, sir. His lordship said to expect you. I trust you had no trouble finding us?'

'None at all, thank you. Lord Wingham's directions were extremely clear.'

Entering the house, he relinquished his hat and gloves and glanced around the well-proportioned hall made cheerful with vases of flowers.

'Lord and Lady Wingham are in the drawing-room, sir. If you will follow me?'

Adam didn't remember meeting Audley's wife but supposed he must have done. She'd have been one of those ladies fussing about Belle at the wedding. He hoped he wasn't going to have to conduct his business in front of her. He already didn't know how much – or how little – he should say to her husband and didn't need additional complications.

'Mr Brandon, my lord,' announced the butler, ushering Adam into a large, sunny room which managed to appear both elegant and comfortable.

A pretty, brown-haired lady sat near the window, a baby on her lap, and the fellow Adam remembered appeared from behind a newspaper. Both wore unrelieved black.

'Welcome to Audley Court,' said Sebastian, striding forward to greet him. 'It's a pleasure to meet you again.'

'Thank you for receiving me, my lord,' replied Adam, shaking the viscount's hand.

'No thanks necessary. You remember Cassandra, don't you?'

'Of course.' He offered the viscountess a formal bow. 'My lady.'

'You're being polite, Mr Brandon,' smiled Cassie. 'We barely met and it was all so rushed I doubt we exchanged more than two words. However … forgive me for not rising but Theo has only just fallen asleep and, after the past hour, we'd rather not wake him.'

'My ears are still ringing,' murmured Sebastian. And to his butler, 'Tea in here for her ladyship, Bradshaw. And coffee in the library for Mr Brandon and me.'

Bradshaw bowed and retreated.

'I see congratulations are in order,' Adam said, gesturing to the baby. 'But please also accept my condolences on your loss, my lord.'

Sebastian's expression clouded. He said, 'We had hoped to have Father with us for some years yet … but are grateful he lived long enough to see his grandson.' Then, seeming to straighten his shoulders, 'Enough of that. I know from Max's letters that everyone at Brandon Lacey is well. And you aren't here to catch up on family gossip, are you?'

'No. There is time for both, however.'

'Well, business first. We'll decamp to the library and you may tell me how I can help.' He crossed to his wife, dropped a kiss on her hair and brushed his son's cheek with one fingertip. 'You'll excuse us, love?'

'Of course.' She smiled again. 'I shall see you at luncheon, Mr Brandon.'

He bowed. 'My lady.'

As soon as the library door closed behind them, Sebastian waved Adam to a chair and reached for the coffee pot. 'Where do you want to begin?'

'At the beginning, my lord. Perhaps with what Lord Alveston has already told you?'

'Fine. But for God's sake stop my-lording me. I haven't got used to it yet and, to me, Lord Wingham is still my father. Sebastian will do.' He handed Adam a cup of coffee and crossed to his desk, returning with a folded paper. 'Alveston's letter. Read it for yourself.'

Adam took the letter but instead of opening it, said, 'I'm happy to take your word.'

'I'm glad to hear that – but read it anyway. Inevitably, his lordship had his doubts about my … reliability. I'm assuming he said as much to you when he told you to seek me out.'

'No. Aside from informing me that you'd recently inherited your title, he merely asked if we'd met. Why would his doubts be inevitable?'

'You don't know?'

Adam shook his head.

'That makes you a rarity,' said Sebastian wryly. 'Well, then … after university I spent eight years earning the kind of reputation no sane man would want. Lord Alveston is naturally wondering if I've grown out of it. Now read the damned letter, will you?'

My dear Wingham, Goddard had written …

Allow me to repeat my condolences on the death of your father and to apologise for taking the liberty of writing to you in respect of another matter at this difficult time.

After a protracted absence, my niece is returning to her home at Dragon Hall near New Romney. I have certain concerns regarding this and shall be sending a young acquaintance of yours, Adam Brandon, with her – ostensibly to act as her escort on the journey from London. In point of fact, Mr Brandon comes with other, additional orders with which he may need help. I refer, of course, to matters protected by the code of silence which I believe still prevails on Romney Marsh.

I come to you due to the proximity of your estate to the area in question. Quite simply, both I and the government department which I serve will be in your debt if you can render Mr Brandon whatever assistance lies in your power. This matter is and should remain confidential. But if and when he calls upon you, you may assure him that he has my permission to divulge information which he considers vital to the success of his mission.

Respectfully Yours,

Alveston

Adam looked up into the viscount's slightly amused blue eyes and said, 'He might have told me that last bit to my face.'

'Didn't he?'

'No.'

'Ah. Possibly because of those doubts I mentioned.'

'I don't follow.'

'He wanted to make some enquiries before he told you to trust me.'

This, Adam realised, sounded all too likely. He said, 'Doesn't that offend you?'

'It might – if I didn't know why he thought it necessary,' came the rueful reply. 'But let's move on, shall we? I suspect I don't need to ask why you're here. Smuggling, is it?'

'Yes. You're the second person in two days to work that out.'

'The other one being?'

'His niece.'

'Matthew Edgerton-Foxe's daughter?' queried Sebastian thoughtfully. Then, 'Yes. My father had some acquaintance with that family but I don't ... neither do I recall ever crossing paths with the lady in London.'

'You'd remember if you had,' muttered Adam.

'Pardon me?'

'Nothing. His lordship told me to keep her in the dark with regard to my enquiries. I've no idea how he thought that might be possible since, better than most people, he knows she's not stupid. Of *course* she was going to guess.'

Setting down his cup, Sebastian looked at him.

'Very well. What do you need from me?'

'Right now? Everything you know about smuggling hereabouts.'

'That won't take long. I've never had any dealings with it and doubt that anyone in my household has. We don't buy smuggled goods – at least, not knowingly. With the best will in the world, one can't always be certain. On the other hand ...'

'What?' asked Adam when he showed no sign of continuing.

'I'll wager a good many of my tenants are involved because they can make a month's wages in a night. Small boats bringing cargo ashore and muscular fellows carrying it inland; farmers who'll look the other way when their plough horses are 'borrowed' for a night; and innkeepers who leave a light at an attic window and the cellar door unlocked.' Sebastian shrugged slightly. 'Like Miss Edgerton-Foxe, I grew up here ... so I've a fair idea of how smuggling works. But knowing, beyond any shadow of doubt, who's doing it is another matter entirely.'

'Because no one talks? Quite. But I've got to find a starting point somehow.'

After a few moments' consideration, Sebastian said slowly, 'There's a Riding Officer in Rye, another in Hythe and one at either Dymchurch or New Romney – I don't know which. If Alveston mentioned them, he probably called them Preventives or Revenue men.'

Adam nodded. 'He told me not to be seen talking to them.'

'Sound advice. Did he also tell you that, if one had to name the worst job in the world, the role of Riding Officer would qualify?'

'No. What's so terrible about it?'

'They are all local men ... so everyone knows who they are and despises them. And as if that isn't bad enough, the poor fellows have wide areas to patrol and no help doing it, so on the rare occasions they actually see a cargo being landed, there's nothing they can do about it. Support, if there *is* any, is always miles away, so it doesn't arrive in time to be useful. If the Riding Officer is rash enough to go in single-handed, he risks a beating – or worse. Personally, I can't think of a more miserable life than riding the coast alone at night and facing neighbours who hate you by day. Frankly, for fifty pounds a year and a horse to care for out of that, I'm amazed anyone does it.'

'Put like that, so am I.' Adam fell silent for a moment. Then he said, 'All right. Those men are my only chance of getting a name ... but I can't seek them out. Can you?'

Sebastian drew a long breath. 'Perhaps. I can certainly try. But not, I think, by going to them. The best option might be summoning them here to me.'

Adam sat up. 'If you do that, I can speak with them myself. And if I could meet all three at the same time, it would be more productive all round. Might that be possible?'

'I don't see why not – though it will take a few days to arrange. Jeavons, the Riding Officer in Rye, will be able to tell me who his colleagues are and where they live. After that, it will be a matter of settling on a day. I'll let you know when I have it.'

'Thank you. That would be a great help.'

'It doesn't sound so to me.' He paused and then said mildly, 'I am getting the impression that you have a plan for how you intend to approach this. Have you?'

'I have an idea, yes. But I'll keep it to myself until I've given it sufficient thought.'

'Fair enough. Is there anything else I can do for you?'

'Educate me about tides and the phases of the moon,' replied Adam promptly.

Sebastian blinked. 'Well, then. There are roughly eight and a half hours between high and low water. And the moon is currently on the wane. I'd guess there's roughly a week before it is dark. Do I take it you're thinking of some night-time reconnoitring?'

'I am if I can work out how to get out of and back into the *Port Arms* without anyone knowing. But at present, that looks somewhere between difficult and impossible.'

'Couldn't you--?' Sebastian stopped on note of laughter. 'No. If you stayed at Dragon Hall with a young, unmarried lady, the old biddies of the district would have you down the aisle before you could blink. Let's see. You can stay here with us, if --'

'No. I mean – it's good of you to offer. But word would get around and, if our acquaintance became generally known, comings and goings here might be watched and any chance of your helping me would be wiped out.'

'Well, we can't have that, can we? What about an isolated cottage? My land extends eastwards as far as the Rother ... but that might be too far away from your centre of operations, not to mention being on the wrong side of the river. And you'd have to fend for yourself, of course.'

'I've a manservant – so I daresay we'd manage. But the distance might create as many problems as it solves. As yet, I don't know the area well enough to say.'

'Well, leave it with me and I'll see what I can come up with.' Sebastian stood up. 'Join Cassandra and me for luncheon. If anything else occurs, we can discuss it later.'

Adam also rose. 'That's kind of you. But wouldn't Lady Wingham prefer --?'

'No. Like me, she'll be glad of a fresh face and new conversation. During these first weeks, we've closed ourselves off from the outside world. Not ready for it yet.'

'No. I recall it being the same with us when we lost my father. But it *does* get easier.'

'So everyone tells me. Come and eat.'

They found Cassie in the dining parlour, investigating the array of chafing dishes on the sideboard. Tossing a smile over her shoulder, she said, 'I hope you don't mind being informal, Mr Brandon.'

'Not at all, my lady.'

'Excellent idea,' said Sebastian, strolling over to catch her in one arm and kiss her.

'*And* I stopped Bradshaw bringing a letter from the Dower House with your coffee.'

He groaned. 'Not another one. What is it this time?'

'Do you really think I'd open it?'

'No. I just *wish* you would.' And to Adam, 'It's from my eldest sister with whom it cannot be said that I get on – which is why she lives in the Dower House rather than here. It's in a good state of repair and perfectly comfortable. But every other day she sends a new complaint. If I go over there myself, I'm likely to throttle her.'

'Which is why you won't,' said Cassie calmly. 'Come and help yourself, Mr Brandon, while Sebastian pours you a glass of wine. And then you can give me the latest news of Arabella and Julian. We enjoyed each other's company during Yule at Sarre Park.'

Over a salmon terrine, chicken fricassee and tiny lamb cutlets in mint sauce, Adam answered questions about his family and asked some of his own about Romney sheep. It wasn't until the syllabub was on the table that Dragon Hall and the name of its mistress was mentioned; and when they were, Cassie immediately said, 'Camilla Edgerton-Foxe? But I --'

'*Camilla*?' spluttered Adam, caught in the act of swallowing a slice of peach. And quickly clearing his throat, 'Forgive me. I interrupted you.'

'Don't apologise. I was merely about to say that I know her – though not especially well. But judging by your reaction, I'd guess that everyone is still calling her Millie?'

'Yes. Her uncle, her grandmother – even her household staff.'

'Well, I can't say too much about that. With the exception of Sebastian, everyone calls me Cassie. I used not to like it very much but now I rather enjoy Sebastian being the only one to use my full name. Perhaps Miss Edgerton-Foxe will find the same one day.'

'How do you know her?' asked Sebastian.

'The usual way. When I made my come-out she was in her second Season so we met at all the same parties. Neither of us accepted an offer that year and I expected to see her again the following one – the year you and I met, Sebastian. Only she wasn't there, of course, due to the tragedy.'

Sebastian's 'Tragedy?' clashed with Adam saying, 'Her parents?'

'You know about that?'

'I know they died in an accident,' said Adam. 'I don't know the details.'

'Their carriage slid off the road into the sea during a particularly severe storm,' Cassie told him simply. 'It was a high tide. No one survived.'

There was a brief silence. But finally Sebastian said, 'That puts things in perspective, doesn't it?'

She stretched out her hand to cover his. 'Yes. It does, rather.' And differently, to Adam, 'Living at Dragon Hall with no one but servants must be lonely. Sebastian and I aren't receiving or visiting at present ... but please tell Miss Edgerton-Foxe that, if she cared to call, I'd be happy to renew our acquaintance.' And after a moment's thought, 'If necessary, assure her that Lord Staplehurst's name will *not* be mentioned.'

'Why would she think it might be – or even care?' asked Sebastian.

'Because she broke off her engagement to him last year and is probably tired of people asking her why.' Cassie looked at Adam. 'You didn't know?'

'I knew about the engagement but not the gentleman's name.'

'I didn't know about either one,' remarked Sebastian, 'but then I don't take much interest in such things. Staplehurst, though? I don't know him well ... but he's an earl and possessed of the sort of looks that all the ladies sigh over.'

'Not *all* of them,' murmured his wife. 'At least half were busy sighing over *you*.'

'Thank you.' He grinned at her. 'So why did Miss Edgerton-Foxe break it off?'

'She didn't say. She left it to Staplehurst and *he* said it was due to a serious difference of opinion.' Cassie hesitated and then added, 'But from time to time there've been whispers about him over the tea-cups. Nothing definite ... just the usual vague rumours.'

'Saying what?' It was Adam who asked – less because he was interested in society gossip than because Goddard and the others had intimated that the broken betrothal had left Miss Edgerton-Foxe with invisible scars. 'Or shouldn't I ask?'

'Your choice, Cassandra,' shrugged Sebastian when she hesitated again. 'I know you don't like scandal-mongering but I think you can rely on Adam's discretion.'

She drew a long breath and then nodded.

'Very well. There were murmurs about a long-standing affair with a married woman who he won't – or can't – give up. I never heard anyone name her though I suspected that some of those doing the murmuring – Dolly Cavendish for one – *could* have done. But the worst of it is that there was also mention of children.'

Sebastian winced. 'If Miss Edgerton-Foxe heard that no wonder she threw him over.'

'Only if she was sure it was true,' argued Cassie. 'And what I remember of her tells me that she wouldn't have taken it on hearsay. She'd have wanted facts. And the only way she could get them would be by confronting Lord Staplehurst directly.'

'You think she'd actually *do* that?'

'Yes,' said Adam before he could stop himself. 'It's *exactly* what she would do.'

'I think so, too,' nodded Cassie. 'Which means that Staplehurst admitted it … or that he lied but failed to be convincing … either of which suggest that it's true since she ended their engagement.'

'Good for her,' grunted Sebastian, re-filling Adam's glass. 'I like her already.'

The conversation moved on to Adam's time in Paris and then to the letters full of helpful advice on land management that Max wrote in response to Sebastian's questions. But after a pleasant hour, Adam prepared to take his leave, thanking Cassie for her hospitality and promising to await word from Sebastian regarding both the Riding Officers and the possibility of alternative accommodation.

Seeing him off in the stable-yard, Sebastian said, 'On another occasion, perhaps we could find time for some swordplay?'

'We could – though I don't generally use foils,' came the blunt reply.

'So Max has told me. And we have a sword to two lying about. What do you say?'

'That I could use the practice.'

'Excellent.' Sebastian patted Hector's flank. 'Nice horse, by the way. Let me know if you ever think of selling him.'

'He isn't mine. And if he was, I wouldn't. Sell him, I mean.'

'I can't blame you for that. Safe ride back, Adam. I'll be in touch.'

Adam set off for New Romney reflecting on the ramifications of what Lady Wingham had said. He realised they told him a great deal about Camilla Edgerton-Foxe. Because, if she had loved this fellow, Staplehurst ... if she'd found out that he had a mistress he couldn't marry but had no intention of giving up ... a mistress, moreover, with whom he had children ... well, if Camilla had found out that those things were true, she was undoubtedly well shut of the man. But it wasn't surprising that the experience had left her with a very jaundiced view of the male sex.

CHAPTER TEN

At Dragon Hall, the campaign of refurbishment continued unabated. With the help of labourers brought in from St. Mary's village, the walls were being transformed from dingy cream to duck-egg blue. And since the fabrics for curtains and bed-hangings had still not arrived from Ashford, Camilla set Mrs Poole and the maids to giving the library a thorough cleaning. Once she'd given strict instructions on the correct handling and dusting of books, she found herself with little to do except to check on progress from time to time, so she shut herself in her father's study with the household ledgers and the farm accounts, all of which needed to be brought up to date. Then, knowing it would be low tide on St Mary's Bay, she took Sheba out for a gallop to blow the cobwebs away.

As she rode, she wondered who Mr Brandon was visiting. He had called the person a gentleman, so there weren't many options. It couldn't be the Lord of the Level because he hadn't known of him until yesterday and by then he'd seemingly been waiting for permission to call on whoever it was. So who might that be? Whoever was deputising for Lord North as Constable of Dover Castle? Sir Victor Amory, just outside Hythe? Lord Blakely at Ashford? Viscount Wingham, the other side of Rye? Which was most likely? The Deputy Lord Constable, perhaps ... but only if Mr Brandon had a letter of introduction from Uncle Hugh. Sir Victor was short of a brain-cell or two and she suspected that nothing in Lord Blakely's cellar had ever paid duty. All of which left the new Lord Wingham. Or, as most people remembered him, the infamous Sebastian Audley.

But he isn't infamous now, is he? He married Cassie Delahaye and by all accounts has turned into a model husband. And he's young – little older, I'd guess, than Mr Brandon himself – so I doubt he'd turn his nose up at a whiff of adventure. She thought for a moment. *Could they have met? Possibly. But wait ... there's someone much more likely, isn't there?*

As usual, the exact words came back to her.

'My sister and brother-in-law spent Christmas with Lord and Lady Sarre at Sandwich,' he'd said.

Sandwich. A longer ride but a stronger connection. Yes. If she had to put money on it, she'd wager Adam Brandon was visiting Lord Sarre … and hoping to enlist his help with whatever Uncle Hugh had sent him to do. Camilla still couldn't begin to guess exactly what that might be. Yes, obviously it had something to do with owling – but what? Because the one thing her uncle must know as well as she did was that nothing and no one was going to stop the Trade any time soon.

* * *

The following morning brought another hastily written note from Guy.

He had left the house-party for London and was staying with Grandmama in Mount Street. Uncle Hugh wasn't being helpful about White's but Dickie Broadbridge had introduced him to another club – Sinclairs – which was almost as good.

Inevitably, there was no word of travelling to Kent. Camilla folded the letter and put it aside to answer later. Guy would come home when he was ready … and in the meantime she had plenty to keep her occupied.

After luncheon, she spent two hours helping in the library and half-regretting the decision to remove all the books so that the shelves could be properly cleaned. It was a massive undertaking and putting everything back where it belonged was going to be equally exhausting. The centre of the floor was covered in piles of books and the air was full of dust, making everyone sneeze. It was a relief, therefore, when Coombes announced the arrival of Mr Brandon … or rather it *would* have been a relief had she not been as grubby and dishevelled as she'd been the last time he had seen her. A moment's reflection as she whipped off both apron and headscarf was sufficient to remind her that, since she had no more interest in Adam Brandon than she had in any other man, what he thought of her was immaterial. But still, it would have been nice to have met him looking tidy for once.

He, by contrast, looked as neat as he always did. He also combined his bow with the words, 'Bad timing, Miss Edgerton-Foxe? If so, you need only say and I'll leave.'

'Why would you think this a bad time?'

'You're wrinkling your nose at me.'

'I'm not – or if I am, it's because of the dust.'

'That's a relief.' Tilting his head consideringly, he pulled something from his pocket. 'I brought toys. But we can play with them another day, if you prefer.'

Camilla stared at the split-ring from which dangled seven or eight slender lengths of irregularly-shaped metal and then into enigmatic cobalt eyes. 'Lock-picks?'

'Lock-picks,' he agreed. 'I promised. Or you said I did. But if you're busy --'

'I'm not. At least, I *was* – but the maids can get on without me.' Eagerness written all over her and already heading out of the room, it took her a moment to realise he wasn't following. 'Are you coming? The chests are still where we left them.'

He had assumed that. But if the maids were elsewhere, he suspected the housekeeper would take a very dim view of him being alone with her mistress in a bedchamber. He said, 'Don't you want someone to ...' But stopped, realising how stuffy it was going to sound.

'To what? To chaperone me?' Camilla demanded impatiently. And then, 'Oh – for heaven's sake! You're not intending to pounce on me, are you?'

'I hadn't thought of it, no.'

'Good. And, though it may be a struggle, I believe I can restrain myself from pouncing on you either. But if you need added security --'

'I don't, thank you. The no pouncing agreement is quite sufficient.'

'If you *do*,' she continued firmly, 'Mr Sutton and his son are up there painting the walls. Now – are you coming or not?'

'Yes, ma'am. I thought I'd already said so.'

She narrowed her eyes at the innocent tone and then laughed.

'Having the last word, Mr Brandon?'

'Always,' he agreed.

In the bedchamber, the older man gave her a polite nod and said, 'Coming along nicely, Miss Millie. Aiming to get the first coat done before the light goes.'

Camilla nodded back. 'Don't mind us, Mr Sutton. We have work of our own.'

Adam knelt down before the first chest and gestured for her to join him on the floor. When she had done so, he held up the ring of lock-picks and said, 'Unless there's a problem inside the lock, opening it isn't as difficult as you may think. The first job is to decide which pick to try first.' He pointed to one shaped roughly like the letter L and deftly removed it from the ring. 'This is usually a good one to start with.'

Camilla watched him lay down the ring and push the other picks aside to leave a space for the one in his hand. Pointing to it, she said, 'Why did you do that?'

'Always keep your picks in the same order. Lesson One for if you ever need to work in the dark. Now, I'm going to open it and then re-lock it so you can try. The trick is to persuade rather than insist. But I imagine that part will come easily to you.'

'Why?'

'Dainty hands and a more sensitive touch,' he replied absently. 'Playing the harpsichord might be an advantage. Do you?'

Dainty hands? Forcing down a silly rush of pleasure, she said dryly, 'I was taught. I wouldn't call what I do *playing*.'

With a sideways half-smile, Adam said, 'Well, *I* haven't picked a lock since my lessons with O'Malley – so right now I'm hoping for the best.'

He slid the pick gently into the lock … telling her when it encountered the tumbler, when he began to turn it and in which direction. Then, instructing her to listen carefully, his fingers continued their smooth, almost infinitesimal movement; she heard a small but very distinct click … and the padlock fell open.

So did Camilla's mouth.

She said, 'I'm impressed. I thought it would take much longer.'

He shrugged as he withdrew the pick and snapped the lock shut again.

'It helped that the lock is in good condition.' And handing her the pick, 'Your turn.'

She re-settled herself on the floor and eyed the padlock with grim determination.

Amusement threading his voice, Adam said mildly, 'Don't glare at the poor thing. It's not your enemy. Think of it as a cat. Stroke it and it will purr for you.'

About to insert the pick, Camilla's hand stilled and she said witheringly, 'That is the most stupid thing I ever heard.'

'Is it?'

'Yes. Clearly, you know *nothing* about cats. Now stop talking, please.'

Since agreeing to teach her this particular skill, Adam had from time to time doubted his sanity. Now, however, he had to admit that he was enjoying her expression of gritty concentration; an expression that said, *I* will *do this. I shall get it right if it kills me*. He wondered if she approached everything with this passion to succeed. That, as he contemplated the soft skin of her cheek, currently adorned with a lock of dark brown hair and the curve of that undeniably splendid bosom, inevitably brought another, quite different, question to mind. He watched her carefully inserting the pick into the lock ... and told his unruly brain to behave. There had never been a frisson of innuendo during all the times he'd practised with Fergus O'Malley and there was no reason to find one now. She was holding the pick so tightly, her hand was shaking. Adam swallowed and managed to say, 'Relax your grip. Yes ... that's better. Do you feel the tumbler?'

'Yes.'

'Good. Now slowly turn it to the right ... and a fraction more --'

The lock sprang open so suddenly she dropped the pick. 'Oh!'

'Well done,' he said simply.

Camilla turned to him, pink with delight. 'I did it, didn't I?'

'Yes. You really did.'

'Thank you!'

The wide, dazzling smile all but scorched him and made him decide it was a good thing she didn't use if often. 'It was my pleasure.'

'No – it was mine. I haven't had so much fun in – well, in ages.'

If that was true, it didn't say much for her life in general. 'You haven't?'

'No. Didn't *you* want to crow when you did it the first time?'

He didn't say to her, as Fergus had to him, *Don't get too excited. It was only a simple padlock.* Instead, he said, 'I don't recall. What I *do* remember is the time he had me sweating over a combination safe for the best part of a day until I could open it in under three minutes.'

'That's just cruel.' She snapped the lock shut. 'I want to do it again.'

'And so you shall – with the other one when I've checked it.' Rising, Adam held out his hand to her. 'It's not that I don't think you can do it. It's just that if there's a build-up of dust or fluff or, God forbid, a touch of rust, it will thwart you.'

She nodded, accepted his hand and let him pull her to her feet.

The padlock on the second chest proved as cooperative as the first. Leaving her happily opening and closing it, Adam retrieved the ring holding the rest of the picks and waited patiently for her to return the one she had been using. When she did so, he replaced it among its fellows and then held the ring out to her, saying, 'I can't imagine I'll need these in the near future, so you may borrow them to practise with, if you wish.'

'May I?' She clutched them to her bosom, apparently as happy as if he'd handed over the keys to the Crown Jewels and told her to help herself. 'Really?'

'Yes – as long as you promise not to get adventurous with them.' He looked around for his hat rather than face that smile again. 'There's a right tool for every job. Use the wrong one and you'll probably damage it.'

'I'll be careful.' She hesitated. 'Can – can I offer you wine by way of thanks? Or ale, if you prefer. I know it ought to be tea but that doesn't seem very ... celebratory.'

'*Are* we celebrating?'

'Yes. At least, *I* am. I plagued Mr O'Malley for *months* to show me what you just have and he said he would but then never found the time – deliberately, I always thought. So a glass of wine at ...' She glanced at the clock, '... at four o'clock in the afternoon with some of Cook's macaroons seems suitably decadent. What do you think?'

That you don't know the meaning of decadence. But he said, 'Since it's not a question I've ever considered, I won't argue.'

Camilla nodded decisively, led him down to the parlour and rang for the butler. When he appeared, she said, 'Chambertin, Coombes.'

For a second until he conquered it, the butler's expression was as shocked as if she'd asked for hemlock. 'Chambertin, Miss Millie?'

'Yes. And macaroons, if they're fresh; whatever Cook baked yesterday if they're not.' She waved a dismissive hand and, as soon as he had gone, said, 'He still thinks I'm five.'

No. He thinks I'm leading you down the slippery slope to ruin, thought Adam ruefully. But he said merely, 'That is the problem with family retainers who have known you since you were. Ours are no different.'

Setting the lock-picks carefully on a table, she sat down and gestured for him to do the same. 'Does it ever annoy you?'

'No. There's no point being annoyed by things you can't change.' He watched her eyes roaming the room and added helpfully, 'If you're looking for some other lock on which to try your new skill, that small casket by the window would probably surrender to the narrow pick with a slight hook at the end of it.'

'Would it? Shall we try?'

'Not today. Stick to the padlocks until your hands don't need your brain.'

Camilla gave a tiny, startled laugh. 'Does that happen?'

'Only with lock-picking. Escaping from an upper-floor window requires every faculty you've got – and some you haven't.' Catching a speculative glint in her eyes, he said quickly, 'And no, I won't teach you to do *that*.'

'I wasn't going to ask you to. But I'd quite like to see *you* do it.'

Adam shook his head. 'Not a chance, I'm afraid.'

'But --' She stopped as Coombes returned with wine, glasses and a plate of macaroons.

Radiating disapproval, he poured the wine and said, 'Will there be anything else?'

'Nothing – though you might offer Mr Sutton and his boy some refreshment. They've been hard at work for hours.'

'Certainly.' He bowed and withdrew.

'He's sulking.'

'I can see how that upsets you.'

'He'll get over it.' She offered him the plate of cakes and took one herself. 'Was Lord Sarre able to receive you yesterday?'

Adam blinked. 'I beg your pardon?'

'Should I not have asked? If so, you needn't answer.'

'I know that. And if it *was* so, I wouldn't.'

'And *I* know *that* – so there's no need to be so pointed about it.'

He lifted one eyebrow. 'Pot calling kettle, Miss Edgerton-Foxe?'

She opened her mouth, closed it again and finally said firmly, 'I will not quarrel with you today.'

Unless I say the wrong thing, he thought. *Or do I mean the right one?* But after a moment, he said, 'It wasn't Sarre I went to see. It was Lord Wingham.'

The grey-green eyes widened, suddenly reminding him of mist over grass.

'Sebastian Audley?' she asked.

'Yes. We have some slight acquaintance and I wanted to add my own condolences to those my brother will already have sent by letter.'

Camilla thought, *That's not all you went for, is it?* But she merely nodded. 'I see.'

'I gather that you know his wife?'

'Sufficiently to say that Sebastian Audley is quite possibly the last gentleman in the world I'd have expected her to marry.'

'How so?'

'Even in her first Season, Cassie Delahaye was renowned as a pattern card of proper behaviour. And Mr Audley ... well, I never met him but that hardly mattered when for years his exploits were plastered all over the scandal rags.' She shrugged. 'I can only assume that Cassie has reformed him.'

'Perhaps he reformed himself,' suggested Adam. And then, 'What sort of exploits?'

'Women and wagers. Apparently the former couldn't resist him and *he* couldn't resist the latter. He turned the traditional sowing of wild oats into an art form. And if he did even *half* the things he's credited with, it's amazing he didn't break his neck or wasn't shot by some outraged husband. However ... judging by your expression he's changed.'

'Somewhat. He and his wife are in full mourning for the late viscount. But her ladyship said that, if you wished to visit, she would be happy to see you.'

Her expression was suddenly guarded. 'That is kind of her. Is that *all* she said?'

'No.' It didn't take a genius to know that telling her the truth was a sure road to disaster. 'She also told me that your name is actually Camilla.'

He saw that surprise her and thought, *Good.*

'What did you think it was?' she asked.

'Millicent. Or perhaps Mildred. It had to be something even worse than Millie – or why would you let people call you that?'

This raised a smile. 'Probably because by the time I was old enough to object, the habit was so well established it might as well have been set in stone.'

He nodded, understanding this. 'My sister's name is Arabella but the only person I can think of who doesn't call her Belle is her husband.'

'I doubt she minds. Belle is a good deal nicer than Millie.'

'True. But so is Camilla. Hasn't anyone *ever* used it?'

Adam saw his mistake immediately.

The smile vanished, her face closed up and she turned away. 'No.'

Yes, he thought. *And I can guess who. Damn.* But said only, 'That's a shame.'

'Isn't it?' Her tone was coolly discouraging. 'If you were thinking I might allow *you* to use my given name, think again. I won't.'

'I wasn't ... but I'm glad we've cleared that up,' he replied equably. 'Going back to the point where we digressed, if you should decide to accept Lady Wingham's invitation, it's likely I'll be going back to Audley Court myself at some point and could --'

'To repeat your condolences?' she cut in sweetly.

'No. To indulge both Sebastian and myself with a little swordplay.'

Camilla sat back in her chair and gave him the kind of look he'd last seen on his mother's face when he was ten and she'd caught him out in a lie. Resisting the impulse to fidget, he kept his mouth shut and waited.

'*Another* convenient excuse?' she asked.

'No. Why do you suppose it might be?'

'Because you said you were visiting a gentleman you needed to speak to. *Needed to*, Mr Brandon. Sympathy calls don't fit into that category. Neither does swordplay.'

Adam made no comment, aware that if you left a silence long enough, the other person would eventually fill it. He did, however, make a mental note not to forget that memory of hers when choosing his words in the future.

'You visited Lord Wingham to ask for his help with your current mission for M Section,' Camilla insisted. 'And if you're going to see him again, it's because he's promised it.'

The smile that returned to her face was the complete antithesis of the one that had floored him earlier. It reminded him in no uncertain terms why he'd originally found her impossibly aggravating. It did not, however, entirely obliterate the warm, laughing girl of less than an hour ago because he suspected he knew exactly what she was doing. Picking a quarrel to divert him from the forbidden ground he'd inadvertently strayed close to.

He said, 'I see you've got it all worked out.'

'Are you denying it?'

'Is there any point – with you so convinced you know all the answers?'

'Not *all* of them.'

'Ah. Is *that* what this is about? Fine. Personally, I don't waste time banging my head against the wall but if you do, go ahead.' He rose and picked up his hat. 'This seems like a good time to take my leave. Pity, really. It had been such a pleasant afternoon. Don't bother ringing for the butler. I know the way.'

Hot colour flooding her cheeks, Camilla also got to her feet.

'Don't forget your lock-picks. Doubtless – the afternoon having gone so rapidly downhill – you'll want to take them with you.'

'Not unless you're inclined to take out your ill-temper on inanimate objects. Are you?'

'No! Of course I'm not.'

'Then they'll presumably be safe enough.' Adam bowed. 'Good day, Miss Edgerton-Foxe.' And was gone before she could reply.

Camilla sank back into her chair and stared at the place where he'd been. Her first semi-coherent thought was, *Infuriating man!* Her second, some little while later, was to wonder where the conversation had descended into the quarrel she'd vowed they wouldn't have. And her third, when she found the precise moment, was to recognise the inescapable. He had accidentally touched the still raw nerve that Stuart had created … and from that point on, she'd metaphorically pulled up the drawbridge and marshalled all her defences. *Mr Brandon* hadn't quarrelled. *She* had.

She made herself consider whether he even knew about Stuart. Had Cassie told him? The Cassie Delahaye she remembered hadn't been inclined to gossip … and since she was now married to a man whose name had been a by-word across the whole of Europe, that was unlikely to have changed.

Without thinking what she was doing, she reached for the lock-picks and held them in her lap to trace the shape of each individual one with her fingertip. He was right. It *had* been a pleasant afternoon ... the most enjoyable one she could remember for a very long time ... and she had ruined it. She wasn't even very sure *why* she had. If he'd actually mentioned Stuart, there might be some excuse. But he hadn't. And he'd made it clear from the beginning that he wasn't going to discuss Uncle Hugh's orders with her – so what had been the point of making an issue of it? Of, as he'd said, banging her head against the wall?

For a long time, she sat there feeling faintly depressed and more than a little annoyed with herself. She ought to apologise. But after today he probably wouldn't call again until he wanted his lock-picks back ... and she could scarcely seek him out at the *Cinque Port Arms*, could she? Word would spread across the marsh like wildfire and half the folk who heard it would think she was running after him – which, she assured herself, *was* not and never *would* be true. She'd been finished with men the day she walked out of Stuart's house on Hanover Square. Spinsterhood mightn't be much fun but at least one knew what one was getting and there was a lot to be said for that. She wasn't going to risk her heart being trampled on a second time.

But did that necessarily mean she couldn't have *any* kind of relationship with a man? Unless she was completely misreading him, Adam Brandon was no more interested in either flirtation or marriage than she was. The idea that he might be was actually laughable. But this afternoon he'd held out a hand in friendship ... and she'd all but cut it off.

Sighing, she shut her eyes and let her head fall against the back of the chair.

Really, she thought, *I have to stop this. And I can't go on judging every man I meet by Stuart. Surely, God can't have made more than one of him?*

CHAPTER ELEVEN

Although Adam thought about Camilla Edgerton-Foxe more often than he either liked or considered necessary, he did not go back to Dragon Hall. This wasn't because the previous visit had ended acrimoniously. He knew perfectly well why that had happened. But if, in more than a year, she hadn't got over Staplehurst, Adam didn't think that there was much he or anyone else could do about it. She had to *want* to put the past behind her; and on present showing, she seemed to prefer wallowing in it.

He was also busy making plans for how best to use the two nights before and after the dark of the moon. A note from Sebastian had informed him that getting the three Riding Officers to set a date for convening at Audley Court was proving problematic.

The Dymchurch fellow is laid low with marsh fever and the Hythe officer has been called to Folkestone. The chances of getting all of them together this side of the new moon are remote but I'll keep trying. Regarding the cottage, the best I can offer is one a couple of miles from Playden, just this side of the Rother from East Guildford but it requires repairs. I'll set the work in hand – it needs to be done anyway – and it will give you time to decide whether it will suit though I suspect not. I'll write again when I have further news.

From Adam's point of view, it would have been helpful to be working in concert with the Riding Officers over the four nights he suspected the gentlemen of the Trade might be active. On the other hand, if the Dymchurch officer was in bed, at least there was little risk of bumping into him by accident. It would be ironic – not to mention highly inconvenient – if he got himself arrested on suspicion of smuggling.

He had three days in which to prepare and the first task, since he couldn't get a map, was to learn the terrain as best he could by heart. His forays would have to be made on foot because if he took Hector, everyone at the inn would know he was out and about. This reduced both the amount of ground he could cover and the time he could spend doing it. He had to leave when all was quiet and return before dawn ... so he decided to concentrate on the area between New Romney and Dymchurch because, if *he* knew the local Riding Officer was incapacitated, it was a foregone conclusion that the smugglers knew it too.

He and Finch rode the Dymchurch Wall, identifying the places most commonly used to cross it and following the tracks inland to see where they led. Adam had no intention of trying to catch a smuggler or two. If the lone Riding Officers couldn't do it, neither could he; and in any case, he didn't believe it would achieve anything of value. His plan, such as it was – and assuming he was lucky enough to see a cargo being landed – was to track some part of it and hope it might lead him to the men behind the operation. The men who Goddard believed were also assisting French spies.

He could barely resist shuddering when he contemplated the number of things that could go wrong. He was already an object of curiosity so if anyone glimpsed him skulking around in the dark he'd be done for. Everything depended on how well he'd learned his lessons in Wilfred Street, on good preparation ... and most importantly of all, on luck.

After two days of following trails inland from the coast, he began to draw a few loose conclusions. All the well-beaten paths led to a village – specifically, those of Snargate, Ivychurch and Brookland. Each village possessed a tavern and taverns generally possessed a cellar. But Adam didn't suppose for a minute that contraband would be hidden in the first place a Revenue man would look for it. If it was being brought to these villages, it was being stored elsewhere ... and the only other possibility offering sufficient space was, as Goddard had suggested, the church. Each village had one of those as well and he'd explored all three of them inside and out without finding anything at all since he couldn't risk being caught poking about. But the most intriguing one of all was the church of St Thomas à Becket at Fairfield, which stood quite alone in the middle of nowhere ... with a track leading directly to its door. It was also kept locked. At this point, it occurred to Adam that he might need the lock-picks after all.

The most pressing problem had always been how to get out of and then back into the *Cinque Port Arms* undetected. Reluctantly, he had decided that his best – indeed, his *only* – chance lay through the window in Finch's bedchamber. His own room overlooked the busy stable yard which meant he might as well stroll out through the front door. Finch's window was one of two opening on to a narrow alley which ran down the side of the inn and Adam had discovered that the window below was that of the brewery, a room only ever in use during the day.

The alley led to the back gate of a cottage. He had strolled its length several times and never met a soul. This was encouraging. Less so was the fact that Finch's window was on the second floor and the wall between it and the ground offered not a single useful hand or toe hold. There was some sort of straggly creeper that he doubted would take the weight of a cat ... and nothing else. Adam suspected that even Rainham, skilled as he was, might have a problem here. And since silence and speed were the order of the day, he sent Finch to nearby Lydd – a place they had yet to visit and were therefore unknown – to buy twenty feet of good rope.

On a night when the moon had shrunk to the merest sliver and praying he'd thought of everything, he behaved exactly as he had done on every other evening, dining with Finch in the coffee room and lingering over a tankard of ale until the crowd in the taproom began to disperse. Then he went upstairs and prepared for his first excursion.

Dressed in black and with the perspective glass Goddard had lent him tucked in a pocket, he said, 'It's finally quiet below. Douse the lamp and check that the lane is empty.'

Finch, who had been unhappy about this from the beginning, looked gloomy.

'I'll say it again, Mr Adam. This is a mad plan.'

'Not the best, I grant you – but tonight is for testing the theory. So just do as I ask and let me get on with it.'

Finch nodded, plunged the room into darkness and opened the window to lean out.

'It's clear, sir.'

'Good. Let down the rope – and please keep a good hold of it.'

'You can count on me.'

'Yes. That's exactly what I will be doing.'

The window wasn't large so getting his shoulders through it took some manoeuvring but eventually he was astride the sill and, with the aid of the rope, able to slither out of the room and start his descent. This was one of many moments when he *really* didn't want to be seen so he made it quick, thanking God that Finch was built like an ox. Once on the ground, he paused for a second to watch the rope disappear into the bedchamber ... and then, taking the shortest route out of town, headed for the sea.

All seemed quiet on the marsh. His senses on full alert, he followed the paths he'd memorised until he could hear the soft advance and retreat of the surf. Then he stopped and remained perfectly still for several minutes, eyes searching the dark and ears straining for any sound other than the sea. He neither saw nor heard anything untoward and began to breathe more easily. The Wall loomed in front of him and he jogged alongside it in the direction of Dymchurch, then climbed to the place he'd chosen for his vigil.

Wishing he had a better idea of what he should be looking for as well as the optimum place to look for it, he pulled the perspective glass from his pocket and scanned the horizon. Nothing. No ships, no small fishing boats, no lights. Adam shifted, attempting to make himself more comfortable. He decided to give it an hour here before taking an exploratory walk. As he had said to Finch, tonight was mostly about judging time and distance ... and whether he could accomplish the whole expedition with no one any the wiser and without falling into a drainage ditch. All of this would be useful information which might make repeating the exercise tomorrow a little less nerve-racking.

The hours crawled by. The sea remained empty of vessels and the only sounds were the gentle lapping of the waves upon the beach and the occasional bleating of sheep. When he could feel his concentration beginning to flag, he stood up, stretched and decided to call it a night. He hadn't expected his first attempt to prove fruitful and it hadn't – but neither had it been a waste of time.

Back in the alley outside the inn, with the first fingers of dawn starting to touch the sky, a small, well-aimed pebble brought Finch to the window and the rope to where Adam could reach it. Climbing up was as easy as climbing down had been but squeezing back through the window was a good deal more awkward. He finally managed it head-first on to the floorboards with Finch dragging his feet clear of the sill and simultaneously pulling the rope in. Adam rolled on to his back and lay there for a moment, catching his breath. Then he said, 'Well, that was an interesting experience ... if completely uneventful.'

'Nothing happened?'

'Not a thing. But now I know it can be done, I'll hope for better luck tomorrow.' He rolled to his feet. 'And before you cavil – yes, I *do* intend to do the same thing again tomorrow night and the next one as well, if necessary. So please don't argue.'

* * *

On the morning following Adam's midnight excursion, the Dragon Hall refurbishment moved on apace with the arrival of the bronze and delphinium brocade from Ashford. By mid-afternoon, Widow Erdsley and her assistant from Ivychurch were hard at work on curtains and bed-hangings while Camilla was directing the maids and footmen in the replacing of carpets and furniture in the library.

When she heard the pealing of the doorbell, she felt a brief, gut-wrenching mixture of hope and anxiety. She had spent the last five days waiting for an opportunity to apologise to Mr Brandon whilst simultaneously failing to mentally compose the right words. Now, since hiding wasn't an option, she took off her apron, smoothed her hair and walked into the hall, summoning a smile.

It wasn't Mr Brandon. It was a tall, loose-limbed young gentleman wearing an exceedingly fashionable coat and a faintly sulky expression.

'*Guy*!' she exclaimed incredulously, crossing to hug him. 'What a wonderful surprise! I hadn't expected you home for weeks yet.'

Having returned the hug, he stepped away, saying, 'I hadn't intended to come.'

'Then why – oh, never mind. The library is all at sixes and sevens, I'm afraid – so come up to the parlour and you can tell me everything over tea.'

Guy Edgerton-Foxe made no reply but followed her up the stairs, letting her enthusiastic welcome wash over him. A part of him was glad to be home ... but another part wasn't looking forward to explaining *why* he was. Throughout the journey from London he'd tried to work out how little he could get away with telling his sister and had come to the depressing conclusion that it wasn't very much. If he lied, she'd know because she always did. And what *he* didn't tell her, she'd probably hear from Grandmama or Uncle Hugh.

Having rung for tea, Camilla sat by the empty hearth and watched him wandering about the room, picking things up and putting them down again. This told her everything she needed to know about his current mood. He always got fidgety when he was in trouble.

She said, 'Guy? Why don't you sit down and tell me what's wrong?'

'Why must you assume that something is wrong?'

'Isn't it?'

He shrugged and said nothing.

'All right. Why aren't you still in London?'

'Does it matter? I thought you were happy to see me.'

'I *am* happy to see you. But judging by your behaviour, you're not happy to *be* here – so naturally I'm wondering why you've come.'

Guy huffed an impatient breath and dropped into a chair.

'Uncle is being awkward,' he muttered. 'There's no reasoning with him and --' He stopped abruptly when the butler arrived with the tea tray and said instead, 'Hadlow at the *Port Arms* is sending my luggage over in his cart, Coombes. And the horse I arrived on needs to be returned to Jem Butler at the forge.'

'I shall see to it. Mrs Poole will have your room ready directly.'

'And a bath, please.'

'Certainly, sir.' Coombes bowed and withdrew.

Reaching for the teapot Camilla said, 'So ... Uncle is being unreasonable. About what?'

'Everything.'

'Such as?'

'Oh –for God's sake, Millie! I've only just arrived. Can't the interrogation wait?'

She rather thought it couldn't but merely said, 'If you wish. How did you get here?'

'On the Mail – which is why my things were left at the inn.' He accepted the cup she offered him and tossed in three lumps of sugar. 'It was a dashed tedious journey, I can tell you. I shan't travel that way again in a hurry.'

'Why didn't you hire a post-chaise?'

'Couldn't afford it, thanks to Uncle,' came the bitter reply.

Camilla suspected she was beginning to see the light.

'Has he stopped your allowance?'

'No. But he won't --' Another abrupt halt and then, 'It's not important.'

'Since you're here and in a foul mood, clearly it is,' she retorted. And then, 'Guy ... you're going to tell me sooner or later what the problem is so why don't you just do it now and get it over with? Because if you're going to continue growling, I'd rather you did it somewhere else.'

'I wasn't growling.'

'You were.'

For the first time, the merest vestige of a smile dawned. 'Wasn't.'

'Were.' She smiled back and, knowing they were his favourite, pushed the cherry tarts towards him. 'Have a cake and tell me what is wrong.'

He picked up a tart, stared at it and mumbled, 'None of it would have happened if Uncle had sponsored me at White's.'

Putting aside the obvious question for a moment, she said, 'Why didn't he?'

'He says not until I'm twenty-one.'

'Oh. Well, that's not long to wait, is it? Just a few weeks.'

'You don't understand. My friends were all members and it was embarrassing not being able to join them. But then Dickie took me along to Sinclairs as his guest and --'

'Wait. Please don't tell me Mr Broadbridge introduced you to a gaming hell?'

'What? No! Nothing of the sort.' He dropped the uneaten tart back on the plate. 'Sinclairs is highly respectable – not a whiff of dishonest play. Half of White's members go there. More than half, probably.'

'So what went wrong?'

He took so long to reply that she thought he wasn't going to. But finally he said reluctantly, 'We started off at the hazard table ... but it got boring, you know? So Dickie suggested going to one of the upstairs rooms where it was all basset and ecarté and so on. We joined a table with Lord Sandwich and the Earl of March and some others and everyone was pleasant and welcoming and it was every bit as good as White's would have been.'

By now, Camilla had a fair idea of what was coming. 'But?'

'The cards weren't running my way and the play was ... deeper than I'd expected.'

'You're saying you lost?'

'Yes. Not enough to signify at first.' He shrugged. 'The company was good, I was enjoying myself and the luck was bound to turn eventually. So I carried on playing.'

He stopped. She waited and, when he showed no sign of resuming, prompted gently, 'And *did* the luck turn?'

'Not really. I won the odd hand now and again but mostly I carried on losing. And bit by bit I started to realise I was getting pretty badly dipped. Not so badly I wouldn't be able to pay, of course! But I knew I ought to stop before it got any worse. I meant to, Millie. I even *wanted* to but ...'

Another pause and this time she filled in the blank herself. 'But you didn't.'

'No. Someone called for another bottle and someone else started telling a long and very funny story. And somehow quitting the table felt awkward when everybody else was continuing to play – even March who'd lost nearly as much as I had. So I ... stayed.'

You carried on throwing good money after bad because you didn't know how to walk away? Camilla wanted to shout the words at him but she held them back. Instead, she said calmly, 'How much, Guy?'

He flushed and looked anywhere but at her. 'Altogether? Just under five thousand.'

'*Five thousand*?' She stared at him. 'Were you drunk?'

'No.'

'Temporarily unhinged?'

'No.'

'Then what on earth were you *thinking*? You must have known you couldn't pay such a sum until at least next quarter.'

'It can't wait that long,' he mumbled. 'Gaming debts have to be settled immediately. And I owed Lord Sandwich, Viscount Stockwell and a fellow named Penhaligon. So I asked Uncle Hugh to advance me the money out of my capital. I mean, as you said, it's only a matter of weeks before my birthday and --'

'Stop!' she said, her face a mask of incredulity. 'Let's be clear. You asked him if you could borrow against your inheritance?'

'Yes. But he wouldn't have it. He said it was against his principles both as guardian and trustee to let me start squandering the estate before I own it,' said Guy bitterly. '*Then* he said there was a lesson to be learned and he wanted to make sure I remembered it.'

'Good,' said Camilla stonily. 'But what are you doing about the gaming debts?'

'*He's* paying them.'

She gave a sigh of relief. 'Yes. Of course he is. And you should be grateful.'

'I *am* grateful. But --'

'You don't sound it.'

'That's because of the way he's *doing* it. He's paying it directly to the men I owe.'

'So?'

'So they'll know that I was playing beyond my means. Uncle's making me look an utter fool! Oh – and that's not all. I'm to pay him back – the bulk of it after I've inherited but the first instalment now with what's left of this quarter's allowance. Not that there was much of *that* after he made me settle with my tailor and bootmaker. He's left me without a feather to fly with, dammit.'

'Hence the Mail coach and your presence here, I suppose?'

'What else could I do?'

'Nothing. But whose fault is that?'

He surged to his feet. 'I don't need a lecture, Millie.'

'You don't need sympathy, either – though you appear to want it,' she retorted, rising to face him. 'You say Uncle has made you look a fool but it seems to me that you did that yourself. As for paying him back, surely you didn't need to be *told* to do that?'

'Of course I didn't! What do you take me for? But there was nothing stopping him from giving me the money so I could discharge the debts myself, was there? He didn't have to insist on handling the matter on my behalf as if I wasn't to be trusted.'

'That isn't why he did it. It's nothing to do with trust --'

'That's not how it will look to Sandwich and the rest of them!'

'What does that matter? Uncle wants to teach you not to be so – so *feeble* in future. Honestly, Guy … continuing to play just because everyone else did? You're almost twenty-one – not ten.'

'It's pointless talking to you. You've no idea what it was *like*.'

'No. I haven't. On the other hand, unless you were tied to the chair, standing up and walking out doesn't sound very difficult.'

His eyes narrowed and he stared furiously at her for a handful of seconds. Then he said, 'No. It doesn't, does it? So watch me.' And he swung away towards the door.

'Oh – for heaven's sake! Running away is no answer.'

'It will do for now. If my things have arrived, I'm going to bathe and change and take myself off to somewhere more convivial. The *London* at Dymchurch, I think. With a bit of luck I'll find a few old friends there – so don't hold back dinner for me. I'll eat at the tavern.'

And he strode out, slamming the door behind him.

* * *

To Camilla's surprise, he returned earlier than expected that night and went directly to bed. More surprising still, he joined her for breakfast on the following morning looking extremely cheerful. The explanation for this came when he said casually, 'I'll be out again tonight and doubt I'll be back until the early hours. But I'll take a key so no one needs to wait up.'

She sighed. 'You'll dine at home, though?'

'Can't. I'm engaged with some fellows in Dymchurch.'

'Engaged to do what?'

'Whatever takes our fancy,' he replied somewhat impatiently. 'I don't have to account for my every movement, do I?'

'No. Of course not.'

'Good.' He rose, preparing to leave the table and added, 'If you must know, somebody said there's a prize fight in Hythe ... so we might go over there if nothing else beckons. I'll see you tomorrow.'

* * *

Adam's second night on the marsh had been no more productive than the first. Nothing stirred except the sheep and, with little else to occupy him, he considered the news of Guy Edgerton-Foxe's unexpected arrival which was on everyone's lips at the *Port Arms*. Distantly, he wondered if the young man knew of his sister's involvement with M Section. He hoped that he didn't – because if he *did*, there was a possibility Adam's own name might be mentioned in connection with it and he would really much rather that didn't happen.

On the third night, a light drizzle was falling and he almost decided not to go out ... but the fact that the sky was inky black made him force himself to stick to his plan. He sat for an hour or more getting steadily damper while the only thing of note was when a sheep blundered into him, causing him to nearly jump out of his skin. His nerves had barely begun to settle again when he glimpsed a flash of blue light out at sea.

It was pure chance that he saw it at all. It was gone in an instant and wasn't repeated. Squinting through the perspective glass, he thought he could make out a dark shape on the horizon but he couldn't be sure. However, logic dictated that the odd flash had to have come from somewhere and also suggested that it was a signal to the shore. Adam turned the glass on the coast either side of him.

Nothing. No. Wait. The merest hint of light over to the left. A dark lantern? Yes, possibly. How far away? Seven or eight hundred yards ... maybe a bit more. He thought rapidly. *How close can I get? More to the point, how close* dare *I go?*

One thing was certain. A cargo was coming ashore tonight and he wasn't going to learn anything at all by staying where he was. On the other hand, it would be foolish to leave his current position until he had a clearer idea of what was going on.

He watched and waited. The distant shape came closer and resolved itself into a ship, most of its poles bare and therefore scarcely discernible from the darkness around it; a small fleet of small fishing boats left the beach to meet it; Adam heard the splash of oars and once or twice the distant sound of a voice. One at a time, the little boats returned ... more slowly, he thought, and riding lower in the water ... all heading for the place that glint of light was showing. He stood up and began moving cautiously towards it.

After perhaps half the distance, he decided he was close enough to observe in relative safety. If he lay flat on top of the Wall, he reasoned that it ought to be possible to see what was happening on the beach below. Getting into position was easier said than done but he finally managed it without sending any loose stones clattering. Then he peered over the edge ... and his breath leaked away.

In the patchy light of a handful of torches, he counted upwards of fifty men. With brisk efficiency, boats were being unloaded. Boxes were strapped, pannier-style, to more than a dozen ponies; packages of all shapes and sizes made their way on to carts; and pairs of barrels were harnessed to the chests and backs of brawny fellows who immediately trudged off inland.

The whole operation, so far as he could see, was running on well-oiled wheels and with scarcely a sound. The various components of the cargo were all leaving the beach along the same track. Adam knew where it went. It led towards Ivychurch – from which there were roads to Snargate, Snave and Brookland. The only way to find out where the goods ended up was to follow but with so many men and so much activity all around Adam knew that doing so would be the height of stupidity. Those who had set off first would presumably either be heading home or back for another load. Not all of them would be moving in the same direction so his chances of not bumping into somebody were slim to non-existent.

* * *

Down on the beach, Guy Edgerton-Foxe was fizzing with excitement and blessing his good fortune in arriving home when he had. If he'd got back just a day later, he'd have missed tonight. This wasn't the first time he had helped with a run. During holidays from university, he had joined the owlers whenever it was possible. It made Guy proud that they trusted him and treated him exactly as they did each other. As for the run itself ... there was nothing like it. Standing shoulder to shoulder in the dark with the other fellows; tense and silent, waiting for the signal out at sea that told the land crew it was time.

His friends at Oxford talked openly about their families buying smuggled brandy and tea. It amused Guy to think of their reaction if he were to tell them how those goods got there. Not that he ever would. Knowing the secret was more important than boasting about it ... and he knew what happened to men who told.

But the organisation of a run was a beautiful thing. The date and time of it were set in advance but the landfall location wasn't fixed until the eleventh hour. Tonight, thanks to the Dymchurch Riding Officer's attack of marsh ague, they were all assembled at Globsden Gut waiting for that all-important blue flash.

It came at last and was answered with a signal from the beach.

Tonight's cargo and the vessel bringing it were correspondingly large so the ship would come as close to shore as it could and await the flotilla of small boats. Guy watched them go. Everyone had their own task. His was that of unloading the boats as they returned from each trip and reloading their cargo on carts and ponies. Tea, tobacco and costly silks came ashore in parcels of varying size wrapped in oiled cloth. A double row of batsmen armed with clubs lined the beach from the waterline to the Wall, ready to protect the tub carriers with their barrels of gin and brandy should it be necessary. The first loads set off inland the instant they were complete ... and the whole operation took place with speed, efficiency and in near silence.

By the time his job was done for the night, Guy knew he'd be drenched in sweat with an aching back but he didn't mind. He'd wanted to spend these weeks with his friends in London ... but since he couldn't, being part of the run was wonderful compensation, even without the money he'd earn from it.

* * *

Above on the Wall, Adam was wet, cold and had cramp in his muscles from lying still for so long. He wanted a hot bath more than he had ever wanted anything but knew it would be hours before he could have it. As he set off on the weary slog back to New Romney he tried to comfort himself with the knowledge that at least he didn't have to do this again tomorrow night. It didn't help very much.

CHAPTER TWELVE

Next morning whilst eating a solitary breakfast and without any idea what time her brother had come home or even *if* he had, Camilla wondered what company he was keeping. There were a number of young men of a similar age, many of whom he'd known nearly all his life. Some were the sons of shopkeepers, solicitors or merchants. Others were fishermen, weavers and farm-labourers. Friends he'd played with as a boy. But she was fairly sure that among them were a few from whom he would be wise to distance himself just a little as he approached his majority.

She was particularly uneasy about the clientele at the *City of London* whither Guy had said he was bound the night before last. Rebuilt four years ago and renamed after the ship which had been swept over the Wall and demolished it, the tavern had become very popular with the younger men. More to the point, Camilla had heard rumours suggesting that some of its regular patrons included men in whom Adam Brandon might well be interested. And if that *was* the case, it would be much better if Guy got drunk elsewhere.

He finally put in an appearance just after eleven when she was about to help the maids hang the new curtains in the master bedchamber. Unable to help herself, she said, 'What time did you get home last night? Or should I say this morning?'

As soon as the words were out of her mouth she wished them back.

His smile evaporated and he said curtly, 'Does it matter? I thought we agreed my comings and goings were my own business.'

'We did and they are. I only asked because I imagine most of your companions from last night have work to go to today.'

'Some do, some don't.'

She sighed and continued trying to sound conciliatory.

'How was the prize fight?'

'It was called off.' He followed her into the bedchamber and stopped dead, absorbing the changes and not looking remotely pleased about them. 'What's going on here? This is Father's room.'

'It *was* Father's room. It ought now to be yours so I thought --'

'Well, you thought wrong.'

Her expression growing troubled, she said gently, 'Guy ... I don't expect you to move in here immediately, if you'd rather not. But in due course --'

'I said no. My present rooms suit me perfectly well and I'd prefer to keep them.' There was a very good reason for that but it wasn't one he could tell Millie. His rooms were on the other side of the house and close to the back stairs – which made getting in and out unseen a damned sight easier than it would be from the master suite. 'So if all this is for my benefit, you've wasted your time. I don't want it.'

The maids all stopped work and stared.

Camilla had a sudden urge to smack him. To stop herself doing it, she grabbed his arm and hauled him out of the room. Then, her voice low and hard, she said, 'I'll give you the benefit of the doubt and assume this attitude is because it feels like replacing Papa. I understand that. Do you think I don't miss him every bit as much as you? I do. Mama's rooms are still as she left them because I go and sit there sometimes. But whether you like it or not, in six weeks' time you'll be head of the family and you'll have to start *acting* the part. Move into these rooms or don't – it's up to you. But leave the sulky boy in the tavern, if you please, and for God's sake *grow up*!'

Throughout this diatribe, Guy had grown steadily whiter. Finally he said, 'Is this about the money? Because if it is and you intend to go on nagging --'

'It's nothing to do with the money,' she snapped back. 'It's gone – and there's an end of it. It's about ducking your problems by running off to drink yourself silly --'

'You think that's what I spent last night doing?'

'Didn't you?' began Camilla. And then stopped, struck by something she should have noticed right away. He looked a little underslept, yes ... but otherwise clear-eyed and alert. Nothing like the way he looked when suffering the after-effects of over-indulgence. She said slowly, 'No. My mistake. But if you weren't drinking until all hours of the morning ... what *were* you doing?'

He raised derisive brows and smiled. 'Enjoying myself in other ways. Do you really want me to spell it out? Or would you rather I spared your blushes?' And with a brief laugh, turned on his heel and walked away.

* * *

At around the time Mr and Miss Edgerton-Foxe were losing all patience with each other, Mr Brandon was woken by the noisy arrival of the Mail coach. He groaned and shoved his head under the pillow despite knowing it wouldn't help. Once awake, he always stayed awake so it was just a matter of surrendering to the inevitable.

He had arrived back at the inn at a little after four in the morning and, having thrown off his wet clothes, immediately sat down to scribble a note to Sebastian, describing what he'd seen and asking that the information be passed on to the Riding Officer in Rye. Then he'd told Finch to deliver it first thing and collapsed into bed for some much-needed sleep.

Now, hauling himself to his feet and dragging on a chamber-robe, he rang the bell and ordered a bath, followed by breakfast. Mrs Hadlow's mouth compressed into its usual grim line and she said, 'A bath, sir? Now?'

'Yes. Now. Is there some problem with that?'

'Well, no. But --'

'Good,' said Adam. 'As soon as possible, if you please.'

She quit the room with an expression that suggested to Adam that he ought to employ caution if breakfast included mushrooms.

Half an hour later and sitting in blissfully hot water, he let his mind drift over everything he'd seen on St Mary's beach. The number of people involved suggested a bigger operation than he'd expected. This, in turn, told him something else. A large cargo of contraband had made landfall last night ... and presumably, its French or Dutch suppliers had demanded payment before handing it over. Consequently, the smugglers must have access to substantial amounts of capital – significantly more than groups of sheep farmers, fishermen or even local gentry would be able to raise. So who was providing the money? One man? Two? A syndicate? And who amongst these was managing the spy chain?

He dressed, sat down to a very belated breakfast – mercifully without mushrooms – and concluded that a note to Goddard wouldn't go amiss. All along, he'd had the niggling feeling that he hadn't been told everything. But if Goddard had any suspicion of who might be involved in the espionage side of things, Adam wanted to know who it was. As soon as he'd finished eating, he wrote the note – which, aside from his questions, included assurances of Miss Edgerton-Foxe's safety and well-being – addressed it to Mr Goddard of Wilfred Street and left it for collection by the afternoon Mail. Then he took Hector from the stables.

He let the horse have his head along the beach and then turned inland on the track used by last night's caravan of smugglers. As he'd expected it was even more well marked than usual thanks to the wetness of the ground; also as expected, it wound past Ivychurch to the Brenzett crossroads ... and on towards Snargate. There was no sign of activity on the roads to either Snave or Brookland and so, recalling the painting of a galleon on the north wall opposite the main door of St Dunstan's at Snargate which had struck him as the equivalent of a smugglers' welcome mat, Adam decided to start there.

Like most of the other marsh churches he had seen, St Dunstan's was a medieval structure with a square tower that had probably been added later. It had a wood-beamed, gabled nave with the usual aisles either side. But, as Adam knew from his previous visit, a rear portion of the north aisle was separated from the main body of the church by a fixed partition. He had wondered about that at the time. Now he wondered about it even more because the flagstones between it and the porch door were wet, as if they had been recently washed. Having already failed to find a way past the screen from inside the church, Adam resolved to take a closer look at the outside. But first, another damp trail ended at the door to the belfry steps ... and since he appeared to have the place to himself, now seemed as good a time as any to investigate.

Finding the door locked was no surprise. But it was annoying to realise that he could have been through it in less than two minutes if —

'Was you looking for something?'

The voice startled him but he turned smoothly to face its owner, a burly fellow carrying a pair of shears, and said, 'I'd thought to climb up for the view. You don't happen to have the key, do you?'

'Old Hollins keeps it. He's fussy about his bells and don't like folk messing with 'em.'

'Ah. Understandable, I suppose.' And with a shrug, 'No matter. Another day, perhaps.'

'Aye. Maybe.' Both tone and expression clearly said, *Don't count on it.*

Taking the hint, Adam strolled towards the door saying pleasantly, 'I'll be on my way, then. Good day to you.'

The reply was a surly nod and for a moment the man didn't seem inclined to move. But when Adam was almost toe to toe with him, he reluctantly stepped aside.

Damn, thought Adam as he walked outside. *If I try examining the walls now, he's going to ask what I'm doing. It will have to wait – by which time, if there* is *anything here, they'll have moved it. Perhaps, if that chatty vicar is away tending his flock, I'll have better luck at Ivychurch.*

He rode back and into the village, fingers metaphorically crossed.

The *Bell Inn* lay beside St George's, so he paused there for a half of home brewed and watched through a window for anyone going in or out of the church. When after ten minutes there had been no sign of life, he left Hector at the tavern and sauntered across the churchyard. Inside, the church was cool and silent. Adam took a long, thoughtful look around. Nothing appeared out of place or odd. If the place was being used as a temporary hiding place, the contraband was either in the tower or the crypt – presuming there was one. The stairs to the tower lay open so he squeezed up the narrow spiral to the belfry and found … absolutely nothing.

Back in the nave, he searched for a door or any possible opening in the floor that might lead to a vault. Once again, he drew a blank. If there was a hiding place here it was extremely well concealed and the longer he went on looking, the greater the chance of being caught doing it. Time to go.

He was about to leave when something about the floor of the Lady Chapel caught his attention. Unlike the nave, it was composed of rough bricks unevenly laid. But a few yards from the altar was a single slab of pale stone with a hole in each corner … around which, and at the end of a trail from that outside door in the north wall, was the same tell-tale dampness he'd seen at Snargate. Adam frowned at the slab and gave it an experimental tap with his boot. Those holes suggested that there was a way of lifting it. But even if he dared risk being caught tampering with the floor, there was no way he could lever that stone out unaided. What he needed to do now was leave before the blasted vicar came in and started asking awkward questions. But one thing was annoyingly certain. He couldn't walk here at night when the cargo – if there *was* a cargo – was being moved onward. Aside from it being too great a distance, he would almost certainly be caught.

He collected Hector from the *Bell* and set off in the direction of Dragon Hall where he hoped to find Miss Edgerton-Foxe in a less tetchy mood than last time he'd seen her and prepared to surrender his lock-picks – though preferably *not* in front of her brother.

* * *

Guy Edgerton-Foxe had just returned from an errand in Dymchurch which, in turn, had bred a second one in Lydd. Both had stemmed from the previous night and neither had been at all onerous – though he did wonder why *he* had been asked to do them. Not that it mattered. He was happy to do anything that got him away from the house and his intensely aggravating sister.

He was in the stable-yard giving orders to Brewster when he saw the horseman riding down the avenue and said, 'Who's this?'

The young groom followed his gaze and frowned.

'It's that Mr Brandon, sir. Him as came down with Miss Millie from London. Been here a time or two since, an' all.'

'Has he indeed? Well, see to his horse out here in the yard ... and deal with the other thing as soon as you can. Meanwhile, I'd better warn my sister to expect company.'

Camilla was overseeing the replacing of the books on the library shelves when Guy stuck his head around the door to say, 'There's a fellow riding up the drive – name of Brandon, I believe.'

'What?' She swung to face him. 'Now?'

'That's what I said. Who is he?'

Busy consulting the mirror, Camilla said absently, 'Uncle Hugh sent him to see me safely here from town.'

'But you've been home nearly a fortnight, haven't you? So why is he still here?'

'I've no idea. Perhaps he has nothing better to do.'

Guy folded his arms and leaned against the door jamb, watching her tidying her hair and tugging the bodice of her apricot dimity gown into place. 'Are you *interested* in him?'

'Interested? In what way?'

'As a potential husband. Isn't that the only way ladies are *ever* interested in men?'

She turned around with a brief, sardonic laugh. 'Some, perhaps. But not this one.'

'Then why are you flapping about how you look?'

'I'm not *flapping*. It's just that the last time he called, I was smothered in dust.'

'Mm. Well ... if you say so.'

'I *do* say so. Now please tell Coombes to send Mr Brandon to the yellow parlour, then serve tea – for some reason, the bell in there wasn't working yesterday so we can't rely on it.' She glanced over her shoulder at him. 'I take it you'll join us?'

'Wouldn't I be *de trop*?' he asked provokingly.

'Oh – for heaven's sake. Haven't I just *told* you? No!'

'In that case, I will. I suppose I ought to meet the fellow.'

Admitted to the house by the butler, Adam said, 'Good day, Mr Coombes. Could you please tell Miss Edgerton-Foxe that if I have once again called at an inconvenient time, there is no need for her to receive me. I merely came to retrieve something I loaned her for a while.'

'It is not inconvenient at all, sir. She has been informed of your arrival and asked for you to join her upstairs.'

'Oh. Good.' He wondered if it was. 'Thank you. You needn't show me up. I know the way well enough.'

Since the parlour door stood open, he paused briefly on the threshold absorbing two things. First, that Camilla ... *When did I start thinking of her as that?* ... was wearing a particularly fetching gown and that the thick, dark hair was arranged with a becoming neatness that made his fingers itch to restore the inviting dishevelment of their last two encounters; and second, that a young man – presumably her brother – was perched casually on the window-seat and surveying him critically over folded arms.

'Mr Brandon.' Hiding her sudden quiver of nerves, Camilla rose and walked towards him, hand outstretched. 'Please – do come in.'

He strolled forward, accepted her fingers and bowed over them.

'Thank you, ma'am. But you have company and I'm intruding.'

'Not at all. Allow me to introduce my brother. Guy ... this is Mr Brandon. As I told you, he is an acquaintance of Uncle Hugh.'

Taking his time about it, Guy sauntered over to shake hands with Adam and immediately follow it up with, 'Pleasure, sir. But you and our uncle must be more than mere acquaintances if he chose you as Millie's escort.'

'Not really. It was more a matter of convenience and timing. And naturally I was happy to do Lord Alveston a small favour.'

'I'm sure he's grateful. As to the convenience ... does that mean you have other business in the district?'

'Not as such. Just no commitments requiring my presence elsewhere at present.' *And that's enough of that*, thought Adam, turning to Camilla. 'Your brother's home-coming must have been a pleasant surprise. I understood you didn't expect him for some weeks yet.'

'I didn't. But happily his plans changed.'

The glint in her eye was *not* one of unalloyed delight. Adam wondered if whatever had been going on between the two of them was responsible for Guy Edgerton-Foxe's palpably suspicious attitude towards himself.

'Ah – tea,' said Camilla, trying not to sound relieved. 'Thank you, Thomas. Please sit, Mr Brandon. A little milk and no sugar, was it not?'

He agreed that it was, knowing she hadn't needed to ask and wondering why she had.

While she busied herself with the tea things, Guy dropped into a chair, smiled at Adam, and said, 'So how are you entertaining yourself hereabouts?'

'Enjoying some exhilarating gallops along the beach and admiring several rather fine churches. Also, I'm finding your sheep worthy of interest.'

Camilla made a tiny spluttering sound and dropped a teaspoon.

Not bothering to hide his disbelief, Guy said, '*Sheep*? Surely you're joking!'

'Not at all. My brother farms sheep on our estate in Yorkshire ... but ours are very different. I think Max might like to experiment with your Romney breed.'

Guy wasn't sure he believed that. He wondered if the fellow was hanging around here to sniff after his sister or for other reasons entirely. On the whole, he hoped it was the former because Millie could probably be relied upon to give Mr Brandon his marching orders in words of one syllable.

Unaware of the trend her brother's thoughts were taking, Camilla handed Adam a cup of tea saying, 'If you're serious about that and can arrange transport, we'll give a pair for your brother to breed from.'

'Thank you. That's very generous – though I'm sure Max would insist on paying.'

'In which case, we'll let him,' remarked Guy, reaching for a slice of fruit cake.

This time his sister's eyes shouted, *What is the* matter *with you?* so clearly she might as well have said it. Smiling inwardly, Adam took a sip of tea and decided to lend a hand.

He said, 'I understand you've recently left Oxford, Mr Edgerton-Foxe. Do you miss it?'

'Not a bit. Who does?'

'I did, a little – though it was Cambridge in my case.'

Guy blinked, as if surprised that Adam had attended a university at all. But he said, 'Three years of dusty books and doddering tutors were enough for me, thank you. But then, I don't claim to be any sort of academic.'

'I don't believe that I made any such claim either,' returned Adam mildly. 'But though I won't pretend I went to *all* my lectures and tutorials, I did attend most of them.'

Not quite under his breath, Guy muttered something sounding suspiciously like, 'Good for you.' Fortunately, Camilla chose the same moment to say acidly, 'From what I've heard of university students, that would make you an exception.'

He smiled slightly. 'Less an exception than a member of the minority.'

'Love of learning? Or did you need a good degree for future employment?'

Guy again, still with that faintly derisive note which, once again, Adam chose to ignore.

'Neither. I studied partly because it was what my father would have expected of me. And partly because I suspected I'd regret wasting opportunities which many men don't get.'

'Opportunities which no women *ever* get,' cut in Camilla.

'And why should they?' demanded her brother impatiently. 'What good would university have been to you? You can't enter a profession, after all. Girls just get married.'

'Not,' she said between her teeth, 'all of them. *I* haven't and don't intend to.'

'You say that *now* but things change. Though Lord knows why you broke --'

In reaching for a honey cake, Adam's cuff somehow managed to overset the milk jug. Coming hurriedly to his feet and snatching up a napkin, he said, 'I'm so sorry, Miss Edgerton-Foxe – how clumsy of me. Allow me to --'

'Please sit, Mr Brandon.' Camilla rose and, taking the napkin from him, began calmly dealing with the spill. 'It is of no moment, I assure you. Guy, ring for more milk – oh, you can't, can you? But doubtless Thomas is hovering in the hall. Go and see, will you?'

With a sigh and a shrug, Mr Edgerton-Foxe sauntered from the room.

The second he was through the door, Camilla abandoned the napkin in favour of reaching for something concealed behind the cushions on her chair. Then, holding out Adam's lock-picks, she hissed, 'You can explain why you did that tomorrow morning at eight on St Mary's beach. Meanwhile, I suppose you came for these?'

He nodded and stowed them swiftly in his pocket. 'I didn't expect to need them --'

'It doesn't matter.' With a glance at the doorway, she went back to mopping the tray. 'Be careful. Guy doesn't know about Uncle or the Section or – well, any of it.' Then, resuming her normal tone and as if continuing a conversation, 'Which of our churches have you found most impressive?'

'Probably the one at Fairfield – though I haven't been inside it yet.'

'And of those you have?' Guy asked, re-entering in time to hear this.

'St Nicholas's in New Romney. It's remarkable to think that it was once on the harbour front. And I was considering visiting Brookland and perhaps Snave.'

'There's nothing special about either of those,' began Guy. 'But --'

'Of course there is,' cut in Camilla, staring at him. 'The belfry at Brookland --'

'Oh yes. I'd forgotten about that. But All Saints at Burmarsh has got the Magdalen bell, hasn't it?' He flashed a hard smile at Adam. 'Although if you're returning to London soon, you won't have time to visit quite all our churches, will you?'

Adam eyed him thoughtfully. Had Guy's dismissive remark about Brookland been designed to keep him away from the place? If so, why? And he hadn't been pleased when his sister corrected him, had he? Deciding that this was something to consider later, he said, 'My plans remain flexible – which suits me as I have other acquaintances in the area.'

'Oh. You do?'

'Yes. Lord Sarre, for example.'

For a second, Guy looked nonplussed. Then, recovering, he said, 'Oh – I see. You met our uncle through him, I suppose?'

Camilla opened her mouth and then, thinking better of it, closed it again. Exactly how *had* he met Uncle Hugh?

'Not at all. Lord Alveston and I met in Paris.' Rising from his seat, Adam smiled lazily and with intent. 'At the time, I was doing a little specialist tutoring at a friend's *Salle d'Armes*.'

Guy also rose. 'Specialist?'

'Yes. Swordsmanship – as opposed to fencing. It's a particular passion of mine.' He watched the younger man absorb that but resisted the temptation to smile. 'And now I should go. Thank you for the tea, Miss Edgerton-Foxe – and once again, apologies for my clumsiness.' His bow included both her and her brother. 'A pleasure to have met you, sir.'

'Likewise,' muttered Guy, no longer sounding quite so superior.

Adam enjoyed a moment's satisfaction and then, with another slight bow, walked out.

When the door closed behind him Guy fixed his sister with a hard stare and said, 'What did he come here for?'

'Must there have been a reason?'

'Unless you and he are on cosier terms than you've admitted to – yes. How many times has he been here?'

'Including today? Three. But --'

'But nothing. Grandmama said you'd vowed to neither visit nor receive visitors – yet *he* seems to be running tame around the place. Why?'

'You're exaggerating. He's only --'

He cut her off with an abrupt gesture, saying, 'I don't like the fellow, Millie.'

'I noticed. I expect Mr Brandon did, too.'

'I don't give a tinker's curse if he did or not. I --'

'Doubtless he's aware of that as well.' She stood up and shook out her skirts. 'Whether you like him or not is immaterial. You know better than to be rude to a guest – or at least, you used to. And I've a feeling that Mr Brandon isn't a gentleman to tangle with.'

'What's that supposed to mean? You surely weren't taken in by him boasting about his swordsmanship, were you? *God*, Millie – I thought you had more sense.'

'I do. Enough, at least, to know he wasn't boasting. He usually wears a sword as a matter of course. I've seen it and it's no toy, so I'd advise you to take him seriously. Clearly Uncle Hugh does – otherwise Mr Brandon wouldn't be here at all, would he?'

'No. I daresay he wouldn't. But since you've no objection to receiving him – and if you can stop turning the house upside down for a little while – I'd like to invite some of my own friends to dine.'

Not any of your drinking cronies from the City of London, I hope, she thought. But said calmly, 'Of course. Anyone in particular?'

'George Derring, Mark and Peter Blane ... maybe a couple of others of similar ilk.' He raised sardonically challenging brows. 'I take it they'd be respectable enough for you?'

Mr Derring senior was the local Squire and, in addition to his son, was blessed with three unmarried daughters. The bachelor Blane brothers ran the offices of their grandfather's bank. Both families were looking for social advancement. Camilla shuddered inwardly. Mrs Derring and Mrs Blane would choose to view their sons dining at Dragon Hall as an invitation to call there themselves ... and it wasn't difficult to guess why.

'By all means,' she said, rising to leave the room. 'But please find a tactful way of telling them to keep their mothers at bay. As I said earlier, I'm not in the market for a husband – any more than I imagine you're looking for a wife.'

CHAPTER THIRTEEN

Back at the *Cinque Port Arms*, Adam found Finch ironing shirts and cravats with the kind of excruciating care he imagined was usually reserved for intricate surgical procedures.

Staying well out of range in case of accidents, he said hopefully, 'Is there no one at the inn who could take care of that, Harry?'

'Only Hadlow's eldest girl. And her Ma wants rid of us so bad there's no saying what she might do deliberate-like.'

There was no saying what Harry might do accidental-like either… and Adam couldn't afford the loss of another shirt so he said, 'Well, leave it for a few minutes and tell me how it went with Lord Wingham.'

Finch obediently set the iron on the trivet. 'He's lent me a horse so I could take the hired one back to the inn. And in case you wanted to move to his cottage, I reckoned as I'd better get a bit of laundry done now.'

'What about the information I sent him?'

'Said he'd pass it on.' And, pointing to the night-stand, 'He's sent you a letter.'

'Good. Thank you.' He picked it up, broke the seal and then, since the room was like an oven thanks to the fire Harry had lit to heat the iron, said, 'I'll read it outside while you finish what you were doing.'

Sebastian's note was brief.

The cottage is ready and yours if you want it. Meanwhile, I'm pulling rank and ordering the three Riding Officers here at noon the day after tomorrow so you can give them a first-hand report. Hopefully something useful will come of that. Cassandra asks if you passed on her invitation to Miss Edgerton-Foxe and suggests that the lady might care to ride over with you and keep her company while we attend to business. Having warned her that you may prefer our association to remain private, I leave that decision to you.

Adam was glad to finally have a chance to meet the local authorities, such as they were. The cottage was a different matter. It was near to the coast at Rye but quite a distance from the marsh. It was also, though he tried not to let this weigh with him, quite a distance from Camilla Edgerton-Foxe – a fact which ought not to matter but somehow did. And though he'd be happier knowing that he'd climbed in and out of windows at the *Cinque Port Arms* for the last time, he couldn't have it both ways.

As for inviting Camilla to go with him to Audley Court, he supposed it might not be the best idea ... but since she'd almost certainly refuse, there was no harm in making the offer. He'd decide about that tomorrow when he saw her.

He contemplated the following day's assignation, already aware what the first hurdle would be and considering the various ways of clearing it safely. He was also uncomfortably conscious of looking forward to it more than was probably wise.

* * *

The next morning dawned dry and bright but decidedly chilly. Having expected to arrive on the beach first, Camilla was surprised to see Mr Brandon cantering towards her from the other direction, his hair windswept and a hint of colour warming his cheeks. She waited for him to come up with her and said, 'Good morning. Have I kept you waiting?'

'Not at all. I woke early and preferred to be away from the inn.' He smiled, noting the smart blue habit and frivolous little hat. 'Shall we ride before you chastise me or after?'

'Before. Don't think I'll forget, though.'

'I know better than to hope for that.'

Her nod of acknowledgement was accompanied by that scorching smile.

'Race you to the end of the Wall.' And she kicked her mare into a gallop.

Adam set off in her wake, knowing she had no chance of beating Hector but willing to allow her to think she might. Across the beach they flew, setting the sand flying and jumping the low groynes with ease. He heard her laugh, the sound seductive, exuberant and full of life. It almost persuaded him to let her win ... but *only* almost because, if he did that and she guessed that he had, nothing but trouble could come of it. So he gained steadily on her, drawing level around the half-way point before giving Hector his head and sweeping past her with a teasing grin.

Halting where the Wall ended, he watched her ride up to him. Her cheeks were flushed, her eyes bright and she'd lost a number of hairpins. Adam felt a sudden urge to dismount, lift her from the saddle and kiss her until she kissed him back. Banishing it, he said, 'I should have named a forfeit.'

'So you should,' she agreed. 'A wasted opportunity.'

And not the only one, he thought. 'It would have been an unfair advantage. I knew I would win.'

'So did I – though for a moment there I wondered if you were going to let me.'

'And if I had?'

'I'd have gone home and been done with you.'

'And I'd have deserved it.'

Camilla's brows rose. 'You would?'

'Is that so surprising? I don't appreciate being patronised either.'

This time she looked at him as if he was an alien species. Then, shaking her head and frowning a little, she said bluntly, 'You see it. Most gentlemen don't. They think they're being indulgent or, worse still, gallant.'

Adam shrugged. 'Quite a lot of ladies expect that – prefer it, even. Neither sex has a monopoly on idiocy, I find. Shall we start back? Or do you want to haul me over the coals for my little mishap yesterday?'

'That was no mishap,' retorted Camilla, setting Sheba in motion. 'You are possibly the least clumsy person I have ever met.'

'Thank you.' And with a suspicious glance, 'You did mean least clumsy *gentleman*, didn't you?'

He saw her repress a desire to laugh.

'That would be telling – and don't change the subject. You spilled the milk to create a diversion. Why?'

'You know why,' sighed Adam, bringing Hector alongside her. 'The atmosphere was already sufficiently strained without your brother putting both feet in his mouth.'

She took her time thinking about this but finally said wryly, 'You're right about the atmosphere. For reasons of his own, Guy was being deliberately annoying. But if you guessed what he was going to say it means someone must have told you something about me that I wasn't aware you knew. Who was it?'

Adam glanced at her face. She neither looked nor sounded as if touching on this subject was tantamount to driving a red-hot poker into an open wound ... but he supposed there was still time.

'Your uncle. He didn't supply details and I didn't ask for any. He merely said that you'd been engaged but had ended it. From an earlier conversation, I had the impression that you prefer not to discuss it ... but your brother seems not to know that.'

'Guy and tact are barely on nodding terms,' she muttered. Then, hauling in a bracing breath and looking him squarely in the face, she said, 'You're right, of course. I *don't* discuss it – and that's my privilege. But over-reacting ... growing angry and defensive the instant I sense a possibility of the subject being mentioned ... that's a different matter.' Still holding his gaze and after a second's hesitation, she added, 'I owe you an apology on that score for the way I behaved last week. I didn't stop to think. I just opened fire because I thought the conversation was heading towards *questions*. But it wasn't, was it?'

'Not then, no.' Adam hesitated and then said slowly, 'But I'd like to ask just one question now, if I may.'

Camilla looked back warily. 'You can ask. I might not answer, though.'

'That's fair. Well then ... I wondered if you regret it.'

'Regret what? The betrothal?'

'No. Ending it.'

She turned away from him to stare along the beach. Her fingers, he saw, were clenched hard on the reins. Finally she said, 'No. There was no other choice. At least ... there wasn't for me. So regret would be pointless, wouldn't it?'

'Regretting something you can't change generally is. But knowing that doesn't stop one wishing things had been different.'

'No. No, it doesn't.' Camilla waited, half-expecting him to ask something more. But when he didn't ... when he simply rode on in silence, she heard herself blurting, 'Guy doesn't know the circumstances. Neither does Uncle Hugh.'

Adam thought that was probably true of her brother. Young Mr Edgerton-Foxe had struck him as fairly self-absorbed. But Goddard? He doubted it. Goddard had the resources to find out anything he wanted to know. He could certainly learn anything Cassandra Wingham had heard over the tea-cups and a good deal more besides. So if Camilla believed him ignorant, it was presumably because he wanted her to.

'They don't?'

'No. If they'd known the truth, they'd have interfered. And it wouldn't have helped.'

He slanted a grin at her.

'Interfering in your life is what relatives are for. They do it because no one else can and because, having put up with it themselves, they don't see why you should be spared.'

Her shoulders relaxed a little. 'That is one way of looking at it.'

'It's the easy way. The other – acknowledging that they do it because they care – is harder to ignore. But that's where not telling them everything comes in.'

Camilla had a sudden, inexplicable urge to tell *him* everything. The down-to-earth manner along with the vault-like discretion made him seem the ideal confidante. More persuasive still was the fact that he wasn't asking – and showed no signs of intending to do so. *Could* she tell him, she wondered? Did she want to? And if she did ... would she regret it afterwards?

Caution won. She told herself that, thus far, she'd restricted the truth to Grandmama and there was no reason to change that. Also, just because she was beginning to like Adam Brandon rather more than she'd anticipated, there was no reason to suppose he would be interested in her erstwhile fiancé's sordid goings-on. So she decided to put the whole subject away and said instead, 'Guy doesn't tell me anything these days. He's out at all hours of the night, sleeps most of the morning and on the rare occasions I see him generally behaves the way you saw. It's becoming very tedious.'

'Nearly all young men are tedious. They leave university feeling very worldly and grown-up and thinking they know everything.' He grinned at her. 'Fortunately, most of us grow out of it fairly quickly.'

'I shall cling to the hope that Guy is one of them.'

They were almost back to the place where their ways parted; the point where Camilla could ride home and Adam, back to New Romney. He hesitated briefly and then, deciding to cast the dice and see what came of it, said, 'If your brother is busy with his own pursuits and you have time for mischief of your own … may I make a suggestion?'

'Mischief?' echoed Camilla, doubtful but curious. 'Yes. If you wish.'

'I'm going to Audley Court tomorrow and Lady Wingham has repeated her invitation to you. If you want to accept it, I'll be at Brenzett Corner at eight o'clock and we can ride there together.' His eyes challenged her. 'Guy doesn't need to know.'

* * *

Adam annoyed himself by spending much of the rest of the day wondering if she would come or not. On balance, he suspected probably not. She had refused to consider the idea when he'd mentioned it before. Indeed, she appeared to have retreated to Dragon Hall like a crab into its shell and was living the life of a recluse … except, oddly enough, with him. In the beginning, he'd half-expected her to tell Coombes not to admit him. He wondered why she hadn't. But whatever the reason, she couldn't go on shutting herself away from everyone forever. It wasn't healthy. And Lady Wingham struck him as a kind, sensible woman; the sort who would listen if one wanted to talk but wouldn't pry if one didn't – which, in his opinion, was precisely what Camilla needed.

As for concealing his own activities from her, he was coming to the conclusion that there was a case for not doing so. If she'd managed to keep her involvement with M Section and their uncle's part in it from her brother, she could presumably keep his own doings equally secret. And nothing he told her would come as any great surprise. She'd guessed most of it anyway. She knew

Goddard had sent him to investigate smuggling on Romney Marsh, so revealing how he was going about it and what he had learned couldn't do any harm and might even be helpful. Not taking advantage of her local knowledge made no sense. The only thing *against* enlisting her expertise was the possibility that she might try to take a more active role in the business ... but Adam felt fairly confident that he could scotch any such notion before she acted upon it.

Would she come? Or would he arrive at the crossroads to find it deserted? It wasn't until he changed his mind about which coat and vest to wear on the morrow and then changed it back ten minutes later, that he began to suspect he might be worrying about entirely the wrong things.

* * *

Camilla told herself that she ought not to go. She *really* ought not. She knew exactly what Grandmama would say.

Gallivanting about the countryside with a young man? Unthinkable! People will see you, tongues will wag and in no time at all two and two will be making forty.

All true, of course. But did it really matter? She wasn't ever going to marry. She'd given up on that possibility over a year ago. So why worry about her reputation? What was the point of playing by society's rules when one no longer cared about being part of its club? None at all that she could see.

Why *shouldn't* she do as she pleased? As soon as Mr Brandon had suggested it, the word *yes* had been hovering on her tongue. And in the same moment, she'd somehow been confident that he wouldn't interpret her acceptance of his invitation as permission to take ungentlemanly advantage. For some reason, she felt sure that his morals were as good as his manners. And even if they weren't and she *did* interest him in that way – which, not having attempted to persuade her to go with him, she clearly *didn't* – she could easily discourage him. Not that she had wanted him to try influencing her decision, she assured herself. Indeed, there was something extremely refreshing about his leaving her to make up her own mind.

Hang other people's opinions, she thought rebelliously. *What good have they ever done me? I'm a twenty-three year old spinster not a silly girl out to catch a husband. There's nothing to stop me visiting Lady Wingham in the company of a single gentleman – one, moreover, who my uncle considered suitable to escort me on a three-day journey from London. I want to go, so I shall. What's more, I'll have Martha unearth that green velvet habit from my trousseau. In fact, she can unpack* all *of it. I've got trunks full of new clothes so I may as well wear them. And it will keep Martha busy tomorrow while I play truant.*

* * *

That evening, while Camilla made her escape plans for the morrow, Guy Edgerton-Foxe was sitting around a table at *The Ship* in New Romney with three friends. In truth, the only one of the trio that he knew well was George Derring, the Squire's son. Mark and Peter Blane were several years his senior and until recently had moved in different circles. The invitation to a card party hosted by one of their cousins a couple of days ago had therefore been surprising ... and the evening itself extremely congenial. He'd left the tables a moderate winner and made his way home thinking that civilised company sometimes made a pleasant change from the more robust crowd at the *City of London*.

Tonight's gathering had been suggested by Mr Derring and Guy took the opportunity to invite his friends to dine at Dragon Hall any evening they were all free.

'That would be most pleasant.' Mark Blane inclined his head, courteously sombre as always. 'I would be delighted.'

'As would I,' drawled his brother. 'This will be the first time you have entertained since the death of your parents, won't it?'

'Yes. There's been no opportunity until now. What about you, George? Will you come?'

'Do you need to ask?' grinned Mr Derring. 'Millie's home, isn't she?'

'She is,' agreed Guy, trying not to sound as if this was a mixed blessing. 'But she's not going out and about much at present. Too busy turning the house upside down.'

Peter Blane laughed. 'But she'll meet old friends surely? She's been away far too long and has always been the fairest flower in the district. The Assemblies in Rye and Hythe just haven't been the same without her, have they, Mark?'

Mark gave his brother a repressive look.

'Miss Edgerton-Foxe's presence graces any event.'

'You can't know her very well,' remarked George lazily. 'If you did, you wouldn't talk about her as if she was somebody's great-aunt.'

'And you *do* know her well, I suppose?' asked Peter, sounding less self-satisfied.

'Yes. We played together as children. And Millie's got more spirit and sharper wits than any other girl I ever met.'

'She's got a sharper tongue, as well,' muttered Guy.

'That's sisters for you,' offered George flippantly, re-filling his glass and pushing the bottle across the table. 'Be grateful you haven't got three of them.'

'Oh I am – trust me! As for Millie, I thought she'd have married by now.'

'Yes,' remarked Peter thoughtfully. 'And she may still do so.'

'Not the way she's going,' muttered Guy. 'She won't even pay calls.'

'At all?' asked Mark, surprised.

'No.'

Frowning slightly, George said slowly, 'If Millie's keeping to herself on account of what happened in London last year, she needn't. No one here gives a rush. And a lady's entitled to change her mind.'

'Forgive my asking,' said Peter, 'but *did* she? Change her mind, I mean?'

'That's out of line!' snapped Mark, frowning. 'You've no business asking that – let alone questioning a lady's word.'

'I wasn't questioning it. I was merely wondering if rumour has the right of it.'

There was a small, awkward pause into which George said stubbornly, 'If Millie says it was she who broke the engagement, then it was. What's more, she'd have had a damned good reason for doing it.'

Guy stared moodily into his half-empty glass. A distant and slightly uncomfortable feeling suggesting that Millie ought not to be a topic for discussion over the card table warred with an urge to admit that she baffled him. At this point, it occurred to him that none of these men were part of London's *beau monde* and probably never would be. This emboldened him to say, 'I expect she did. But I've no idea what it was. As for Lord Staplehurst – the whole thing happened so fast that I never met him. All I know is what he put about afterwards. That he and Millie broke their betrothal by mutual consent.'

'She doesn't talk about it?' asked George.

'Not a word.'

'As is her prerogative,' observed Mark disapprovingly. 'And in my opinion, this conversation has gone on quite long enough.'

Guy flushed and took refuge in his glass.

'Oh – don't be such a stuffed shirt,' said Peter. 'We're all friends, aren't we? So cheer up, Guy. Some appreciative male company is all the ladies ever need.'

Guy scowled. 'She already has male company – and not the sort I like. Our uncle sent him with her from London on escort duty and he's still hanging around. She says she's not receiving visitors but she receives *him*.'

'Who is he?' asked Peter.

'Some fellow named Brandon – a younger son, I think – and too full of himself in my opinion. According to Millie, he swaggers around wearing a sword, for God's sake! But what *I* want to know is why he hasn't gone back where he came from.'

'You think he's trying to fix his interest with her?' asked George.

'I can't think of any other explanation.'

'And is she likely to let him?'

A surly shrug and then, 'She says not. But I wouldn't wager on it.'

'Well then,' declared Peter. 'Our course is clear, gentlemen.'

'Is it?' asked Guy warily.

'Of course! You wish to be rid of Mr Brandon?'

'I'd be happy to see the back of him, yes. But --'

'Then we shall eclipse him with our collective wit and charm.'

George gave a snort of laughter. 'And wealth and excellent connections?'

'Those things don't matter. If Brandon's a younger son, he won't have them either. But the three of us shall show Miss Edgerton-Foxe that there are plenty more, vastly superior fish in the sea. Between us, we'll soon send this interloper off with his tail between his legs.'

CHAPTER FOURTEEN

Adam arrived early at the crossroads, thankful that the day was dry and, as best he could tell, looking set to remain so. He smoothed the cuff of his coat and ordered his hands to stay away from his cravat. His pocket-watch told him it wanted a few minutes to eight. It was still possible that she'd come.

And then he heard hoof beats approaching and seconds later, she appeared from around the bend. This time the elegant riding-habit was deep forest green and cut to emphasise and flatter both bosom and waist, while a jaunty tricorne with a floating veil sat on the glossy dark curls. Something inside Adam unexpectedly shifted a little. He decided the only sensible thing to do was ignore it.

'Good morning, Miss Edgerton-Foxe. I'm glad you decided to join me. The ride will pass quicker and more pleasantly with company.'

'Well, I've vowed to be on my best behaviour – so let us indeed hope so.' She continued to gaze at the only thing about his appearance that had so far struck her. 'I see you've come armed today. Are we expecting footpads?'

'Not *expecting* them ... though one never knows. The sword is because I promised Sebastian a bout.' He smiled suddenly. 'That wasn't a lie, you see.'

Camilla coloured faintly. 'I never supposed it was,' she began. And then, under that amused slate-blue gaze, huffed, 'All right. I *did* suppose it and I still think it's only half the truth. But at the time you said it, I was feeling ... tetchy ... and *you* were busy covering your tracks. Admit it.'

'I'll admit that you were definitely tetchy.'

She scowled at him and then laughed. 'Keep this up, sir, and my good intentions may be very short-lived.'

Don't tempt me, thought Adam. But he said, 'In that case – since we've some distance to cover – perhaps we should put some of it behind us while the roads are still quiet?'

'That would probably be wise,' she agreed, nudging Sheba into a canter.

Wise … but disappointing, was his inevitable reaction as he set off in her wake.

They reached Brookland without seeing another soul and paused briefly for Adam to see the triple-flounced belfry which sat beside the church rather than on top of it.

'According to local legend,' Camilla told him, 'it fell off in shock when a virgin bride came to be married.'

He laughed. 'And the real reason?'

'If it had been over the church, the marshy ground probably wouldn't have supported the weight. Personally, I prefer the legend. Shall we ride on?'

She led the way through a network of narrow tracks until they reached the Guildford Lane. There was more traffic on the roads now and, recalling from his previous trip that this might be their last chance for any speed, Adam suggested picking up the pace again. Camilla nodded and they trotted in companionable silence as far as the ditch marking the Sussex border.

Once more slowing to a walk and having had long enough to reach a decision, Adam said, 'I'm not going to Audley Court purely for an hour's swordplay with Sebastian.'

She turned, gazing at him out of eyes wide with sardonic amusement.

'*Aren't* you? Good heavens – I'd never have guessed!'

Adam met her look with one of his own. 'Fine. If you don't want to know why I *am* going, let's talk about the weather instead.'

'Does that mean you were actually going to *tell* me?'

'I'd thought of it, yes.'

She stared at him with a mixture of bafflement and incredulity. Finally she said, 'Why? I mean, why tell me *now*? Come to that, why tell me at all?'

'Partly because you already know and have done from the beginning,' he shrugged. 'I didn't confirm your suspicions because Goddard told me not to and because I didn't know you well enough to take the risk. Now, however, I suspect you could be helpful – if only by keeping your eyes and ears open.'

'Thank you, kind sir. I'm flattered.'

He flashed her a grin. 'No. You're not.'

'All right. I'm not. So tell me. Why *are* we visiting Lord Wingham?'

'Because he's arranged for me to meet the three local Riding Officers. And before you ask – no, you will *not* be joining us. The fewer people openly involved, the better. But afterwards I'll want your thoughts as well as Sebastian's on what they tell me.'

Have you any idea how unusual that makes you? thought Camilla. *I don't believe Rainham and the rest of them have* ever *asked my opinion. Not once – even when I've been working with them. Oh, my* memory *comes in useful. But I've sometimes wondered if they realise there's a brain attached to it.*

She said slowly, 'Can I ask what you've learned so far?'

'Less than I'd like and nothing that leads where I want to go with this. But three nights ago, I watched a large cargo being landed between New Romney and Dymchurch.'

Her jaw slackened with shock for a second before she said weakly, 'You went out on the marsh ... on a night there was a run? And you stayed to watch? Are you *completely* insane?'

'Not quite. It's why I'm here --'

'If the owlers had caught you, you'd be dead.'

'But they didn't and I'm not,' replied Adam reasonably. 'I'm never going to find out anything unless I take the occasional risk, am I?'

She shuddered. 'Don't even *think* of doing it again. You were lucky. Next time you might not be. God knows how they failed to spot you. Don't you realise that they have look-outs posted *everywhere* when a cargo is due?'

'I rather guessed that they might.'

'They have watchers on the coast, looking for revenue cutters,' she snapped as if he hadn't spoken, 'and watchers inland looking for Preventives. They are *organised*, Adam. They don't leave anything to *chance*. It was a miracle you even left the inn without being seen and followed.'

'I was careful.'

'If you'd been caught, they'd have slit your throat and disposed of your body.'

'Exceedingly careful?' he hazarded meekly.

'Stop that!' exclaimed Camilla, thoroughly exasperated by what she glimpsed in his eyes. 'It's no laughing matter!'

'I know. Don't you want to hear how I got out of the inn?'

'No!' And then, relenting a little, 'Oh all right. Yes. How did you?'

'Down a rope from my manservant's window. But please don't tell Rainham that.'

'Promise you won't do anything so foolhardy again and I won't.'

Adam shook his head. 'I never make promises I might have to break.'

'Make an exception.'

'I can't. But I thank you for the warning and will be sure to bear it in mind.' He smiled suddenly. 'You called me by my given name a few minutes ago. Does that mean I have leave to use yours?'

'There you go again – trying to distract me,' she retorted. 'It won't work.'

'Pretend it has – unless you *want* to argue all the way to Audley Court?'

'I don't want to argue at *all*. I just want to make you aware of the risks you're running.'

'Consider it done. If it's any comfort, I've written to Goddard. If he thinks I'm out of my depth, he'll either send help or recall me. Now … may I *please* stop calling you Miss Edgerton-Foxe?'

Her sudden unexpected gurgle of laughter burned through Adam's chest like brandy. His brain still wasn't sure how much he liked her. For reasons of its own, his body liked hers very much indeed.

'It gets a bit wearing, doesn't it?' she agreed. 'On my ears as well as your tongue.'

He wished she hadn't mentioned tongues. It was putting ideas in his head he really didn't need just at present. Clearing his throat, he said, 'Was that a yes? If it wasn't, I'll just have to resort to ma'am in future.'

'Don't do that. It makes me feel like Grandmama.' She hesitated, almost shyly. Then, 'So yes ... Adam. You may call me Camilla, if you wish.'

* * *

They arrived at Audley Court a little after eleven, having paused briefly in Rye.

Greeted warmly by both Lord and Lady Wingham, Camilla found herself promptly whisked away. Left alone with Sebastian, Adam said, 'Thank you for this – and for lending Finch a horse and offering the cottage. It's good of you but --'

'No it isn't. It's just encouraging you to further bloody stupid exploits,' came the grimly forthright reply. 'I must need my head examining. *You* certainly do.'

'Not you as well,' groaned Adam. 'I've had that lecture most of the way here.'

'From Miss Edgerton-Foxe? You *told* her?'

'Yes. She's not stupid. But about the --'

'Good to know that *one* of you isn't.'

'-- cottage,' finished Adam. 'I'm grateful. But I believe it's too far out.'

'Yes. I suspected as much – but we can discuss that later if needs be. The Officers will be here soon and I've told Bradshaw to bring them up immediately. That gives you and I a short time in which to plan how best to work this – and the first thing, in my opinion, is to make it plain that you're not merely poking around out of nosiness.'

'Perhaps. But I'd thought to keep you out of it by seeing them alone.'

'There's little point in that, is there? I passed what you told me to Jeavons and he'll have doubtless told the other two. Come into the library. Cassandra is taking care of Miss Edgerton-Foxe.'

Upstairs in a guest bedchamber and perching on a window-seat while her maid put Camilla's hair to rights, Cassie said, 'You and I never got to know each other as well as I'd have liked. I'm glad to have the chance to rectify that.'

'It's good of you to invite me at such a time. May I say how very sorry I was to hear of Lord Wingham's death?'

'Thank you. We miss him. And I'm sad to think that Theo will never know him.'

'Theo is your son?'

'Yes. Not quite three months old and already bidding fair to be as much trouble as his father.' Cassie tilted her head, smiling. 'That wasn't meant seriously, by the way. Sebastian isn't the man you may have read about in the scandal sheets – and hasn't been since before I met him.'

Camilla had the uneasy feeling that anything she said at this point might be misinterpreted so she ducked the issue by thanking the maid and rising from her seat by the mirror saying, 'May I see him? The baby, I mean?'

It was the right choice. Cassie beamed at her. 'Of course. I do *try* not to be the kind of doting mama who foists her offspring on everyone – but it's surprisingly difficult. I do, however, promise to leave him in the nursery so we can enjoy some adult conversation.' She paused on the threshold and said hesitantly, 'You don't have to answer this ... but since receiving Mr Brandon's note, Sebastian has been worried. Is he right to be?'

'Yes. But on Mr Brandon's account – not his own or yours.'

'I see,' said Cassie. 'Well, naturally I'm relieved to hear that ... and also sorry.'

'Sorry?' asked Camilla. 'Why?'

'Because I suspect that you're worried, too.'

* * *

On the floor below, three extremely uneasy men were being shown into Lord Wingham's library. Rising to meet them and dismissing Bradshaw with a nod, his lordship said, 'Welcome, gentlemen. Jeavons – perhaps you would introduce your colleagues?'

Jeavons, a heavy-set fellow with a straggly pepper-and-salt beard, gestured to the other men in turn. 'Ned Hindley from Hythe, m'lord, and Don Tranter from Dymchurch.'

Hindley, skinny and prematurely bald, managed something akin to a bow. Tranter crushed his hat in his hands and stared at the carpet.

Indicating the chairs placed near his desk, Sebastian invited the trio to sit and when they had done so, said, 'Thank you for coming. You all know who I am. Mr Brandon here is a friend of mine who has been sent from London with official backing at the highest level. He is also the gentleman who witnessed a large cargo of contraband being landed at St. Mary's Bay three nights ago.'

All three looked at Adam and quickly away again.

'I take it,' continued Sebastian, 'that, but for Mr Brandon's information, none of you were aware of this event?' They shook their heads. 'What – not even a whisper?'

'No, m'lord,' said Jeavons gloomily. 'Not even that.'

'I understand that's normal,' remarked Adam. 'No one talks.'

'No, sir, they don't.' It was Hindley who spoke. 'We can ask questions till we go blue but nobody sees nothing nor hears it neither.'

'That must be very frustrating for you.'

'Not near so frustrating as being spread so thin we couldn't do nothing even if we'd seen what you did,' said Jeavons bluntly. 'If I might make so bold, sir, how *did* you catch wind there was to be a run?'

'I didn't. I went out and watched and waited. On my third attempt, I got lucky.'

'The luckiest bit was them not catching you at it.'

'A fact which has been brought home to me very forcibly,' agreed Adam. He glanced at the other two officers. 'I take it you've all been told what I saw?' They nodded. 'Good. Then I'd like you to take me through it, if you would – explain the process.'

Tranter was still examining the carpet. Jeavons looked blank.

'The process, sir?' asked Hindley. 'You mean ... what happens when?'

'Exactly. The first thing I saw was a single flash of blue light. Let's start there.'

'That'd be the spotsman on board ship telling the land crew they were off-shore,' offered Jeavons, looking happier now he understood what was required. 'Very distinctive that blue light is. Look-out can't fail to see it.'

'How is it done?' asked Sebastian curiously.

'Flint-lock pistol without a barrel, m'lord. Charge the pan and pull the trigger. Simple.'

'But inventive,' murmured Adam. 'And the land crew show a light to indicate they're ready and waiting?'

'Not just that, sir. The ship-master has to bring his vessel in on a fixed day and time but won't know exactly where landfall is to be because it's not decided till the last minute. That's another thing as makes our job harder,' said Jeavons bitterly. 'Even if there *was* an informer, he wouldn't be able to point us to the right spot in time to do anything about it – 'cos even the *ship* don't know where to weigh anchor till they get the signal.'

'And that is given how?' asked Adam. 'I caught something I *thought* was a light ... but it was so faint I couldn't be sure.'

Jeavons looked at Hindley. 'Spout lantern, d'you reckon?'

'Most like,' Hindley agreed. And when Adam looked enquiringly at him, 'The lantern has a long spout in front of the flame and a glass bullseye to focus the beam. Sends the light where you want it without much over-spill. Very useful to the owlers, that is.'

'I can imagine,' murmured Adam. Then, looking across at the Dymchurch officer, 'You're very quiet, Mr Tranter.'

'I ain't much for talking,' Tranter muttered.

'Not even when the cargo I saw came ashore on what must be your patch?'

'That's not my fault. I was laid up, wasn't I?'

'Of course. Marsh fever, I believe?' The answer was a terse nod. 'I hope you are fully recovered?'

'Till the next time,' grunted Tranter. 'Comes and goes, it does.'

Adam let the silence linger for a few uncomfortable minutes before turning back to Jeavons and Hindley. 'I know you gentlemen have other occupations and don't wish to take up too much of your time, so let's move on. I saw the unloading from the ship and re-loading for onward transport. What I'm principally interested in from that point is where the goods go. I have my own suspicions but I'd like to hear yours. Mr Jeavons?'

'Some of it gets no further than Tenterden or Ashford. But the bulk of it – the silks and laces, tea and brandy – is for London.'

'Does it begin its journey immediately or is it stored locally for a time?'

'It's here alright – probably till the next night,' said Hindley sourly. 'There's various places they stow it. Hidden cellars and churches, as often as not. But any time we go round looking, the bloody stuff's not there no more – begging your pardon, m'lord.'

Sebastian waved this aside, 'Which churches?'

'St Thomas's at Fairfield,' answered Jeavons. 'Nearly caught up with it there one time. And I'd put money on Ivychurch – though I can't figure out where they hide it.'

'Snargate and Brookland,' grunted Hindley. 'Makes you wonder, don't it? Half the sextons hereabouts must be taking a sweetener to look the other way. If we had more men … if there was dragoons nearby and more than a couple of Revenue cutters patrolling the coast … well, then we *might* be able to do something about it. But there ain't, so we can't. And with respect, Mr Brandon, I can't see you doing any better.'

'Neither can I. But digressing slightly … I expected to see large kegs rolling ashore. Instead I saw a great many small casks carried off two to a man. Brandy, was it?'

Hindley nodded. 'And gin, sir. It's in small barrels because it comes in raw.'

'Raw?'

'Yes. Neat, if you like. Take your throat out if you drank it like that so it's let down to drinking strength when it gets where it's going.'

'You mean it's diluted?' asked Sebastian. And with horrified incredulity when Hindley nodded, 'With *water*? In *London*?'

'Yes, m'lord.'

'Then God help anyone who drinks it!'

'London's water is that bad?' grinned Adam.

'In some places, you wouldn't even *wash* in it,' replied Sebastian, shuddering. 'However … have you any further questions?'

'Yes.' The cobalt eyes travelled to each of the Officers in turn. 'There were roughly fifty men on the beach that night. Can any of you put a name to even *one* of them?'

They exchanged glances and once more it was left to Jeavons to answer. He said aridly, 'Between us, I reckon we could probably name all fifty, sir – but it wouldn't do no good. *Everybody* is involved in it one way or another and they don't see nothing wrong with it 'cos who's it hurting? They're just earning a bit extra for themselves bringing in tea and baccy what folks can afford. *Where's the harm in that?* they say. *We're doing everybody a favour, ain't we?* And Peter won't peach on Paul 'cos he knows Paul won't peach on him.'

'I'm not interested in Peter and Paul,' said Adam crisply. 'I'm not even especially interested in the tea and tobacco. What *does* interest me is the man or men whose money floats the entire enterprise. Buying a cargo as large as the one I saw requires a good deal of cash and it has to come from somewhere. Any ideas on that score?'

All three shook their heads.

Hindley said, 'Some London gent, like as not.'

'Who probably never sets foot round here,' nodded Jeavons sourly.

Adam's gaze settled on the silent third man. 'Still nothing to say, Mr Tranter?'

'No. How would I know where the money comes from?'

'No more than your colleagues, I daresay. But surely you have an opinion?'

'Well, I haven't. I just do my job best as I can.' He glanced at the others, his expression sullen. 'So a run come in and I missed it. So what? You missed it an' all, didn't you? And *you* wasn't sick in bed like I was.'

Blinking, Hindley said, 'Nobody's blaming you, Don.'

'Ain't they?'

'No.' It was Adam who spoke, his tone perfectly bland. 'And I've no idea why you would think so. But if I've hurt your feelings, I apologise.' He paused, rising from his seat, aware that Jeavons was turning a snigger into a cough. 'I need a name, gentlemen.

Just one name; someone who might know something and be willing to talk to me in confidence. If any such comes to mind, you can leave word for me with Lord Wingham. But for now, I thank you for both your time and your help.'

* * *

Left alone again, Sebastian looked thoughtfully at Adam and said, 'Well ... what did you make of that?'

'Jeavons and Hindley were as helpful as one might reasonably expect.'

'And Tranter? Something off-key there, wouldn't you say?'

'Yes. He might have come here expecting blame. He might feel aggrieved that an amateur did his job for him. He might feel guilty because he wasn't ill at all that night – merely malingering.' Adam grimaced. 'Or he might know a lot of things he's not telling us.'

It was a long time before Sebastian spoke but finally he said, 'It could be worse than that. It's not completely unknown for Riding Officers to accept bribes in return for going suddenly blind and deaf on the night of a run.'

Adam stared at him. 'Please tell me that's a joke.'

'It's not.'

'Hell.'

'Quite. If that's true of Tranter – and I'm not saying it is, mind – he could conceivably pass on some or all of what was said here this morning.'

'Now *there's* a jolly thought.'

'Isn't it?'

Both men fell silent for a moment, contemplating the various ramifications.

'Malingering is the most likely thing,' said Adam at length. 'Let's hope it *is* just that – because I don't imagine keeping an eye on him is a viable option. Do you?'

'Not really.' Sebastian stood up and grinned. 'Sufficient unto the day, do you think? I was going to suggest joining the ladies in the drawing-room. But since you've brought your sword, perhaps we might enjoy ourselves first?'

'By all means. Where?'

'The rear courtyard. The ground is level, there's plenty of space and it's well away from the stable-yard and any potential audience.'

Adam lifted one brow. 'Shy, my lord?'

'No. But if you're going to humiliate me, I'd sooner not have witnesses.'

CHAPTER FIFTEEN

In fact, Cassie hadn't taken Camilla to the drawing-room but to a smaller, less formal parlour that got the afternoon sun. They drank tea; and though conversation was a little stilted at first, it soon flourished. They discussed mutual acquaintances, compared Cassie's awful sister-in-law with Camilla's annoying brother and speculated on what was going on in the library. Cassie talked about Christmas at Sarre Park and was just telling the tale of how a little girl and a goat had been instrumental in restoring the Marchioness of Amberley's sight when she became aware of the chime and scrape of metal drifting in through the open window.

Turning towards the sound, she said, 'What on earth ...?'

'Swords.' Camilla was already on her feet. 'Adam said he'd promised Lord Wingham a match or a bout – or whatever it's called.'

'And they weren't going to tell us so we could watch?' Grabbing her hand, Cassie hauled her over to the window. 'Oh my goodness. Perhaps *that's* why.'

Below them in the small courtyard, an assortment of masculine clothing adorned a bench. And in the centre of the space, stripped down to breeches and boots, Adam and Sebastian circled each other at sword-point.

Sunlight turned red hair to flame and wheat-blond to silver-gilt ... but what held Cassie and Camilla transfixed were two firm, perfectly-proportioned torsos, lightly but undeniably tanned and strapped with neat, well-defined muscle.

Oh, thought Camilla dizzily, her eyes drinking in Mr Brandon's shoulders and arms, chest and flat stomach. *He is ... spectacular. Like the statues at Montagu House only better. I had no idea*. And then, as Sebastian made a sudden lunge which Adam parried almost lazily, 'I presume they won't hurt each other?'

'Not deliberately.' Cassie's gaze was equally avid. 'I never get used to it, you know.'

'Get used to what?'

'How beautiful Sebastian is.' And then, with critical amusement, 'Though it has to be said that Mr Brandon is almost his equal.'

'*Almost*? You're just biased.'

'Yes. Aren't you?' And proudly, without waiting for an answer, 'Sebastian fences with Rockliffe who is said to be brilliant. So Mr Brandon may have a challenge on his hands.'

'So he might if they were fencing,' agreed Camilla. 'But they're not.'

'What?'

'Those aren't foils – they're swords. Didn't you see the one Adam was wearing when we arrived?'

'No. I barely saw *Mr Brandon*, let alone noticed what he was wearing,' retorted Cassie, peering down to where the fight – such as it was – had begun to gather pace. 'Good Lord! You're right. Actual *blades*! They'll maim each other.'

'But only by accident,' murmured Camilla dryly. 'They won't, though. From what I understand, Adam is an expert. If that's true, he won't touch Lord Wingham or give Lord Wingham the chance to touch him.'

'Well, that's a comfort. But call him Sebastian, please. As yet, he still prefers it.'

Below in the courtyard, Sebastian tossed a laughing remark over their crossed blades … and promptly found his sword spinning from his hand. He stopped laughing, watched it sliding across the stone paving and then, looking at Adam, said, 'What the hell was that?'

'A little trick of my own.'

'Show me.'

Adam smiled and did so, demonstrating the precise angle required and explaining as he went before inviting Sebastian to try.

Sebastian nodded and concentrated on recreating Adam's instructions exactly – only to have Adam step back, sword still in hand. Frowning, he said, 'What did I do wrong?'

'Nothing. It's easy to avoid when one is expecting it. Try again.'

Sebastian did so and gave a grunt of frustration when he achieved the same result.

Adam shrugged. 'I don't want my blade damaged.'

'Unfair! And I notice you weren't showing mine the same respect.'

'I'll respect it when you do. How long since it was last oiled?'

'No idea,' admitted Sebastian. Then, 'I fence tolerably well but I'm finding this more difficult than I expected.'

'It's a different skill.' Adam lifted his sword. '*En garde*.'

This time they engaged in a longer bout which eddied and flowed about the courtyard.

Above them, two ladies hung out of the window to watch, admire and occasionally suck in a breath when one or other of the swordsmen seemed in danger of mutilation.

Cassie whispered, 'Why aren't we ever allowed to see men do this?'

'Violence and naked male flesh?' retorted Camilla sardonically. 'We're *ladies*. We can't possibly *enjoy* this sort of thing. We'd have the vapours and faint.'

The swords rang, hissed and slithered in counterpoint until Sebastian was breathing unevenly and sweating. Finally, after some fifteen minutes of it, he stepped back dropping his point to the ground and gasped, 'Enough. My shoulder and arm are screaming and I've cramp in my hand.'

'You're not accustomed to the extra weight,' began Adam. Then stopped, as enthusiastic applause broke out from above their heads.

Sebastian looked up, laughed and gave a flourishing bow. 'How long have you been watching?'

'Long enough,' responded Cassie. 'We thought it splendid, didn't we, Camilla?'

'Splendid,' agreed Camilla, watching Mr Brandon turn away to sheathe his sword and reach for a towel. He didn't glance up and his movements looked suspiciously casual. She thought, *Is he embarrassed? Why?* He *isn't the one who's been caught gawking.*

Having briskly rubbed down his neck, arms and shoulders, Adam pulled on his shirt. Sebastian, meanwhile, was still standing there bare-chested and bantering with his wife until she said, 'Do put something on, darling. If you walk through the house looking like that the maids will faint.'

'Ah – but from shock or admiration?' he retorted, catching the towel Adam tossed at him. Then, 'Have Bradshaw send up some ale, will you? We'll join you as soon as we're fit to be seen.'

'You're fit to be seen *now*. That's just the trouble – is it not, Camilla?'

Feeling herself flush, Camilla muttered something that sounded like, 'Stop dragging me into it, will you?' and withdrew into the room.

Cassie followed, rang for the butler and said severely, 'Don't you *dare* go all coy and ladylike now. You were salivating just as much as me – though mostly over Mr Brandon, I hope. Admit it.'

'Yes. All right – I was. But there's no need for *him* to know that, is there?'

'Why not? He'd probably like it.'

'Not necessarily. And that's beside the point.'

'Which is?'

'I ... I'm not sure,' she lied, while a little voice in her head supplied the truth.

This is dangerous. I don't mind liking *him. That's harmless enough. But I do* not *want to become attracted to him. I'm done with all that – and it's almost certainly the last thing on his mind anyway. Only it's quite difficult* not *to warm to a man who listens to one's opinion and, in many respects, generally behaves as if one Is his equal. And it's even* more *difficult when the man in question teaches you to pick a lock, uses a sword as if it was an extension of his own body and has the musculature of a sculpture by Michelangelo.* She drew a long breath of mingled anxiety and irritation. *I don't want to develop feelings for him. I really,* really *don't. But I'm not sure it isn't already happening. Damn.*

The ale arrived and some minutes later the gentlemen walked in laughing.

Cassie said judiciously, 'I'm not sure you deserve ale. Why didn't you invite us to watch instead of sneaking off to have your fun in secret?'

'Why do you think?' grinned Sebastian, heading for the jug and pouring two tankards. 'Adam was being gentle – but he might just as easily have wiped the floor with me. You think I wanted you to see that?'

'Since your swordplay wasn't the bit we liked best, it wouldn't have mattered in the least.'

'Hussy,' he replied. And handing one of the tankards to Adam, 'Despite being a blow to my self-esteem, I found that extremely enjoyable. I hope we can do it again.'

'So do I.' Adam took a drink, still carefully avoiding Camilla's eye. 'If you wish, I can show you some exercises that will help you get used to the weight of the blade and adjust your balance. You'll be surprised at the difference it will make.'

'Thank you. I'd appreciate it.' Sebastian looked across at his wife. 'No doubt you want chapter and verse on our meeting with the Riding Officers?'

'Since Camilla and Mr Brandon have the whole ride home in which to discuss it, the gist will do for now. Was it helpful?'

'In some ways,' replied Adam. 'But less than I'd hoped.'

'And what exactly *had* you hoped for?' asked Camilla.

He finally made himself meet her eyes and was relieved to find them perfectly serious.

'Something that might lead to those in charge of the operation. Specifically, to those who finance it. It seems to me that smuggling will never be stopped at ground level. But it *might* be stopped – or at least drastically reduced – by cutting off the money.' He shrugged slightly. 'What do you think?'

'I agree entirely,' she said. 'It's probably the only thing that might work. But getting names isn't going to be easy. Or safe.'

'I realise that.'

Camilla turned to Cassie. 'What *that* means is that he realises the *not easy* part. The *not safe* part probably won't register until somebody has a pistol to his head.'

'That's because he doesn't believe it will happen,' nodded Cassie sagely. 'Men are like that – though it's mostly for show.'

'You think so?'

'Oh yes. They need us to think them clever and daring and fearless ... knights riding into battle, in effect. So they have to keep up appearances.'

'Appearances are fine. Clever, daring and fearless are also fine. It's the *I am indestructible* bit that is the problem.'

Adam murmured, 'I'm sitting right here, you know.'

'Of course we know,' grinned Cassie. 'This wouldn't be any fun if you weren't.'

He looked at Sebastian who had been silently laughing throughout all this.

'I don't suppose you'd consider helping?'

'I wasn't planning to. But since you're asking ... you wanted to talk about the cottage.'

'Yes. As I tried to tell you, I'm grateful for the offer and sorry if I've put you to unnecessary trouble --'

'You haven't. I told you that. The place was no use as it was. Now it's habitable.'

'What cottage is this?' demanded Camilla.

'One of mine at Pleyden,' Sebastian told her. And to Adam, 'I'm not surprised you decided against it. So ... what will you do instead?'

'Stay at the inn, I suppose. There's not a great deal of choice and as long as I don't need to go out and about at night or --'

'I thought I made it clear why that kind of thing had to stop,' cut in Camilla. 'Which part of those reasons didn't you understand?'

Cassie sent Sebastian a look which caused him to take refuge in his tankard.

'I understood all of them,' said Adam. 'Which part of *I can't promise to stay safely tucked up in bed* did *you* not understand? It's why a cottage would make life easier.'

'If you wanted a cottage on the marsh, why didn't you ask *me*, for heaven's sake?'

He raised interested brows. 'Would you have given me one?'

'Not if you're going to use it to get yourself killed.'

'Not intentionally. Not at all, if I can help it.'

'Oh good. That makes it *so* much better, doesn't it?'

'From my point of view it does.'

Seizing the moment that Camilla spent glaring fulminatingly at him, Cassie said, 'If the two of you want to carry on bickering in private --'

'We're not bickering!' snapped Camilla. And to Adam, 'Are we?'

'Well, *I'm* not. Which,' he added quickly as she opened her mouth on an objection, 'by implication, means you aren't either – since bickering requires two people.'

Sebastian gave a crack of laughter and stood up.

'Entertaining as this is, I'm calling a truce until after luncheon. Cassandra?' And as she nodded and went to ring for the butler, 'But in my unaccustomed role as referee, allow me to observe that you both have valid points. As Miss Edgerton-Foxe says, prowling the marsh at night is likely to be the death of you, Adam. But if, knowing that, you're going to do it anyway, some of the risks could be reduced by moving from the *Port Arms* to a place where your comings and goings can escape notice more easily.' He grinned. 'You can continue bickering – I beg your pardon! – *debating* the pros and cons on the way home. Right now, let's eat and talk about something less contentious.'

* * *

In fact, there was no further argument on the ride home because, as soon as Audley Court was behind them, Camilla said abruptly, 'Sebastian is right, isn't he?'

'About what?'

'Although living somewhere other than the inn makes it easier for you to indulge in more hair-raising exploits, it eliminates at least *some* of your chances of being caught.'

'I believe so, yes.'

'Then I suppose I'd better find you a cottage.'

Adam looked at her. 'Are you sure?'

'Yes. I don't pretend to like it. But I like the idea of you climbing in and out of windows in New Romney even less.'

'I'd certainly rather not do so. But what will your brother make of you providing me with accommodation?'

'Nothing, probably.' Camilla had already considered this. 'Guy has yet to show any serious interest in the minutiae of our holdings. As long as he doesn't actually *see* you, he's unlikely to find out.'

'But your people? The steward, for example. He's bound to know, isn't he?'

'Yes. And if Guy asked, Robson would tell him. But he won't ask.' She caught his expression and added, 'Yes. I know I ought to be encouraging him to start assuming his responsibilities and I will – just not right now. So forget Guy for a moment. He and Robson aren't the main difficulty.'

'They're not?'

'No. I can't make a cottage properly habitable – by which I mean clean and fully equipped – without the assistance of my household.' Her brow wrinkled in thought. 'I'm confident they can be trusted to do as I ask and hold their tongues afterwards … and I believe I can also persuade them that Guy should know nothing about it.' She stopped and nodded decisively. 'Yes. That should work.'

'What should?'

She smiled suddenly, that sunburst smile that slammed through Adam's chest.

'Liberal use of Uncle Hugh's name. Fortunately, I received a letter from him yesterday. I can tell Coombes and Mrs Poole that it brought a request to help you, if asked.'

'You appear to have it all worked out,' he said in not quite his normal tone.

'Yes. You find that surprising?'

'Not in the least.' He paused, thinking, *For God's sake! Pull yourself together. It was a smile. Nothing more.* 'No. The only surprise is that you're prepared to help me despite disagreeing with my methods. Thank you.'

'You can thank me by not getting yourself killed,' she retorted. 'Now … you said the Riding Officers suspect particular churches are being used. Which ones?'

'Ivychurch, Fairfield, Snargate and Brookland. Why do you ask?'

'If the owlers *are* using those, you don't want to be too nearby.' Another pause and then, 'There's a place near Orgarswick that might do. It's isolated, in good repair and larger than most cottages. It's also still empty because I'd planned to offer it to Robson's son and new daughter-in-law.' She smiled wryly. 'They married in July and the baby is due next month. But by then, I imagine you'll have returned to London.'

'Yes,' agreed Adam, aware that the notion was less appealing than it ought to be. 'I suppose I will. But if I may have the cottage in the meantime ...?'

'Yes. Meet me at St. Mary's in the Marsh at eight tomorrow. I'll show you the way to it and give you a key – but allow me tomorrow and the next day to make it ready. With a bit of ingenuity, I may even be able to keep you provisioned from Dragon Hall throughout your stay.' She awarded him another, but this time distinctly sardonic, smile. 'I've a suspicion any of my maids would fall over each other for the chance to come each day and cook for you. Shall I ask them?'

* * *

Back at the *Port Arms*, he found Finch in a mood of unaccustomed twitchiness over the arrival of a new guest.

'Got a very nice horse, Mr Gilbert has. And a lot of luggage and a valet brought in on the Mail Coach. But what's *really* rum is how much interest he's taking in *you*, Mr Adam. First, he asked Hadlow if you was still staying here. Then his valet asked me where you was and when you'd be back – not as I told him owt. But what bothers me is how he knew you was here in the *first* place.'

'Yes. That is odd,' agreed Adam, his mind busy with several possibilities. 'Presumably the gentleman is somewhere about?'

'In the coffee room, like as not.'

'Then I'd better go and find out what he wants, hadn't I?'

'Not like that, sir,' objected Finch quickly. 'Your coat's all creased and your cravat's gone limp – not to mention you smell of horse.'

'So? I'm going to meet the fellow – not escort him to a ball,' said Adam, heading for the door. 'He can take me as I am.'

'But he's terrible elegant and his valet thinks I'm *your* valet and – and I'll never be able to hold my head up if you go down as you are. Please, sir. At least change your clothes?'

Adam didn't give a fig for what Mr Gilbert's valet thought or didn't think but he hadn't the heart to ride roughshod over Finch's anguish.

'Oh God,' he muttered. 'All right, Harry. But let's make it quick, shall we?'

Inevitably, it took much longer than it would have done without Finch's enthusiastic assistance. Adam shed his clothes, washed and pulled on a fresh shirt and breeches. He even managed to drag a comb through his hair and re-tie it. So far, so good. But after that nothing would dissuade Harry from helping.

'You got to let me, Mr Adam,' he said earnestly. 'Or how'll I learn?'

So, refraining from pointing out that Harry's ham-like hands were about as suited to valeting as they were to embroidery, Adam submitted to having his cravat tied. The first attempt nearly garrotted him and, by the end of the second, the cravat was in a worse state than the one he'd been wearing all day. Then came the disaster with the vest. Refraining from pointing out that he'd been managing buttons since he was six, Adam stood perfectly still while Harry fastened them ... and sent one flying across the room when it came loose from its moorings. Harry went in search of it, vowing to put matters right.

'Do so, by all means,' said Adam grittily. 'But I'd like to meet your Mr Gilbert this evening if at all possible ... so I'll wear the other vest. And no, thank you. I believe I can finish dressing on my own.'

Ten minutes later, he entered the inn's coffee room to find it occupied by only one person; a large gentleman in coat of fine, blue wool who stood by the window, in apparent contemplation of the stable-yard but who turned, grinning and said cheerfully, 'Where the hell have *you* been all day?'

It was Viscount Rainham.

Not as surprised as he might have been since he'd been half-expecting Goddard to send someone, Adam shut the door behind him and strolled over, offering his hand. 'Mr Gilbert, I presume?'

'None other. Depending on the task in hand, the title can be a blasted nuisance and Gilbert's my given name so I don't have to think twice before answering to it.' He paused and added quietly, 'Is it safe to talk here?'

'To a degree, if we're careful. After all, you've already let Hadlow know that we're acquainted, haven't you?'

'I'm sorry about that – but it couldn't be helped. Your note to Goddard spoke of possibly removing from here and, for all I knew, you might already have done so. As for your valet, I'd no idea you had one with you.'

'He's not a valet,' muttered Adam. 'But please don't tell your man that – both for Finch's sake and mine.'

'My own man went back to Town on the afternoon Mail. He was only here to ensure that my luggage arrived intact.' Rainham sat down and waited for Adam to do the same. Then he said, 'I've read your note to Goddard so I know your progress so far. What is the current situation?'

In as few words as possible, Adam recounted that day's meeting with the Riding Officers, not omitting his and Sebastian's doubts about Mr Tranter. Then he said bluntly, 'I should also tell you that Miss Edgerton-Foxe knows why I'm here.'

'She does? But Goddard said --'

'I know what Goddard said. But keeping her in the dark when she'd guessed most of it was a farce. And she can help.'

'How, exactly?'

Adam looked at him, noting the scepticism in Rainham's eyes. He said, 'Right now, by enabling me to move out of this inn to somewhere more discreet. But in other ways, too. She may not be party to what goes on around here but she knows about it. She also knows precisely how dangerous it is and how much trouble I'll be in if I'm found out. She's discreet. And, in case you've never noticed it, far from stupid.'

'I daresay,' agreed the viscount laconically. 'But her brother is neither. And he's back home now, having blotted his copybook in London.'

'How?'

'The usual way. Heavy losses at the card table. Uncle was *not* pleased.'

'No. I would imagine not. Did *he* tell you this?'

'Goddard?' Rainham shook his head. 'I had it from one of the gentlemen he paid off in the young fool's stead. I mention it because --'

'I know why you've mentioned it and it's unnecessary. Cam – Miss Edgerton-Foxe will not confide in her brother so his misdoings are of no consequence.'

It was too much to hope that Rainham wouldn't notice the slip. He said, 'Dear me! On first name terms, are we? I'm impressed. I thought she'd still be snarling at you.'

'She says what she thinks – as do I,' replied Adam curtly. 'I wouldn't call it snarling. However, since I'm told you brought half of your wardrobe --'

'Not the half my valet is familiar with. What I have with me are largely what you might call ... working clothes.'

'Disguises, you mean,' said Adam, having heard about Rainham's fondness for dressing up. 'Well, I wouldn't unpack just yet. With luck, we'll be moving to a cottage on the marsh the day after tomorrow. At least, I assume you're staying to lend a hand?'

'To lend a hand ... whilst giving you the benefit of my vast experience,' agreed the viscount. And before Adam could respond to the provocation, 'Also, to pass on Goddard's more recent sundry musings ... and suggestions regarding our investigations which I suspect will not prove especially helpful.'

* * *

Later that same night, long after darkness had fallen in the *Cinque Port Arms* and New Romney as a whole, a group of some seven or eight men gathered at the ruined Hope Chapel a little way outside the town.

The meeting had been called by one of their number. The fellow who, earlier that day, had claimed not to be a great one for talking, was now surprisingly loquacious. He relayed the Audley Court meeting in some detail and followed it up with both his impression of Mr Brandon and the little he knew about him. Then, he turned a respectful eye on the leader of the group and said, 'What d'you reckon we ought to do about it, Captain?'

The man to whom this had been addressed took his time about answering. Finally, he said, 'About the new viscount – nothing. Audley Court has had no dealings with us since the old lord passed. As for Brandon ... also nothing until we have orders to the contrary from above. If he does indeed have official backing in London, moving against him is likely to draw unwelcome attention.'

'But *does* he?' asked one of the others. 'Could've been a lie to guard his back.'

'Could've been,' agreed Tranter. 'But there's summat else. Brandon weren't the only one at Audley Court. Young Mr Guy's sister was about somewhere.'

The captain frowned at him. 'Are you sure?'

'Yes. I seen her mare in the stables. And Brewster over at Dragon Hall says Brandon's been visiting. Makes you wonder if Mr Guy hasn't let summat slip, don't it?'

'It does. But it tells us who sent Brandon here. Guy Edgerton-Foxe's uncle is the Earl of Alveston; a powerful man with great influence in government circles. Consequently, if his lordship is Brandon's employer, I suspect we have only two choices. Either we watch but don't touch; or we ensure that he disappears without a trace. You will do nothing until I give the order.'

'And what about young Guy?' said someone. 'He's always been reliable – one of us, you'd say. But there's another run in four nights' time. What if he's turned informer?'

'I doubt – knowing what the consequences would be – he is that stupid. But like Brandon, he will also bear watching – as will Jeavons and Hindley, in case they make contact with either of them. I shall see to that.' The captain paused, clearly debating some further point. Finally he said, 'But there is a loose end that perhaps should be tied up without delay. The late viscount's valet was pensioned off and given a cottage near his niece at

Peasemarsh. Tranter ... did you hear anything to suggest that Wingham might have already spoken with him?'

Tranter thought about it, his brow wrinkled in concentration. Then, shaking his head, he said, 'No. Nothing. Why?'

'Because Mr Perkins always purchased the old lord's brandy from me personally and I would prefer that he did not share that fact with the current viscount.' He glanced around the assembled faces and added negligently, 'Thompson, Sedge ... see to it, will you? And sooner rather than later.'

'Yes, sir. Would that be permanent-like?' asked Thompson.

'Do you really need to ask that?'

The pair exchanged glances. Then Sedge said, 'No, sir. I reckon not.'

CHAPTER SIXTEEN

'Rainham's here,' was Adam's greeting when Camilla met him outside St. Mary's church the following morning. 'Well, not *here* precisely. But at the *Port Arms*.'

'Good. For a nasty moment I thought he was lurking behind a tombstone, waiting to leap out shouting "*Surprise*!"'

His mouth twitched. 'You did?'

'No.' She frowned a little and sighed. 'He'll try to take over.'

'I know. He's already started.'

'Of course he has.' Setting Sheba in motion, Camilla waited for Adam to come alongside her and then said, 'Stand your ground. If you give him an inch, he'll take the proverbial mile.'

'I know that, too. But there's a limit to what I can achieve on my own so an extra pair of hands and eyes will be helpful. Also, he's brought word of certain rumours Goddard has picked up in London.'

'What, exactly?'

'Subterranean rumblings within the East India Company.'

'There's nothing new about that. Internal squabbles are a way of life there.'

'This is something else. Apparently, secret enquiries are being conducted.'

'Not secret enough if Uncle Hugh has heard about them,' she observed. 'And the Company *certainly* doesn't want M Section poking its nose in. It likes to keep its house in order without outside interference and is powerful enough to do it. However ... enquiries regarding what?'

'There has recently been an increase in the quantity of smuggled tea – though how anyone can know that is a mystery to me,' he shrugged. 'But the Company is considering the possibility that some of its own ships' captains are responsible.'

'*Considering the possibility*?' echoed Camilla incredulously. 'If any of their captains are breaking bulk they'll *know* because it will show up on the bill of lading.'

'Breaking bulk? What's that?'

'Selling a part of the ship's cargo for themselves.'

'Ah. That isn't what they're doing,' murmured Adam. Then, 'I'm impressed. How do you know things like that?'

'How do you think? The amount of trivia lodged in my brain thanks to M Section is staggering. But never mind that. If the captains aren't pilfering, what *are* they doing?'

'Taking advantage of cargo space the Company allows them for personal use. The suspicion is that a substantial number of them are bringing in nothing *but* tea and selling it to the smugglers through some sort of agent – probably in France or Holland.' He paused and then added, 'If there's a further run, Goddard wants Rainham and me to look out for tea boxes coming ashore which bear the company's mark.'

'Oh? And how exactly does he suggest you do that?'

'He doesn't. He leaves it to our ingenuity.'

'Very helpful,' she snapped acidly. 'Does he want anything else?'

'Yes.' Adam drew a long breath and added, 'M Section is currently working closely with the Intelligence Service.'

'On *what*?' demanded Camilla. 'Or no. Let me guess. They want to know how much espionage is going on under cover of smuggling. Yes?'

'Yes.'

'And you've known that since the beginning, haven't you?'

'Again, yes.'

'But you didn't mention it because Uncle Hugh told you not to. So why tell me now?'

A faint smile touched his mouth. 'I realised it wouldn't come as a surprise. And it's the reason Goddard has sent Rainham.'

This time she merely stared at him, worry and disbelief mingling in the misty-green eyes. Finally, she said darkly, 'He's sent Rainham. Lovely. That's bound to make *all* the difference, isn't it? But let me see if I have this right. The pair of you are supposed to find out who's behind the smuggling ... and where the spying trail starts and ends ... and then put a stop to both of them? Are those your instructions?'

'More or less. Sounds something of a tall order, doesn't it?'

'That's not a tall order – it's insanity! Is he trying to get you both *killed*?'

'I hope not.' He glanced sideways at her. 'I'm gathering that you think we can't do it. But you've forgotten our secret weapon.'

'I never forget anything – more's the pity,' she said crossly. '*What* secret weapon?'

'You,' he said simply.

Camilla's jaw went slack. 'Me?'

He nodded. 'Purely in a planning and advisory capacity, of course – leaving anything risky to Rainham and me. Why not?'

'You don't honestly think that Rainham will consent to that, do you?'

'I won't be asking his permission,' came the cool reply. 'In fact, I've already told him that I've taken you into my confidence – though not about the spies.'

'And he didn't throw a fit?'

'He wasn't happy. But, to be fair to him, he was more concerned about Guy finding out – and his discretion thereafter.'

'He needn't worry about that. Guy won't find out – or not from me.'

'That's what I told him.' Adam looked sideways at her. 'Speaking of your brother ... what did you tell him about yesterday?'

'Nothing.'

'He didn't ask?'

'Oh he *asked*. But he knew I hadn't taken one of our grooms so if I'd admitted riding to the other side of Rye, he'd have asked who *had* escorted me. Rather than tell him, I said that I'd make him privy to *my* activities when he made me privy to *his*. He said *he* doesn't disappear for an entire day. I replied that no, he disappears for an entire *night* instead.'

Adam's mouth curled. 'At which point the honours were even?'

'Quite. So he changed tack in favour of endless complaints about me going off without a word and leaving him to endure a visit from the mother and younger sister of one of his friends.'

She smiled suddenly. 'Since I'd previously told him to take steps to prevent that particular eventuality, I had no sympathy for him – at which point he decided to sulk instead.' Camilla pulled Sheba to a halt in front of a sprawling single-storey cottage. 'This is it. Will it suit, do you think?'

There wasn't another building in sight; just acres of marsh, sheep and one of the broader drainage ditches.

'Admirably,' said Adam, dropping from the saddle and reaching up to her help down from hers. Then, when she was on the ground and he'd forced his seemingly reluctant hands to release her, 'Where are we exactly?'

'Roughly a mile from Dymchurch. You can easily approach the Wall from either side of town,' she replied, hiding the heightened colour in her cheeks by fussing over the skirts of her habit. 'And it's a similar distance from Dragon Hall, when travelling there directly.' She produced a key from her pocket and unlocked the door. 'It's been empty for a month or two but was put in good repair after the previous tenants left. Come in and see for yourself.'

He followed her into what was clearly the main room, low-ceilinged and dominated by a large fireplace. On one side of it, a door led to the kitchen-cum-scullery; on the other lay two very small bedchambers, the second accessed through the first. Furniture throughout was meagre but adequate. Adam said, 'You can't imagine how relieved I am not to have to share a bed with Rainham.'

Camilla laughed. 'Oh, I think I can. Not that either of you will have much privacy and your manservant will have to sleep on a pallet in the family room. The necessary is in the yard by the barn which you can use for stabling ... and the water-pump is there, too. It's all very basic, I'm afraid.'

'If Rainham's too delicate to rough it a little, he can stay at the *Port Arms*. As for Finch and me – we'll manage.'

As he spoke, Adam was conscious of little save that they were standing extremely close together in a tiny room, the bulk of which was taken up by the bed. Inevitably, his body resumed the conversation it had begun with hers when he'd helped her from the saddle. Camilla, by contrast, seemed supremely unaware of this fact and, having produced a small notebook from her pocket, was busy making a list. Peering over her shoulder, he read,

Linens, pillows

Kettle, Crockery, Cutlery, Skillet, Soap

Basic foodstuffs – tea, bread, cheese, eggs, ham etc.

He knew an impulse to laugh. She was thinking like a housewife; he was thinking like a man. He said, 'While you're busy with that, I'll take a look around the yard.'

Camilla's reply was a seemingly absent nod. But when she heard the outer door close behind him, she shut her eyes and drew a long, steadying breath. Then, opening them again, she gave herself a mental talking-to.

All right. Everything about his character appeals to me and he's also attractive. Not wildly handsome, perhaps – but undeniably attractive. However, none *of that explains what just happened. He didn't touch me. He was merely standing rather close. Nothing more than that. Yet every bit of me was so – so* aware *of him I could scarcely breathe. That shouldn't –* can't *– be allowed to happen. But I don't know how to stop it. And what any of this says about what I truly felt for Stuart, I daren't contemplate.* She gave a despairing groan. *I shouldn't have gone with him yesterday or be here with him now. I ought to get the cottage ready and then stay well away from him. Only I* won't *because working with him and Rainham is just too tempting to resist.*

Stiffening her shoulders, she swung back into the main room as Adam strolled back in from the yard. Glimpsing her expression, he said, 'Is something wrong?'

'Not at all. But there's a great deal to be done so I need to get started. We should have the place ready for you by the day after tomorrow.'

He eyed her consideringly. 'I'm happy to lend a hand, you know.'

'I daresay. But my girls will get on quicker without … distractions.'

'What you implied yesterday suggested the opposite,' he remarked. And thought, *It would be nice to think* I *distract* you. *But I don't, do I? Not even a little bit. You won't permit it.* Then, seeing her chin lift, he added, 'But I won't argue. I'll just say thank you.'

'You already did.' She slid past him and out through the door. 'Make sure Rainham knows what he's in for, won't you? Ah.' She paused, frowning. 'You didn't say and I forgot to ask ... but has he come as the viscount or something else?'

'He's currently masquerading as Mr Gilbert – but he's brought a lot of luggage.'

Camilla gave a brief laugh. 'I can imagine. You'd better tell him not to call at the house. Guy may never have actually *met* him but Rainham's almost certainly been pointed out to him in London. He's the younger gentlemen's role model.'

'He is? Why?'

'The usual reasons. He boxes, fences, shoots, drives to an inch and his stables are second to none. He's also exceedingly fashionable so every idiosyncrasy of style is slavishly copied.' She glanced into Adam's face. 'You knew none of that?'

'No. The first time I met him, he looked like a dock hand and was sporting a black eye.'

'Oh? Well, that's the other side of him. The side which makes him marginally less aggravating.'

* * *

Once back at Dragon Hall and establishing that, as usual, her brother was out, Camilla lost no time in summoning both the butler and the housekeeper and explaining – briskly but not entirely truthfully – what she wanted.

'A *cottage*, Miss Millie?' Coombes looked horrified. 'Gentlemen can't possibly live in a cottage. It simply isn't fitting.'

'Normally, no,' agreed Camilla crisply. 'But I have shown it to Mr Brandon and he has declared it acceptable. Also, it is what my uncle requires.'

'That's as maybe,' said Mrs Poole tartly. 'But his lordship's not the one staying there. And *he* hasn't got the job of trying to provide the poor gentlemen with a few comforts.'

'No. But he's confident we'll manage – and so am I. On a separate issue, Lord Alveston wishes no word of the matter to reach my brother. Without having been apprised of all the details, I gather that whatever Mr Brandon and Mr Gilbert are engaged in is not without risk. And Guy, as we all know, is still young enough to equate danger with fun.' She paused and when neither the butler nor the housekeeper spoke, added, 'It goes without saying that no word of this is to go beyond the household. I have absolute faith in *your* discretion and I believe I may also rely on Martha's. The question is … dare I trust the housemaids?'

Mr Coombes stiffened. 'Every servant in Dragon Hall knows my rule about *gossip*.'

'The girls are devoted to you,' stated Mrs Poole. 'And since they've done nothing but sigh over that Mr Brandon, a smile and a word from him should do the trick.'

'Yes. I thought as much myself. Now … we'll need the gig, Coombes, and I'll drive it myself. But we'll also want the cart to carry goods. Tell Dawson to get it ready but have either Thomas or Ned available to drive it when needed.'

'Certainly, Miss Millie.' The butler bowed as if to leave and then hesitated. 'You recall that tomorrow evening is Mr Guy's bachelor dinner?'

'I do. But though the timing is unfortunate, it isn't catastrophic. The library and the dining-room are in good order; Cook has the menu well in hand; and I'll be back in plenty of time to attend to any last minute details.'

'Very good, Miss Millie.' He bowed again and left.

Camilla turned briskly back to the housekeeper. 'The first job will be cleaning, so please assemble brooms, mops, buckets and so forth. Also, linen for three beds. Then, while the girls and I set to work at the cottage, I'd be grateful if you'd gather the other things the gentlemen will need. I began a list but feel free to add anything you think necessary.' She rose and handed over a sheet of paper. 'I leave it in your capable hands, Mrs Poole – and I thank you. Now … give me ten minutes to speak to Martha and shed my riding habit, then send Molly, Susan and Jill up to me.'

Martha, who had spent the whole of yesterday unpacking Miss Edgerton-Foxe's hitherto unworn trousseau, was at first not pleased to be asked to perform the kind of menial tasks she considered beneath her station. She said stiffly, 'Of course, I'll help if you wish it, Miss. But I've my hands full here. There's still another trunk to be emptied and where I'm to put the contents I just don't know. Your closets are already overflowing and --'

Camilla held up a hand to stem the tide.

'I know ... and I have an idea about that.' She smiled. 'You've always rather liked the blue polonaise, haven't you? And I suspect the pink *robe d'Anglaise* would look rather well on you – as would the striped cherry taffeta. Or perhaps there are others you'd prefer? You must have first choice before I offer a gown to each of the maids.'

Needless to say, this banished Martha's reluctance. She beamed and said, 'Oh Miss! Are you sure? I don't reckon you've worn any of them more than three times apiece.'

'No. Probably not.' *I haven't needed my prettiest clothes for quite some time*, came the unspoken thought. 'But they're yours if you want them – so put them to one side before the girls get here.'

Upon learning that they were each to receive the gift of a gown in return for helping their mistress to scour a cottage, Molly, Susan and Jill did not need to be asked twice.

'Whatever you need, Miss Millie,' said Molly promptly. 'The gowns'll be much appreciated, I'm sure – but we'd help without 'em.'

'Thank you. I knew I could count on you. Now ... Coombes and Mrs Poole are aware of the situation. But I do not want *any* word of this leaving the house to cause gossip in the neighbourhood. For one thing, it puts me in an awkward position. Worse still, it may endanger the two gentlemen for whom we are preparing the cottage.' She allowed herself a dramatic pause. 'One of them is Mr Brandon.'

Four pairs of eyes grew very round.

'*Anything* for Mr Brandon,' sighed Susan.

'Yes.' Jill nodded enthusiastically. 'Anything at all.'

'Two real gentlemen living in a *cottage*?' snorted Martha. 'What's wrong with the inn?'

'It is too public.' Camilla lowered her voice conspiratorially. 'Mr Brandon and his colleague have been sent on a delicate mission by Lord Alveston. And his lordship asks *us* to help.' Another pause to watch this sink in. 'I haven't met the other gentleman yet. But Mr Brandon insisted I pass on his thanks for the extra work and also for keeping what you know to yourselves. Naturally, he looks forward to expressing his appreciation in person.'

* * *

The rest of the day passed in a whirlwind of activity and a great deal of what Mrs Poole called elbow grease. By the end of it, Camilla and the maids were exhausted but secure in the knowledge that they had worked wonders. After an onslaught of sweeping, mopping and washing, windows gleamed, the stone-flagged floor was spotless and there was no longer a cobweb or speck of dust anywhere. Logs, cut by Thomas, were piled up beside the hearth; mattresses had been aired and turned; extra chairs had been sent for and the tiny scullery had acquired pots, pans and a kettle. Even the privy in the yard had received a thorough scouring after Molly had taken one look and pronounced it disgusting. They all agreed that tomorrow could largely be devoted to finishing touches such as hanging the freshly washed curtains, making up the beds and filling the shelves with a generous supply of foodstuffs, plates and cutlery.

Once back at Dragon Hall, Camilla had hoped to avoid Guy until she had washed and changed. It was sheer bad luck that he walked out of the library just as she was taking the stairs to her bedchamber.

'*Millie?*' He stopped, shutting his mouth and staring at her wildly straying hair, old cotton gown and filthy apron. 'What on *earth* have you been doing?'

'There was a minor emergency at an estate cottage. But it has been sorted out so --'

'An emergency? Why didn't *I* know anything of it?'

'Partly because I didn't know where you were and partly because we didn't both need to be there.' She smiled and shrugged. 'There'll be time enough for you to take over the reins of the estate after your birthday and I'll be happy to hand them to you. But for now, I thought you wanted a holiday – time to enjoy living in your own home again.'

Guy flushed a little. 'I do, I suppose. But I oughtn't to let everything fall on you.'

'And in a little while you won't.' She gathered her limp skirts to continue on her way. 'And now I'm off to take a bath and have Martha put me to rights. Will you be dining at home this evening?'

'Yes – though I'll be going out directly afterwards. I promised to join a few fellows at the *London* for a hand of cards. And before you say anything, we play for shillings not guineas so I won't be coming home up to my neck in debt.'

'I didn't suppose you might,' she said over her shoulder. 'But I'm glad to hear it.' And reached the safety of her room hoping she'd turned his mind away from the fictional emergency.

* * *

The second day at the cottage, though less grubby and not quite as hectic as the first, was still remarkably busy since one or other of them continually thought of some small comfort or task that had so far been overlooked. But by mid-afternoon, there was nothing left to be done except leave Thomas putting down fresh straw in the barn. The maids, inevitably, went back to Dragon Hall feeling cheated at not seeing the gentlemen.

In truth, Camilla rather wished that the evening ahead was not one on which guests were expected. True, she need do little more than check that all was in order downstairs and put in a token appearance when the gentlemen arrived ... but that still meant formal dress and a head full of hairpins when all she wanted was to wallow in a scented bath before curling up by the fire in a chamber robe with a book and her dinner on a tray.

This, however, was not to be. So at a little before seven that evening, she joined her brother in the drawing-room to await their guests, beautifully coiffed and clad in a green tulle-over-taffeta polonaise.

Had she but known it, Guy was looking forward to the evening ahead a good deal more than he might have done had not the night at the *City of London* been so ... odd. All the same crowd was there and no one said anything to suggest he wasn't welcome; but somehow he'd got the feeling that men he regularly drank or played dice with weren't quite as friendly as usual. Since he couldn't account for this, he'd spent most of today telling himself that he'd imagined it; that it was merely the extra buzz of tension which often heralded a run. Down on the beach, the night after tomorrow, everything would be normal again. But still, he felt a certain relief at the prospect of spending an evening among gentlemen who knew nothing of his secret life.

'You look pretty,' he told Camilla. 'New gown?'

'Just one I haven't worn before.' She smiled at him. 'But I won't intrude on your evening. When I've greeted your guests, I'll leave you to enjoy yourselves.'

Feeling vaguely guilty, he said, 'You could at least join us for a glass of wine.'

'Briefly, then.' She raised sardonic brows. 'Do you *really* want Coombes and Mrs Poole having fits over the fact I haven't got a chaperone?'

Guy gave a snort of wry laughter. 'No. Perhaps not.'

First to arrive was George Derring. The same age as herself, he bowed over her hand, grinned at her and said, 'It's good to see you, Millie. Glad to be back?'

'I believe I am,' she replied. And with mock severity, 'And it's Miss Edgerton-Foxe to you, sir. We are no longer ten years old.'

He cast her an appreciative look. 'No. I can see that.'

She shook her head at him and said, 'Please tell your mama I was sorry I missed her.'

'If you like. But she had the chance to parade Clara before Guy – which is what she came for even though I *told* her it'll be years before he looks for a leg-shackle.'

'Who's looking for a leg-shackle?' asked Guy, crossing the room in time to hear this and handing each of them a glass of wine. 'Not you, surely?'

'Not,' agreed George, fixing Camilla with a soulful gaze, 'unless I had some hope that my childhood sweetheart might say yes.'

'Was that a proposal?' she asked.

'If you took it as one and said yes, he'd be thoroughly ditched,' said Guy. 'Now, stop flirting with my sister, there's a good fellow and --' He turned away, hearing sounds betokening arrival. 'Ah. Perfect timing, wouldn't you say?'

'Depends on one's point of view,' murmured George irrepressibly. And in an undertone as the Blane brothers were announced, 'Drive with me tomorrow, Millie?'

'I can't. Another day, perhaps.' And walked away to greet the newcomers.

She didn't know Mark and Peter Blane well and was surprised that Guy did, since they were several years older. She herself had only ever met them a handful of times at assemblies in Rye or Hythe. Both were of similar height, brown haired and brown eyed. But where Mark dressed with elegant restraint, Peter had a taste for bright colours and great quantities of trimming. And while Mark was unfailingly correct and somewhat ponderous, Peter clearly fancied himself witty, modish and irresistibly charming. The fact that he also expected every female he met to think the same grated somewhat.

Mark bowed over her hand and murmured a conventional greeting.

Peter seized both of her hands and carried them to his lips before saying extravagantly, 'Miss Edgerton-Foxe – what an utter delight to see you again! And looking lovelier than ever, if I may say so.'

Quelling an impulse to observe that he already *had* said so, Camilla withdrew her hands and, making sure her smile encompassed both brothers, said, 'Welcome to Dragon Hall, gentlemen. I hope your family is well?'

'Very well, thank you,' replied Mark with a small smile. 'Both Mother and Grandmother would like to call – but I believe you are not receiving as yet?'

'No. We are still settling in and busy refurbishing the house. But soon, I hope.'

'Meanwhile,' cut in Peter swiftly, 'all work and no play isn't good for anyone. Let me take you for a drive. We could go to Hythe or Rye – whichever you prefer. But you must have *some* fun, ma'am. I insist upon it!'

'Insist away,' said Guy, offering glasses of wine to the brothers. 'It won't do you much good. Stubborn as a mule, my sister, when she sets her mind to it.'

'Thank you, Guy – but I can answer for myself. And thank you for the invitation, Mr Blane, but the answer is no just at present.' She smiled brightly at their guests. 'It's a great pleasure to see you again, gentlemen – but now I shall leave you to enjoy your evening.'

'Must you ?' asked Peter, assuming a stricken expression and pressing one hand over his heart. 'So soon?'

'Yes. I'm afraid I must.' And she walked away, aware that while Mr Derring and Mark Blane moved aside with civil bows, Peter had reached the door ahead of her to wait, one hand on the latch and the other outstretched, ready to take hers. Camilla prevented that manoeuvre by holding her skirts and waited pointedly for an instant before saying, 'Is there some difficulty with the door, sir?'

'No, no. A thousand pardons, Miss Edgerton-Foxe.' He finally pressed the latch. 'I am merely desolate to lose your company so soon.'

'That is unfortunate,' she replied. And softly, with an acid-edged smile for the irritating fellow at her side, 'But I'm sure you'll get over it.'

And was gone.

CHAPTER SEVENTEEN

On the following morning, the gentlemen prepared to quit the *Cinque Port Arms*. Over a belated breakfast, Adam was scribbling a note giving Sebastian his new direction when Rainham joined him, saying, 'You will not believe what that fellow Hadlow wants to charge for hiring his wretched cart for a day – and extra, if you please, for allowing me to drive it.'

'Well, if you *will* insist on bringing a mountain of luggage --'

'Working clothes,' tutted the viscount. 'I told you that. And even if they weren't, we can't *all* manage for weeks on end with three suits and a half-dozen shirts.'

'Four shirts,' came the muttered reply. 'Finch has burned holes in the other two.'

Rainham laughed and tossed down a letter inexpertly sealed with a clod of brown wax.

'This came for you.'

Adam signed and folded his note to Sebastian and opened the other. Ill-written and atrociously spelled, it was from Riding Officer Jeavons and, translated into English, said, *Heard a whisper. Might be nothing, but could be a run the night after tomorrow. Maybe Dymchurch, maybe towards Hythe; maybe neither. Have sent word to Hindley. He'll ask for dragoons if you agree. You'll find him next to The Spotted Pig, far end of Hythe High Street – he makes bridles and suchlike.*

Adam frowned at it for a moment then, regretfully giving up his usual second cup of coffee, rose from the table. A deceptively sleepy gaze encompassed him and Rainham said, 'Going somewhere?'

'Hythe.' Adam tossed him the note. 'And possibly also Dover. Come, if you wish. Actually, come even if you *don't* wish.' He paused, briefly absorbing the other man's austere grey suit and black vest. 'I'll speak to Hindley since I've met him and you haven't. But if we have to talk the Constable of Dover Castle into turning out some troops, I suspect the viscount will have a better chance than Mr Gilbert. So a different coat, perhaps?'

Rainham handed the note back and stood up. 'Unnecessary. I can play myself as well out of costume as in it. Shall we go? Or no. Since we may have a long day ahead of us, we'd better get all our gear loaded on to the cart and have your fellow drive it to the cottage so we needn't come back here. Does he know where he's going?'

'No. But if he follows us as far as Dymchurch, I can point him in the right direction.'

'Good. Then let's get to it.'

* * *

Leaving Finch with instructions to unload everything at the cottage and then return the cart to the inn in order to reclaim the horse Sebastian had loaned to him, Adam and Rainham rode on to Hythe at a brisker pace. On the previous day, Adam had said as little about the cottage as possible. Now, he decided to pass the ride by describing it in detail in order to enjoy Rainham's increasingly pained expression. When he finished explaining about the privy in the yard, he said cheerfully, 'Not quite what you're used to, I imagine.'

'And you are?'

'No. But I've probably more acquaintance with inferior lodgings than you have. So if you'd rather not leave the comfort of the inn --'

'No, no. If Millie has gone to some trouble, it would be churlish to find fault. And if the information we are currently pursuing proves accurate, there's a chance our time here may be brought to a speedier end than previously seemed likely.'

Adam didn't agree but it seemed a shame to put a damper on Rainham's optimism if he got comfort from it, so he said, 'When I've spoken to Hindley, we --'

'Yes. About that. Will he want to be seen talking to you?'

'Why not? He's a loriner, isn't he? And I think Hector's reins need replacing.'

They parted company at the *Swan Inn* half way down Hythe's busy High Street and Adam rode on alone until he reached the *Spotted Pig* and the adjacent lorinery. The door stood open, giving a clear view of Hindley working at a bench while a young apprentice swept the floor of wood shavings. Dismounting without haste to give the Riding Officer time to notice him, he pulled off his gloves and ran his fingers back and forth over a section of the horse's reins, frowning.

'How can I help you, sir?' asked Hindley, wiping his hands on a rag.

'See for yourself,' replied Adam, stepping back and passing him the reins.

Hindley examined them. 'Ah. Quite a bit of wear, isn't there?' And over his shoulder to the apprentice, 'Jimmy! Go in the back and find them reins I made for the vicar that he never collected. They're the best we got and this gentleman don't want to wait.'

'Yes, sir!' The boy sped off.

'About this whisper Jeavons has picked up, is it?' asked Hindley quietly, hands and eyes still busy with Hector's reins.

Adam nodded. 'Have you heard anything?'

'No. But that don't mean Jeavons ain't right. And God knows it's rare enough we catch wind of anything afore the event so it'd be daft to ignore this'n.'

'We don't know the precise when and where. Jeavons *thinks* the night after tomorrow but my opinion is we should be on the alert as of tonight. What's yours?'

'The same.' Hindley scratched his head. 'But I doubt I'll get dragoons out from Dover two or mebbe three nights in a row no matter *how* hard I argue for it. And even if I do, there won't be enough of 'em to make a difference.'

'Who do you --?'

Adam stopped abruptly as Jimmy ran towards them, clutching the new reins.

'Found 'em, sir!' he said proudly.

'Good lad. Now finish unpacking that box of bits what came this morning.' And to Adam, 'Want me to swap 'em for you, sir? Won't take but a minute.'

Adam was fully capable of exchanging one set of reins for another and equally aware that there was nothing wrong with the existing ones. But he nodded and said, 'By all means. How much do I owe you?'

'Eight shillings, sir.' And then, head bent over his work, 'You was saying?'

'Do you apply to the Constable of Dover Castle for soldiers?'

'Lord North?' Hindley gave a snort of laughter. 'He's too busy being Prime Minister to spend time at the castle. No. I ask Major Levinson and he says yea or nay, depending.'

Adam eyed him thoughtfully. 'Would it help if I tried? Or, more particularly, the senior colleague Lord Alveston has sent from London to assist me?'

'Might. If'n he can come over snooty enough.'

'Snooty is his speciality.'

'Do it, then. You and him got more chance than me.' Hindley stepped back. 'There you go, sir. All done.'

'Thank you.' Adam handed over the eight shillings and added a couple more for good measure before climbing into the saddle. 'I'll see you're kept informed.'

A nod and a glance over his shoulder to check the whereabouts of his apprentice, then, 'Best not tell Tranter, sir. There's summat off about him, if you know what I mean.'

'I do. And I agree. Take care, Mr Hindley.'

The Riding Officer gave a mock salute. 'And good luck to you, sir.'

* * *

'Dover?' sighed Rainham. 'Today?'

'Yes. I need you looking down your nose with icy disdain.'

'Ah. Well, in *that* case ...'

The journey took over an hour. They were stopped at the castle gates by a youthful Captain – who passed them rapidly on to Major Levinson, who wilted under the viscount's lordly manner and frigid gaze and summoned Colonel Barker.

'I wish,' said Rainham for the third time and sounding utterly bored, 'to see whoever is deputising for the Lord Constable. Who is it?'

'General Hawthorne, sir. But --'

'Then kindly ask the General to receive me on a matter of some urgency.'

'Who shall I say --?'

'You may say that I come with full authority to speak on behalf of the Earl of Alveston.'

'That may well be, sir, but --'

'I shall give General Hawthorne my name. *You* do not need to know it. Now – go. I do not have all day.'

Colonel Barker walked unhappily away. Rainham grinned at his retreating back.

Adam said nothing since he didn't know who might be listening.

The Colonel returned to announce that the General would see them. Rainham's reaction clearly said he'd expected nothing less. They were shown into a comfortable room that was part-library and part-office. An imposing, grey-haired officer rose from behind the desk and said, 'You make quite a mystery of yourselves, gentlemen. Lord Alveston's name is recommendation enough for me to receive you – but now I would like yours, if you would be so good.'

Holding out his hand, Rainham supplied both his name and his title. Then he said, 'My companion is Mr Brandon. And since he has been engaged in the business that brings us to you longer than I have, I would ask that you give him your attention, sir.'

General Hawthorne waved them into chairs and resumed his seat. 'Well?'

With swift, relentless economy Adam explained his brief from Lord Alveston and what he had learned so far before coming to the point of their visit. Hawthorne listened without interruption and, when Adam ceased speaking, said curtly, 'How sure are you that a smuggling run is imminent?'

'Not remotely sure. But information of this kind is too rare to be ignored on the chance that it may not be correct. The Riding Officers who brought it to my attention believe that dragoons should be on stand-by. I agree. Furthermore, I believe it should begin tonight in case the run takes place earlier than expected.'

The General's expression remained sceptical.

'And the same thing tomorrow night if it doesn't, I suppose?'

'And the night after that. Yes.'

'You ask a great deal, Mr Brandon.'

'I don't believe so, sir. But if I do, surely the stakes warrant it?'

There was a brief silence into which Rainham eventually said, 'Well, General?'

'I daresay,' came the reluctant reply, 'that I could detail half a dozen men to --'

'No,' said Adam, crisply. 'That won't do at all. I want at least forty.'

'That is outrageous, sir!'

'Far from it. I saw upwards of fifty men on that beach last week, General. If we are to stop the run, hopefully capture some of the smugglers and also seize their cargo, we need to go in with sufficient force. Anything less would be a waste of everyone's time.'

Silence fell again while the General went steadily red in the face. As before, it was Rainham who spoke first. He said, 'I would point out, sir, that Lord Alveston's interest in the Trade stems from concerns raised by both the East India Company and the Intelligence Service. I imagine that Lord North cannot be ignorant of these. I further imagine that his lordship wants those concerns dealt with. Would you not agree?'

Mention of the Prime Minister had its effect. General Hawthorne opened his mouth, closed it again and finally snapped, 'Very well. I shall order forty troopers to the old barracks outside Hythe. The townsfolk are accustomed to us using it for training purposes so are unlikely to think anything untoward. I will instruct Major Levinson to put two captains on watch tonight and for the next two. I trust that satisfies you, gentlemen. Equally, if it turns out to be a wasted exercise, on your heads be it.'

Once outside the Castle again, Rainham said, 'Well ... that was fun.'

'Good – because tonight won't be.'

'Let me guess. You want us to lurk wraithlike in the dark, keeping a look-out for smugglers who are probably sleeping soundly in their beds.'

'Yes. But at least we won't have to climb through a window.' Adam cast a dubious glance at the sky. 'And we can always *hope* it doesn't rain.'

Rainham groaned.

* * *

They arrived at the cottage to a mouth-watering smell and the sight of Finch diligently stirring a pot hanging over the fire.

'Hidden talents, Harry?' asked Adam, tossing his hat down on a chair that he didn't recall having been there before.

'Not me, sir,' grinned Finch. 'Beef stew. They sent it from the house a bit ago.'

'Excellent. Any trouble?'

'No. I've unpacked your gear but didn't like to touch Mr Gilbert's. Was that right?'

'Perfectly,' said Rainham absently. Having wandered from room to room, he re-joined Adam saying, 'Well, it's miniscule and we'll be tripping over each other ... but it could be worse, I suppose.'

'You didn't see it yesterday,' retorted Adam. 'It's warm, it's clean and there's a hot meal waiting. What more do you want?'

Rainham threw up one hand in a gesture of surrender. 'Ale?'

'It's in the scullery,' answered Finch. 'And there's cups and plates and such in that cupboard over there. If you get 'em out, I'll cut some bread and dish up.'

The viscount blinked, laughed and obediently set about laying the small table.

'This,' he remarked to no one in particular, 'will be a whole new experience.'

The three men sat down and ate together. Adam told Finch that he and Mr Gilbert would be out most of the night and why. Finch scowled into his stew and said he hoped the pair of them were going to be careful. Rainham reached thoughtfully for another piece of bread and said nothing.

While Finch cleared away the remains of their meal and washed the dishes, Adam and Rainham tried to get a few hours' sleep. Adam didn't know whether Rainham managed this or not. For his own part, his mind was too busy weighing up options and potential problems to let him doze so, in the end, he got up and sat by the fire with Finch, watching raindrops starting to spot the windows.

When the viscount joined them he was unrecognisable. Already a large man, two or three inches over Adam's own not-quite six feet and broad through the shoulders and chest, he now looked both dangerous and massive. A shapeless felt hat was pulled low over greasy black hair and a face that appeared not to have seen a razor in several days. Below that loomed a bulky figure in a long, tattered greatcoat and a pair of boots so battered it was a wonder the uppers were still attached to the soles.

Finch stared, open-mouthed, at this apparition.

His teeth far too white in the swarthy face, Rainham executed a neat pirouette and said, 'Well? Too much, do you think?'

'That depends,' said Adam, 'on which effect you're aiming for.'

'Meaning?'

'The smugglers will give you tubs to carry and the Redcoats will shoot you on sight.'

'Very droll.' Rainham glanced at Adam's head-to-foot black. 'You, of course, look like a bloody highwayman.'

'I look unobtrusive – which is the general idea.' Adam watched the viscount lift a pair of exquisitely engraved and clearly expensive duelling pistols from their case and shove one of them into his belt. He said slowly, 'You don't think those rather spoil your disguise?'

'That's immaterial. I am not going out unarmed,' replied Rainham grimly. And, pushing the other pistol towards Adam, added, 'Neither are you.'

'Naturally not,' came the mild reply. 'My sword and the knife in my boot will suffice. I'm afraid I don't much care for pistols.'

'You can't shoot?'

Adam sighed. 'I can shoot. I'm just not fond of noisy weapons that give someone the chance to kill you while you're re-loading. Shall we go?'

Outside, darkness had fallen and the moon, still in its first quarter, was largely obscured by cloud. The rain had almost stopped but an eerie, greyish mist hovered over the marsh.

Striding along beside Adam, Rainham presently muttered, 'What a godforsaken place this is. Why Millie's forebears chose to settle here of all places is a mystery.'

Adam merely shrugged and said, 'Where's *your* home?'

And with a wry laugh, Rainham said, 'On the Welsh Marches – which a good many people probably consider as godforsaken as here. But I love it.'

'Is that where your lady wife is now?'

'Yes. London is insupportable at this time of year.'

Glancing sideways through the dark, Adam said, 'And where does she think you are?'

'Here,' replied Rainham, surprised. 'Why? Did you suppose I lie to her?'

'Given your attitude towards Camilla, it was a possibility.'

'No. It wasn't. I do not lie to my wife. Vivian knows what I do but takes no part in it. Millie is a different matter. If she gets involved in *this* and gets hurt, Goddard will have your head and mine. And now I suggest we change the subject.'

'Or perhaps stop talking altogether?' returned Adam. 'We're skirting Dymchurch.'

In no time at all, the Wall was towering above them – twenty feet of lashed pilings and packed stone. Adam led the way up to the track at the top and then over the seaward wall to a place he'd identified a few days ago; uncomfortable but well concealed.

'Here,' he murmured. 'It's a better position than I had before. We can see the entire coast from Hythe to Denge light ... and the tracks leading back into the marsh are some distance either side of us so we're unlikely to be discovered.'

Rainham shrugged as if to say he'd take Adam's word for it. Then, finding a reasonably flat stone, he sat down, leaned his forearms on his knees and prepared to wait.

Adam wondered whether General Hawthorne had kept his word and sent the promised troops to Hythe ... and, if he had, whether the Major's officers would stay alert. At the first sign of activity at sea or on the beach, he'd like the comfort of knowing reinforcements would be on their way. He decided to check on the Hythe barracks tomorrow. He might get another brief word with Hindley at the same time.

The night remained dark and still. Beside him, Rainham shifted slightly but stayed silent, presumably as aware as Adam how voices travelled in the open air. Time passed and the tide came in to lap against the base of the Wall. At length, Rainham said, 'How high does the water come?'

'To the top.'

'Literally?'

'Yes.'

'Then I'm assuming we'll have moved before that happens?'

'Yes. Don't worry. I won't let your boots get wet.'

Rainham gave a grunt that might have been laughter.

A further half hour slid by without any sign of activity other than the rising water.

Coming stiffly to his feet, Adam said, 'Nothing is going to happen now. Let's go.'

'Thank God. I think this rock is going to be permanently etched on my backside.'

'I know the feeling.'

Trudging back to the cottage, Rainham said, '*How* many times did you do this?'

'Three.'

'I'm impressed. Personally, I'd sooner not spend two more nights like this one at all, let alone to no good purpose – so I hope Jeavons' information proves accurate.'

'So do I. And tonight was merely a precaution – or a rehearsal, if you prefer.'

'In which case, roll on opening night tomorrow.'

Back at the cottage, Finch had built up the fire and set bread, cheese and wine on the table. 'Anything?' he asked.

Adam shook his head at both the food and in answer to the question. He merely drained a cup of wine and took himself off to bed.

* * *

He woke in the late morning to the scent of coffee and fresh bread. Heaving himself out of bed and hauling on shirt and breeches, he left his tiny room to find Rainham already at the table and, nodding a good morning, said, 'Where did the bread come from?'

'The footman brought it a bit ago,' said Finch. 'And a note for you.'

Adam sat down, poured coffee and read the brief missive.

It's best that, like Rainham, you don't come to the house. If you need to speak to me – or I to you, for that matter – St Mary's is probably the best place. Some sort of greenery on the grave nearest the gate means meet at eight the following morning. Tell Rainham or not. It's up to you. Yrs. ***C.E.F.***

Adam frowned a little, wondering if something had happened to make Camilla feel that additional precautions were necessary. Then he shoved the note in his pocket and reached for bread and a slice of ham, saying, 'I'm riding over to Hythe again to check on the situation with our support troops. It shouldn't take more than an hour or two. And I think we'll both feel more comfortable for knowing back-up is actually there.'

Rainham nodded. 'And the note?'

'Camilla – extending your embargo on Dragon Hall to me. She doesn't say why – but I imagine it's to do with her brother.'

'In which case, she's wise to be cautious.'

'Yes. I only met Guy once but the antipathy was mutual. However ... I take it you don't want to come to Hythe?'

'No. I'll spend an hour or two getting to know the district. And *you* will take either your sword or Finch with you. No – please don't argue. Some risks are unavoidable but others are not. You will ride to Hythe armed or with company. And that is quite final.'

Looking thoroughly irritated, Adam opened his mouth, closed it again and snapped, 'Fine. The sword, then.'

'Thank you,' nodded Rainham. 'And please ... do give my love to Major Levinson.'

* * *

Adam didn't pass on Rainham's flippant remark. He could well imagine what the response would be and didn't want to spoil his own accord with the major who, as far as he could see, had everything under control and three of his best men on scout detail. Adam did, however, take the opportunity to pass on other information.

'If, as we hope, we catch a run in progress and should any of the cargo elude us, I have a couple of suggestions as to where you might look for it afterwards.'

'Go on,' said Levinson.

'A section of the nave at St Dunstan's in Snargate is sealed off from the body of the church for no obvious reason. And in the floor of the Lady Chapel of St George's in Ivychurch, there's a stone slab which I believe can be lifted. You can't miss it.'

'Churches,' muttered the Major. 'God.'

'Exactly.'

Adam left the barracks feeling optimistic, then rode into Hythe to catch Hindley's eye from across the street and give him a nod affirming that all was in hand. Hindley nodded back and Adam made his way to the *Swan*, left his horse in the stables and walked into the taproom for a mug of ale.

It was empty but for a couple of local tradesmen haggling over something or other near the counter and four youngish gentlemen gathered in a corner by the window. Adam took his ale to an empty table and sat down to mind his own business. His peace was short-lived.

One of the gentlemen – flamboyantly clad in peacock velvet, gold lacing and quantities of lace – drawled, 'Do you see what I see, Mark? A fellow with a sword, no less.'

One of the other men, more conservatively dressed but otherwise bearing such a striking resemblance to the speaker that he could only be his brother, glanced fleetingly across the room. 'Yes. Let it go.'

'Do you know ... I don't think I will.' The colourful gentleman rose and took a couple of steps in Adam's direction. 'I've heard talk about some mountebank with a sword. You, is it?'

Sighing inwardly, Adam curled his fingers around his ale pot and remained seated. This sort of thing happened from time to time. Inspired by wine-fuelled bravado, some young idiot *would* insist on trying to show off in front of his friends. It was tedious and annoying but rarely had to end in a fight. And so, ignoring the question, he said pleasantly, 'Don't let the sword alarm you. Neither it nor I have any interest in you, sir.'

'But *I've* an interest in *you*. Your fame precedes you, you see.'

'What're you talking about, Peter?' asked one of the gentlemen behind him fuzzily. 'Do you know him?'

'I know *of* him,' replied Peter, swaggering a little closer. 'Mr Brandon, I presume?'

Letting boredom invest every muscle, Adam nodded. 'And you are?'

'Leave it, Peter!' snapped Mark again. 'There's no point to this.'

'I'd listen to your brother, if I were you,' advised Adam before the popinjay could get a word out. 'I'm fairly resistant to provocation ... but not completely immune.'

'Who the *hell* do you think you're talking to?' spluttered Peter.

'Since you've yet to introduce yourself, I have no idea.'

'My name is Peter Blane, damn you!'

'Congratulations. Should I have heard of you?'

'Perhaps not. But you *will* do.'

'I'll look forward to it. But for now, I'd like to drink my ale in peace.'

Mr Blane floundered for a second, clearly unsure how to deal with this. Then, rallying, he said, 'Be warned, Brandon. You've been sniffing about a lady of my – of *our* – acquaintance. Her brother doesn't like it. And neither do I.'

There was a brief, abrupt silence into which the fourth man asked, 'What lady?'

'*Don't!*' warned Mark as Peter opened his mouth.

'No, really. Don't.' Adam finally rose from his bench, his tone less mild than before. 'A gentleman doesn't bandy a lady's name about in the alehouse. Furthermore, you are clearly under a misapprehension. But even if you were not --'

'A misapprehension? Is *that* what you call it?'

'Even if you were not,' finished Adam calmly, 'you are taking issue with something that is none of your concern.'

'*Not my concern*?' Peter advanced to within three feet of him. 'I will have you know, sir, that I – I intend to make the lady in question my wife!'

This time the silence was one of utter shock which, to Adam's mind, spoke volumes. Even Blane himself seemed to be wondering where the words had come from. Then Mark muttered disgustedly, 'Oh for God's sake! Just shut up and sit down.'

Peter didn't. Glaring haughtily at Adam he said, 'What do you say to *that*?'

'Only one thing immediately springs to mind. Does she know?'

Both of the cupshot friends tittered.

Mark growled, 'Enough, Peter. You're digging a hole for yourself. Stop now.'

'Oh you can't leave it there,' encouraged Adam. '*Does* she know?'

Peter opened his mouth, closed it again and finally avoided the question by saying stiffly, 'It is not perhaps ... *entirely* ... settled, as yet. But --'

'She doesn't, then.' Adam watched the idiot's fists clench and thought, *Go on. Take a swing at me. I know you're lying. I just don't know what you expect to achieve by it. Give me an excuse to find out.* Smiling sympathetically, he said, 'Scared I might cut you out, Mr Blane? Understandable. But making unfounded claims won't help you. And this conversation is over.' He gave a casual nod and picked up his hat. 'Good day to you.'

'Don't walk out on me, damn you. I'm not finished with you yet.'

Adam pivoted to face him so quickly he took a step back.

'Yes you are. You want to hit me but you won't do it. If it's the sword that is worrying you, it need not. I promise I won't draw it. But I *will* hit you back. And that should worry you a good deal more. Only think of the damage it might do to your pretty coat.'

And with a last and very genuine grin, he strode out.

* * *

Adam rode back to Orgarswick by way of St Mary in the Marsh, drawing rein by the church wall while he considered laying a branch of laurel on the grave nearest the gate. If Mr Mouth-Almighty Blane was known to Camilla – as, presumably, he must be – she might like to know about their imminent betrothal. Then he recognised that this must wait. If the run took place tonight, there was no predicting what the hours following it would require of him thus making it impossible to meet Camilla at eight the following morning.

Regretfully, he turned Hector's head in the direction of the cottage.

CHAPTER EIGHTEEN

Adam had barely finished assuring Rainham that Major Levinson's arrangements were faultless when there were sounds of a horse in the yard, swiftly followed by a thunderous knocking. The viscount laid one of his pistols on the table and Finch, upon receiving a nod from Adam, opened the door.

Lord Wingham stood on the threshold, pale and unaccustomedly grim. Striding into the room, he took in Rainham's presence, came to an abrupt halt and said curtly, 'Forgive the intrusion, Adam – but I need a private word.'

'No, you don't,' responded Adam. 'Alveston has sent Mr Gilbert to assist me.'

'That won't wash,' said Rainham, calmly sliding the pistol out of sight. 'His lordship and I are acquainted. How do you do, Wingham?'

'Not well, as it happens. Gilbert, is it?'

'For the moment, yes.'

'Fine.' Sebastian turned back to Adam. 'My late father's valet has been murdered. Oh – they *tried* to make it look like an accident but nobody who knew Perkins would believe he got drunk, fell in a drainage ditch and drowned. And the hell of it is that, if I'd made the connection sooner, he'd still be alive – and *you* might have a name.'

Adam laid a hand on Sebastian's shoulder and pressed him into a chair. Frowning, he said, 'Slow down and start at the beginning. Your father's valet, you say?'

'Yes. He'd been with Father forever – I've known him since I was a child. But when Father died, he wanted to retire and live near his niece and her children and – and grow flowers. So I bought him a cottage at Peasemarsh and pensioned him off. And yesterday morning his body was found face down in a bloody *ditch*.'

'I'm sorry to hear it,' said Rainham quietly. 'But what makes you think you could have prevented it?'

'The brandy,' replied Sebastian bitterly. 'If I'd remembered about that I'd have recognised the danger ... but I didn't and now it's too late.'

Placing a cup of wine near Sebastian's hand and sitting down beside him, Adam said, 'What *about* the brandy?'

'It was Father's favourite tipple. But after his first apoplexy, Blanche – my sister – wouldn't let him have it. So Perkins supplied him on the quiet. They kept it hidden behind Shakespeare's histories,' he said with a shaky laugh. 'Father wondered how Perkins knew good brandy from bad when he never touched it himself. What *I* should have wondered was how he came by it. But the answer to that is fairly plain now, isn't it? He got it from the owlers – probably one in particular. A man he knew.' Sebastian's eyes met Adam's. 'Do I really need to say it?'

'No. You might have spoken to Mr Perkins about this at any time. But the smuggler he dealt with didn't worry about it until he learned that you and I had met the Riding Officers. One of them must have talked – Tranter probably.'

'Yes.' Pushing his untouched wine aside, Sebastian stood up. 'So now he's got the hang of it, let's see if he'll talk some more.'

'Wait.' Adam's gaze travelled to Rainham and back again. 'I'm sorry, Sebastian. Much as I'd like to help you knock seven bells out of Tranter, we can't. Or not today, anyway.'

'Why?'

'Because Jeavons thinks there may be a run tonight and we've got forty dragoons standing by at Hythe. We can't do anything to jeopardise that.'

Sebastian swore under his breath.

'On the other hand ...' murmured Rainham, meditatively.

'On the other hand *what*?' asked Adam.

'If a run *is* due in tonight, Officer Tranter knows. I'm wondering how difficult it would be to lay him by the heels without any of his fellow smugglers thinking anything is amiss.' He smiled slowly. 'Imagine how very helpful he could be if only he allowed himself to be ... persuaded.'

'I'll persuade him,' said Sebastian flatly. 'The constable at Rye is investigating Perkins' death and I've got people of my own looking into it but I've little hope of anything coming of any of that. Wringing information out of Tranter is the best chance I have.'

'Well then,' said Adam, sitting down again. 'I suppose we'd better figure out how we're going to get hold of him ... and how we're going to make him talk.'

* * *

At Dragon Hall, Camilla was half-way through adding a column of figures when Coombes tapped at the study door to inform her that Mr Blane had called. Tossing down her pen with a huff of impatience, she said, 'Which one?'

'He did not give me a card,' replied the butler with a hint of disapproval. 'But I believe Mr *Peter* Blane, since he is somewhat flamboyantly clad.'

'Wonderful,' muttered Camilla. Then, drawing a bracing breath, 'Very well. You'd better show him up to the drawing-room. Ask Mrs Poole to prepare a tea tray and tell Martha to come and keep me company.'

'Very good, Miss Millie.' The butler hesitated briefly. 'If you've no objection, I will leave Thomas outside in the hall.'

Her brows rose. 'By all means. But why?'

'I ... suspect the gentleman may have been drinking.'

'He's *drunk*?'

'No! Dear me - if that were so, I would not have admitted him to the house!' said Coombes, shocked at the very idea. 'But I detected wine on his breath.'

'In which case, he's no business coming here at all,' said Camilla flatly, sailing to the door. 'And if he is not very careful, I shall tell him so.'

She entered the drawing-room with Martha at her heels and left the door open. She noticed that Mr Blane did not look pleased by either – though he quickly pasted a too-bright smile on his face. For her own part, Camilla had to stop herself blinking at the garish turquoise coat with its flashy gold braid.

'My dear Miss Edgerton-Foxe,' he exclaimed, crossing towards her, hands outstretched. 'How very good of you to receive me!'

'Not at all,' she returned with a courtesy she hoped he understood meant absolutely nothing and evaded his grasp by the simple expedient of waving him to a chair and sitting down herself. 'What may I do for you?'

'Do? Why – nothing. I was merely passing nearby and had a sudden impulse to see how you did. But indeed I need not ask. You have never looked better.'

'How kind of you to say so.'

'Not at all. You are blooming. Kent obviously agrees with you.'

'Since it is my home, one would certainly hope so,' said Camilla dryly, as Thomas entered to set the tea tray before her. 'I trust your mother is well, sir?'

'Oh yes. Mama never ails. She sends her good wishes and hopes you will permit her to call in the near future.'

'Of course. As I believe I explained to you before, when the refurbishments are complete, I shall be at home to all my neighbours.' She passed him a cup of tea with one hand and offered a plate of lemon tarts with the other. 'Cake?'

'Thank you, no.' The smile with its full array of teeth remained firmly in place. The cup rattled on its saucer and he had to use both hands to set it back on the table. 'Miss Edgerton-Foxe, I was hoping ... oh dash it all! Miss *Millie* – I may call you that, may I not?'

'No. You may not.' She watched his jaw slacken with shock and thought, *Coombes is right. He's not drunk but he's clearly heading that way if he seriously thought I'd say yes. Still, at least I've wiped the smile off his face for a moment.* 'However ... you were saying?'

'I – yes.' He rallied, beaming anew. 'May I persuade you to drive with me one day?'

'I'm afraid not. Once again, I believe that I refused that invitation the other evening.'

'I hoped you might have changed your mind.'

'I haven't.'

The smile faltered again but the wretched man was nothing if not persistent.

'Come riding then. Along the beach one day? There's no harm in that, is there?'

'None at all, if I wanted to do it. But I don't.'

'Why *not*?' he demanded. And this time without any vestige of a smile added sulkily, 'You've been seen out riding with that Brandon fellow, after all.'

'Where I go and with whom,' replied Camilla icily, 'is no concern of yours, Mr Blane. And *that Brandon fellow* is both a gentleman and known to my uncle, the earl.'

She watched this hit home, followed by the moment his mouth bypassed his brain.

'Your uncle didn't hear the way he was talking at the *Swan* in Hythe a couple of hours ago. He wasn't much of a gentleman *then*, I'll have you know!'

He's met Adam? How? She felt a remote stirring of amusement. *I'd like to have seen that. I doubt he came out best. But for now, it's time to put an end to this.*

She set down her cup and stood up, thus forcing him to do the same.

'He at least knows better than to call on a lady after he's been drinking – which it appears you do not. And now, since you have said quite enough, I suggest you leave.'

Belatedly realising that he'd blundered, Mr Blane resumed his smile and said, 'I beg your pardon. It's just ... after seeing you again the other evening I've been unable to think of anything *but* you. And I wanted ... I hoped ... that you would allow me to further our acquaintance. Only then I ran into Brandon and his – his insolent attitude towards you all but overset me.' He surged towards her, narrowly missing the table. 'I have not spoken to Guy yet but I am sure he would be happy if --'

'Stop, please,' said Camilla flatly, holding up a staying hand. 'Let us be clear, sir. Are you ... intimating ... that you wish to *court* me?'

'I – yes. It was always my wish but --'

'Why?'

He blinked at her. 'Why what?'

'Why do you suppose you might like being married to me? Or is it my *connections* you'd like to be related to?'

'No! Perish the thought, dear lady! How could you – that is, my attraction to you is of a long-standing nature but, in the past, there was never an opportunity to – to pursue it. And when you became engaged to Lord Staplehurst, all hope seemed to be at an end. But now ... *now* it seems I may have a chance at last. Will you not allow me that, at least?'

'No. I will do you the favour of telling you not to waste your time. I am not interested in marriage. Perhaps not ever and *certainly* not with you.' Since it appeared she had finally broken through what was either monumental conceit or a remarkably thick skin, Camilla decided to drive the point home. 'You do not know me at all, sir. If you did, you would know better than to stand there spouting arrant nonsense at me. There has been no long-standing attraction. As for being unable to stop thinking about me, I advise you to try – because if you call on me again, my butler will have orders not to admit you. Good day, Mr Blane. Thomas will show you out.'

As if waiting for his cue, Thomas appeared promptly in the doorway.

'This way, sir.'

Blane remained very still, staring at her. The incessant smile turned into something very different and he said, 'So that's the way of things. Think you'll get a better offer from Brandon, do you? Well, keep hoping. I know his sort. And any offer *he* makes won't come with a wedding ring. You can count on that.'

And he swept out, shouldering Thomas from his path as he went.

'Nasty little weevil,' said Martha, moving to Camilla's side. 'Are you all right, Miss?'

'Perfectly, thank you.' She gave a sudden unexpected choke of laughter. 'And you're quite right. Nasty little weevil describes him *exactly*.'

'The cheek of it! Thinking you'd ever look at the likes of *him*? And as to what he said about Mr Brandon – that was nothing but a pack of lies.'

'I know. Thank you, Martha. Please tell Coombes that although Mr Blane may visit my brother, I shall not be receiving him in future.'

Martha curtsied and left the room. Camilla sank slowly into a chair, her mind busy with several questions. Since it was unlikely that anyone had introduced Blane to Adam – after all, why should they? – the wretched man had presumably recognised him from something Guy had said. She'd have something to say to her idiot brother about that. She'd also give a great deal to know what had passed between Blane and Adam ... and had no doubt at all that Adam would tell her, if only she had the opportunity to ask him. The trouble was that she'd told him to stay away unless a meeting was strictly necessary.

It had only been three days since she'd last seen him but it seemed longer. She told herself that she merely missed their conversations. She refused to acknowledge that it was rather more than that. *Was* Peter Blane's intrusion sufficient excuse to ask for a meeting? Probably not. From the little Thomas was able to tell her, it seemed that Adam and Rainham were exceptionally busy and rarely to be found at the cottage. Much to their disgust, none of the maids had yet clapped eyes on either of them. Camilla wondered what they were up to; then she wondered how long it might be before Adam wanted to meet her; and finally she returned to the question of whether or not to risk sending him a note.

* * *

Over tankards of ale, discussion on how to get Mr Tranter where they wanted him didn't take the gentlemen very long.

'We'll need to keep him somewhere he'll be neither seen nor heard,' said Rainham, 'which makes here our only choice. The difficulty is how to get him here without him shouting blue murder every step of the way.'

'I have an idea,' said Sebastian. And, with a slight shudder, 'He's a rat-catcher, apparently. Summon him to deal with an infestation.'

'That could work.' Adam thought about it. 'He won't be taking part in the run – assuming it happens. But his neighbours will know about it and not be surprised if he's out all night, so nobody will miss him before tomorrow. But Rainham and I need to be on watch at the Wall by ten at the latest. If he hasn't talked by then --'

'Perish the thought.' Rainham stood up and stretched. 'I feel sure that, between us, we'll have Mr Tranter chatting merrily in no time. And with that settled, I intend to snatch a couple of hours' sleep before he gets here.'

In the end, it was decided that Finch should go to Dymchurch and lure Tranter to the cottage with the promise of a generous fee for disposing of the fictitious rats.

'What if I can't find him?' asked Finch. 'Can't go around asking, can I?'

'No,' agreed Adam. 'But at seven in the evening – if he's not at the address Lord Wingham has given you – he'll be in the nearest tavern. You're sure you'll recognise him?'

'Yes. Stringy little fellow with red hair and a bit of a limp. Shouldn't be hard to spot.'

'Hopefully not. Spin whatever yarn you like, but get him here. And be careful.'

'Don't you worry about me, sir. I won't let you down.'

'I know that, Harry. You never do.'

* * *

By the time Finch was expected back, Adam had changed into the unrelieved black he wore for night expeditions. Rainham, on the other hand, emerged looking every inch the viscount in deepest violet silk.

'You're not coming out on the marsh like that, are you?' asked Adam.

'No. Tranter will refuse to talk because he's more afraid of the smugglers than he is of us. We have to reverse that – and intimidation is the first step.'

When horses were heard outside, followed by Finch's voice, Adam took a seat by the hearth while Rainham and Sebastian temporarily made themselves scarce. Then Finch was ushering Tranter through the door and remaining to lean against it while the Riding Officer stared in horror at Adam.

'*You*!' he said, and immediately turned to flee only to be prevented by Finch's burly form behind him. 'What d'you want with me? There ain't no rats here, I'll be bound.'

'Only one.' Adam rose and gestured to a chair. 'Sit down, Mr Tranter. My friends and I are eager to have a little chat with you.'

'I got nothing to say to you,' he began. Then stopped, aghast, as Sebastian and the imposing figure of Rainham materialised from the bedchambers. 'M-My lord? What's this? I haven't done nothing – I swear.'

'Perhaps and perhaps not,' shrugged Sebastian, his tone edged with frost. 'But you *know* things, don't you? And you are going to share those things with us.'

'Beginning,' added Rainham, 'with whether or not a cargo is making landfall tonight.'

'A – a cargo? H-How would I know that? But if you've heard summat you gotta let me go to – to do my duty.'

Rainham made a sound suspiciously like a growl and, picking up Tranter by his collar as if he weighed no more than a rabbit, rammed him down on the chair Adam had placed in the middle of the room. Then, while Finch tied him to it, he said, 'But you *don't* do your duty, do you? You ride about, well away from anything that may be happening on the beach. Then you go home, close the curtains and hide your head under the covers till morning.'

'No! I look out for the smugglers and --'

'You do indeed,' remarked Adam. 'You look out for them exceedingly well. And not merely by turning a blind eye. How much did they pay you for telling them all about your meeting with Lord Wingham and me?'

'What? No! It's a lie. I never --' He stopped. 'Look. If somebody blabbed, it must've been Hindley or Jeavons. It weren't me.'

'It was you – and a man is dead because of it,' snapped Sebastian. 'You are implicated in that death and in danger of hanging for it – if they don't hang you for being in league with the owlers whilst simultaneously taking pay as a Riding Officer. Now answer the original question. Is there a run tonight?'

Tranter's eyes flickered from one to the other of them – partly through fear, Adam thought, and partly to determine which of them was most likely to be persuaded to believe him. Finally, in something akin to desperation, he mumbled, 'There's mebbe a chance of it.'

Rainham and Adam exchanged glances. 'Go on,' said Adam.

'That's all I got, mister. The owlers don't talk. You know that.'

'And yet you heard something.' It was not a question.

Tranter licked his lips nervously.

'I – I thought I might've caught a – a whisper in the tavern but it weren't no more'n that and I could've been mistook.'

'But equally, you may not have been – in which case, it was your duty to share this information with someone in authority. Why didn't you?'

'Who's going to listen to the likes of me? Tell me that.'

'We are listening, Mr Tranter,' replied Rainham. 'I can assure you that we are listening *intently*. But so far, I believe we are all finding you a touch unconvincing. Gentlemen?'

'More than a touch,' said Adam.

'Hardly helpful at all,' agreed Sebastian.

'So can we hurt him now?' asked Finch, stepping away from the door with just the right note of eagerness. 'I've got the iron nice and hot on the trivet and I fetched the pliers in like you told me, Mr Gilbert, sir – and you promised I could have a turn this time.'

'I did and you may ... but all in good time. And while you're waiting, why not fetch the meat-hook in case it's needed.'

'Yes!' said Finch, rushing to the scullery and back again. 'That was a good trick you told me about, sir. I'd *like* to try that one.'

Even though it had been rehearsed, Adam had to bite his lips and avoid Rainham's eye in case he laughed. As an apprentice torturer, Harry was worryingly convincing.

Tranter thought so, too. His eyes nearly starting out of his head, he said chokingly, 'You're not doing nothing to me with p-pliers nor anything else. You're *gentlemen*.'

'We are,' agreed Rainham. And then, 'Oh dear. Did you imagine that gentlemen don't play rough? How naïve of you. We have an absolute arsenal of dirty tricks and very few scruples about using them. But whether or not we do so on this occasion is up to you.'

Sweat was beading the Riding Officer's brow and the wild-eyed gaze again travelled over the four of them. Nothing he saw was comforting. Finch hummed cheerfully as he busied himself with the iron; Sebastian idly examined his fingernails; Adam's hand strayed lovingly over his sword-hilt; and Rainham perched on the edge of the table, managing to look both dangerous and faintly bored.

'Well, Mr Tranter?' he said at length. 'What is it to be?'

'I c-can't,' he moaned. 'If I t-talk they'll kill me!'

'And if you *don't* talk, we'll hurt you until you do. Either way, we *will* have our answers.'

'Look on the bright side,' suggested Adam persuasively. '*They* don't have to know you talked. We certainly won't tell them.'

'But they'll find out. They always do.'

'Very well,' sighed Rainham. 'Finch ... how would you like to start?'

'Well, there's the meat-hook,' replied Finch longingly, 'or I could iron his fingers.'

'Or both?' shrugged Rainham. 'Best get on with it, then. We don't have all night.'

'No!' screamed Tranter, as Finch bore down on him, hook in one hand and flat-iron in the other. 'No! I'll tell you – I will. Just keep him away from me!'

'Hold, Harry,' said Adam, strolling round to drop on his haunches in front of Tranter. 'Let's find out if he means it. Is there a run tonight? Yes or no.'

'Y-Yes.'

'And making landfall where?'

'Between Brockman's Barn and Marshland Gut,' mumbled Tranter miserably.

'Well done. That hardly hurt at all, did it?' said Adam, rising to pull out his watch. 'It's a half after eight. I've just time to warn Levinson and get back before --'

He stopped as Tranter's cry of 'You got *dragoons* waiting?' clashed with Sebastian's, 'Don't be an ass! You can't.'

Adam looked at his lordship. 'Why not?'

'Because there'll be groups of owlers heading across the marsh all over the damned place – and, whichever road you take, you'll have to ride right through them.'

'But --'

'No.' Rainham this time. 'He's right. You're no use to us dead. And if Levinson is as organised as you say, he'll see the activity for himself once it starts. So sit down and let's finish this with Mr Tranter. Sebastian ... your turn, I think.'

Sebastian nodded and, pulling up another chair, sat astride it to face the Riding Officer.

'You told your smuggler friends about last week's meeting, didn't you?'

Tranter shut his eyes and released a heavy breath. 'Yes.'

'And one of them ordered the murder of my late father's valet.'

He flinched and his eyes flew open. 'I had nothing to do with that!'

'Then who did?' And when Tranter didn't immediately answer, '*Who*?'

'It – it was Thompson and Sedge. The captain told 'em to ... to silence him for good.'

'The captain?' cut in Rainham. 'Who is he?'

'Don't know. I don't know his name and I ain't never seen his face proper. None of us have. He meets us in the dark, wearing a hood. We just call him the captain because he brings the orders.'

'He *brings* the orders?' queried Adam. 'Brings them, not *gives* them?'

Tranter nodded. 'Somebody's above him. Don't know who they are neither.'

'So ... what *can* you tell us about him?' asked Rainham. 'How does he speak?'

This took some thought. Then, 'More like you than me, I reckon.'

'An educated man, then? Possibly even a gentleman?'

'Could be.' Tranter fidgeted, straining against his bonds. 'Look. I'm sorry about the valet. I'd never heard of him till the captain said the old man knew his name – so how was I supposed to guess anyone'd want to kill him? And now I've told you everything I know --'

'Not a half nor even a quarter of what you know,' said Adam. 'I'm quite sure you could name every man in Dymchurch who is an active smuggler. But we --'

Panic stirred. 'I won't! No. Somebody'd cut my throat for sure.'

'But we won't ask you to do that,' finished Adam calmly. 'This is how our future relationship is going to work. You will keep us informed of the smugglers' activities … and you will tell the smugglers only what we *tell* you to tell them. You will mention our presence here to no one at all. And when contact is necessary, you will make it through Mr Finch who, I should warn you, has become very attached to his pliers.'

Tranter dissolved into wordless moaning.

'Cheer up, man,' said Rainham bracingly. 'It's not all bad news. We might pay for your services if they warrant it. And now, if Adam and I are to go out again, I should change.'

'But not into Smuggler Jim, for God's sake,' begged Adam.

'Certainly not. On this occasion, plain Mr Gilbert will suffice.'

'And what about me?' wailed Tranter. 'You're going to let me go, ain't you?'

'And risk you running off to warn your old friends? Not a chance. You'll be our guest until morning,' replied Adam. 'But fear not. Lord Wingham and Finch will be keeping you company.'

CHAPTER NINETEEN

When Adam and Rainham arrived at the Wall, the beach below still appeared deserted.

'Could Tranter be wrong?' murmured Rainham, frowning.

Adam shook his head. 'I don't think so. They'll be there but staying out of sight until they get the ship's signal. Look out for a blue flash. That's when things begin to happen.' He shifted, frowning a little. 'I still wish I'd been able to warn Levinson.'

'Well, you couldn't – and it would have been asinine to try, so forget it. He's done this before, hasn't he?'

'Once. He said he'll move his men into place as soon as there are signs of activity and invade the beach as the first of the cargo makes land.'

'Upon which, I presume, you and I join in the fray?'

'Unless you'd rather sit and watch?'

'Very droll,' muttered Rainham. And fell silent.

* * *

Below them and a few hundred yards away, Guy also waited for the fun to start ... except that, like the other evening at the *London*, nothing felt quite right. He'd caught a number of strange glances and Dan Clements, his friend and partner for the unloading, wasn't his usual cheerful self. Eventually, when incomprehension became a mixture of hurt and unease, he could keep silent no longer.

'Dan ... have I done something wrong?'

'I don't know. Have you?'

The blunt question and the hard look that accompanied it rocked Guy on his heels. He said, 'Such as what, for example?'

'How would *I* know if *you* don't?'

'But that's the thing. I don't. I mean, I *really* don't.'

Clements eyed him narrowly for a moment and then said slowly, 'You've not let anything slip, then? Maybe at home?'

'What? *No*! Of course not!' replied Guy hotly. And lowering his voice in response to the angry hissing noises around him, 'How could you think that? I've been one of you on and off for years and never said a word to anyone.'

'That's it though, isn't it? On and off, like you said. Mostly off.'

'I couldn't help that. And it's different now.'

'Yes. You've not had to creep about under your sister's nose before.'

Something lurched unpleasantly in Guy's chest. He said, 'Millie's doesn't know *anything*. I make damned sure of that. And anyone who says different is a liar.'

'If you say so,' shrugged Clements. 'All I know is, her name came up somewhere it shouldn't and, far as we can see, there's only one way that could have happened.'

'Shut up,' said a voice from behind them. 'Ship's here.'

For a while after that everything happened in well-ordered silence. Men poured on to the beach, some leading ponies or driving carts, and boats were dragged down to the water. Forcing himself to ignore the uneven thundering of his heart and the knot of worry numbing his mind, Guy concentrated on the tasks required of him thinking, *Dan has it all wrong. Millie doesn't know. She* can't. *I've always been careful about that. Somebody's made a mistake – but it wasn't me*.

The first incoming boats were being unloaded and their contents transferred for transport when they heard the sound of horses racing along the sand toward them.

'*Dragoons*!' someone shouted. 'Defend yourselves!'

And then all hell broke loose.

Shots rang out as an orderly line of horsemen bore down on the smugglers who, encumbered by boxes, packages and small kegs, were caught unprepared. A dozen men fell where they stood. Others froze for a second, unsure which way to turn and some still tried to get their loads to the carts or ponies. But the majority threw the goods aside – just in time to meet the onslaught of a further twenty redcoat infantry swarming over the Wall. The silent world of the beach was all shouting, flashes of light from pistols and the clash and slither of steel.

At the first sign of Levinson's dragoons, Adam and Rainham left their position and scrambled down towards the mêlée. Rainham had a pistol in each hand and Adam, his sword. By the time they reached the action, a battle royal was in full swing. Trying to form a defensive line to protect both their colleagues and the cargo, batsmen fought troopers off with clubs and flails. Away to his left and over the din of confusion, Adam could hear Levinson roaring out orders to hold formation ... and then he came under attack from a fellow wielding a long-handled spade.

He ducked, reached out and grabbed the stave. The man wrenched it from his grasp and swung it at his head. Adam ducked again, swerved underneath and clipped the man who held it under the chin with the hilt of his sword. He went down, taking the spade with him ... and Adam immediately found himself facing an ancient cutlass in the hands of a massive fellow with tattoos. Adam didn't generally like fighting with a blade in each hand but this was no time to be finicky. Keeping Goliath and his cutlass at bay just long enough to draw the knife from his boot, he launched into a swift series of moves designed to disarm if he could, wound if he couldn't. Even now, he preferred not to kill anybody unless he absolutely had to.

Goliath kept on coming. Adam danced out of reach. With a roar of derision, Goliath charged ... and blundered harmlessly by when Adam side-stepped, spun and sent him staggering with a boot to the back. At this point, Adam became aware of another fellow bearing down on him armed with a flail and realised he couldn't deal with both of them. Hurling his knife at Goliath before he had a chance to turn around, he saw it embed itself in his shoulder. Then, without wasting a second, he leapt at the other man and delivered a slash to his right forearm. The flail hit the sand and the man howled.

Aided by a couple of dragoons, Rainham was attempting to stop a second gaggle of smugglers escaping by boat. The first was already some thirty yards from the beach. He had discharged both his pistols and had no time to re-load ... but he doubted the smugglers knew that and hoped that one or other of the dragoons had a shot left. Aiming a pistol in each hand, he roared, 'Stand or I fire!'

Three men dropped their clubs and raised submissive hands. But two others spun round and splashed frantically towards the waiting boats. Neither of the dragoons fired. One remained where he was, clumsily trying to re-load his musket. The other hurled himself after the escapees and, wielding his musket like a club, brought one of them down. Cursing wildly, Rainham ploughed after him and managed to fell the other with a sort of flying dive. Face down in three or four inches of water, the fellow gurgled and struggled until a slight relaxation in pressure allowed him to lift his head sufficiently to haul in some air.

Wet and annoyed, Rainham arose, hauling his captive up by the collar.

'You!' he snapped to the dithering trooper. 'Help secure these men – now and quickly.'

'Sir!' The soldier jumped to obey, looking shamefaced.

Leaving them to it, Rainham turned back to the ongoing chaos and tried to assess the situation. A few of the ponies were missing and also, he thought, one or two of the carts which meant that some contraband had left the beach. There were still pockets of fighting here and there, punctuated by the occasional shot. Quite a few men of both sides were down, some dead but by no means all. Levinson's troopers seemed to be closing in on roughly two dozen smugglers who hadn't managed to flee and some of his officers were working to secure the scattered cargo. He couldn't see Adam anywhere.

Beyond the as yet incomplete circle of redcoats and having just disabled a fellow intent on staving his skull in with a cudgel, Adam was taking a moment to catch his breath when his attention was caught by a man who was attempting to crawl, inch by inch, up the beach. Frowning, Adam dropped on one knee beside him, taking in the quantities of blood from a bullet wound in his back. Turning him over as gently as he could and discovering a second and clearly mortal wound to the stomach, he said, 'Be still. You won't make it.'

The man blinked at him out of pain-glazed eyes and muttered something incoherent. Then, more lucidly, he said raggedly and in French, 'I must. I cannot be ... taken.'

Adam's breath snared but he answered coolly and in the same language.

'You won't be. I'm very sorry, monsieur.'

'I ... I am dying?'

'I fear so.' Feeling rather sick, he folded the man's hand in his own.

'Soon?'

'Very soon.'

The Frenchman managed a wry grimace. '*Merde.*'

'Indeed. May I know your name, monsieur?'

'C-Corbeau. Gaston Corbeau. You?'

'Adam Brandon.'

Silence. Then, so faintly Adam barely heard it, 'You are ... not French ... I think.'

'Does it matter?'

This time the silence was even longer. 'It seems ... not. My papers ...'

But even as Adam leaned closer to listen, Corbeau expelled a long, sighing breath.

Slowly, Adam folded the dead man's hands over his chest and was just about to get to his feet when he saw the small, sealed packet protruding from the Frenchman's torn coat. He removed it and dropped it in his pocket. Then he stood, suddenly conscious of the painful blow he'd taken to his left elbow and the throb in his cheekbone that might be heralding a black eye. Around him, something approaching order was gradually being restored with prisoners being marched away while the wounded, both redcoats and smugglers, were loaded into waggons. Turning, he saw Rainham heading his way and said remotely, 'Still in one piece, I see.'

'Yes. You?'

'A scratch or two.' And gesturing to the Frenchman, 'Better than Monsieur Corbeau, here.'

Rainham's gaze sharpened. 'A spy?'

'It would seem so. I have his despatch. But that's for later. First we'd better thank Levinson for his assistance and come to some arrangement about his prisoners.'

'Yes. But for God's sake, let's make it quick. I'm looking forward to a bath.'

Adam sent him a pitying glance.

'*Keep* looking forward to it. Given our current living conditions, it's the nearest either one of us will get.'

* * *

A short while ago, Guy Edgerton-Foxe had recovered consciousness to the confused sensation of being in a boat. He opened his eyes, but hurriedly shut them again when his skull throbbed as if it was about to split. Had someone hit him? And why was he in a boat? Cautiously, he opened his eyes again. He was jammed in the rear of one of the small boats used to ferry cargo and it was being rowed very fast towards ... what? Guy tried to think. The last thing he remembered was the descent of the dragoons and shots being fired. He'd been with Dan. A wave of relief came over him. It was all right then. Dan had somehow got him off the beach before he could be wounded or captured. He was being rescued. Thank God. Except ... something wasn't right, was it? No. It definitely wasn't. His hands were bound.

'Back with us, are you?' growled Dan Clements over the splash of oars from the other end of the boat. 'Good. That'll save me carrying you up the ladder.'

'Ladder?' asked Guy. And then, fear slamming through him, 'Where are you taking me?'

'Never you mind,' came the cold reply. 'A lot of us'd like to know what you've told and who you've told it to. So we're going somewhere you'll have plenty of time to explain all about your sister and Brandon and them bloody dragoons. I'm looking forward to it.'

* * *

By the time Adam and Rainham got back to the cottage, the first fingers of dawn were touching the sky. Both of them were tired, dirty and increasingly aware of a variety of aches and pains. It didn't help that they were also aware that their work wasn't done for the night.

They found Finch alert and ready with cups of wine, Tranter dozing uneasily, still tied to the chair and Sebastian preparing to leave.

'What happened?' he asked as soon as they walked in. 'Did it go as planned?'

Adam nodded wearily. 'More or less. Nineteen smugglers are under arrest and a further handful, either wounded or dead. Some of the cargo got away but most didn't. Rainham or I will confer with Levinson later today. What of you? Has our friend here given you all the information you need for the apprehension of Mr Perkins' murderers?'

'He's told me where to find Messrs Sedge and Thompson. And he knows that if he tips them off he won't like the results.'

'I said I wouldn't, didn't I?' muttered Tranter sulkily. 'It's getting light. Can I go now?'

'Yes – though if you're wise you'll lie low for a few hours,' replied Adam. 'Untie him, Harry, and see him on his way. You should leave, too, Sebastian. There's nothing more you can do here and your lady will be worried.'

Sebastian nodded and reached for his hat.

'My thanks for your help – and I'll keep you informed.'

When he and Rainham were alone, Adam brought out Corbeau's packet and removed the protective wrapping to reveal a direction he didn't understand. He lifted the seal as he'd been taught so as not to break it and spread the sheets out on the table. One glance at them was all it took to see the next problem.

'It's in code,' he said.

'Of course it is,' agreed Rainham a touch irritably. 'But neither one of us is in any state to start trying to break it now.'

'No. Pity Vincent isn't here. How good were *you* at his lessons?'

'Moderate. You?'

'The same. So it's going to take time. Damn.'

They fell silent and, by the time Finch walked back in, were sliding towards sleep. Taking the situation in at a glance, Finch said, 'Go to bed, the pair of you. You'll be neither use nor ornament later on if you don't.'

'True.' Rainham heaved himself to his feet and waved a hand at Corbeau's despatch. 'That will still be there in four or five hours' time. We'll attack it then.'

Adam nodded and watched him trudge from the room. Then, recalling an earlier thought, said, 'Harry … might someone from the Hall bring bread again today?'

'Aye. That footman – Thomas, his name is. Probably be here around seven.'

'Good.' He pulled paper, pen and ink towards him. 'Give him this note for his mistress. Tell him to make sure she has it before she goes out and not to let the brother see it.'

Camilla, he wrote

Do not on any account go to the beach today. I need to see you and will explain then. He hesitated and then, in case it wasn't imperative enough, underscored *on any account* before considering what to write next. *I can't get to the church early today – but if you think it safe to meet at dusk, I'll see you then. If not, it must be tomorrow.*

In haste,

Adam

He folded the sheet, sealed it and pushed it across to Finch. Then he went in search of his bed, saying over his shoulder, 'Wake me at nine if I'm not already up. And get some sleep yourself, Harry. You did brilliantly last night.'

* * *

As on the previous morning, he arose to the welcome aroma of fresh bread and coffee just as Rainham came in from the yard, towelling his hair. They nodded to each other but didn't speak until they each had a steaming cup in their hands. Then Adam said, 'About Corbeau's despatch … I've an alternative we might try.'

Rainham reached for the butter. 'Go on.'

'After last night, the smugglers are probably still in disarray. Right now, I doubt they know who escaped, who was lifted and who died. If that's so, they won't know Corbeau's current status and will hope he's merely delayed … which gives us a few hours' grace.'

'To do what?'

'Figure out where the despatch is supposed to go … and deliver it.'

'*What*?'

'Think about it. Delivering it gives us a chance to identify this co-called Captain of Tranter's or someone even more senior,' persuaded Adam. 'And letting the smugglers believe their chain is still intact gives us a further advantage. Isn't that worth a try?'

'Without knowing what might be in the despatch? Absolutely not.'

'Quite. So I wondered if it could have suffered in transit. Water damage, perhaps?'

Rainham stared at him in silence. Then he said grudgingly, 'Yes. I suppose that *might* work. But we need an accurate copy before we can ruin it and it's two closely-written pages! With the prisoners to question and everything else that needs to be done today, how do you – oh.' He stopped abruptly. 'Of course. You want to take it to Millie.'

'Yes,' agreed Adam. 'She memorises it and makes a copy while the largely unreadable original goes where it's supposed to – if we can work out where that is.'

'We'll come to that presently. Aside from a copy for you and me to work on, we should send one to Wilfred Street for Vincent and to keep Goddard informed.'

'How? Neither you nor I can take it – not with things possibly reaching boiling point here.'

'No.' Rainham's eyes were cold and focussed. 'So we send it the one way it can't fall into the wrong hands. Inside Millie's head.'

For a long moment, Adam simply stared at him. Then he snapped, 'No, we damned well won't – or not unless I go with her.'

'You can't. You just said as much yourself.'

'That was before you decided to risk Camilla. If she goes, *I* go.' Even as he said it, he had the uneasy feeling that she might have her own views on the matter. Drawing a steadying breath, he said, 'I suggest we postpone this argument in favour of more immediate issues – such as where to take the original. I sent Camilla a note suggesting a meeting early this evening though there's a chance she may not be able to come. Assuming she is, you'll need to be ready to move the despatch onward.'

'Me? Why not you?'

'Because a buffoon I met yesterday recognised me from Guy Edgerton-Foxe's description and, for all I know, there may be others who can do the same. Also, *you're* the one who enjoys dressing up. So ... what do you make of the direction?'

Still looking both unconvinced and reluctant, Rainham reached for the outer sheet.

To await collection by
Erasmus Brooke Esq.
at Woolland Pack

He said, 'Woolland Pack? Is that a location? The name of a house? What?'

'It could be either,' returned Adam, 'though if it's a village, it's not one I know. But how many men do you think there are called Erasmus?'

'You're taking it at face value. Don't.'

'No. I suppose not. Perhaps Camilla may have some idea.' He poured a second cup of coffee and reached for the ham. 'Here's the deal. You start working on the code and I'll go to Hythe to start questioning whichever prisoners seem most likely to know something useful and can also be persuaded to share it.'

'Probably none of them,' remarked Rainham. 'But I admire your optimism.'

CHAPTER TWENTY

Camilla read Adam's note at the breakfast table and couldn't prevent a very real frisson of pleasure at the prospect, not just of seeing him, but also at the rather touching knowledge he was worried about her. He had concerns connected to the beach – to which she was absolutely *on no account* to go. The underscoring made her smile a little but also made her wonder if there had been a run last night. That had to be a possibility; though why Adam thought there might still be dangers lurking on the beach, she couldn't imagine. By now, there wouldn't be any sign of whatever might have happened under the cover of darkness. Owlers didn't leave things to chance. And anything they couldn't hide would disappear with the next high tide.

There was no sign of Guy – which was no surprise since he was rarely home before the early hours of the morning and never came downstairs before noon. She was aware that this was a habit he needed to break before it became thoroughly ingrained ... but if she started doing something about it now there was a chance he'd poke his nose into places she'd rather he didn't.

The day seemed to be dragging its feet and although there were things she could busy herself with in the house, none of them held her attention. By mid-afternoon she was too restless to sit still and, on her way to change into her riding-dress, she sent a message to the stables asking for her mare to be saddled. Then, telling Coombes that she might be some time but would be back for dinner, she set off on a leisurely round of tenant visiting, the aim of which was to arrive at St Mary's in good time for her assignation.

It was unfortunate that the afternoon which had begun so pleasantly grew steadily cloudier and eventually, just as Camilla left the Brownlow smallholding at Paradise Bush, turned to drizzle. However, she refused to let this dampen her spirits. She could find shelter for Sheba beneath the trees around the graveyard and for herself in the church porch. And with something to look forward to, she didn't mind waiting.

* * *

Having, as Rainham had predicted, returned empty-handed from Hythe and subsequently drowned his frustrations under the chilly water of the pump in the yard, Adam arrived at St Mary's earlier than he'd intended only to be surprised by the sight of Camilla's mare contentedly cropping the grass beneath the trees. Something inside him warmed to the possibility that she was as impatient to see him as he was her. He'd like to *think* she was ... but knew better than to hope for it.

She met him in the doorway with the wide, sizzling smile that never failed to temporarily scatter his wits and said, 'You're early!'

He swallowed and smiled back. 'So are you.'

Uneasily aware that she had perhaps made her pleasure at seeing him a little too blatant, Camilla lifted one nonchalant shoulder and turned to walk back into the porch. 'Because of the rain.'

It wasn't what he'd hoped for but he said merely, 'I, too.'

It wasn't what she'd hoped for either but she hadn't known that until he said it. Opening her mouth on the first thing that came to mind, she said, 'How is the cottage? Are you moderately comfortable?'

'Yes. At least, *I* am. Rainham is struggling to come to terms with the absence of a bathtub along with a couple of footmen to fill it with hot water.' And without waiting for her to speak, 'You stayed away from the beach this morning?'

'As you told me to. But why --?'

'I had advance word of a cargo coming ashore last night so we arranged for a troop of dragoons to be on hand to meet it – you can guess with what result. And I wasn't sure how long it would take to clear away the signs of it.'

Camilla stared at him, finally taking in first the shadowy bruise on his cheekbone and then the bandage around his right hand. She said starkly, 'You were hurt?'

'No more than you can see. Neither was Rainham. But --'

'Good. Just for future reference, I don't faint at the sight of blood.'

'I never supposed you did.' He drew a mildly impatient breath. 'Camilla ... I need you to do something and it's important. Can we sit down somewhere while I explain?'

'Yes, of course. I'm sorry. Let's go inside. There's no one there – I checked. And if someone comes, we'll hear them.'

He followed her into the small church and looked around. Like others he'd visited, it had box pews – these of natural wood and lovingly polished – and the same royal Coat of Arms he'd seen elsewhere. But it also boasted a pipe organ flanked by a pair of boards on one of which was written the Lord's Prayer and on the other, the Ten Commandments; and, on the floor beneath it, a pair of late-medieval brasses. He said, 'This is ... nice. Peaceful.'

Camilla nodded. 'Yes. St Mary's has always been my favourite. But you're not here to admire ecclesiastical architecture, are you?'

'No.' He unlatched a pew at the back of the nave and, when they were both seated, produced Corbeau's packet. 'This fell into my hands last night. It's a French despatch and it's in code. Obviously we need a copy for decryption purposes. But I want to render this one virtually unreadable in order to send it on its way and --'

'How?' she asked. '*How* are you going to make it illegible?'

'Water damage – as if the man carrying it was in the sea at some point. But I can't do that until we have a copy to work with. It's a long shot and Rainham's not convinced but --'

'But you hope doing so will lead to more information,' she said. 'More specifically, the identity of the person who receives it?'

'Yes.' He was surprised she'd seen his intention so quickly, then realised he shouldn't have been since he already knew her mind moved fast. 'So I wondered if you might --'

'I know what you want.' She waved a dismissive hand at him and spread out the pages. 'Go and explore the church, if you like.'

'Thank you. I'm happy where I am.'

In truth, she was happy where he was as well, his shoulder pressed companionably against hers. 'Fine. But I have to read it.'

Read it? he thought. *Read a collection of apparently random letters and numbers and* remember *it*? But he said only, 'I'll be quiet then, shall I?'

She glanced at him then and, though she couldn't help smiling, muttered, 'If you can manage it, that would be helpful.'

'I'll try, ma'am.'

This time his reward was a tiny gurgle of laughter. Then she settled down to concentrate. It took a little while but, even so, she passed the pages back to him a lot sooner than he expected, saying, 'All right. I have it. Meet me here tomorrow morning and you shall have your copy. Was there anything else?'

'Yes,' he said. And then, 'I'm sorry. Do you *know* how impressive that is?'

'I can imagine how impressive it *looks*,' she agreed. 'But I'm used to the fact that a bit of my brain works differently to most people's. Now ... the other thing?'

'This.' He showed her the direction. 'Do you have any idea where it might be?'

Camilla looked at it, blinked and then gave a tiny chuckle. 'Yes. Haven't you?'

'No.' He eyed her warily. 'It's that easy?'

'Let's put it this way. The only people around here who *wouldn't* put two and two together are the ones who couldn't read it anyway.'

'I see. Thank you for generously sparing Rainham and me official idiot status.'

'You're quite welcome.'

'And so?'

'Mr Erasmus Brooke at Woolland Pack,' she read, eying him encouragingly as if she expected the penny to drop. Then, 'I don't know who Erasmus is. But he's expecting to collect this at the *Woolpack* tavern in Brookland.'

Adam shut his eyes and groaned. 'Excuse me for a moment while I go and bang my head against a wall.'

'Don't be too hard on yourself. You can't be familiar with quite *every* tavern on the Marsh. At least, I hope you're not.'

'Not yet. I'm still working on it,' he replied absently. Then, opening his eyes again, 'But I should have seen Brookland. Now you've said it, it's staring me in the face.'

'The extra E at the end of Brook probably misled you.'

'Stop. Being kind just makes it worse.'

'Kind? Me? I thought you knew me better than --'

'Shh!' his hand closed hard over hers. 'Someone's coming.'

Camilla hadn't heard anything. Now, however, she caught a female voice saying, '… not going to stand out here getting wet.'

'Down,' hissed Adam, shoving the despatch into his pocket with one hand while pushing her off the pew with the other. 'On the floor. Lie flat.'

'Why?' she whispered. 'They won't see us if we just --'

He didn't bother to answer. In one smooth move just as the porch door swung wide, he pinned her to the floor by the simple expedient of lying on top of her, effectively jamming them both in the tight space between their pew and the one in front. Camilla huffed in surprise and tried to heave him off. She might as well have tried dislodging a boulder. Realisation that she was lying beneath a great deal of warm, nicely-made masculinity stilled her immediately; that and the fact that there were two people roughly twelve feet away.

She looked up, met an intent slate-blue gaze and raised her brows in silent enquiry. He shook his head and braced himself on his forearms, seemingly in an attempt to relieve her of some of his weight. If she'd dared speak she would have told him not to worry on her account. She was already discovering that being pressed from chest to knee against Adam Brandon was not a hardship. His mouth, she realised, was inches from her own.

From somewhere near the pulpit, a disgruntled male voice said, 'All this creeping about is stupid, Izzy. And for what? *You're* free, *I'm* free. We're both old enough to know our own minds – and have been for a good while now. So why --?'

'You *know* why. My Pa hasn't … warmed to you yet.'

'It's nothing to do with not *warming* to me. He just wants to keep you at home, looking after him, selfish old bugger.'

'Mind your mouth, John Trot!'

'Sorry. But ten years I've been trying to court you – and a right fool it's making me look!'

Gazing down into a pair of wide green eyes, Adam mouthed, 'Ten *years*?'

Camilla's mouth quivered appreciatively.

'I don't mean it to,' Izzy was saying placatingly. 'But I can't go against my Pa.'

'Why not?' And when she said nothing, 'For God's sake, Izzy – you're *thirty-nine*.'

Camilla gave a tiny gasp, laughter filling her face and forcing her to press her lips together to stop it escaping. Adam fixed her with a warning frown which, probably because he couldn't quite disguise that he, too, wanted to laugh, didn't work as well as it might have done. Feeling tremors of mirth beginning to ripple through the supple body beneath his, he laid a cautioning finger against her lips.

It might have been enough if Izzy hadn't chosen that moment to say huffily, 'A proper gentleman wouldn't refer to a lady's age.' Giving John the chance to growl, 'If'n I *wasn't* a proper gentleman, Izzy Baker, I'd have tumbled you long since and got you in the family way and we'd have been married by now, you daft bat!'

It was too much. Camilla made a desperate choking sound and her whole body started to shake. Realisation that suppressed laughter was about to escape in an infectious and seductive ripple effectively quenched most of Adam's own amusement. For her sake more than his, being caught in a compromising position on the floor of a church clearly couldn't be allowed to happen. There was only one thing that might avert certain calamity and, without further hesitation, he did it.

The shock of his mouth descending on hers was great enough to banish both the desire to laugh and the recollection of having wanted to. Her sudden stillness woke an annoying little voice at the back of Adam's mind telling him that it wasn't necessary to take this further. But her mouth was soft and sweet under his; she wasn't trying to push him off; and being plastered against that splendid bosom was sweet torture. Moreover, he'd wanted to do this for a while now and might never have another opportunity ...

so he didn't even consider stopping. He just waited until her eyes fluttered closed and he felt the suspicion of a sigh and then he let the kiss gradually deepen.

Camilla didn't hear Izzy stamping out in disgust and wouldn't have cared if she had. She had been kissed a few times but not like this. Not with temptation and persuasion and heat ... and a hand lightly cupping her cheek as if she was some rare and wonderful creature. He kissed her with his whole attention and without haste ... as if he had infinite time in which to do so. It was beautiful beyond her wildest imaginings and took away thought, leaving only sensation in its wake. She opened her mouth and kissed him back.

Pleasure rumbled in Adam's throat. He'd wanted to kiss her and had expected to enjoy it ... but not as much as this. She was all enticement and welcome and something else he couldn't put a name to but which he dimly suspected was just *her*. He retained enough sense to keep his hands under control but only because, if he didn't, he might forget to stop. But he couldn't prevent himself trailing kisses along her jaw and down her throat before capturing her mouth again ... even though he realised that, by now, she must know what his body was telling her.

In the end, it was the sound of the porch door banging in a gust of wind that brought them both to their senses. Slowly, reluctantly, Adam lifted his head as if listening and said what he'd known five minutes ago. 'They've gone.'

'They have?' Camilla blinked up at him. 'Oh. I suppose we can get up then.'

'Yes.' He didn't move. 'I suppose we can.'

A faint blush stained her cheeks and the merest hint of a smile dawned. 'Now?'

'What? Oh. Yes. Of course. Forgive me. My mind wandered for a moment.'

Feeling every bit as foolishly gauche as he no doubt sounded, Adam peeled himself off her with some semblance of his usual grace and, reaching out to help her up, said, 'I'm sorry. Throwing myself on top of you probably wasn't the best idea – just the best I could come up with at short notice.'

The blush intensified and she concentrated on shaking out the crushed skirts of her habit. 'You needn't apologise.'

'Need I not?' he asked bluntly. 'For anything?'

'No.' Some of the lovely glow of the last few minutes seeped away and reality slid insidiously back, bringing logic and disappointment with it. Presumably, all men kissed differently and inevitably some did it better than others ... *ergo* she shouldn't read too much into the fact that Adam Brandon possessed skill beyond the ordinary because it wasn't necessarily anything to do with her personally. Clearing her throat, she said clinically, 'I was about to betray our presence which, at best, would have resulted in us looking very foolish. You had to stop that happening and you didn't have many options – hence the kiss. It's quite all right. I'm not about to slap your face.'

He eyed her thoughtfully, aware of the change. 'That's a relief.'

'Yes. I'm sure it must be.' She awarded him a brief, tight smile. 'Please don't give it another thought. I understand perfectly.'

Adam gave swift but serious consideration to what he was tempted to say, aware that the possible consequences could be massive but equally aware of something deep within himself that didn't want to be silenced.

Although he'd sewn all the usual wild oats during the year or so after Cambridge, sex for its own sake had quickly palled and these days, such liaisons were relatively rare. Those he *did* indulge in were ... enjoyable ... but, in essence exactly the same as each other. Physically satisfying but emotionally lacking. The last one had been eight months ago in Paris, since which time he'd neither missed the intimacy nor been remotely tempted. Until now. Until Camilla Edgerton-Foxe had stirred something inside him that was both different and, he suspected, significant. At the back of his mind was the suspicion that the knowledge ought to be alarming, yet somehow wasn't.

'Actually,' he said slowly, 'I'm not sure you do.'

'Oh – for heaven's sake!' Camilla stood up. 'There's nothing further to say.'

'I disagree.' Reaching out, he pulled her back on to the pew beside him. 'Do you know when our unwelcome visitors left?'

'What? No. Not precisely. Does it matter?'

'It has a certain bearing, yes. Izzy stormed out, chased by Mr Trot, about thirty seconds after my mouth met yours and you forgot you'd wanted to laugh.'

She scowled at him. 'What are you saying?'

'I'm admitting, for the sake of clarity, that I need not have kissed you at all – let alone taken the opportunity to make the most of it.'

The scowl slowly vanished but she continued to stare at him as if he'd spoken Chinese. Finally, still searching his eyes, she said, 'If that's a joke, it's a poor one.'

'Then it's fortunate it wasn't. Why do you think it might have been?'

'Isn't it obvious?'

'Not to me. I'm afraid you'll have to explain.'

'Because I – I'm not the sort of female from whom, given the chance, men steal kisses. And please don't contradict me. I know what I'm talking about. I had three marriage proposals from men who only really wanted my dowry. And I was betrothed to one I thought loved me except that it turned out he didn't.'

'All of which says a great deal more about them than about you.'

'Oh – don't be obtuse, Adam. It's not just that I'm no great beauty. Everything about me is sharp and – and *pointy*.'

Adam repressed a tiny quiver of laughter and, letting his gaze stray appreciatively over her, murmured, 'Not quite *everything*.'

She either ignored this or it sailed harmlessly over her head.

'I'm not charming. I don't know how to flirt with my fan or flutter my lashes – and I don't want to learn.'

'Thank God.'

'Worse still, I don't behave the way young ladies are supposed to. I'm no good at pretending I don't have any opinions and I can't help saying what I think.'

'I know.'

'Often it comes out more – more forcefully than I mean it to.'

'I've noticed.'

'And if I don't agree with something, I argue.'

'So you do.' He wondered how long it would take her to listen to the tone of his voice as well as the words and recognise what he was really saying. 'Anything else?'

'Gentlemen don't care to be told they're wrong, even when they are.'

'In most cases, *especially* when they are.'

She nodded eagerly. 'Exactly! So they prefer ladies with perfect manners and a head full of feathers to someone like me. *Now* do you see?'

'Not entirely. What has all this to do with whether or not I wanted to kiss you?'

She threw up her hands. 'Haven't you been *listening*?'

'Yes. And here's what I heard. You're not a blue-eyed blonde with a rosebud mouth. So what? If every man wanted one of those the world would be in a sorry state – so it's fortunate some of us don't. You have beauty of your own; and just because it's different, doesn't make it *less*.'

'*Now* who's being kind?'

'You think? Then try this. Your smile melts my brain and you have the most erotic laugh I've ever heard. As for your body, you may have noticed that it was recently giving mine unsuitable ideas.' Her jaw dropped and he went on before she could recover herself. 'You have opinions and are prepared to stand by them. Good for you. You have an excellent – even remarkable – mind, so why *shouldn't* you use it? And there's nothing wrong with strong, capable women, Camilla. My mother is one. So, fortunately, is my sister – since strength and practicality are prime requirements for marriage to Julian Langham.' He paused to grin at her. 'Is any of this getting through to you?'

'I – yes.' She looked as dazed as if she'd been poleaxed. 'Only I don't think --'

'Then don't. Consider those men you mentioned earlier and tell me whether I'm remotely similar to *any* of them.'

She shook her head and continued to stare at him as if he were either an alien species or a potentially lethal explosive device. 'You aren't. Not at all.'

'Hallelujah.' He pulled her to her feet. 'You might like to give what I've said further thought – but not now. We've been here long enough. And there's still one other thing which we can talk about while we walk back to the horses. Peter Blane.'

It took a second for the change of subject to register. Then she said, 'Oh. Him. Yes. He told me he'd met you.'

'Did he? But of course he did. When?'

'That same day. How did it come about?'

'I was wearing my sword and he guessed who I must be. Guy, I suppose?'

'Without doubt. And then?'

'He threw a few insults designed to provoke me and ended by informing me and his three companions that he intended to marry you.'

'*What*?' Camilla gaped at him. 'The little *toad*. What did you say?'

'I asked him if you knew. He couldn't hide the fact that you didn't – which explains his visit to you. He had to try covering his back. What did he say?'

'He spouted some drivel about being struck by my manifold charms and an urgent desire to court me. Loosely translated, that means he likes the idea of being related to the Earl of Alveston.' They had arrived where the horses were tethered and she sighed wistfully. 'I don't suppose you hit him, did you?'

'No.' Adam lifted her into the saddle and mounted Hector.

'Pity. He really is unspeakably dreadful. Who were the other men with him?'

'Two of them were equally stupid and more than a little foxed. The only sensible, sober one of the quartet, I took to be his brother. Who are they?'

'A banking family. No shortage of money and perfectly respectable but lacking the kind of connections they'd like and would find useful.' She stopped, realising that he was riding beside her. 'What are you doing? Your road lies in the other direction.'

'I'm escorting you to the end of your drive. And yes, we've established the fact that you argue. But now isn't the time and you won't win.' He sent her a beguilingly lazy smile. 'I have opinions too, you see ... and, as my brothers would doubtless inform you, an uncommon degree of obstinacy.'

* * *

As he had been since the early hours of the morning, Guy Edgerton-Foxe was tied to a chair in a damp hovel reeking of fish. He was glad of the respite. They had asked him the same questions over and over and he'd given the same answers since they were the only ones he had. No, his sister knew nothing of his night-time activities. He hadn't told her and she hadn't guessed. No, he hadn't known that Adam Brandon was under orders from Lord Alveston or in league with Viscount Wingham. No and no and no.

The answers hadn't gone down well. Guy's jaw throbbed and was still swelling and, judging from the screaming agony in his midriff, he thought he might have a cracked rib. He told himself he was lucky it hadn't been any worse ... but it didn't help much because he knew it still could. He also tried telling himself that they wouldn't touch Millie ... but he didn't dare trust that either.

When he first regained consciousness he'd thought they intended to put him on the ship and send him to France. That they hadn't was a relief – until he realised where they *were* going. He knew more or less exactly where he was; the bleak, godforsaken wasteland of Denge Marsh, populated only by sheep and the odd, solitary fisherman. No one came to this inhospitable place if they didn't have to. Guy knew he had about as much hope of rescue here as if he'd been chained to a rock in the middle of the sea.

He was hungry, hurting, alone and aware that his erstwhile friends weren't finished with him yet. He didn't know if he would get out of this alive or how much danger Millie was in. What he *did* know, irrefutably, was that he had no one but himself to blame.

CHAPTER TWENTY-ONE

After bidding Adam farewell at the end of Dragon Hall's drive, Camilla rode on through the gathering dusk, with the things he'd said ringing in her head and her mind in a hopeless tangle. Had he meant any of it? *Could* he have done? And what did he expect her to make of it? She didn't know. But even without the answers, she couldn't help smiling.

Inside the house, she pulled off her gloves and had just set one foot on the stairs when the butler appeared behind her, saying, 'Miss Millie – a word, if I may?'

She turned. 'Of course. What is it, Coombes?'

'Mrs Poole and I are concerned about Mr Guy. He didn't come home last night.'

'Oh.' She stepped back to face him. 'Well, that hasn't been unusual recently, has it?'

'No, Miss. But he generally returns at some point. On this occasion, his bed has not been slept in and he hasn't returned to the house at all since he left yesterday evening.'

'Not even for a change of clothes?'

'No.'

Camilla frowned. 'That *is* odd, certainly. He said he was meeting the usual group of friends and would probably be home very late – but he ought to have been back by now. You'd better send the young groom to Dymchurch to ask --'

'Begging your pardon, Miss Millie, but that's another thing. Dawson informs me that Brewster did not present himself for work today and sent no explanation.'

The last thing of interest to Camilla just now was the groom having taken a day off. Trying not to sound impatient, she said, 'Then send Thomas. Tell him to ask at the *City of London*. That is Guy's usual haunt. And though he's unlikely to still be there, someone must at least know when he left – or even where he might have been going. And Coombes …?'

'Yes, Miss?'

'Don't be too worried just yet. Guy acts on impulse. It's possible he went to stay with someone or other who could lend him a clean shirt and will wander home later tonight. But in the meantime, we should try to discover his current whereabouts if we can.'

Coombes bowed. 'I will see to it.'

'Thank you. And please have dinner set back half an hour, would you? It's been a long afternoon and I'd like to sit down with a cup of tea before changing my dress.'

In truth, it wasn't tea she wanted. It was the chance to sit quietly and contemplate the strange and wonderful things Adam had said to her and to decide whether she dared believe them. Her most immediate reaction was less that she *couldn't* than that she *shouldn't.*

Your smile melts my brain and you have the most erotic laugh I've ever heard.

Erotic wasn't a word she'd ever heard anyone say out loud and to have it applied to herself was impossible to take in. And yet ... Adam Brandon used words sparingly and with precision. She also hadn't previously known him to lie. Then there was the tone in which he'd spoken. She'd heard plenty of empty compliments over the years and they were always delivered with the same jarring note of overdone sincerity. Adam had sounded so completely matter-of-fact he might have been discussing the weather.

That last thought caused her to smile, shake her head and wonder if that was the way he usually went about sweeping a girl off her feet. Except ... there was also that thing he really, *really* shouldn't have said.

As for your body, you may have noticed that it was recently giving mine inappropriate ideas.

The words had the same effect now as they had when he'd said them, producing a wave of heat that she suspected wasn't purely embarrassment. The truth, of course, was she *had* noticed. Even through several layers of clothing, glued together as they were, she had been aware of the change in his body. But that wasn't the problem. The implication of what Adam had said was that she'd not only *noticed* that change but also understood what it signified. And he knew as well as she that she ought *not* to understand it. It was one of many things of which ladies were supposed to remain ignorant until their wedding night. Even at the age of eighteen, Camilla had found that particular taboo utter nonsense and during her first husband-hunting Season had secretly purchased a medical tract in order to acquire a basic understanding of male anatomy and how it worked. But *he* couldn't have known that … so she shuddered to contemplate what he might be thinking.

Pushing all of this aside as best she could, she let Martha help her into a simple gown of pink tiffany and sat down to pick absently at her dinner. She was in the library, starting to write out the code in her head when Coombes came to inform her that Thomas was back from Dymchurch.

Camilla laid down her quill and turned, trying to clear her mind of the intense concentration required by the task in hand. 'Good. Send him in, please.'

With Coombes at his heels, Thomas entered the room looking windswept and unhappy.

'I'm sorry, Miss Millie. I haven't found out anything really. I went to the *London*, like you said, but nobody'd talk to me. There was a funny mood all round. When I walked in, everybody went quiet then turned their backs on me and carried on talking. All I could get out of the innkeeper was that Mr Guy *might* have been there for a bit early evening but he didn't know when he'd left or where he'd gone – and *that* was like pulling teeth.'

This, Camilla thought, was no surprise. Given what Adam had told her, of *course* no one would talk. Nearly everyone in the tavern had probably been on the beach last night. They must all be convinced that there was an informer in their midst and speculating on who it might be. The local Riding Officer was doubtless quaking in his boots.

She said, 'I'm sure you did your best, Thomas – and thank you for trying. There's nothing more we can do before morning except hope Guy returns overnight. If he doesn't, I'll send word to his friends tomorrow.' *And if* that *fails,* she thought, a knot of anxiety expanding in her chest, *the next step will be the magistrate. And Adam, thank God.* Summoning what she hoped was a reassuring smile, she said, 'He'll turn up full of excuses, just you wait and see. Meanwhile, don't stay up all night worrying.'

Coombes nodded but didn't look convinced. Thomas said abruptly, 'A good few of 'em in the *London* had bandages and bruises – and there were some empty stools.' He hauled in a deep breath. 'Miss Millie ... I think there might have been a run last night.'

She *really* wished he hadn't said that.

'It's possible, I suppose,' she shrugged. 'And if there was, it could account for Guy's apparent change of plans. But let's not get carried away until we know more. Thank you both. That will be all.'

When they had gone she sat for several minutes staring into space. Surely Guy had more sense than to get involved with the owlers? Knowing how dangerous they were, even *he* couldn't be that stupid. Could he? Of course he couldn't. And how on earth would he get away with that kind of activity with no one in the house any the wiser? No. She was being ridiculous and letting her imagination run away with her. If he'd got wind of a run – which in itself was unlikely – he'd have stayed well away out of the way of it. Her first thought had probably been the right one. He'd spent last night with friends – hopefully the Derrings rather than the Blanes – and would be home, if not by morning, then at some point tomorrow. She tried not to wonder why, if that was the case, he hadn't sent a note. It was most probably Guy's usual lack of consideration. And meanwhile, she had a job to do.

She finished transcribing the despatch just after eleven, still with no sign of her errant brother and had gone to bed, not expecting to sleep. In fact, she fell into an uneasy doze a little before dawn and awoke to her maid's presence and the aroma of chocolate.

Sitting up and yawning, she said, 'Martha ... has Guy --?'

'I'm sorry, Miss Millie. Mr Coombes says there's no news.'

Camilla's heart sank. 'I see. Tell him he will find two letters on my desk – one to Mr George Derring and the other to Mr Mark Blane which should be delivered without delay. Then lay out my blue riding habit and send a message to the stables asking for my mare to be saddled. I have to go out.'

While Martha went to pass on her orders, she sipped her chocolate without tasting it and fretted. Then Martha reappeared and held out a sealed letter, saying, 'This just came for you, Miss. Mr Coombes said a boy from New Romney brought it.'

Camilla took the folded paper and broke the seal, praying it wasn't from Adam, cancelling their appointment. Not today ... not when she really needed him.

It wasn't from Adam. It was much, much worse than that. Her knees turned to jelly and she dropped awkwardly on the dressing stool.

We have your brother, it read. *You can waste time looking for him if you wish but you will not find him. At present, he is in good health. Whether or not this continues depends on two things. Firstly, the speed and honesty with which he admits the precise extent of his indiscretion which, on the night before last, resulted in financial loss, imprisonment and some deaths. I am sure you know to what I refer. And secondly, on your ability to remain silent regarding anything he may have told you whilst also distancing yourself from the authorities and those persons taking too great an interest in matters which do not concern them. Once again, I believe you will understand me. Your brother has been exceedingly foolish, Miss Edgerton-Foxe and may yet pay the price for it. Take care that you do not follow in his footsteps ... and, if you are wise, show this message to no one.*

By the time she'd read to the end of it, Camilla's heart was racing and she felt sick. But her mind was crystal clear on one thing. Until she could see her way through this mess more clearly, she had to hide the true situation from the household. So she said, 'It appears that Guy may not be back for a few days yet. I am not entirely sure of the details ... but he seems to have got himself into some kind of romantic entanglement.'

'Oh Miss!' gasped Martha. 'Never say some harpy's got her claws into him?'

'I'm not sure yet.' Camilla was relieved to hear her voice emerge sounding cool and faintly exasperated. 'Still, I daresay it can all be sorted out – though doubtless it will be I who has to do it. But it will have to wait until later. I have an appointment elsewhere this morning and no idea how long it may take.'

Half an hour later, downstairs and itching to be off, she remembered the notes she had ordered delivered. Fortunately, Thomas had barely returned from his morning trip to the cottage so she was able to tell Coombes not to send them after all and then repeat the same fabrication she'd given to Martha. Coombes, inevitably, was shocked, causing her to waste more precious minutes smoothing his feathers. But finally, the painstakingly transcribed despatch safely in her pocket along with the threatening note, she was able to make her escape.

She found Adam waiting beside Hector in the shelter of the trees. She reined in beside him and said, 'Thank God! I was afraid you mightn't come – and I need help.'

'Slow down.' He reached up and lifted her from the saddle and, his hands still resting on her waist, said, 'Breathe. Then tell me what's wrong.'

Camilla merely shook her head and shoved the note at him. 'Read that.'

Swiftly and with a gathering frown, he did so. Then he said, 'When did you get this?'

'About an hour ago. We were starting to worry why Guy hadn't come home – but I never dreamed it could be anything like this.'

Adam looked at her. She was white-faced and shaking. His immediate impulse was to put his arms around her and simply hold her close for a moment or two ... but he suspected that, being who she was, she'd repudiate that. She had come to him for help, not comfort. So he said evenly, 'You had no idea he was involved with the smugglers?'

'If I'd known, do you think he would have been?'

'No.' A stray recollection came back to him. 'Has Mr Medley of North Farthing asked you to house his ponies while his barn roof is repaired?'

She stared at him somewhat wildly. 'I have no idea what you're talking about.'

'That's what I thought. It means that your young groom has been helping Guy help the smugglers. I believe I'll have a word with him.'

'You can't. He hasn't been seen since --' She stopped as the truth hit her.

'Since the run,' finished Adam aridly. 'All right. Forget him for the moment. Have you shown this letter to anyone else? Mr Coombes, for example?'

She shook her head. 'I made up a lie about Guy being mixed up with a woman. But that won't hold water for more than a few days if we can't get him back – and he could be *anywhere* by now.'

'I know. And I won't pretend he's in less trouble than you think.' Adam thought fast, mentally listing the possibilities. 'But we're not powerless. There are things we can do.'

'Such as what?'

'To begin with, start a search. And --'

'A search? *How*?' she demanded impatiently. 'With only you, me and Rainham?'

'No. With the half-dozen dragoons I believe Major Levinson will give me if I ask. No – don't interrupt. Just listen to me. One; we start a search. Two; you go to the local magistrate and also the Lord of the Level and report your brother's abduction. Guy isn't *nobody*. He's head of one of the district's leading families and the Earl of Alveston is his uncle. The authorities will take this very seriously, trust me.'

'If I do that,' she said slowly, 'I'll have to tell my people the truth.'

'Yes – but you can trust them so it's a small price to pay.' He stopped as a further thought occurred to him. 'The note you received this morning won't do for the authorities. If Guy isn't to be rescued from the smugglers only to be arrested afterwards as one of them, we'll need something different.'

Camilla rubbed a hand over her face. 'How many other lies will I have to tell?'

'A few, I imagine. But at least you'll have no difficulty remembering them. Now … where was I? Yes. Three; you offer two separate rewards. Fifty pounds for information leading to Guy's recovery and a hundred to the person who finds and rescues him.' He smiled grimly. 'There must be men who would sell their grannie for that.'

'I daresay. But their grannie is one thing – their own neck, another,' objected Camilla. 'A hundred pounds is no good to you if you're dead.'

'Don't be so defeatist,' he said severely. 'It isn't helping.'

'I'm *not* being defeatist,' she snapped. 'Shutting your eyes to reality isn't helpful either.'

Glad to see that some of the colour had returned to her face, Adam took her hands and gently squeezed them. 'That's better. Are you ready for Number Four? It's the pick of the bunch, I promise you.'

Her fingers clung briefly to his and then withdrew. 'Tell me.'

'We bargain for Guy's release directly with the smugglers through Mr Erasmus at Brookland,' he said simply. 'By now, they've had time to realise Corbeau hasn't shown up and they'll be worrying about what may have happened to his despatch. My guess is that they want it quite badly – and the beauty of it is that they don't know that we intended to give it to them for nothing. Actually, asking for something in return will probably look less suspicious. Rainham can handle that part. He can wear one of his disguises and tell them he's doing it for the reward money you've offered. Yes. That will work.'

Shaking her head a little, Camilla pulled out her copy of Corbeau's despatch and stared down at it, thinking furiously. She said, 'You were going to make the original one illegible.'

'And I still will. Without knowing what's in it, there's no choice --'

'But that won't work if you're going to offer it in exchange for Guy! Don't you see? Someone is going to insist on *seeing* it. And that someone has to believe it's worth having.'

Adam's eyes narrowed and it was a moment before he replied. Then he said, 'Yes. You're right. Do you have an alternative suggestion?'

'Yes. How long do we have before Rainham might be forced to show it to them?'

'At the very earliest? Tomorrow, I should think.'

'Very well, then. What we need is a different version of *this*,' she said, restoring the transcript to her pocket. 'One that *looks* perfectly all right but is so hopelessly jumbled and filled with inaccuracies that no one will ever make sense of it. It doesn't even need to be complete – and it has the added advantage of keeping the original intact for M Section.'

Adam nodded slowly and eyed her with simple admiration.

'That,' he said, 'is quite brilliant.'

'Let's hope so. But it will be easier and safer if I make it from my original transcript rather than out of my head. I'll have both for you by noon tomorrow.'

'Good. And now ... come with me to the cottage so we can sit down with Rainham and work out our next moves. What do you think?'

I think I'm both incredibly glad and incredibly fortunate that you're here, was the first thing that came to mind. But she nodded and said, 'Yes. Let's do that.'

* * *

Once Rainham had got a pithy denunciation of Guy's intelligence off his chest, matters progressed briskly. Adam put Corbeau's despatch to one side until it could be replaced by Camilla's scrambled version; Rainham wrote a threatening ransom note demanding money in return for Mr Edgerton-Foxe's person; and Camilla helped Finch to prepare a belated breakfast.

When they were crowded around the table and the men were demolishing plates of egg and slices of fried ham while Camilla nibbled absently at a piece of toast, Adam voiced the thought that he'd so far been keeping to himself.

'The writer of this morning's letter believes you know something, Camilla. And *persons taking too great an interest in matters which do not concern them* must be a reference to Sebastian and me. What this adds up to is the possibility that Guy was already under suspicion and was snatched from the beach the instant those suspicions were confirmed by the arrival of the dragoons.' He paused, letting the words sink in. 'But my point is this. You didn't know anything and therefore had nothing to pass on. So why do the smugglers suppose otherwise?'

There was a long silence while everyone thought about it. Then Rainham said laconically, 'Another little chat with Mr Tranter might answer that question. Some small nugget he passed on to the smugglers but didn't share with us, perhaps?'

'That sounds likely,' agreed Adam. 'But the immediate tasks are engaging the help of both the military and the authorities and getting the reward posters printed. Logically, I should see Levinson and you should go with Camilla – preferably in full viscount mode. And if we draft the reward notice now, Harry can take it and find a printer.'

'I'll do that.' It was the first time Camilla had spoken since sitting down to eat. 'There is a printer in Dymchurch. And I have to go there to see Sir Cuthbert.'

'Sir Cuthbert?' asked Rainham. He was finding the way Adam and Millie were studiously avoiding each other's eyes extremely entertaining and wondering what, precisely, was going on between them. 'Is he the magistrate?'

'No. He's the Lord of the Level. The magistrate is Squire Derring.'

He nodded. 'You are acquainted with both of them?'

'Of course.'

'And do you think what Adam calls *full viscount mode* is strictly necessary?'

'I'm sure you can intimidate them well enough without it.'

'I'm comforted. Thank you.'

'Don't mention it.' She rose, gathering up empty plates. 'So ... is that our current plan?'

'In most respects. We'll divide the tasks as Adam has suggested. But as of tonight, I think he should take up residence at Dragon Hall.' Rainham pretended not to notice how quickly two pairs of eyes collided with each other before fixing on him instead. 'You're a possible target, Millie. And excellent though your household staff may be, they are no substitute for the protection of a gentleman. Either one of us would do, of course –

but your people don't know me. What do you think, Adam? Do you agree?'

It was what Adam had been thinking about for the last hour ... what he'd known he wanted but ought not to. He said, 'Would that be all right with you, Camilla?'

She continued clearing the table, her colour slightly high. 'Why not? I'm sure Coombes will be delighted. And my maids certainly will be.'

'Good. Then that's settled,' said Rainham, getting up. 'Let's get cracking, shall we?'

* * *

In Hythe, Major Levinson still had details out searching for and reclaiming any contraband which had slipped through the net on the night of the run. He was also extremely busy with the numerous organisational matters that had to be taken care of before he could transfer both his men and their nineteen prisoners back to Dover. He therefore regarded Adam with weary resignation and said, 'I won't ask you to explain the connection between the abduction of this young man and the business the other night. Clearly there is one. I'll merely point out that it will be like looking for a needle in a haystack.'

'I'm aware of it – which is why we need help.'

Levinson drew a long breath. 'Very well. I'll assign you six troopers and a lieutenant to coordinate their activities and liaise with you. That's the best I can do.'

'Thank you, Major. Tell your officer he can leave word for me with Miss Edgerton-Foxe at Dragon Hall. And you may be sure I'll make Lord Alveston aware of your help.'

'Yes. Since my colonel is going to have something to say about me overstepping my authority, I'm counting on that,' came the wry response. 'Now ... let us decide how best to organise this. I assume you have some ideas?'

'One or two. Yes.'

* * *

In Dymchurch, a substantial bribe from Rainham persuaded Mr Maize the printer to put his other work aside in favour of the reward leaflets. He promised a dozen within the hour and a further fifty by the following morning.

At the New Hall, the Lord of the Level listened to Camilla in growing outrage.

'Your brother – a *gentleman* – held for ransom? Disgraceful – utterly disgraceful! I shall order the parish constables to make finding him and arresting those responsible a priority.'

'Thank you, sir,' said Camilla gratefully. 'I am offering a reward for useful information – a reward which your officers will be as entitled to claim as anyone else.'

'I'll see they're made aware of it, ma'am.'

'Please do,' drawled Rainham. 'And also ensure that Miss Edgerton-Foxe is kept abreast of any such information or further developments. Her uncle, the earl, will naturally be monitoring the situation.'

'Lord Alveston may rely on me to do everything within my power,' replied Sir Cuthbert earnestly. 'Everything!'

At Farthing Manor, Squire Derring stared at them, apparently stricken silent by shock.

His wife, on the other hand, crushed Camilla to her bosom, saying tremulously, 'Oh my! Oh you poor, *poor* dear! *What* you must be going through, I cannot imagine! Is no one safe?' And over her shoulder, 'William! You must *do* something!'

'I intend to,' snapped her husband. 'Let the girl go before you suffocate her, Iris. And you, my lord ... tell me how I can help aside from sending my son out with a search party.'

'Spread the word that a reward is being offered for information leading to Mr Edgerton-Foxe's safe return,' replied Rainham. 'You might also let it be known that anyone coming forward may do so in complete confidence, if you take my meaning.'

'I do. And that *could* do the trick ... but I wouldn't care to rely on it.'

'No, sir. Sadly, neither would I.'

* * *

Rainham escorted Camilla to Dragon Hall and then, leaving her to break the bad news to her household, took a circuitous route homewards via several taverns in order to distribute eleven of the twelve reward sheets. He arrived at the cottage only a few minutes before Adam and, having compared notes on progress thus far, the two of them sat down to plan their next move.

Pushing the sheet he'd kept back towards Adam, Rainham said, 'I've left one of these at the *Woolpack* in Brookland. With luck, word will get to Erasmus and bring him out of the woodwork tonight. If so, I'll show him the outside of the despatch but refuse a closer look. Nothing will be agreed at a first meeting since one assumes he'll have to consult his superiors.'

'True.' Adam frowned slightly. 'But since we don't know what you'll be facing, you'd better take Harry to watch your back. Or me. Or both of us.'

'Why not Levinson's dragoons as well?' drawled the viscount. 'No. I'll take Harry because, if Erasmus puts in an appearance, I want to know where he goes afterwards. But I can take care of myself, thank you. And *you* may remove yourself to Dragon Hall where you and Millie can either continue avoiding each other's eyes or find out what it is you want with each other.'

Adam felt himself flushing. 'I don't know what you're talking about.'

'Yes you do.' Rainham stood up and stretched. 'Just behave yourself. That's all I ask. Or I'll put your head through a wall before Goddard has the chance to do something worse.'

CHAPTER TWENTY-TWO

Although shocked and understandably worried about Guy's safety, the Dragon Hall staff took the news that he had been abducted and was being held for ransom more calmly than Camilla had expected. She realised that this would assuredly *not* have been the case had she told them of the smuggling connection which was why she hadn't. Instead, she explained the measures that Mr Brandon and Mr Gilbert had set in hand in the hope of catching the perpetrators and rescuing Guy and ended by saying, 'Of course, if there is no other alternative I shall pay what these people ask. But the gentlemen are averse to giving in to them if it can possibly be avoided.'

Everyone nodded and there was a general murmur of approval.

Steeling herself for what she expected to be the trickiest hurdle, Camilla informed them that, in addition to everything else, it had been decided that Mr Brandon should take up residence in the house until the situation was satisfactorily resolved. Then she held her breath and waited for Mrs Poole and Coombes to object.

Neither of them did.

'And a good thing too, if there's going to be kidnappers and men with guns running about,' said the housekeeper indignantly.

'I think that unlikely, Mrs Poole. It's merely a precaution.'

'A sensible one,' stated the butler. 'Until Mr Guy is back safe and sound, I will be happier knowing Mr Brandon is here during the hours of darkness.'

'As will we all, I'm sure,' agreed Camilla weakly. 'But I don't believe he expects the house to come under attack. It is more a case of this being our headquarters. All information will be directed here – and we'll all have our roles to play.'

More nods of agreement and straightening of spines while, at the back of the room, the maids exchanged excited whispers. Able to guess what *that* was about, Camilla said quickly, 'Mr Brandon will probably arrive later this evening so we should prepare one of the guest bedchambers. Which would be the most suitable, Mrs Poole?'

'The blue room,' came the prompt reply.

This was a surprise. She'd thought Adam would be given a room on the other side of the house – not one just down the corridor from her own. 'Why that one?'

'We turned it out and gave it an airing only a week ago so the girls can have it ready in a trice. Now ... shall I tell Cook to hold back dinner for Mr Brandon? I'm thinking that with all this nastiness going on, you'll be the better for a bit of company, Miss Millie.'

This was even more surprising and Camilla couldn't help blinking. Before she could open her mouth, Coombes said, 'And please ask him how we, the staff, can help.'

An odd thought occurred. *Can they possibly think this a chance for a bit of matchmaking? Because if so, I can only suppose that the news about Guy has unhinged them.* But she said, 'Yes – delay dinner and have the blue bedchamber prepared. I have work to do and don't wish to be disturbed. But let me know when Mr Brandon arrives.'

* * *

Leaving Rainham to his preparations and Harry putting together a scratch meal, Adam packed only the more respectable of his clothing, reasoning that if he needed what Rainham called working clothes he could change at the cottage. Then, wishing both of them good luck, he set off for Dragon Hall.

He spent the ride trying to determine precisely what he expected to come of closer and more prolonged proximity to Camilla – particularly under the current circumstances. He hoped he could keep the worst of her anxiety at bay but wasn't sure she'd let him. He also hoped, after what had happened in the church, she wouldn't imagine she needed to be on her guard in case it was repeated. Most of all, he hoped that the jumble of thoughts and feelings she created inside him might actually begin to make sense.

The head groom took charge of Hector and Coombes welcomed him warmly.

'Good evening, Mr Brandon. Miss Millie told us to expect you. I believe she is currently changing her gown but I will see that she is informed of your arrival. Leave your bags here and they'll be attended to, sir. In the meantime, please go up to the parlour and make yourself comfortable. Thomas will bring wine.'

'Thank you. I apologise for the intrusion and any extra work it may cause but --'

'Do not *think* of it, sir. We are relieved to have a gentleman in the house – and grateful for everything you are doing to rescue Mr Guy. Allow me to take your hat.'

Adam surrendered it with a half-smile. 'I'm usually asked to leave the sword as well.'

'Not here, sir. Under the circumstances, I would prefer *that* remained at your side.'

In the parlour, candles had been lit but the curtains not yet closed against the last of the light. Adam stood at a window overlooking the garden and reminded himself that he was here to help protect the household and collate information as and when it arrived. Anything of a more personal nature had, for the time being, to remain in the background.

He turned as the door opened. Camilla hesitated on the threshold for a moment, as if she was as unsure of her ground as he was. Then she crossed the room in a subtle rustle of dark green taffeta and said baldly, 'How did it go with Major Levinson?'

'Successfully. He's allocating half a dozen troopers and a lieutenant to finding Guy. I've recommended he make them extremely visible by billeting them at *The Ship* in Dymchurch. And – forgive me – I promised that Dragon Hall would bear the cost of that.'

'Perfectly right.' She sat down, waited for him to do likewise ... and paused again when Thomas arrived with the wine. Then, when they were alone, she said abruptly, 'I've begun work on the fake despatch but I've come to the conclusion that my uncle ought to see the real one. And if we don't get Guy back in the next two days, he needs to know about that as well. I can make a further copy or you can send the original.'

'A further copy if you can bear it. Rainham and I agree Wilfred Street should have one.' He watched her pleating and re-pleating a fold in her skirt with fingers that clearly wouldn't stay still. Then he rose, poured a glass of wine and handed it to her. 'Try not to worry. At least *one* of the avenues we've set in train will work. But in case this experience isn't sufficient to keep Guy out of trouble in future, I hope you won't mind if I apply some additional punishment of my own when we have him safe.'

'Not at all – so long as you wait your turn. If he comes through this in one piece, I'll probably murder him. *Smuggling*, for heaven's sake! He must be insane.' She broke off. 'Oh – the staff don't know about that. I thought it best to stick to the ransom story.'

'I agree. There's no point in alarming them more than necessary.'

Camilla took a sip of wine, set the glass aside and noticed something.

'You're not drinking?'

'No. But perhaps a glass with dinner – if I'm invited to join you?'

'Of course. Did you think I'd send you to eat in the kitchen?'

'I hoped you wouldn't. But I recognise that the situation isn't entirely proper and that Mr Coombes and your housekeeper might have ... opinions ... on the matter.'

'They do. Just not the sort you might expect,' muttered Camilla. 'I suspect they may have what you might call *expectations*. But I'd rather not know for certain.'

Adam's brows rose and he considered asking what she meant but the moment was lost when Coombes appeared to summon them to table. Over crab terrine followed by Romney lamb in a port and rosemary sauce, he watched Camilla picking at the food on her plate instead of eating it. To distract her, he talked a bit about Paris until, laying down her knife, she said abruptly, 'Paris was where Goddard recruited you, wasn't it? How did that happen? How did he even *know* about you?'

'I did a favour for the friend of a friend,' he replied a shade ruefully. 'A gentleman whose sins had come back to haunt him and were giving him his just desserts. But Emile-Henri begged me to help so, not without a certain amount of reluctance, I did. And the result was that the man in question was so impressed with my skills that he went singing my praises to a friend of his – namely, your uncle.'

'So it was pure chance?'

'Yes. What about you? When did you start working for the Section?'

'At the end of my first Season. During the course of it, I'd overheard something that seemed potentially damaging to a senior member of the government and I told Uncle Hugh about it. Then, at the end of the Season, I was invited to a house party that Uncle said would be attended by a gentleman who was of interest to him. He asked me to see who that man met and listen to his conversations when I had the chance. I did. Two months later, he and another gentleman were arrested for selling shares in a non-existent canal project. And by then, of course, Uncle Hugh knew all about my trick memory.'

'He didn't know before?'

She shook her head. 'No one did, really. I learned relatively early that it was something best kept to myself.'

Adam frowned. 'Why?'

'Because all it ever seemed to do was get me into trouble,' she replied. 'It began with my governess when I was seven. She gave me a passage to learn by heart. I read it through, told her I knew it and recited it. She chided me for not admitting it was a piece I already knew. I insisted that it wasn't – that I'd just learned it. She rapped my knuckles and called me a wicked girl for lying so naturally I argued and that only made it worse. I didn't understand I was different, you see. I thought *everyone* could do what I could.'

'But what of your parents? Surely *they* knew?'

'Not really. They thought it was just a case of little pitchers having big ears. One time, Guy cut all the illustrations out of my favourite book and I called him a name I knew must be rude because one of my boy cousins used it – and Papa heard me. But that wasn't absolutely the *worst* thing.'

'It wasn't?'

'No.

'No. One Christmas we had house-guests and there was to be an impromptu soirée. Everyone gathered in the drawing-room to discuss it and I said ...' She stopped. 'No. I can't. I didn't understand it when I was nine and I don't understand it now – but I *do* know it has some dreadful underlying meaning that only gentlemen are aware of.'

'Please?' coaxed Adam. 'I won't tell a soul – I promise.'

'You'd better not,' she replied darkly. And then, a speculative gleam entering the green eyes, 'Very well. I'll tell you on condition you explain what it means.'

Thinking, *How bad can it be?* he said, 'It's a deal.'

'Well, then ... I suggested that if Lord Renley couldn't persuade Lady Anderton to play his flute, perhaps he might play it himself.'

Adam's jaw dropped and for a second he just stared at her, transfixed. Then, in a strangled voice, he said, 'Don't stop there. What happened next.'

'Some of the gentlemen sniggered and one of them said, "I didn't know you were a flautist, Renley – or you either, Rosie. How long have you been playing?"'

'Go on,' yelped Adam, his shoulders shaking.

'Lady Anderton turned scarlet and fled with her husband in hot pursuit; and Lord Renley told my father that he ought to "muzzle that bloody child." Then *he* stamped out as well and slammed the door. After that, the gentlemen gathered on the other side of the room amidst gales of laughter while the ladies looked blank and pretended nothing had happened.'

By now, Adam was helpless with laughter ... and Camilla impaling him with a look that could kill did nothing to quell it. Wheeling away from the table, he tried to stifle his paroxysms in a cushion but they didn't dwindle until he was gasping and hiccupping.

Finally able to make herself heard, Camilla said frigidly, 'It's not *that* funny. All I said was that Lord Renley could --'

'Don't!' begged Adam, wiping his streaming eyes and trying to catch his breath. 'Please don't say it again.'

'Then tell me what it means.'

'I c-can't.'

'We had a deal. You *promised.*'

'I know. But that was before ...' He stopped and sat up, his face flushed and still vivid with laughter. Then, hauling in a calming breath he said unsteadily, 'I'd tell you if I could. Truly, I would. But I doubt there's a man alive who could explain that to a lady without dying of embarrassment. *I* certainly can't. And I – I'd very seriously advise against asking Rainham. Sorry.'

* * *

The man who slouched into the *Woolpack* that night bore no resemblance at all to the aristocrat who had called there earlier in the day. The long, flapping coat increased both height and bulk; a battered, old-fashioned hat shadowed an unshaven face; and filthy, straggling hair and grime-encrusted fingernails had the half-dozen customers already enjoying their ale hoping the newcomer didn't sit anywhere near them. He didn't. He glanced about the taproom, swept the reward leaflet from the wall beside the counter and growled an order at the innkeeper before taking possession of a settle in a dim corner.

'Ale. And if Erasmus is about, tell him I've got what he's looking for.'

Finch, already comfortably established near the fire, hid a grin in his ale pot.

Half an hour passed and then an hour. Finally, when Rainham was starting to wonder if he might be wasting his time, the door opened on a well-dressed but otherwise nondescript man somewhere in his middle-thirties, who nodded to the innkeeper then walked directly over to Rainham's corner. Tossing his hat on the table, he said quietly, 'I hear you've got something for me.'

'Might have,' came the gravelly reply. 'Depends who you are.'

'You can call me Erasmus.'

'And you can call me Your Majesty,' retorted Rainham, lazily scratching an armpit, 'but it don't mean I'm the bleeding King, does it?'

The landlord set a small mug of brandy on the table and hurried away. Seeming to make up his mind, Erasmus hooked a stool forward with his foot and sat down, saying abruptly, 'Why isn't Raven here? Where is he?'

Raven? thought Rainham. And then, smothering a laugh, *Corbeau. Of course*.

'Safe – or was yesterday. But he's hurt bad and lying low. Got a sword in the gut t'other night on the beach. Touch and go whether he'll make it, if you ask me. But he paid me to bring you this ...' He edged enough of Corbeau's packet from inside his coat for Erasmus to see it. 'I was going to an' all – until I saw *that* and got a better idea.' He slapped the reward sheet on the table between them. 'You got him, ain't you?'

'I beg your pardon?'

'Cut line, mister. I dunno who you are and I don't care. But the fact you're here for Raven's packet tells me what your business is. You got *him*.' He stabbed the paper with one finger. 'Edgerton-Foxe. What's more, I know why.'

'You think so?'

'Plain as the nose on your face. Nobody in their right mind kidnaps an earl's nephew for ransom and thinks to get away with it – least of all somebody in your line of work.' Rainham tutted and tapped the paper again. 'I seen three of these already. By tomorrow, there'll be dozens of 'em and the Marsh is going to be crawling with troopers and constables and folks trying to get their hands on the reward.' He leaned back in his seat and took a swill of ale. 'You've got him all right but not for the reason *that* says. If I had to guess, I'd say you lifted him 'cos you think he brought the dragoons down on you t'other night.'

'You're fishing,' shrugged Erasmus, 'and I've heard enough. Just hand over Raven's packet and be done with it.'

'Not so fast, my buck. You can have the Frenchie's report when I get what I want.'

'Which is what?'

'Ain't it obvious? I want to claim that hundred pound reward.'

Erasmus gave a sharp, derisive laugh. 'You're deranged.'

'Not me, friend. Think about it. If the boy had ratted, would he have been on the beach when it happened? Course he wouldn't. Unless he's *really* stupid, he'd have been as far away as he could get. And you can stop acting all innocent-like. We both know it ain't going to wash with me.'

There was a long, chilly silence. Then Erasmus said, 'Very well. Stupid or simply indiscreet – it makes no matter which. Quite aside from the debacle of the other night, I have two useful operatives in gaol for murder. Someone has obviously talked and we have reason to believe it was Edgerton-Foxe.'

'What reason?'

'You don't need to know. Suffice it to say that the matter has to be addressed.'

'Granted. But I'd lay money you're barking up the wrong tree. It's no skin off my nose - but if I'm right, you ain't never going to find your informer, are you? Thing is, you jumped to conclusions and it's left you with a quandary. Right now you got a choice between killing the young bugger – which really *would* put the fat in the fire – or letting him go and hoping he don't talk. Trouble is, the longer you keep him, the more chance there is of somebody else sneaking off to the redcoats and pointing the finger.'

'You, for example?'

'No. Not me. I got a better plan. A plan where you get your letters, I get that hundred pounds and young Guy goes home all nice and tidy with the fear of God in him about what'll happen to his sister if he puts a toe out of line.'

'And how, exactly, do you expect to make that work?'

'All you gotta do is tell me where to find him and get your men to look the other way. I can take care of the rest.' Rainham drained his tankard and stood up. 'Tell whoever's in charge that they got until tomorrow night to decide. After that, I'll think about getting my money some other way – at Dover Castle, maybe. Your choice, mister. It's all one to me.'

And tossing a few coins on the table, he touched his hat and walked out.

* * *

At Dragon Hall, Adam and Camilla had returned to the parlour and were debating whether or not to start trying to decipher Corbeau's despatch.

'Vincent taught me where one starts with decoding – the only thing, I might add, that I *was* taught – but you probably know more about it than I do. Perhaps --'

She stopped as a tap at the door heralded Coombes who said hurriedly, 'I beg your pardon, Miss Millie – but there is a dangerous-looking person below stairs insisting he has information for Mr Brandon.' Fixing his gaze on Adam, he added, 'Thomas has the old musket trained on him, sir. It doesn't work, of course – but it'll hold him till you get there.'

'Very good, Mr Coombes.' Adam rose and held out a hand to Camilla. 'Coming?'

'Yes!' She was on her feet in a second.

'Miss Millie, I don't think --' began Coombes unhappily.

'I daresay. So don't.' Taking Adam's arm and sweeping from the room at his side, she said, 'I didn't dare hope for results so soon. Did you?'

'No. But let's wait until we hear what this fellow has to say, shall we?'

In the kitchen, Mrs Poole, Cook and the maids all stood in a huddle on the far side of the room while Thomas grimly pointed an ancient flintlock at their visitor. This individual leaned nonchalantly beside the door, arms folded across his chest and looking faintly bored. But when Adam and Camilla appeared, he growled, '*Fine* sort of welcome this is.'

'What did you expect?' asked Adam. And on a long-suffering sigh, 'I suppose you *had* to turn up here looking as if you'd cut anybody's throat for tuppence?'

'Yes. It was on my way,' said the apparition, in suddenly perfectly rounded aristocratic tones as he swept off his hat. 'And if it's no trouble, I'd like a hot bath.'

The fact that the matted black hair came off along with the hat caused a collective gasp of shock. Unfortunately, it also caused Thomas's finger to jerk on the trigger of the musket which went off, blowing a hole in the wall above the visitor's head. Cook screamed, the under-footman swore and the little scullery maid went into hysterics. Thomas turned perfectly white and threw the still-smoking weapon down as if it was red-hot.

Camilla, however, said incredulously, '*Rainham*?'

He tutted and calmly brushed off plaster dust. 'Gilbert, darling. Try to keep up.'

'I'm s-sorry,' stammered Thomas. 'It wasn't s-supposed to work.'

'And perhaps it *also* wasn't supposed to be loaded,' suggested Rainham dryly, picking up the musket and placing it in a corner. He winced as the scullery maid's hysterics rose to a crescendo. 'Will someone please stop that child's infernal caterwauling so that we can all hear ourselves think?' And with a lifted eyebrow as the housekeeper hustled the girl away, 'What's the matter, Millie? Didn't you recognise me?'

'I doubt your *wife* would recognise you right now,' she retorted. And turning to the assembled servants, 'It's all right, everyone. This is Mr Brandon's colleague – and I can assure you that he doesn't usually look like this.'

'You'd better come upstairs,' said Adam. 'But given your present state, I'm sure everyone would prefer that you did *not* make contact with the furniture.'

'I'm not infested,' complained Rainham mildly, 'but I'll do anything you like in return for that bath I mentioned.'

'Fine,' said Camilla impatiently. And having issued the necessary orders, along with that of finding Mr Gilbert a clean shirt, she swept out leaving the two gentlemen to follow her.

'Where's Harry?' asked Adam.

'I sent him back to the cottage. We didn't both need to come.' Lowering his voice slightly and gesturing to Camilla's back, 'How is she bearing up?'

'Surprisingly well so far. But then she was never going to sit around wailing and wringing her hands, was she?'

'Very true. Do you wish she was?'

'No.' Adam cast him an irritable look. 'I know you've just nearly been shot, but at least *try* not to be an ass, will you?'

Rainham shook his head and laughed.

When they were all gathered around the fire with glasses of wine, he said, 'In a nutshell, Erasmus turned up half-expecting to meet Corbeau – who, predictably, he refers to as Raven. The fellow's respectably-dressed and well-spoken so there's a chance he's Tranter's 'captain'. My guess is that he's also somebody's secretary or valet. He was understandably coy to begin with but eventually admitted that he and his associates have Guy. They think he's an informer, although he wouldn't tell me *why* they think it. I did my best to cast doubt on this belief as well as nurture concerns about the problems that abducting an earl's nephew are likely to cause but I don't know how successful I was. He's eager to get hold of Corbeau's despatch but hasn't the authority to surrender Guy in exchange for it. I've given him until tomorrow night.'

'So we just have to wait?' asked Camilla, her fingers clasped tight in her lap.

'Yes, but we expected that. It's why you have until tomorrow to finish your nonsense version,' replied Adam. And to Rainham, 'Were you able to follow him?'

'Up to a point. He rode to Lydd.'

'And?'

'And he entered one of four large houses on a road running parallel to the churchyard – thus supporting my secretary or valet theory. Unfortunately, since I couldn't risk him seeing me, I don't know precisely *which* house.'

Camilla sat up, frowning. 'I know who lives in all of them. Sir Edmund and Lady Morton; he's in his seventies and bed-ridden. The Misses Wesley; a pair of spinster sisters who knit more socks than the poor have feet; Arnold and Dorothy Marshall; still mourning the death of their only son. And ... the Blanes.'

Adam looked at her. 'Blane? As in the idiot I met the other day?'

'Yes. Grandparents, mother ... and two sons. Mark and Peter.'

Rainham looked at Adam, 'Tell me about the brothers.'

'The one I met uses his mouth more than his brain.'

'And the other?'

'I've no idea. Camilla?'

'I don't know either,' she sighed. 'Mark is more intelligent than Peter. But the Blanes are a respected banking family so it doesn't seem likely that they would be involved – even at several removes – with the owlers.'

'The sick old man, the couple in mourning and the sock-knitting sisters sound even less likely,' Adam pointed out.

'Well, yes. I suppose so. But Mark and Peter are Guy's *friends*, for heaven's sake! Would they really have him kidnapped?'

'Stranger things have happened,' remarked Rainham. 'Smuggling is highly lucrative, remember. But whichever house Erasmus entered, he may merely be employed there in some innocent capacity. It doesn't necessarily follow that one of the family is up to his neck in smuggling and espionage. Equally, it doesn't mean that they are not.' He looked at Adam. 'However, the street would bear watching, don't you think?'

'Yes. But who is going to do it? You can't, I can't, Harry can't do it single-handed ... and posting a dragoon across the street will ring alarm bells.' He thought for a moment. 'Lydd isn't so far from Audley Court. Perhaps Sebastian might supply help?'

Rainham gave a sudden, short laugh. 'I think that highly likely. I almost forgot; Erasmus said two of his men had been arrested for murder – which has to have been Sebastian's doing. One of us had better --'

'*Murder*?' said Camilla sharply. 'Of whom?'

Adam and Rainham exchanged glances and Adam said reluctantly, 'Sebastian's late father's valet. We think he had dealings with the smugglers and knew something.'

'So they had him killed?' She stared at him looking suddenly sick. 'Oh God. If they'd do *that*, what are they doing to Guy? Starving him? Beating him? *What*?'

'There's no point in pretending that they're handling him with kid gloves,' replied Rainham grimly, 'but they won't kill him.'

'You mean,' she said shakily, 'they won't kill him until they've got the despatch.'

'Not just that, Millie. They know who his uncle is and won't want to bring fire and brimstone down on their heads if it can be avoided. And in the meantime, we're moving heaven and earth to get Guy back. You know that.' He turned to Adam, 'I'll see Sebastian tomorrow while you tell Levinson's lieutenant about Erasmus. And someone has to --'

'Wait,' said Adam. 'While you're in Rye, get permission to interrogate the alleged murderers. Fear of the noose might loosen their tongues or you could play one off against the other. And though they may not know anything about Guy, they'll know other things.'

Rainham nodded slowly. 'Now why didn't I think of that?'

'I'm sure you would have eventually. And in the meantime, the reward bills need to be collected from the printer and circulated.'

'I'll do it,' said Camilla. 'I'll take Thomas with me.'

'You won't go at all,' corrected Adam. 'No risks, remember?'

'It's only to Dymchurch and back,' she began, only to stop in response to a tap at the door and the appearance of Coombes who announced that Mr Gilbert's bath was ready.

'Thank God.' Rainham rose with alacrity. 'I can put up with a great many things when needs must – but sluicing myself down with cold water is not one of them. Be good, children. I shall return a new man.'

'We'll look forward to it,' murmured Adam, watching him go. And, as soon as the door closed behind him, 'Distance isn't the issue, Camilla. For the time being you're not going to the end of the drive and back without adequate protection. And Thomas *isn't* adequate.'

'I suppose not.' She drew a shuddering breath and wrapped her arms about herself as if suddenly cold. 'I think … I think the reality of all this is finally catching up with me.'

Adam thought so too. Rising, he crossed to sit beside her and put his arm around her. 'That's hardly surprising. You've done wonderfully so far … but it's been a hell of a day.'

'It has.' She leaned her head against his shoulder. 'I want to ask you to promise that it will all be all right. But you can't, can you?' She gave an unsteady laugh. 'It would be one of those promises you don't make because you might have to break it.'

'Not this one, if I can possibly help it.'

'I know.' Camilla remained where she was, comforted by his warmth and strength and, for the first time she could remember, wanting to curl up inside it. She said awkwardly, 'I – I'm glad you're here. I'm glad of Rainham too, of course. But he'll keep things from me and refuse to let me help. And I *need* to help. If I have nothing to do, I'll go mad.'

'I can understand that. If it were one of my brothers, I'd feel the same. But at present, all you can usefully do is finish the fake despatch and keep up morale in the house. Then, if Rainham doesn't have better luck tomorrow night, you should write to Goddard. In fact, I'm not convinced we should wait that long.'

'Neither am I. Waiting is more sensible ... but I'm not feeling very sensible right now.'

He nodded and said slowly, 'Would engaging your uncle's help make you feel better?'

Camilla lifted her head to look up at him. 'Perhaps. Yes. I think it might.'

Adam had been congratulating himself on sticking to a mere brotherly hug despite everything inside him demanding something quite different. But when those silvery-green eyes met his, all notions of proper behaviour flew out of the window. Sliding both arms about her and pulling her close, he whispered, 'Then do it, sweetheart. Do it.'

And kissed her.

As soon as his mouth touched hers, Camilla knew with bone-deep certainty that this was what she had been wanting ... even waiting for. His kiss was slow and sweet and inviting; and she welcomed it without hesitation, reaching up to cup his nape and hold him to her. But much sooner than she would have liked, he raised his head to look at her and said apologetically, 'I promised myself I wouldn't do that.'

'Did you?' Of its own volition, her free hand rose as if to touch his cheek and then hovered irresolute at his shoulder. 'Why?'

'This ... isn't the right time.'

'It isn't?'

'No. I could be said to be ... taking advantage.'

'Surely that's for me to say. And I'm not.'

'No?'

'No.'

'Oh.' Something changed in his eyes and he shifted to wrap his fingers around the hand at his shoulder. 'That's encouraging.'

'In what way?'

A tiny wry laugh shook him. 'It encourages me to hope that you like me. Just a little bit.'

'Don't be absurd. Of course I like you.'

'Good.' He dropped a last, fleeting kiss on her parted lips and drew her to her feet. 'Take that thought to bed with you and try to sleep. I'll see Rainham on his way.'

CHAPTER TWENTY-THREE

While Adam was conferring with Lieutenant Prentiss, Camilla wrote a letter to her uncle. She kept it brief, was careful not to sound as frightened as she felt and exhorted him not to tell her grandmother. At that point, a new thought caused her to put it aside rather than sending it to catch the morning Mail coach. It occurred to her that, once she finished the fake despatch, they'd no longer need her complete copy – which meant that, if Adam agreed, it could be sent to Uncle Hugh along with her letter.

Yes, she thought. *The sooner Vincent starts deciphering it, the better. I can always write out another one and we'll still have Corbeau's original.*

Throughout all of this, she steadfastly kept her mind off Mr Brandon, along with the memories and feelings which had kept her tossing and turning for nearly two hours after she'd gone to bed last night. She was just settling down to continue turning the despatch into gibberish when the first of the neighbours started to arrive.

She realised then that she ought to have expected them. She'd managed to keep visitors at bay for over a month which, in a country district, was a remarkable achievement. But with the Marsh already buzzing with word of Guy's abduction, nothing was going to stop the trail of people coming to commiserate with her and ferret out details.

First to arrive was George Derring with his mother and all three of his sisters. George squeezed her hands and said simply, 'This is a dreadful business, Millie. But standing here telling you how sorry I am won't do any good. I've left our steward assembling a search party and I'm going back to join it. If and when we discover anything, I'll see you have word immediately.'

Appreciating his good sense and touched by his thoughtfulness, Camilla said, 'Thank you, George. That is very good of you.'

'It's the least I can do. If there's anything else, just ask.' And he was gone.

Unfortunately, Mrs Derring and her daughters did not leave with him. Although the two younger girls were largely silent in between irritating bouts of whispering, seventeen-year-old Clara joined her mother in asking far more questions than was polite. Camilla could feel her nails digging into her palms and her company manners growing very thin.

Next to come were the Reverend and Mrs Hooper from Old Romney, closely followed by Doctor and Mrs Quinn from Dymchurch and finally Mr and Mrs Thorpe from Cheyne Court. The parlour began to feel very crowded and Camilla was losing her ability to smile. She dropped several hints to the Derring ladies, none of which found their mark.

Eventually however, Coombes came to her rescue.

'I beg your pardon, Miss Millie,' he murmured, 'but some of the tenants' wives and daughters are in the kitchen. They don't wish to intrude but they have all brought small gifts for you – pots of preserve and posies of flowers, that sort of thing. I thought you would wish to know and perhaps take a moment to --'

'Yes.' She was out of her seat before he could finish. 'Yes, I would indeed.' And to the assembled guests, 'Forgive me, everyone – but my presence is required below stairs. The tenants are understandably anxious. But thank you all *so* much for calling. I cannot tell you how much I appreciate it.'

And she whisked herself out of the room before anyone could say a word.

'Thank you, Coombes!' she hissed. 'Another minute and I think I might have strangled Clara Derring with her own sash. Do what you can to get rid of them, will you?'

The gathering of women in the kitchen was entirely different from the one in the parlour and Camilla tried not to dwell on the fact that many of their husbands and brothers had probably been on the beach the night Guy had been snatched. Each of them expressed anger or shock at the abduction of poor Mr Edgerton-Foxe and begged Miss Millie to tell them if there was anything – anything at *all* – that they could do to help. Then they curtsied and went away, leaving the table covered with their offerings.

Once she was certain that the upstairs visitors had also departed, she returned to the library and her task. A bare half hour later, Coombes came to tell her that Mrs Blane the elder and Mr Mark Blane had called.

She laid down her quill and looked at him, her mind racing. This was probably no different to the previous visits; sympathy liberally laced with curiosity. On the other hand, there was a small possibility that it might be more than that. She barely knew old Mrs Blane and could probably count on one hand the number of times they had met. Of course, she didn't know Mark well either. But at least they hadn't brought Peter with them. *Or perhaps*, she thought acidly, *he knows better than to show his face here.*

She found Mark standing stiffly by his grandmother's chair, his countenance as dourly impassive as it always was.

Camilla curtsied and said dutifully, 'How kind of you both to call. I need not ask what brings you. I believe the whole Marsh must be aware of our troubles by now.'

'It is an appalling business,' replied Mark. 'Is sufficient being done?'

'Everything that *can* be ... but in circumstances like these, nothing is ever enough.'

'Of course it ain't,' averred Mrs Blane. And lifting an imperious finger, 'Come here, child. I haven't seen you this age and my eyes ain't what they were.' And when Camilla stood directly before her, 'Ah yes. I remember now. Just like your mother. Nothing commonplace or milk-and-water about either one of you. All character and spine.' She nodded. 'But why ain't you married, Miss? Ought to be by now.'

Camilla managed a smile. 'Thank you, ma'am. But I have no plans in that direction at present.'

'Time you did, then. Don't want to end up like Jane and Annie Wesley, do you? Mad as bats, the pair of them. No, child. Find a man you fancy while you're still young enough to catch his eye – and let him know he'll be lucky to have you. That's my advice.'

'Thank you, ma'am. I will give it some thought. Now ... will you take tea?'

'Not today, I thank you. You've too much on your mind for chit-chat and we'll not stay long. I only had Mark bring me to find out how you're bearing up – but I see I needn't have worried.'

'Do you have any indications at all about who may have taken Guy?' asked Mark.

'Nothing definite as yet. But Squire Derring and Sir Cuthbert are making strenuous enquiries and the Dover garrison has sent dragoons to help search. Also, I am offering a reward for information so I am hoping we will learn something soon.'

He nodded, frowning a little. 'Sorry as I am to say it, I cannot be entirely surprised at this unfortunate turn of events.'

'Now, Mark,' chided his grandmother. 'This ain't the time for that kind of talk.'

Camilla smiled briefly at the old lady but said, 'Really, sir? Why not?'

'I have cautioned Guy time and again about associating with the riff-raff that patronise the *City of London*. Although one could never have predicted *this*, there was always a possibility that some of the men he thought were friends were nothing of the sort.'

Camilla surveyed him thoughtfully.

'You think the plot to seize Guy might have originated in the tavern?'

'I fear it cannot be discounted. After all, what other likely possibility is there?'

'I don't know. But Guy has known those men since he was a boy.'

'I daresay. But he is no longer a boy – and neither are they.' Mark hesitated and then added, 'Who knows what nefarious activities they get up to ... or might persuade Guy to participate in?'

She was aware that he was watching her as carefully as she was watching him. She said flatly, 'I collect you're talking about smuggling.'

'Talking through his hat is what he's doing,' cut in his grandmother tartly. 'The very idea, Mark! I reckon Miss Millie is scared enough without you making it worse.'

'That was not my intention,' he said weightily. 'However, the notion cannot but occur. We all know it goes on.'

'We do,' agreed Camilla. 'But Guy would never be so foolish as to get involved in that. And if he *was*, either I or a member of my staff would have some inkling of it – which we don't.' She allowed her eyes to widen as if at a sudden notion. 'Oh! Are you suggesting that Guy has been snatched by smugglers?'

'Not at all!' he said, looking shocked. 'I would never think such a thing, let alone alarm you with such a dreadful idea. And clearly it cannot be the case, can it? I don't imagine that smugglers are in the habit of making ransom demands.'

'No,' she agreed. 'It does sound unlikely. But if that *were* to be the case, I would hope that fifty pounds – or even a hundred – might be sufficient temptation for someone to come forward.' She favoured him with a bright smile. 'As was said to me only yesterday, there are men who would sell their grandmother for that.'

* * *

For some time after the Blanes had left, Camilla found it impossible to concentrate on the French despatch. Had Mark been dissembling or merely disingenuous? In either case, what had his remarks been designed to achieve? And was he – *could* he be – Erasmus's master? Half of her said not; that he was too staid and too conscious of the bank's reputation to risk damaging it with criminal activity. The other half wasn't so sure; it reminded her how little she knew him and that a good many people weren't what they seemed. Stuart hadn't been, had he?

Stop that, she admonished herself, picking up her quill again. *You promised this would be done – so concentrate and get on with it.*

A little while later, Adam found her staring down at the pages in front of her and shaking out the cramp in her hand. His gaze watchful and suspecting that she was as conscious as he about last night, he said lightly, 'Is it finished?'

'Yes. I've altered letters and groupings; I've missed out words, made up and inserted others at random; and in places, I've omitted whole chunks of the thing. With any luck, it's complete nonsense now.'

'And will give someone a monumental headache.'

'Since it's given *me* one, I certainly hope so. But now it's done, I'd like to send the full version to Uncle Hugh along with my letter about Guy. It needn't go by Mail. There's a courier service in Ashford that we could use. What do you think?'

'I think that's an excellent idea and I'll be happier knowing it's in Goddard's hands.' He paused, then added, 'Coombes says you've had visitors.'

'Yes. Various neighbours and tenants. Also Mark Blane with his grandmother.'

'Ah. And?'

'He was at pains to remind me of Guy's folly in associating with *riff-raff* and perhaps joining in their *nefarious activities*.'

Adam's brows rose. 'Interesting. Did he mention smuggling?'

'No. I did.'

'Even more interesting. Why?'

'Sit down and I'll give you the conversation from the beginning – excluding old Mrs Blane's marital advice.'

'Are you sure you ought to omit that? It might be crucial.'

'It's not.' She sat facing him, told him to pay attention and recited what both she and Mark Blane had said. And, at the end, added, 'I'm still trying to decide what to make of it.'

'Did you get the feeling he knew the ransom story was a lie?'

'That's just it. I couldn't tell. Everything he said came out in that disapproving *I know best* way of his – yet he wouldn't have referred openly to smuggling if I hadn't done so. And when I asked point-blank if he thought smugglers were responsible for Guy's disappearance, his reaction was one of shock – though I wasn't sure how genuine it was.' She brooded over it for a moment and then said slowly, 'This morning, I asked a few questions about the Blanes' neighbours. Mrs Derring told me Sir Edmund isn't expected to last out the year and his much younger lady is reputedly having an affair with one of the officers at Dover.

The vicar's wife says the Marshalls' house is still draped in black crepe but Dorothy has been seen driving about in a fancy new carriage. And though not *entirely* as mad as bats – which is how Grandmother Blane described them – the Wesley sisters are definitely *odd* in that they never receive male callers. All of that boils down to what you said last night. The most likely suspects are the Blane family.'

'Mark,' he agreed. 'Or perhaps his grandfather?'

'Yes. I suppose we shouldn't rule him out.'

'We can't rule anyone out until we know for sure which of the four houses Erasmus entered last night. Meanwhile, what do you know about Grandfather Blane?'

'Not a great deal. Although he has handed over nominal control of the two banking offices to his grandsons, I believe he's continued as Chairman of both the Marsh Drainage and the Wall Maintenance Committees.'

'Still very active, then?'

'It would seem so.' She sighed and rubbed the space between her brows. 'How was your morning?'

'Lieutenant Prentiss has divided the area up into sections and has his men out in pairs, searching each in turn. No result so far, unfortunately. And I've taken the precaution of asking him to send two of them to the *Woolpack* tonight – out of uniform, of course – in case Erasmus brings friends along to take the despatch from Rainham by force.'

'Did you *tell* Rainham you were going to do that?'

'No. He'd have argued. But they've had time to plan and prepare since last night and he could be walking into a trap.' From the moment he'd walked in and she had turned to face him, Adam had been acutely aware of her pallor and the shadows under her eyes. He said, 'Did you have Thomas collect the reward handbills?'

She nodded and gestured wordlessly to the neat heaps on the table.

'Then change into your riding-dress and come with me to distribute them. We can leave your garbled forgery at the cottage for Rainham at the same time.'

Her breath caught and light flared briefly in her eyes. Then it was gone and she said, 'I'd like to. But I'd better not. There's Uncle's letter to be finished and sent on its way … and I might be needed here.'

'Not for anything that won't wait an hour or two,' he said firmly. 'You can't stay cooped up in the house for the duration, Camilla. You need air and exercise. So finish your letter, put on your habit and don't argue. In case you haven't noticed, I get enough of that from Rainham.'

* * *

At Audley Court, upon understanding what Rainham wanted, Sebastian immediately ordered his steward to find four men willing to undertake special duties in Lydd for a few days. Then he bore his guest off to the gaol in the castle and demanded access to Sedge and Thompson.

'As yet, we've got nothing out of them but useless denials,' Sebastian had said grimly, 'but I don't think the warden has been applying sufficient pressure.'

'Separate them,' suggested Rainham. 'Let's try divide and conquer.'

Upon learning that the smuggling fraternity, to which his prisoners assuredly belonged, was suspected of abducting the nephew of an earl, the castle warden needed no persuasion to offer their lordships *carte blanche*. Thus, Sebastian spent the next hour alternately threatening and cajoling Sedge, while Rainham employed similar tactics with Thompson. At the end of it, by prior agreement, they called a halt to compare notes.

'Anything?' asked Rainham.

'Not much. A slip of the tongue confirmed that Guy Edgerton-Foxe *might* have been involved with the owlers … but Sedge claims to know nothing about the abduction and is still denying Perkins' murder. You?'

'Mention of Raven rendered Thompson mute for a full minute. I think,' said Rainham, 'it's time you and I changed over and let each of them think the other is blaming him for the murder. Then, once the image of the noose is dangling in front of them, we casually mention that Lord Alveston is on his way, looking for blood. That might shake something out of them.'

Sebastian shrugged. 'It's worth a try. But perhaps we should ask the warden to get the thumbscrews and pincers ready.'

'All in good time. Ah, I nearly forgot – toss the name Blane into the conversation and see what, if anything, comes of it.'

'Blane as in Blane's Bank?'

'Yes. It came up last night and may be nothing – but one never knows.'

The next hour proved more productive.

Rainham broke through first by saying bluntly, 'Your friend has finally admitted being party to the murder of the valet. However – since he doesn't want to hang alongside you – he claims that it was *you* who did the deed. Furthermore --'

'What? *No*. That ain't true and he never said it! *He wouldn't*.'

'Furthermore,' continued Rainham imperturbably, 'Mr Edgerton-Foxe's uncle, Lord Alveston, is currently on his way from London. His lordship is not a patient man. He will want answers; he'll want them quickly; and he'll begin with you. If you want to spare yourself pain, I suggest you start talking now.'

'I don't know nothing about Edgerton-Foxe. If he's been lifted, it ain't no doing of mine. I didn't even *know* about it till Lord Wingham told me – and that's the honest truth.'

'A tiny part of it, perhaps. Clearly, Mr Edgerton-Foxe fell under suspicion. Why?'

'I don't know that neither!'

'No? Here's what I think happened. Lord Wingham and a colleague of his by the name of Brandon had a meeting with the three local Riding Officers. Somehow that information made its way to you and your fellow smugglers. I could even hazard a guess as to *how* it did.' Rainham paused, seeing the increased alarm in Sedge's face. 'I know you were present when it was disclosed because that was when you got the order to kill the valet. But what I don't know – and what you are going to tell me – is what was said to raise suspicion about Lord Alveston's nephew.'

Sedge stared at him, his face perfectly white. He said, 'I don't *know*, I tell you!'

'Do you *want* to swing? Because you will, you know. Don't think we'll make the mistake of letting you be tried in a local court. We know how rarely those get a conviction. Lord Alveston will ensure you go for trial at the Old Bailey ... followed by a short trip to Tyburn.' He paused again, letting the words sink in. 'Your only hope of avoiding the noose lies in telling me everything I want to know. So think hard, Mr Sedge. My patience is waning.'

'I can't,' groaned Sedge. 'If I talk I'm a dead man.'

'And you'll be a dead man if you don't. This has gone far beyond a few kegs of brandy – though you'll be charged with those as well as murder, abduction ... and treason.'

'Wh-what? *No*! I never – I *wouldn't* --'

'Well, someone has. Did I mention we have Raven's latest despatch?'

If Sedge had been frightened before, he was now visibly shaking.

'I don't know what you're talking about. I swear I don't.'

'We'll see. But for now, let's go back to my original question. What made your friends think that Edgerton-Foxe had betrayed them?'

There was a long, long silence while Sedge fought against the inevitable. Finally, desperation in every word, he said, 'It was Tranter who told about the meeting with Lord Wingham and B-Brandon.'

'Go on.'

'He said ... he said he'd seen Mr Guy's sister's mare in the stables that day so he knew she'd been there as well. And he said that Brandon fellow had been visiting her at Dragon Hall.' Sedge squeezed his eyes shut and added miserably, 'It looked as if Guy'd blabbed. But nothing was said about s-snatching him. I never heard a word about that!'

For a long, excoriating minute, Rainham remained silent. Then he nodded and said, 'Very well. Now let's chat about French spies.'

In a room on the other side of the corridor, Thompson was busy throwing all the blame for the murder of Perkins on to Sedge. 'All right. Him and me was told to get rid of the valet. But it was Sedge as done it, not me. I never touched the old man. And if he says different, he's a bloody liar.'

'Perhaps. Perhaps not. Forgive me if I'm not convinced. Who gave the order?'

'The – the Captain.'

'Why? Why murder an old man?'

'He said ... the Captain said P-Perkins knew his name.'

Sebastian nodded. 'Go on.'

'That's it. The valet got the old lord's brandy from him so he knew who he is.'

'And who *is* he?'

'I dunno.

'I think you do. We believe he sometimes calls himself Erasmus.'

Thompson flinched but said nothing.

'Not his real name, perhaps,' mused Sebastian idly. 'And please don't pretend you don't know what that is. Only a complete imbecile obeys an order to kill without knowing who gave it. So ... who is this fellow you call the Captain?'

'I don't *know*, I tell you!'

'Frightened that if you talk your friends will kill you, Mr Thompson? Don't be. I'm going to see that you hang for murder. My colleague in the next room wants to add treasonable dealings with the French to that. And Lord Alveston is on his way to rain bloody hell down on whoever's kidnapped his nephew. Your smuggling confederates are the *last* thing you should be worrying about right now. So let's try again, shall we? What is Captain Erasmus's real name?'

Thompson was beginning to look decidedly green. 'W-Wilson,' he moaned.

'Thank you. That wasn't so difficult, was it?'

'Oh God. Don't let him find out you got that from me.'

Ignoring this, Sebastian uncrossed his legs and said chattily, 'And now tell me what connection, if any, he has with the Blane family.'

For a second, Thompson stared back with a sort of blank horror ... and then he vomited. Sebastian, who had seen it coming, moved away just in time to save his boots.

'Well,' he said. 'Was that an answer ... or wasn't it?'

* * *

As they rode from village to village and tavern to tavern with the reward handbills, Adam was pleased to see the colour returning to Camilla's cheeks and even the occasional smile. He wondered if she had spent any time at all wondering about what had passed between them on the previous night but suspected that her mind was trapped in a circle of worry about her brother. He, of course, had thought about it a great deal on his way to and from New Romney ... but had drawn only one conclusion. Where Camilla Edgerton-Foxe was concerned, he was in serious trouble.

They were *en route* from Brenzett to Old Romney when Camilla pulled Sheba to an abrupt stop, kicked her foot free of the stirrup and slid from the saddle. Then, skirt snatched up in both hands, she broke into a run, shouting, '*Sheep*!'

Adam immediately saw where she was going – and why. Some thirty yards away, a sheep lay writhing on its back, its legs waving helplessly in the air. He knew what that meant. When sheep rolled into that position, they couldn't get up again. They exhausted themselves trying, panicked and, if they were left that way for too long, they died. Launching himself from Hector's back, Adam went racing after Camilla.

They reached the afflicted animal at the same time. Heedless of the muddy grass, she dropped on her knees at its side and without glancing at him said quietly, 'Have you done this before?'

'Yes.' He grasped two of the sheep's legs. 'You push, I'll pull.'

'Keep hold of her when she's up or --'

'Or she might go down again. Yes, I know. Ready? One ... two ... *three*.'

And just like that, the ewe was on her feet again, swaying woozily between Adam's steadying hands. Camilla sat back on her heels, watching and waiting. After a moment or two, the ewe gave an annoyed-sounding bleat and pulled herself free to totter a little way off before seeming to find her balance. Then, weaving slightly, she lurched across the field to the rest of the flock.

And Camilla burst into unexpected and, to Adam, wholly enticing laughter.

'I love seeing them do that, don't you?' she gurgled. 'She looks drunk.'

'As a lord,' he agreed, offering his hands so he could pull her to her feet. 'A good thing you spotted her – though not *quite* so good for your habit.'

She looked down at the damage and shrugged. 'It's only mud. It will come off. And it hardly matters if it doesn't.' She beamed up at him, her fingers still clinging to his. 'We just saved a life, you and I. Doesn't that feel *amazing*?'

'I don't know about amazing. But satisfying, certainly.'

She released his hands to slap both palms into his chest. 'Oh don't be such a – a *man*.'

He couldn't help but smile. 'Forgive me ... but I can't really do much about that.'

It occurred to Camilla in that moment that she was teetering on the brink of feeling something for him that she'd sworn never to risk again. But it was hard to be cautious when he stood quite still, looking back at her out of cobalt eyes holding the merest suggestion of a smile. And so, for the first time that she could remember, words came out of her mouth without having first gone through her brain.

'I would like to kiss you. But I shouldn't, should I?'

The smile that had been hiding in his eyes suddenly illuminated his whole face.

'No. You shouldn't. Not because I don't want you to or because I wouldn't like it – but because there are things that need to be said. And --'

'And now isn't the time,' she sighed.

'No. But that time will come, I promise.' He reached out to touch her cheek. 'And meanwhile, I thank you for telling me.'

CHAPTER TWENTY-FOUR

As before, Rainham sent Harry Finch ahead of him to the *Woolpack* and sauntered into the taproom himself some half hour later. There were three or four faces he remembered from the previous evening ... and two he didn't, apparently engrossed in a game of dice. Rainham ordered ale and occupied the same discreet corner as last night. Then he settled down to wait, mulling over whether or not to use any of the day's fresh information. The ale, as he'd noticed the night before, was particularly good here so by the time Erasmus finally put in an appearance nearly an hour later, he was broaching his second mug.

Erasmus remained at the counter, chatting to the innkeeper for several minutes before crossing to take the stool opposite and set down two small tankards of brandy. Pushing one of them towards Rainham, he said, 'I have passed on your suggestions. But I am instructed to *see* Raven's despatch before any decision can be made.'

'Don't mess me about,' growled Rainham, ignoring the brandy in favour of his ale. 'You seen enough of it already to know what it is. And if you think I'm letting you get your hands on it without I get what I want first, you got another think coming.'

'That is unreasonable. I'm hardly going to bring Edgerton-Foxe *here*, am I?'

'Never expected you would. But you can tell me where he is, can't you?'

'Hardly. I have no reason to trust you. For all I know, that packet you gave me a glimpse of last night is a fake. I need to see it properly to make sure it isn't.'

'Well, I ain't opened it, so you aren't going to neither.' He pulled the despatch from inside his coat and waved it before Erasmus's eyes so he could see the unbroken seal. 'I'm not having anybody thinking I know what's inside and might've passed it on.'

'If you want your hundred pounds, I suggest you think again. Those pages could be someone's letter to their mother. They could even be blank.'

'Oh that's likely, isn't it? Raven got sent off with empty sheets of paper? I don't think so – and neither do you.' Rainham frowned, tapping the packet against his free hand as if considering the matter. 'All right. Suppose I agree to let you take a look. Got your word you'll swear the seal weren't broken till now, have I?'

'If that's what it takes, yes. Hand it over.'

'Oh no. I think I'll keep hold of it, if it's all the same to you. You can see it well enough from there.' Rather more clumsily than he'd intended, Rainham shattered the seal, unfolded Camilla's neat pages and held them up, muttering, 'Bloody hell. Is this supposed to make sense?'

'Not to you.' Leaning forward, Erasmus took a close look. Then, nodding, 'All right. It looks genuine but my principal won't agree to your terms until he's seen it for himself.'

'Which he ain't going to do till *I* see Edgerton-Foxe,' retorted Rainham, refolding the pages and stowing them back inside his coat. 'Did you think I come down with the last shower? I didn't. I want to know *where* the boy is and I want to know he's still *breathing* or it's no deal. Got it?'

'Yes. And it can be arranged.'

'Good. 'Cos in case you ain't noticed it, time's running out. Them reward posters've spread like weeds since yesterday – and the boy's sister has got the redcoats out looking for him. If you dither much longer, *neither* of us is going to get what we want.'

'Understood.' Erasmus reached for his so far untouched brandy and gestured for Rainham to do the same. 'Shall we drink to a speedy and mutually acceptable resolution?'

'Why not?' grunted Rainham, picking up the tankard and tossing its contents down his throat. 'Tomorrow night. And come with the right answer. I'm done with tripping back and forth to no good purpose and want an end to this business.'

'As do I,' replied Erasmus agreeably. 'And doubtless Mr Edgerton-Foxe is equally eager to return home. I fear he has not found his captivity comfortable.'

'So long as he leaves it in one piece, I don't care if you've kept him chained in a kennel.' Rainham pushed to his feet and reeled slightly. Mentally castigating himself for downing the brandy too fast, he took a steadying breath and fumbled for the coins he knew were in his pocket but which seemed to be eluding his fingers. Then, finding them, he tossed them on the table, nodded a careless farewell to Erasmus and headed for the door.

Erasmus sat back, unhurriedly sipping his brandy. The dice-playing men on the far side of the room finished their game. One remained in his seat ... the other said something about needing a leak and sauntered after Rainham.

Outside, the cool night air hit his lordship like a blow, causing him to stagger. Righting himself with a muffled curse, he thought woozily, *Am I drunk? I shouldn't be. Unless –*

And that was as far as he got before a hefty shove knocked him off his feet, completing his disorientation. A body landed on his back, shoving him face down in the dirt and holding him there; a second pair of hands reached inside his coat; Rainham swore and tried to stop them but couldn't get his hands free.

Then someone yelled, '*Sarge!* Out here! To me!'

And another body landed on top of the first, driving the breath from his lungs. Beyond the roaring in his ears, came the sound of running footsteps. He hoped it was Finch.

And then, without warning, he found himself suddenly free. Struggling to his knees, his head swimming unpleasantly, he saw four men – none of whom was Finch – grappling with each other. The pair he thought looked vaguely familiar already appeared to have the upper hand; the other two were seemingly more intent on getting away than continuing the fight. Rainham wasn't sure who was on his side and who wasn't. So he sat back on his heels, swaying slightly, and waited for whatever was happening to resolve itself.

It didn't take long. Three minutes later, the men he hoped were rescuers rather than attackers had the others pinned down and immobile.

'You all right, sir?' asked one of them breathlessly.

'More or less. Who are you?'

'Sergeant Fisher and Trooper Ellins, sir. The lieutenant sent us in case you had trouble.'

'Right.' Rainham's brain wasn't working any better than the rest of him but he looked around, saying, 'And where's bloody Finch?'

'Here, sir.' Emerging from the tavern, Finch was holding Erasmus in an arm-lock and had a knife pointed at his ribs. 'He was trying to slope off through the back door. I thought it'd be better if he didn't.'

Forcing down an insane desire to laugh, Rainham concentrated on hauling himself to his feet and very nearly fell over again. The dreadful hairy hat had fallen off during the struggle and lay on the ground a few feet away. He pushed back his own hair, rubbed a hand over his face and tried to pull himself together.

'Not yourself, are you, sir?' asked the Sergeant sympathetically. 'I reckon you've been given a dose of summat ... but we need your orders, see.'

'Orders?'

'Yes, sir. What d'you want doing with these three?'

He breathed deeply and attempted to think. It wasn't easy. Finally, he said, 'The two you took down ... and my thanks for that, by the way ... they're un-un --'He stopped and tried again. 'They're not important. The other one *is*.'

'So we should let these two go?' asked Trooper Ellins, plainly disappointed. 'Now?'

'Might as well. If you take them to the lock-up they'll be gone by morning.'

He watched as the soldiers reluctantly released their grip and allowed the captives to take to their heels. Erasmus, he noticed, was staring back at him, white-faced and tight-lipped. Somewhat distantly, he supposed that wasn't surprising ... and, not without difficulty, remembered what he'd been about to say.

'I'm not at my best right now and I can't risk losing our friend here, so your escort as far as New Romney would be welcome. And Harry ...?'

'Sir?'

'Knock him out, tie him up and load him on to his horse. He'll be less trouble that way.'

'Wait a minute!' protested Erasmus, opening his mouth for the first time. 'I can't fight all four --' Which was as far as he got before Finch's fist dropped him like a stone.

'That was for the drugged drinks,' Finch told him. And to Rainham, 'Where are we taking him?'

'Dragon Hall. It's presumably got a secure cellar and I want a word with Mr Brandon.'

* * *

Before dinner, Adam and Camilla had studied Corbeau's despatch in detail. After it, Camilla suggested they might begin decoding it themselves whilst waiting for a reply from Goddard. Adam merely sat back nursing a half-full glass of wine and nodding occasionally.

'These groupings of numbers are probably names,' she said firmly. 'Vincent told me that's a frequently used device in codes.'

'Mm. He told me the same thing.'

'It's the same two groups, over and over – so a lot of this concerns the same two people. Both names are eight letters long and have three letters in common.'

'So they do. And you think that will help?'

'Don't you?'

'Not really. However ... how do you suggest we proceed with the rest of it?'

'Vincent says the most often-used letter is E.' She shot a glance at him. 'Don't say it. I'm sure he told you that as well.'

Adam shrugged. 'Probably. But your memory is better than mine.'

'Much better,' she retorted. 'At least you remembered *that*.'

'I remind myself of it constantly. However ... going back to the letter E?'

'Yes. Well, I suppose we could try and work out which letter is used most often in the code. Perhaps if we took a paragraph each and listed all the letters of the alphabet and then put a mark beside each one as it occurs ...' She stopped, looking discouraged. 'It could take forever, couldn't it?'

'It could.' He sat back and stretched out his legs, looking totally relaxed. 'Also – if you'll forgive me mentioning it – you seem to have overlooked a trifling detail that is likely to prove an added complication.'

Camilla frowned. 'And what is that?'

'Think about it for a moment.' He grinned provokingly. 'I'm sure you'll figure it out. In fact, I'm surprised you haven't already.'

The frown became a scowl. 'There's no need to be so smug.'

'I'm not being smug. I am merely being – as you pointed out earlier today – a *man*.'

That nearly won him a laugh but she held it back.

'You're certainly doing your best to be annoying.'

'Oh I can be much more annoying than this,' he assured her. And thought, *Yes, sweetheart. While you're busy being irritated you aren't worrying about Guy and I'm not struggling to keep my hands to myself*. 'Come on, Camilla. What haven't you considered?'

She stared down at the coded sheets with such fierce intensity Adam was surprised they didn't burst into flames. Finally, she threw herself back in the chair and said crossly, 'I don't *know* – which is hardly surprising when I never claimed to be an expert at this.'

'No more have I. And it isn't about that. Think about what else you know.'

'Such as what? Oh – just *tell* me, will you?'

'You'll kick yourself.'

'No. I'll probably kick *you*. What am I missing?'

He grinned at her and shrugged. 'You're forgetting where the despatch came from.'

'It came from a spy known as Raven,' she began. And then stopped, groaning. 'Oh God. It might be in French. It probably *is* in French.'

'Je dirais presque certainement, Mademoiselle.' Adam tilted his head invitingly. 'You do speak French, don't you?'

'Yes. But not half as well as you, I'm sure.'

'No. I wouldn't think so.' He laughed and held up one hand in a fencer's gesture of surrender when she gave him a look that would have curdled milk. 'I'm sorry. Over the last few years I've spent a lot of time in France --' He stopped as the door opened and Rainham strode in with Coombes hovering helplessly behind him. Rising, he said, 'What's happened?'

During the ride from Brookland, Rainham had largely recovered from whatever drug he'd ingested. It helped that he was feeling inordinately pleased and optimistic with the way the evening had turned out. He said, 'Come downstairs, Adam. I've brought someone with me and he's not really fit for Millie's parlour.'

'Neither are you,' observed Camilla trenchantly, 'yet here you are anyway.'

Adam smothered a laugh. 'I think you'd better explain.'

'Very well.' Turning, Rainham shut the door in Coombes' astonished face. 'Thanks to your two troopers, we still hold the fake despatch. Thanks to Finch, we now hold something even better.' He grinned, his teeth flashing white in his filthy face. 'Erasmus ... alias the Captain ... alias Mr Wilson – which is a name I was given at Rye gaol this morning. He's currently in the hall, bound and under guard by Finch and the footmen.'

'That,' said Adam, 'could change everything.'

'Precisely. We've now got two options. We can try to prise information out of him. And we can coerce him into giving us Guy in exchange for his own freedom.'

'And if he refuses or doesn't know where Guy is?' asked Adam.

'We gamble on his employer being a member of the Blane family and offer *them* the exchange,' shrugged Rainham. 'It may not be so much of a gamble. One of the valet's murderers threw up when Blane's name was mentioned.'

Camilla looked at Adam, her face bright with hope. 'What shall we do?'

'Exactly what Rainham has suggested.'

'Thank you,' murmured his lordship sardonically. Then, 'Is there somewhere we can talk to him privately – by which I mean out of earshot of the servants?'

Camilla nodded. 'There's a small room off the hall that was supposed to be a place for visitors to wait but is actually never used. And my people do not listen at doors.'

'Excellent,' said Rainham. 'Adam – let's go.'

'If you think,' replied Adam, offering his arm to Camilla, 'that she is going to stay here with her hands folded in her lap, you are either an idiot or you don't know her at all. What's more, I'm fairly sure she's as capable of putting the fear of God into Erasmus as either of us.'

At the bottom of the stairs, watched by both footmen, Finch had one of Rainham's pistols pointed at the prisoner. Nodding cheerfully at Adam, he said, 'The troopers you sent came in handy, sir.'

'I'm glad to hear it. Camilla ...?'

'Through here,' she said, throwing open the door of a sparsely-furnished room. 'Candles please, Thomas. And Coombes, assure the household that there is no cause for alarm and that everyone can retire as usual.'

Not looking at all convinced, the butler said, 'But shouldn't one of us stay to --?'

'No. Mr Brandon's man will be more than sufficient, thank you.'

Inside the dismal little parlour, Rainham pushed Erasmus into a chair and set another one for Camilla some distance away; Finch lounged by the door, Adam perched on the corner of a table and Rainham occupied the space before the empty hearth. Throughout all this Erasmus said not a word.

When the door had closed, silence lingered for a moment or two. Then Adam said, 'Perhaps we ought to begin with introductions. I am Adam Brandon; the lady, as I'm sure you've guessed, is Miss Edgerton-Foxe; and you've already met my colleague, Mr Gilbert. Which of the three names we have for you would you like us to use?'

Erasmus said nothing but wariness flickered in his eyes.

'You weren't aware that we knew anything about you? No? Then let me enlighten you. Recently, you've been calling yourself Erasmus. But you're also known to some as the Captain and ... what was that other name again, Gil?'

'Wilson,' came the laconic reply.

Wariness became alarm but still Erasmus said nothing.

'That's right. Wilson. And we know this because ...?'

'One of the fellows he sent to murder the late Lord Wingham's valet told us,' said Rainham obligingly. 'Reluctantly, of course ... but he got around to it in the end.'

'Can we please put the civilities to one side and get to the point?' demanded Camilla. And to Erasmus, 'I don't give a fig who you are. I just want to know where my brother is. And unlike these gentlemen, I have very little patience and even fewer scruples.'

'Did you know,' murmured Adam to Rainham, 'that she has a way with kitchen utensils that would make your hair curl?' And to Erasmus, 'Do I have to spell it out? No one who might help you knows where you are and you're going nowhere until we have Guy Edgerton-Foxe. Silence isn't going to help you; only information will do that. Where is he?'

Erasmus swallowed and finally said, 'I don't know.'

'That won't help you either,' said Rainham bluntly. 'But perhaps you're forgetting a few things. As of now, we can get you charged with the abduction of the Earl of Alveston's nephew, complicity in the murder of Lord Wingham's valet ... and, thanks to Raven's despatch, treason. All three carry the death penalty – even without adding smuggling. So let's try again, shall we? *Where is Guy Edgerton-Foxe*?'

Erasmus started at the suddenly harsh tone but said stubbornly, 'I don't know.'

Seeing Camilla's mouth open on some hasty remark, Adam gave an almost imperceptible shake of his head. Her brows soared but she remained silent.

'I heard those three words a good many times from Thompson and Sedge before they finally recognised the futility of them,' Rainham was saying coldly. 'Since I don't intend to repeat myself, I suggest you listen very carefully. We know Guy has been helping the smuggling fraternity. We also know you became suspicious of him when Tranter told you about Mr Brandon's meeting with the Riding Officers at Audley Court and added that the presence of Miss Edgerton-Foxe's mare in the stables suggested she'd been party to it.'

'What?' gasped Camilla. She stared at Erasmus. 'You decided Guy had betrayed you because somebody saw my *horse*? Is that really all it took? No other explanation for my presence occurred to you?'

He shifted uneasily and wisely kept his mouth shut.

'*Idiot*!' she snapped. 'Mr Brandon escorted me to Audley Court so that I might visit my friend, Lady Wingham. As for Guy's smuggling activities, the first I knew of them was when I received your damned letter. You've kidnapped my brother for *nothing* – because if someone *did* betray you it certainly wasn't *him*!'

'Which is what I tried to tell you last night,' said Rainham. 'But you jumped to conclusions, set someone to watch Guy … and at the first sign of dragoons during the last run, you had him snatched. Wherever he is *now* is where you had him taken. Make no mistake, sooner or later you *will* tell us where that is.'

There was a long, eviscerating silence. Finally Adam said idly, 'This is the point where I'd have thought any sensible man would be proposing a bargain. Something along the lines of '*Let me go and I'll give you what you want*,' perhaps?'

'That assumes both logic and intelligence,' remarked Camilla acidly. 'On present showing, he doesn't have either one.' She stood up. 'I've had enough of this. I'm going to fetch the cheese-grater.'

Adam stared at the floor, clearing his throat.

God, he thought. *Is there another woman anywhere as marvellous as this one?*

Erasmus, who presumably had an active imagination, turned a shade or two whiter. He said, 'Supposing I *could* tell you where the boy is … would you let me go?'

'Immediately?' asked Rainham. 'Not a chance. Not until we have proof that he's alive.'

With a tiny, strangled sound which effectively banished any desire Adam might have had to laugh, Camilla subsided into her chair. He stretched out a hand to her and said softly, 'He had to say it. You know that.'

She nodded and her fingers clung to his for a moment. As soon as she let go, Adam stood up and gestured to the swelling bruise blossoming on Erasmus's jaw.

'Your handiwork, Gil?' he asked.

Rainham shook his head. 'Much as I'd like to take the credit, it was Finch. He laid our friend here out cold for nearly an hour. Nice job, I thought.'

'Mm.' Adam summoned a slow, grim smile and loosened his sword in its sheath. '*Is* Edgerton-Foxe alive? You have five seconds to tell the truth ... or trust me, the cheese-grater is going to be vastly preferable to what *I'll* do to you.'

'Yes,' choked Erasmus, less, Rainham suspected, on account of the sword under Adam's hand than the look in his eyes. 'That is, yes – so far as I know he is. Nobody's been told to – to get rid of him.'

'Pray you're right,' advised Adam. 'And now tell us where the hell he is. Do not, if you want to end today with all your parts intact, even *think* of saying you don't know. You have no idea how much I'd enjoy hurting you.'

Erasmus shut his eyes and gave up. 'He – he's on Denge Marsh.'

Camilla was on her feet in an instant. '*Where* on Denge Marsh?'

'I don't know.' And very quickly, 'I *really* don't know. Somewhere near the Pitts to begin with but they'll have moved him by now. And even if they haven't, I probably couldn't be more exact. If you know Denge Marsh, you'll understand why.'

Adam and Rainham both looked at Camilla. Rainham said, 'Does that make sense?'

'Yes.' She squeezed her eyes shut for a moment and then, opening them again, said, 'The bulk of it lies beyond Lydd. And the only landmark is Lamplough's Tower at --'

'What is that?' asked Rainham.

'The lighthouse. It stands on the marsh's furthest extremity. The rest of it is a vast area of nothing. Just clumps of weed growing out of the shingle and the occasional fisherman's hut. It's as bleak and ugly a place as you could find. The fishermen sometimes stay there overnight but nobody actually *lives* there.'

'Perfect for their purposes, then,' said Adam. 'In the morning, I'll see that the dragoons and anyone else who's been heading a search party is told where to concentrate their efforts.' He smiled at Camilla. 'With luck, we might have Guy home in time for dinner.'

'I hope so.' She gestured to Erasmus. 'What shall we do with him?'

'Lock him in the cellar till morning,' said Rainham. 'I have quite a few more questions for him ... beginning with his full name and that of the person he's working for.'

Alarm flickered behind Erasmus's eyes.

'You won't get that from me – not *ever*!'

'We'll see ... tomorrow. You might want to use the night to contemplate the fact that, in order to hook a really *big* fish, the law is sometimes inclined to let the minnows slip through the net. Not always, of course – but sometimes.'

* * *

It was no surprise to find Thomas sitting on a chair in the hall. As soon as Camilla appeared, he rose saying, 'I waited up in case you needed anything, Miss Millie.'

'Thank you. As it happens, I do. We need secure accommodation for the man Mr Gilbert brought here. It doesn't have to be comfortable.'

'The small cellar, maybe? There's not much in there barring a few empty boxes. It's a bit damp but it's got a stout door and a lock – and the only way out is through the kitchen.'

'Perfect. Show Mr Brandon and Mr Gilbert the way, please.' She turned, and finding Adam at her shoulder said, 'Ought someone to keep watch – just in case?'

'Perhaps. But leave Rainham and me to worry about that. Why don't you go to bed? You look exhausted.'

'I am tired,' she admitted, 'but I don't think I could sleep.'

'Then at least sit down with a glass of wine. I'll join you when our guest is safely bestowed.'

'If Rainham wants to stay the night or leave your man here --'

'Thomas and I will see to it. Just *go*.'

For possibly the first time ever, Camilla merely nodded and did as he told her.

Adam didn't know whether to be glad or worried. As he had done earlier, he found himself dwelling on her courage and remarkable strength of character. She had lost her parents in a freak accident and spent the last forty-eight hours knowing that she might lose her brother as well. Most ladies would have given way to fear and confusion by now. They wouldn't have concentrated on forging a French despatch or gone running across a muddy field to rescue a sheep or let him provoke a ridiculous argument. Camilla Edgerton-Foxe's spine had as much steel in it as his sword ... and that made her unique.

When he entered the drawing-room some half hour later, she was curled up on the sofa but still wide awake. She said, 'What's happening?'

'Rainham has left – mostly in order to shed those disgusting clothes. He'll be back early tomorrow. Finch is staying and he, Thomas and I will share the night watch. There's nothing for you to worry about and nothing at all for you to do ... so give your busy brain a rest. Or, if you can't, tell me about Denge Marsh.'

She blinked. 'There's very little I can usefully say. There are one or two hamlets inland of Lydd but on the main expanse towards the sea, aside from the brick kilns, there's nothing. Just a vast area built up over the centuries from the accumulated silt and shingle brought in by periodic flooding. And it's prone to fog.'

'It sounds charming.'

She gave a weak laugh but said, 'It's not. But ... do you really think we might find Guy tomorrow?'

'Tomorrow might be a bit too optimistic but soon, I hope. First thing in the morning, I'll speak with Lieutenant Prentiss while Rainham visits the magistrate and the Lord of the Level. Then both he and I will spend another hour or so questioning Erasmus before going out ourselves. Everyone will be told to report any findings to you here.'

'I'm not superfluous, then?'

'Absolutely not.'

'Rainham thinks I am,' she grumbled. 'He'd keep me out of this whole affair if he could and wouldn't have even let me in the same *room* as Erasmus if you hadn't made him.'

'He can't help it. His instincts and his upbringing are both geared towards shielding ladies from anything remotely unpleasant.'

'And yours aren't?'

'Mine are more flexible. Not all women flourish inside a protective shell. *You* wouldn't.' He hesitated and then, with a hint of mordant humour, added, 'But obviously I'd prefer you didn't court serious risk … if only in the interests of self-preservation.'

'Meaning?'

'Meaning that, if necessary, I'd put my body in front of yours,' he said matter-of-factly. 'But naturally I'd rather not have to.'

CHAPTER TWENTY-FIVE

Weary as she was, Camilla couldn't sleep. Her mind was spinning with anxiety about Guy and reeling from the discoveries of the evening. But amongst it all, one thing rose to the surface and refused to be set aside.

If necessary, I'd put my body in front of yours. In other words, *I would risk my life for you.* Put like that, it sounded dramatically heroic but that wasn't how Adam had said it. He'd made it sound perfectly ordinary and then turned it into a wry joke ... which, paradoxically, told her how sincerely he meant it.

Not that she would have questioned that. Adam Brandon didn't make grandiose gestures. He was honest, down-to-earth and rock-solid dependable. Truthfully, she wasn't sure how she'd have endured the last few days without him there to make the unthinkable just a little less awful and to hold her fears at bay. He was a bastion of quiet strength ... yet he never had and never would use that strength to dominate her. He was, as she had known for some time, entirely unlike any other man she'd ever met. He certainly was nothing like Stuart – over whom she'd broken her heart and wasted a year of her life and who, she now knew with utter certainty, she hadn't ever truly loved. She'd merely been ... what? Dazzled, she supposed. There wasn't any other way to account for it.

I'd put my body in front of yours. That Adam would say that to her filled her with awe and humility. Oh, he'd die for his mother, his sister and his brothers – that went without saying. But that he would include *her* in the circle of those dearest to him made it impossible for her to continue dismissing the thing he'd hinted at over and over since that day in St Mary's church. Without actually putting it into words, he had been telling her that he loved her ... and she had been stubbornly trying not to recognise, let alone *believe* it because she'd believed it once before and found it false; which was also why she'd so far taken equal care not to examine her feelings for him.

A small sound that was half laugh and half sob escaped her. If she was honest with herself, she didn't need to examine her feelings because there was no escaping them and hadn't been for several days. The better she got to know Adam, the more impossible he became to resist. Looking back, she supposed it had been inevitable. He was clever, intriguing and different ... funny, kind and honourable. He encouraged her to be herself and liked her just as she was. He had a devastating smile and a spectacular body ... *and his room was just down the hall from hers.*

She jerked upright, heart pounding. Where on earth had *that* thought come from? Stupid. Stupid, stupid, *stupid*! It wasn't as if she could trip along and knock on his door ... *could* she? No, of course she couldn't. And what would she say if she did? More to the point, what would *he* say?

Camilla lay down again, ordering her brain to behave. Adam insisted that now wasn't the time to explore whatever was growing between them – and he was right. Unfortunately, knowing that didn't stop the insane idea from persisting.

* * *

In fact, Adam hadn't gone to bed. Since he had promised to relieve Harry in a few hours, it didn't seem worthwhile removing his clothes only to put them on again. It was easier by far simply to doze on the sofa in the parlour ... except that he *didn't* doze. He just lay there, thinking.

For the first hour or so, he occupied his mind with devising strategies for tomorrow; the best way of planning the search and mentally listing all the questions Erasmus hadn't so far been asked. Tonight, their priority had been finding Guy ... but that was only a small part of a much bigger picture. They needed to discover who controlled and financed the entire smuggling operation ... and to learn the contents of Corbeau's despatch. The latter wasn't going to happen without the assistance of a skilled cryptographer and unless Camilla had included a request for Vincent Clive in her letter to Goddard, they weren't going to get one and would have to muddle through on their own whilst simultaneously dealing with everything else. It would be nice to think that, sooner rather than later, the whole mess could be handed over to someone with the authority and man-power to deal with it but right now, that wasn't looking very likely.

Inevitably, as soon as her name popped into his head Adam's thoughts became centred on Camilla. *I would like to kiss you*, she had said. That made him smile and warmed something inside his chest. She shouldn't have said it. She knew that as well as he did. But she'd said it anyway ... and unwittingly given him hope that when the time *was* right, she wouldn't retreat behind a brick wall of obstinacy. Even in the privacy of his own head, he was still avoiding calling what he felt for her by its proper name. He knew that was both ridiculous and cowardly. He also knew he'd eventually have to bite the bullet and say it aloud. But for now he was more comfortable leaving the word tucked away inside his heart until he needed it. It felt ... safer.

He forced his mind back to the business at hand. By tomorrow, Erasmus would presumably be missed – which increased Guy's danger and meant he needed to be found very quickly. And hindsight suggested that perhaps Rainham had made a mistake in not keeping hold of the men who had tried to steal the despatch because there was a chance they might report something which would draw attention to Dragon Hall. *Erasmus* might now know that Camilla had been unaware of her brother's doings – but his superiors did not. Adam didn't like that idea one little bit. With so much else to do, he couldn't be on hand to protect her round the clock and he wasn't sure she could be relied upon to stay at home until he and Rainham knew exactly what they were dealing with.

The clock chimed three, reminding him that it was time to take over from Harry. Adam stood up, yawned and stretched. It was proving a very long night.

* * *

Alone and shivering in the dark, Guy Edgerton-Foxe was struggling to keep track of time. They'd moved him yet again tonight and, in most respects, it was a change for the better. He had spent the previous nights and days, bound hand and foot and often gagged as well, in filthy, pitch-black hovels. His new lodgings were dry, a bit more spacious and, come the morning, there would even be some light. All of this was good. Less so was the fact that *this* time he knew exactly where they'd brought him

... and comforting himself with the knowledge that he was being moved around because people were out hunting for him no longer worked quite as well as it had before.

They'd stopped trying to beat the answers they wanted out of him yesterday. He didn't know if that meant they believed he hadn't betrayed them or merely that they no longer expected him to say anything different. He tried not to think too deeply about what they intended to do with him and instead concentrated on praying that help would come quickly. Millie wouldn't be sitting on her hands. She'd be moving heaven and earth to rescue him. Sooner or later he'd be found ... wouldn't he?

The perpetual cold and the damp of the previous days had brought on a cough which set his damaged ribs on fire. He was brought food from time to time but he'd stopped wanting it and had to force himself to swallow a few bites. The only things he craved were a warm coat, something hot to drink ... and dawn peering through that tiny window he was sure must be there, high in the wall. The dark had begun to creep inside his brain and he wasn't sure how much more of it he could take before he began screaming.

* * *

On the following morning, with all the search parties duly informed where to centre their efforts, Rainham and Adam decided to postpone further interrogation of Erasmus in favour of joining in the search while they could be reasonably certain that Guy was still on Denge Marsh. There was also, as Rainham pointed out, no harm in letting the fellow stew for a few more hours. Leaving Finch on guard in the kitchen and telling Camilla not to leave the house in case new information came in, they set off through the persistent drizzle to Denge Marsh.

It lay beyond New Romney and, as Camilla had said, was land given back by the sea. Adam realised that he had touched the edge of it once before when he'd ridden to the place where the Dymchurch Wall ended but at the time, faced with an empty expanse of apparently barren shingle, he had seen no point in exploring further.

'Hell,' muttered Rainham a mile or two along the shore through patchy mist and having seen nothing but the occasional boat-winch. 'I see what Millie meant about this place. Without a reliable map or even a compass, how the devil can we cover the ground methodically? It we're not careful, we'll end up going around in circles.'

'We could try using the coastline as a point of reference – at least to begin with,' suggested Adam, for want of anything better. 'And from the little we know, it sounds as if Guy has to be hidden in one of the fishermen's huts – which means there aren't that many places to look. So let's get started, shall we?'

At the end of two damp hours, they had persuaded one fisherman to let them into his hut and used their lock-picking skills to get inside two others but found neither Guy nor any sign that he'd ever been there. At the end of three, they ran into a pair of Lieutenant Prentiss's dragoons who had come up equally empty-handed.

'We've worked our way from Lydd down to the coast either side of it,' said one of them. 'Nothing anywhere.'

'Do you know where your fellow troopers have been looking?' asked Adam.

'The sergeant and Ellins set off towards Greatstone, sir, but we ain't seen them since first thing. And Mason and Clay are doing the stretch between the Gut and the lighthouse. We bumped into them a bit ago.'

'Aside from Mr Brandon and me, there should be two other parties of civilians out searching,' remarked Rainham. 'Have you seen any sign of them?'

'Not so far, sir.'

Rainham muttered something irritable under his breath.

Having a fair idea what it was, Adam ignored him and addressed the troopers.

'Well, just keep at it, gentlemen. Today is our best chance of finding him because, by tomorrow, his captors will almost certainly have moved him elsewhere and we'll have no idea where to start.'

The troopers saluted and went on their way. Watching them go, Rainham said slowly, 'It occurs to me that no one has yet spoken with the lighthouse keeper. Should we --'

'Yes,' Adam interrupted, wheeling Hector about. 'Good idea. Let's go.'

The lighthouse was some way inland, suggesting that the coastline had changed significantly since it had been built. The tower itself showed signs of age and weather damage, causing Rainham to wonder how long it had been since Trinity House had sent someone to inspect it. Adam merely shrugged, tried the door and, finding it locked, hammered it with his fist. It remained firmly shut, so he banged on it again.

'What d'you want?' demanded an annoyed voice from above. 'I'm busy.'

Both Adam and Rainham took a few steps backwards and gazed up at the gantry surrounding the lantern where an unkempt head peered at them and the same testy voice said, 'Well?'

'We'd like a word,' said Adam. 'Perhaps you could come down?'

'No. I got work to do up here. And I'm not coming down them bloody stairs only to climb all the way back up again. Tell me what you want or clear off.'

'Perhaps a couple of crowns would pay for the inconvenience?'

'No. I got bad knees.'

'I'll bet I could change his mind,' murmured Rainham. 'A shot past his ear, perhaps ... or we could set fire to the door. Or I could just stand here and sing. People have been known to run screaming.'

Although he couldn't help grinning, Adam said flatly, 'I daresay. But I'd rather you didn't risk shooting him. And even if damaging Trinity House's property *isn't* a serious offence, you won't set fire to anything in this infernal rain.'

'Spoilsport.'

Seeing little other choice, Adam shouted up the same litany they'd given everywhere else. A young gentleman was being held against his will somewhere in the vicinity. Had the keeper seen or heard anything unusual in the last three days?

'No,' came the bald reply. 'I haven't. And I don't come up here to enjoy the view. I come 'cos I got *work* to do.'

'And the times when you're not working?' asked Rainham.

'I mind my own business and leave everybody else to mind theirs. If'n I'd seen summat fishy, I'd tell you. But I haven't. So I'll thank you to bugger off and let me get on with fixing this bloody shutter.'

Adam and Rainham exchanged glances.

'Please tell me how much use you think that was,' invited Rainham.

'Not much,' admitted Adam regretfully. 'But it's the best we'll get – so we might as well do as we've been told and bugger off.'

* * *

At Dragon Hall, the day crawled by. Camilla spent most of the morning in the yellow parlour from which she would be able to see anyone approaching the house. No one did ... and by noon, she was a seething mass of impatience.

With so many people out looking, she thought, *surely* someone *must have discovered something by now? And if they have, why hasn't Adam sent word? He knows I won't be able to settle to anything until I hear what's happening.*

The afternoon passed even more slowly than the morning had done. Knowing that Adam and Rainham had put off questioning Erasmus until later in the day, she contemplated doing it herself. She was fairly sure she knew what questions to ask and it could do no harm to try. But when she went downstairs and asked Finch to bring Erasmus to the little room they had used the night before, his response was a flat refusal.

'I'm sorry, Miss – but Mr Adam would fillet and bread me. No two ways about it.'

'Not if I told him I'd *ordered* you to do it,' she objected.

'Wouldn't make a bit of difference. And the fellow's better left where he is. He's getting twitchy – which is all to the good. It'll do him no harm to sweat a bit longer.'

Quietly fuming, Camilla went back upstairs and tried to occupy herself with the household accounts. By the time she'd added up the same column of figures three times and got three different answers, she felt like throwing something at the wall.

Fortunately, before she actually did so, Coombes appeared to inform her that a man had arrived, saying he had information for her.

'Thank God!' she said fervently, tossing down her quill. 'Bring him up.'

'Here, Miss Millie?'

'Yes. Here. Why not?' And then, through her teeth, 'Have Thomas come as well if you think I need protection.'

The nervous-looking fellow Thomas showed into the room wasn't anyone she knew so she began by asking his name.

'Seth Reed, missus.'

'And who sent you to me, Mr Reed?'

The question appeared to startle him. He said, 'N-Nobody sent me. I come on my own 'cos I know where your b-brother's hid.'

Camilla's pulse gave a single hard thud. 'Are you sure?'

He nodded. 'I seen him. Only for a minute, like – but I seen him.'

'Where?'

'On Denge beach. Looked like they must've took his coat – and coughing something terrible, he was.'

Fear clenched in her stomach but she made herself ignore it. 'Go on.'

'Well, they locked him in this hut. Tied him up as well like as not 'cos after a bit, they went off. So I waited till it was safe and tried talking to him through the door. He said to get you, Missus. You and a warm coat. Begged me, he did. Promised you'd pay handsome.'

'Which I will, if your information results in my brother's rescue,' said Camilla. 'Now … where is this hut?'

'Where?' Reed echoed, sounding baffled. 'On Denge beach, like I said.'

'Yes. But that is a large area so you'll need to be more precise.' He continued to look blank, so she added impatiently, 'Describe the place to me.'

'I can't, Missus – not exactly. But if you was to come, I could *show* you.'

Just for a second, the idea was so tempting – and she so very badly wanted to believe it – that she almost agreed. Then Adam's voice in her head caused sense to prevail and she said, 'I won't come myself. But I'll give you a couple of men and --'

'No,' he said, shaking his head.

'Why not? If you can show me, you can show them.'

'He said to bring you. *Just* you, Missus – nobody else. Can't trust anybody else. Said it over and over he did. And he promised me two hundred if I did what he wanted.'

Temptation and hope were replaced by the beginnings of suspicion.

Why would Guy say that? she wondered. And then, with certainty, *He wouldn't. Not unless he was off his head with fever, in which case nothing he said matters. In his right mind, he'd know I would send someone trustworthy – perhaps even redcoats. He certainly wouldn't want me wandering about Denge Marsh with a total stranger. Something about this isn't right. What is this fellow Reed up to?*

Deciding to test him, she said coolly, 'Lead two of my men to the place where my brother is being held and *I'll* give you two hundred. Take it or leave it.'

'I – I *can't*, Missus,' he said desperately. 'Like I said, it has to be you. I *promised*.'

And that was when Camilla knew without any shadow of a doubt what was happening and was thoroughly annoyed that, for a handful of seconds, she had almost fallen for it ... and might have done so but for those few, vital words.

If necessary, I'd put my body in front of yours. But naturally I'd rather not have to.

Well, he *wouldn't* have to because she wasn't going to do anything stupid. She was going to do exactly what he would want her to.

'Very well, Mr Reed – but wait a moment. Thomas ... is Coombes in the hall?'

The footman glanced over his shoulder. 'Yes, Miss Millie.'

'Good. Ask him to send Mr Finch to me and then please come back yourself.'

He nodded, left the room and reappeared almost immediately, once more leaving the door open.

Camilla contemplated their visitor in silence for a moment and then said, 'Now, Mr Reed ... there is just one tiny problem that perhaps you can help me with.'

'What's that?' he asked warily.

'I don't believe a word you have said.'

He took a half-step backwards and bumped into the table. 'No! It's all true. I --'

'Not one single word. So let us start again. Who sent you?'

'Nobody! I ain't lying – honest, I'm not! Everything I said --'

'Enough. My brother may be foolish but he's not a complete idiot. And neither am I.'

'I've only done what he told me. But it ain't my fault if you won't listen, is it? I tried.' He turned and headed for the door only to find Thomas, with Finch skidding to a halt behind him, blocking it. 'Out of my way, you pair. I'm leaving.'

'Is he, Miss Millie?' asked Thomas without shifting an inch.

'No. Please come in, Finch.'

'Something I can help you with, Miss?' he asked, sliding past Thomas.

'Yes. Someone has sent Mr Reed here to lure me to a lonely spot on Denge Marsh where I may be abducted and presumably imprisoned along with Guy. Naturally, I would like to know who that someone was ... so Mr Reed is going nowhere until I do. Perhaps you and Thomas would like to make a start on persuading him to talk?'

Finch grinned and cracked his knuckles. 'Happy to, Miss. Tom?'

'It'd be a pleasure, Harry.'

Camilla couldn't help giving a tiny choke of laughter.

'I thank you both. And we'll need somewhere to lock him up – but *not* with the other one. Can you --?'

'Yes. You just leave that to us, Miss,' said Finch. And then, 'You! With us – and don't even *think* of running if you don't want a broken leg.'

* * *

By late afternoon on Denge Marsh, the drizzle had become a downpour. Adam and Rainham had roamed back and forth across the entire area more than once. They had investigated every evil-smelling hut they came across and found nothing but hooks, lines, nets and fish scales. By the time the light started to fail, they were both soaked to the skin and had stopped talking to each other some time ago when each of them began suspecting the same thing.

Erasmus had lied. Guy Edgerton-Foxe wasn't here; he was somewhere else entirely.

Eventually however, Rainham said moodily, 'This is a waste of time. Let's go back. I'm going to thrash the truth out of bloody Erasmus.'

Adam grunted. 'Enjoy yourself, by all means. I just want a hot bath.'

'As do I. But first things first.'

They rode on in silence for a few minutes. Finally Adam said, 'Do you think he was ever here at all?'

'I doubt it. Do you?'

'I'm not sure. But you may be right. Certainly, we've seen no sign to suggest --' He stopped, peering through the incessant rain at the pair of approaching redcoats. 'Sergeant Fisher. Any luck?'

'No, sir. And I reckon we've not left a stone unturned.'

'Not to argue, Sarge,' said Trooper Ellins cautiously, 'but I still think there were summat funny at the lighthouse.'

'That weren't nothing, lad,' said the Sergeant. And then, seeing the young man's downcast expression, 'But if it's bothering you, tell the gentlemen anyway.'

'Yes, do,' said Adam encouragingly. 'Anything may be useful. What did you see?'

'I didn't see nothing, sir. But I *heard* summat. We was talking to the keeper by the door – he wouldn't let us in. Said it was against regulations. Only then I swear I heard somebody yell out and there was a sort of thump and it all went quiet again.'

Rainham frowned. 'You asked the keeper about it?'

Ellins nodded. 'He said it was his grandson larking about and he told us to clear off so he could go and wallop the little bugger. Then he slammed the door on us.'

Adam looked at Rainham. 'It might be nothing. Equally it might not. And it's the only thing left. So … a return visit?'

'Yes,' replied Rainham grimly. 'By all four of us. And *this* time, we'll damned well get inside – one way or another.'

CHAPTER TWENTY-SIX

At Dragon Hall, with darkness falling and no word from Adam or Rainham, Camilla trod purposefully downstairs to see what progress Finch and Thomas were making with Reed. Try as she would, she couldn't think who might have sent him or what they expected to achieve by abducting her as well as Guy. Between that and Erasmus's refusal to name his superiors it felt as though they were making no progress at all. Telling herself it was only the fourth day since Guy had been taken didn't help at all against the image of him cold, coughing and, by now, probably despondent.

But she straightened her spine and took a brief detour through the kitchen before stalking into the small ground floor parlour where Mr Reed, with a few blossoming bruises he hadn't had an hour or so ago, was securely tied to a chair.

'Has he said anything useful yet?' she asked Finch.

'Not especially. He's still trying to make us believe he doesn't know who sent him.'

'But I *don't*,' moaned Reed. 'The likes of me ain't told who gives the orders. All we has to do is *follow* 'em.'

'I see.' Camilla nodded and produced the coarse cheese-grater from the folds of her skirt. 'Have you told him about this? It worked quickly enough last night, didn't it?'

'Aye.' Finch grinned at her. 'It did that, Miss. Good idea.'

'I thought so – though Cook was by no means pleased at me borrowing it again. She said it took the scullery maid half the morning to get it clean.'

Reed stared at the grater with mingled incredulity and dawning horror.

'Wh-what the hell's that?'

Smiling, Camilla held it where he could see it clearly and said pleasantly, 'We use it for grating hard cheese. But, as a colleague of yours recently discovered, it grates other things just as well.'

He turned to Finch, his eyes nearly starting from his head. '*No*! You ain't g-going to – to use that on m-me? You w-wouldn't!'

'No,' agreed Finch. 'I wouldn't. But *she* would.'

'*No*!' He yelped as Camilla advanced a couple of steps. 'Don't l-let her near m-me. Don't! I'll tell you – I will!'

She hesitated for a moment, frowning down at the grater as if she was undecided on whether or not to set it aside or was simply reluctant to do so. Then she said, 'Very well. Start talking and make it the truth. I don't have much patience.'

He nodded and swallowed hard, his gaze never leaving her hands.

'Matt Dunne at the *Woolpack* sent for me.'

Camilla and Finch looked at each other.

'Brookland,' she muttered irritably. 'Again.'

Finch nodded but asked Reed if the *Woolpack* innkeeper usually passed on orders.

'No. It oughter 'ave been the – the Captain but Matt said nobody could find him.'

'No,' said Camilla silkily. 'They wouldn't. He's in our cellar.'

There was a horrified silence. Then he wailed, 'You g-got the *Captain*? No, no. You can't have done. Not him. You're lying.'

'She's not,' growled Finch. 'And you should know better than call a lady a liar. Now get on with it. What did Dunne tell you to do? Kidnap her?'

'No! No, I swear it weren't that. I was to – to lead her to the old chapel at Pigwell for – for a special meeting.'

'With whom?' demanded Camilla sharply.

'I don't *know*!'

'And why in such an out-of-the-way place?'

'I don't know that neither.'

'Take a wild guess,' she invited. 'Or let me do it. After all, any honest person wishing to speak to me has only to come to the front door … so the result of your ludicrous attempt at deception wasn't going to be mere conversation. I was to be abducted. Wasn't I?'

'No.' Reed stopped, looking suddenly confused. 'Or if you was, Matt Dunne didn't know. He said as somebody wanted to meet you and they wanted to do it in-- in--'

'In secret?' offered Finch helpfully.

'Yes. But summat else as well. I can't remember the word.'

'Incognito?' suggested Camilla, her brain busy with the implications of this.

Reed nodded. 'Yes! That were it. Dunno what it means – but that's what he said.'

'It means that the person wishing to meet me doesn't want me to recognise them.' She looked across at Finch and Thomas. 'Which, in turn, means that it is someone I know.'

* * *

The small sliver of light that had cheered Guy's day had faded once more into the interminable dark of night. But worse than this was the knowledge that all hope was gone. Twice today, he'd come within a hairsbreadth of rescue ... and twice it had been snatched away. They wouldn't look here again. And if they did, it wouldn't matter because he would almost certainly be moved again tonight.

The first time, Dan Clements had kept him silent by holding a knife against his throat. That a man he'd believed was his friend could do that made him weep inside. The second time, the man who guarded him was someone he didn't know and he'd been sitting in the corner reading the newspaper with agonising slowness, a finger underneath each word. Guy decided to take the risk. Shouting *Help!* as loudly as he could, he managed to make the chair he was tied to bang on the floor. This earned him a massive blow to the head, followed by a kick that drove all the breath from his body. By the time he was able to function again, the gag was back and his rescuers – if that is what they had been – had left.

They wouldn't be back. No one would – or no one who would help him. Instead, Clements and two fellows he hadn't seen before arrived with lanterns and a piece of cold pie he couldn't force down his throat. When they realised he wasn't going to eat, they shrugged, replaced his gag and settled down to a game of dice. But he was grateful at least for the lanterns.

* * *

For Adam and his companions, finding their way to the lighthouse in the dark was made simple by the fact that the beacon was lit.

'Considerate of them,' remarked Rainham. And then, edging his horse closer to Adam's, 'Have you any thoughts on how we play this?'

'Some. Assuming Guy is there, we don't know how many men may be guarding him. So we try not to raise the alarm until we're inside.'

'Then brute force and a thorough search? Yes.' He fell silent for a moment. 'I hope to God he *is* there. If this goes on much longer, Millie will start falling apart.'

'No,' said Adam, 'she won't. Or not in any way *you'd* be able to see.'

'Ah. I take it that means you would. Is that faith, confidence or ... private knowledge?'

'None of your business.' Adam turned an irritable glance on him. 'Do you think we might concentrate on the task in hand?'

Rainham shrugged. 'Just trying to lighten the mood.'

'Save it until later. Better yet, keep the witticisms for those who appreciate them.'

About four hundred yards from the lighthouse, they drew rein, dismounted and tethered the horses as best they could to a solitary bush.

'Quick but quiet from here and pray nobody is watching from the gantry,' said Adam. 'Once there, Fisher, Ellins and I stay out of sight while Mr Gilbert persuades someone to open the door.'

'I'll do my best,' murmured Rainham, 'but it would help if I knew the keeper's name.'

'It's Stubbs, sir,' offered Trooper Ellins eagerly. 'I asked a lad at the brick kilns. Jacob Stubbs.'

'Excellent. Well done.' And to Adam, 'So ... we get inside. And then?'

'You, I and Ellins take the stairs to search, fighting when necessary. And Sergeant Fisher remains below to subdue Mr Stubbs and bar the door to any new arrivals.'

The Sergeant saluted. 'Yes, *sir*!'

'If we find Guy, we get him and ourselves away as fast as possible,' finished Adam. 'Have I missed anything?'

'Yes. Guy may not be very mobile, in which case I'll carry him out. But we'll need a horse to get him away – so I'll ride from here while the rest of you trot.' Rainham grinned. 'Don't worry. I'll give you a head start.'

'Fine. Spread out, gentlemen, and let's go.'

Jogging across uneven ground, most of it shingle, was neither easy nor as silent as Adam would have liked; but at least there was no sign that their approach had been noticed and, in due course, all of them arrived at the tower.

Rainham banged on the door ... and then a second time, calling out, 'Stubbs? You in there, you lazy sod? I got messages.'

'Messages?' came a voice from within. 'From who? And who the hell d'you think you are, calling me lazy?'

'Money for old rope, your job is,' grumbled Rainham. 'Come on. Open the bleeding door, will you? When I'm done here, I gotta go back to Brookland and like as not somewhere else after that. The Captain's in one of his moods and giving everybody a busy night on account of it.'

'The Captain?' There was a screech of bolts being withdrawn. 'Why didn't you say that in the first place? We bin waiting to hear --'

And that was as far as he got because, the instant the door opened wide enough to allow it, Rainham pole-axed him with one blow to the jaw and caught him before he fell.

By that time, Adam and Fisher were at his elbow with Ellins one step behind. Wrenching off his cravat, Rainham passed it to Fisher hissing, 'Gag him with that and find something to tie him up with. Adam --?'

'Yes.' Ellins at his heels, Adam was already on the stairs.

'That you, Captain?' A voice drifted down from some distance above.

'No. He's busy so he sent me,' called back Rainham, climbing the spiral stairs behind Ellins and deciding to keep talking in the hope of covering any additional noise they might be making. 'Name's Pollard – not as it'll mean anything to you. They brought me in from Warehorn. How far up are you, for God's sake? These stairs are bloody tight.'

'Third floor, last before the top,' laughed the voice. 'Too fat for 'em, are you?'

'I'll give you *fat*, you gobby bugger.' He looked up just as Adam, at the turn with his boot on the first step of the third flight, looked back and nodded. 'Hell of a place, this. But at least you're dry – which is more'n I am. Rain hasn't stopped all --'

'Three,' announced Adam calmly.

And then the chaos started.

By the time Rainham erupted into the room, Ellins was grappling with a greasy-haired youth on the floor while Adam took the chatty fellow down with the last of three rapid and well-placed punches. A third man, holding a knife but seeming unsure what to do with it, stood just behind the chair where, bound, gagged and wild-eyed, Guy Edgerton-Foxe sat staring at the intrusion for a few seconds before doubling up, coughing.

'Drop the knife,' growled Rainham, advancing on him. '*Now*!'

'Get Guy,' snapped Adam, drawing his sword. 'Leave that one to me.'

Dan Clements shook his head and, seeming to reach a decision, put the blade against Guy's throat. 'No. Back off. All of you. Back off or I'll kill him.'

'If he starts coughing again, you'll kill him by mistake,' remarked Rainham acerbically as he circled towards them. 'Move the damned knife or kiss your options goodbye.'

Clements hesitated, then withdrew the blade a fraction. 'What options?'

Ignoring him, Rainham said quietly, 'Try to be still, Guy. He won't do it.'

Guy blinked to indicate that he understood but Clements shouted, 'I'll do it if I have to. So stay back. If you come at me, I'll slice him.'

'And then what?' asked Adam. He'd got as close as he dared and was keeping the sword at a deceptively unthreatening angle. 'You've nothing else to bargain with and no chance of getting out of here alive and free – because if by some chance one of us doesn't kill you, you'll hang. Where's the sense in that?'

Out of the corner of his eye, Adam was aware that Ellins had disposed of the youth and was circling Guy and his captor from the left. To the right, Rainham was a mere three feet from them and a couple of steps to their rear. Judging by his flickering gaze, the fellow with the knife was beginning to realise that he couldn't watch all of them at the same time. The trouble was that none of them could do anything while that knife hovered at Guy's throat so Adam continued trying to persuade the fellow holding it to see reason.

'Don't throw your life away over this. If none of us die, there's a chance you won't either. Let us take Guy home. He really *didn't* betray you, you know.'

'No – I *don't* know. If he didn't, who did?'

'Me.' And seeing that Guy's shocked intake of breath was about to set off a fresh paroxysm, added rapidly, 'Move the knife. He's going to cough again.'

The blade drew back another inch allowing Guy to abandon his attempts to control what couldn't be controlled. Clements said blankly, 'You? And who the hell are you?'

'My name is Brandon and I work for Guy's uncle, the Earl of Alveston – as does the gentleman just behind you.' He watched Rainham's hand sliding inside his coat and added, 'He's the one you should be most worried about right now.'

Clements jerked his head round and found himself looking down the gleaming barrel of a duelling pistol. Over it, Rainham smiled coldly and, picking up his cue, said, 'What Mr Brandon means is that he prefers to avoid killing people whereas I have no problem with it.'

'Let Guy go,' said Adam again, his voice as calm as before. 'There's no other choice. Kill him and, one way or another, you're a dead man. Let us have him and you might live.'

For the first time, Clements looked unsure. But he shook his head and muttered, 'Not for long I won't if I do it without permission.'

'Permission from whom?' asked Adam. 'If it's the Captain who worries you, he needn't. He's been our prisoner since last night.'

'*What*?'

'You heard. How do you think we knew to look on Denge Marsh?'

'He – he *told* you?'

'He did. And before long, he'll tell us a great deal more,' responded Adam agreeably. 'Think it over for a moment. And while you do, perhaps you'd consider allowing Guy to pull that filthy gag away from his mouth so he can breathe properly.' He waited, watching the fellow trying to decide and thought, *Do it. If Guy can pull it down around his neck, you'll have to move the knife again and I may have a chance of disabling you before Rainham puts a bullet in your brain*. 'Come on. You must realise that the game is up and your best way out of this mess lies in cooperation.'

There were a further few seconds of hesitation and then Clements said grudgingly, 'All right. Take it off, Guy – but no sudden movements, mind.'

Guy nodded and, reaching up with his bound hands, managed to get his fingernails inside the gag so he could work it clear of his mouth. It was tight so his first attempt merely dislodged it a bit and set him coughing again. Clements swore under his breath and reached for the knot at the back of Guy's head with his free hand.

Risky as it was, Adam knew that this was the best chance he would get.

Gauging the exact second when the fellow was both distracted and imperfectly balanced, he made a lightning-swift lunge ... sending the point of his sword deep into the shoulder of the arm holding the knife. There was a scream of pain; the knife clattered to the floor; and, in the next second, Rainham had Clements' arm twisted high against his spine and was forcing him to his knees.

Adam loosed an uneven breath and sheathed his sword, aware that his hands were no longer quite steady. At the back of his mind throughout the last minutes was the knowledge that, if this turned out badly, he was going to have to explain to Camilla how their attempt at rescue had got her brother killed. Relief didn't even come close to describing what he felt at knowing he wouldn't have to.

Ellins, meanwhile, had picked up the knife and was using it to cut Guy's bonds. As soon as his hands were free, Guy yanked off the gag and spat out residual bits of it. Then, rubbing at his chafed wrists and struggling to speak past the dryness of his mouth, he croaked, 'Is ... is Millie safe?'

'Yes,' replied Adam. And then, because he couldn't help himself, 'No thanks to you, of course – but yes. She's perfectly safe.'

'Thank God. And – and thank you. I'm s-sorry.'

'So you should be,' agreed Rainham. He let Clements drop and dusted off his hands. 'They've obviously knocked you about a bit. Are there any injuries I can't see?'

'It hurts to cough so ... so I think I may have a cracked rib.'

'Very likely. But if that's the worst of it, you got away lightly, you young fool. Now ... do you know any of these men?'

The pair who had been knocked out were starting to come round and Adam was helping Ellins haul them into a corner.

Guy looked across and shook his head. 'Not those two, no.'

'And this one?'

He stared down in silence. Head bent and blood seeping through his fingers, Clements was clutching his wounded shoulder and whimpering. But finally, when he dared to glance up, Guy said stonily, 'Yes. Until a few days ago, I thought ... I thought he was a friend.'

'A rude awakening and a salutary lesson, then.'

Leaving Ellins pointing his musket at the men in the far corner, Adam turned back saying brusquely, 'We need to leave – so we'll tie these three up and leave Fisher and Ellins to guard them. As soon as we're back, I'll have Lieutenant Prentiss send help. Agreed?'

'Agreed. But I imagine we'd better let Stubbs get back to work. It won't do for the lantern to go out.' Rainham cast an assessing glance at Clements, 'And what about him?'

'He won't bleed to death, if that's what you mean,' replied Adam impatiently. 'But I doubt his right arm will be much use to him for quite some time.'

CHAPTER TWENTY-SEVEN

As the hours crawled by and darkness fell, Camilla's restless impatience had turned into gnawing anxiety. Between them, she and Finch had got as much out of Reed as they could – with the result that there were now two men tied up below stairs, awaiting the gentlemen's return. But where were they? They had been out on the Marsh for hours and what could they possibly achieve in the dark? By her calculations, they ought to have been back ages ago – so why *weren't* they? It suddenly struck her that if something had happened to Adam it would be every bit as bad as losing Guy.

Coombes and Mrs Poole tried to make her sit down to dinner but she thought that food might choke her.

'You ought to have something, Miss Millie,' insisted the housekeeper. 'You've had a long, hard day and --'

'And the gentlemen have had a longer one,' she snapped. Then, shutting her eyes for a moment and drawing a deep, steadying breath, she tried to moderate her tone. 'When they get back, they'll be wet and hungry. Tell Cook to see that there is a hot meal ready to serve, start heating water for baths and – and anything else you think will be helpful.'

It was a further hour before the sound of hooves in the stable yard had her running down the stairs. She paused on the turn above the hall, heart beating rapidly and her knuckles glowing white on the bannister.

Please, she prayed silently. *Please let everything be all right.*

Coombes opened the front door … and Rainham stepped over the threshold, half carrying Guy, with Adam two steps behind him.

Just for an instant, Camilla thought she must be imagining it. Then with an odd, inarticulate cry, she flew down the remaining steps and pulled her brother into her arms. 'Oh *God*! We've been searching and hoping but *how* --?' She stopped, swallowing hard. 'No. Questions can wait. It's enough that you're home. I've been so *worried*!'

He hugged her awkwardly. 'I'm sorry, Millie. Really, really sorry.' And had to step back clutching his ribs as he dissolved into a fit of coughing.

'I know you are. Never mind that now. Let's get you comfortable. Heavens, you're wet through and you *reek*. Coombes! A fire in Mr Guy's room, a hot bath, warming pans in his bed and send Ned to valet him. Mrs Poole, something for his chest and broth for later when he's warm and dry. Rainham … can you help him upstairs, please?'

'Yes, ma'am.' He gave a lazy salute as the servants scattered to do her bidding. 'But my price is a very large brandy.'

'You shall have it,' she promised, watching him pick Guy up as if he weighed nothing at all and start up the stairs while her brother protested unconvincingly that he could walk.

Slowly, Camilla turned and finally allowed herself to look at Adam. As he had for several minutes, he was leaning silently against the wall, wet through and looking tired. She gave a tiny sound that might have been a sob and then crossed the space between them to slide her arms about him, saying, '*Thank* you. Thank you for bringing him back. I don't know how you did it but – *thank* you.'

Aware of the sodden state of his coat, Adam set his hands at her waist and held her slightly away from him. He said huskily, 'You shouldn't do this. I'll soak your gown.'

'I don't *care*.' She shook her head, pressed back against him and continued mumbling into his throat. 'You're *safe*. You were gone so long I was frightened that something – something terrible had happened to you.'

'Were you?' Surprised and touched, he let one arm slide about her while the other hand rose to lift her chin. 'Well, it didn't. But you could reward me anyway.'

And then he was kissing her and she was kissing him back, the fear of the last hours transforming itself into an expression of everything she was afraid to say. She didn't care that the entire household might be watching. All that mattered was that he was back with her, safe and in one piece. His mouth trailed a scorching path down her throat and her fingers tangled in his wet hair. Her hand found its way inside his coat only to be frustrated by vest and shirt; he gave a small growl and held her even more closely, his fingers straying over her back. And meanwhile their mouths returned to each other over and over again, neither of them having the will to stop.

Nor did they hear the first tactful clearing of a throat. It took a second, louder one to get Adam's attention. Loosening his grip on Camilla, he reluctantly lifted his head to look past her knowing already who he would see. And there was Rainham, arms folded across his chest and leaning negligently against the large, carved newel post, watching them with ill-concealed amusement.

He had shed his coat, someone appeared to have provided him with a dry shirt and his partly-dried hair hung loose. Without waiting for Adam to speak, he said blandly, 'Guy is receiving every possible care and Coombes wants to know if he can serve dinner. Shall I suggest he waits a further half hour so that the two of you can shed those wet clothes?'

'Yes,' said Camilla over her shoulder. 'Do. And you'll find the brandy in the library.'

'Is that a polite way of telling me to go away?'

'You need it spelled out?' asked Adam.

'No. Do *you* need me to point out that, but for me, it would be Coombes standing here right now?' retorted Rainham. And sauntered back up the stairs.

Adam and Camilla looked at each other. Finally, she said, 'I should let you get dry before you catch your death.'

'I'm not so feeble.' He tucked a stray curl back behind her ear, his touch gently lingering. 'But first I need Finch to take a message to Lieutenant Prentiss. I've left two of his dragoons guarding the men holding Guy and they'll need help.'

Her eyes widened and she said, 'Where? Where did you find him?'

He smiled, dropped a light kiss on her nose and said, 'Later. We'll give you the whole story over dinner. Go and change your gown before *you* catch your death.'

* * *

As soon as she had exchanged the sodden blue taffeta for a lilac and green flowered polonaise, Camilla sped along to her brother's room only to be told that Guy was still soaking in a hot bath.

Nodding, she said quietly, 'How is he, Ned?'

'He's more tired than anything else, Miss Millie. The cough is bad and there might be a cracked rib – which don't help. But he'll mend fast enough now he's home.'

'Yes. Yes, of course he will.'

'I'll stay with him through the night – just in case, like.'

'Thank you. I know you'll look after him – and that he'd rather have you than anyone else. Tell him I'll look in again later but won't disturb him if he's sleeping.'

Downstairs, after a swift wash and change of clothes, Adam had joined Rainham and the brandy in the library. Handing him a glass, the viscount said mildly, 'You can tell me to mind my own business if you like but --'

'Mind your own business,' returned Adam.

'I was merely going to ask if --'

'I know what you were going to ask, thank you. And if I have anything to say to Camilla, I think she deserves to hear it first, don't you?'

'Fine. Have it your own way. But I *will* say one thing. From what I learned about it later, she was well out of it with that stupid bastard Staplehurst but she doesn't need another debacle. So don't mess it up.'

'Finished?' asked Adam, downing a hefty swallow. 'Excellent. *Now* mind your own business.'

Sweeping through the door and reminding herself that she would *not* be embarrassed either by what she and Adam had been doing earlier or by the fact that Rainham had seen them doing it, Camilla absorbed the fact that the gentlemen appeared to be sharing a hard look not far distant from a glare. 'Are you two *arguing*?' she demanded.

'I'm not,' muttered Adam. 'It's Rainham who can't stop talking.'

She surveyed them with mock severity and, gesturing to the depleted decanter, said, 'That's probably the brandy. But don't you *dare* get foxed before you've told me everything! Besides … you're not the *only* ones who have had an interesting day.'

'Why?' Adam set down his glass with a little thud. 'What happened?'

She grinned at him and shook her head. 'You first.'

'*Food* first,' corrected Rainham. 'Neither of us has had anything since breakfast – a fact I took the liberty of mentioning to Coombes.'

'Worried you might not be adequately fed? You needn't have been.' Camilla took Adam's arm and towed him to the door. 'You're the heroes of the hour because you brought Guy home – so Cook will serve the next best thing to a fatted calf or die in the attempt.'

Knowing she was unlikely to get any sense out of either gentleman until they'd got some food inside them, Camilla set her questions aside until they had consumed bowls of creamy vegetable soup and a fish course of cod with mussels. She, finding that she still had little appetite, did no more than toy with either dish and largely occupied herself covertly watching Adam across the table. But by the time he and Rainham were attacking thick slices of beef in a red wine sauce her impatience got the better of her and she said baldly, 'Slow down before you give yourselves indigestion. Where did you find Guy?'

Rainham continued chewing with evident enjoyment. Adam laid down his knife and, smiling a little, said, 'In the lighthouse.'

Her eyes widened. 'Go on.'

'It was a stroke of luck, really. We'd been there earlier in the day and might not have gone back but for Trooper Ellins.' And he proceeded to tell the story in his usual concise fashion, deliberately omitting any mention of how close Guy had been to having his throat cut. Then, at the end of it, he said, 'We may get more information from the three men who I hope Lieutenant Prentiss will soon have under lock and key. But our best chance of finding the man who controls the operation still lies in Erasmus Wilson.'

For a moment or two Camilla said nothing, mentally combing through everything he'd said and wondering about the things he hadn't. She doubted if the rescue had been achieved *quite* as smoothly as he'd made it sound. But the point was that it *had* been achieved – so there was nothing to be gained by pressing for details he'd chosen to withhold. Finally, she said, 'Erasmus and those other three men you spoke of aren't *all* we've got.'

The dark, slate-blue gaze sharpened. 'They're not?'

She shook her head. 'Finch didn't tell you?'

'I didn't give him the chance,' replied Adam. 'Supposing *you* tell me.'

It was interesting – and rather satisfying – to note that Rainham had stopped eating and was regarding her with close attention. She was almost tempted to keep him on tenterhooks for a little while longer. But teasing Rainham was one thing – teasing Adam, quite another. So she said simply, 'A man came here wanting me to go with him to the hut where he claimed Guy was hidden. I didn't believe him. So Finch and I asked a few questions, prised the real reason he was here from him ... and then locked him in the log store for you to play with later.'

Adam relaxed again. 'You didn't threaten him with the cheese-grater, by any chance?'

She smiled modestly. 'As it happens, I did. Who would have thought a humble kitchen utensil could make grown men quake?'

'It isn't the utensil. It's the look of eager anticipation they see on your face that convinces them you'll use it.'

'I must remember that. It could come in useful in all manner of circumstances.'

Adam grinned but, before he could make a suitable retort, Thomas arrived to clear the table for the desserts, fruit and cheese ... so instead he asked if Finch had returned from New Romney.

'Yes, sir. He said to tell you that the lieutenant's taking care of things.'

'Good. Thank you.'

When the footman had retired again, Rainham said, 'Our friends from the lighthouse?'

Adam nodded but said nothing, merely reaching for a small slice of cheese.

'Are they men Guy knows?' asked Camilla.

'One of them is,' replied Rainham. 'A former friend, apparently – though one wouldn't have known it from the way he was behaving.'

'Forget that for the moment,' said Adam, foreseeing questions he didn't want to answer. 'Camilla ... what was the *real* reason for this fellow's visit today? Abduction?'

'No – though that was my first thought. He says someone wants to meet me without being recognised – only of course, he doesn't know who.'

Adam's own gaze narrowed. 'But clearly *you* would if you met them.'

'Yes.' She hesitated for a moment and then added, 'Perhaps that is something we ought to consider?'

'Possibly,' said Rainham firmly. 'As a last resort and having taken every possible precaution. But before we go down that road, I think we'll try shaking a few more answers out of Erasmus. Ah – I take it he's unaware of the other fellow?'

'Completely. I'm not *entirely* stupid.' She stood up. 'However, if you'll excuse me, I'd like to check on Guy and find out if he's managed to eat anything.'

Both gentlemen rose and bowed. Adam said, 'You'll join us in the library afterwards? We ought to consider what to do next.'

She nodded and walked swiftly from the room. When the door closed behind her, Adam said bluntly, 'You do have an unerring knack of rubbing her up the wrong way, don't you? And you're telling *me* not to make a mess of it?'

Rainham muttered something profanely insulting and took refuge in his wine glass.

* * *

Camilla returned to the library looking a good deal happier. She said, 'He's had some of Cook's beef broth, taken a little laudanum and will be asleep by now. But he said you both handled a nasty situation incredibly well and he's concerned he didn't thank you properly. I told him not to worry about that because I'd do it for him.'

'Correct me if I'm wrong,' drawled Rainham provokingly, 'but I thought you'd already thanked Adam more than adequately.'

Adam groaned inwardly and Camilla sent his lordship a frosty glare.

'And to think,' she snapped, 'I've told Mrs Poole to prepare a bedchamber for you because, with the rain and no one having been there all day, the cottage will be cold. I was *even* going to suggest that you quit the cottage altogether and move here for the duration. But if you're going to be deliberately annoying the whole time --'

'Who – me? I wouldn't dream of it.' He laughed at her and said winsomely, 'Darling Millie, please invite me to stay. I promise I'll be good.'

'You'd better be,' she muttered. 'We'll send for your things in the morning – meanwhile, you'll just have to manage. And you may as well come as yourself. Since Squire Derring, the Lord of the Level and half the senior military officers in Kent know who you are, there's little point in keeping up the Mr Gilbert charade here at home.'

'Especially with you calling me Rainham half the time,' he murmured.

'There you go *again*! You just can't help yourself, can you?'

'How can I resist when you provide such an opening?'

Camilla was still drawing breath to retaliate when Adam said, 'If I didn't know better, I'd swear you two were brother and sister. I've never heard adults who weren't related bicker as consistently as you do. Call a truce, can't you? Otherwise, if Rainham moves in here, I'm going back to the cottage.'

This had the effect of silencing both of them, if only temporarily. Then, grinning at Camilla, Rainham said lightly, 'As you're aware, I have two sisters. Neither are half as much trouble as you ... but neither are half as much fun either.'

She pressed a hand over her heart. 'Goodness! Was that a compliment?'

'I suspect it may have been.' He turned to Adam. 'I'm not sure I can face another session with Erasmus tonight. You?'

Adam shook his head. 'No. I recognise that getting Guy back, though one important battle, wasn't the whole war ... but at least there's less urgency now. However, I suppose one of us ought to make the acquaintance of Camilla's visitor.'

Rainham groaned and heaved himself to his feet. 'I'll do it. You more than earned your pay with that perfect time thrust earlier. And then I'm for bed.' And as Camilla started to rise, 'Stay where you are, Millie. I'm sure Coombes will tell me where I can lay my head.'

She stood up anyway and, putting her hands on his shoulders, reached up to kiss his cheek. 'Thank you for everything you've done. You know, don't you, that even though you're the most provoking person I know, I'm rather fond of you?'

He laughed and gave her a quick hug before releasing her. 'And you know it's mutual. Now sit down, let Adam pour you a glass of wine and then go to bed. You look every bit as tired as I feel.' And he walked out, leaving them alone.

Watching Adam pour the wine, Camilla said carefully, 'That was very restrained of him, wasn't it? I expected some witty instruction to behave ourselves.'

'He got something of the sort off his chest earlier.'

'What?'

'Nothing I didn't know already.' He handed her the glass and sat beside her. 'Relax for a little while. And promise you don't intend to sit with Guy *all* night.'

'I don't. I'll pop in, of course, but Ned is staying with him. He's devoted to Guy. Always has been since they were children.' She leaned back, took a sip of wine and then, recalling something, said slowly, 'What is a time thrust?'

Adam had known better than hope she wouldn't ask and been silently cursing Rainham's big mouth since the second he'd opened it. He said, 'I'm sorry?'

'You know perfectly well what I mean. Is it a fencing term?'

'Yes – though technically speaking, what I did wasn't a time thrust at all. It was merely ... similar.' He stopped, then added quietly, 'Can we please not talk about this?'

'Why not?'

Because I suspect I hit the exact spot which will leave that man with a largely useless arm for the rest of his life, he thought queasily. *But mainly because, after what happened earlier, the 'right time' I've been waiting for appears to have arrived ... and I'm not sure I'm ready for it.*

During the course of the evening, several things had occurred to him. Although he would be damned before he'd let Rainham force his hand, he couldn't ignore the fact that his lordship had seen what he'd seen. Neither could he deny that whatever was happening between himself and Camilla needed to be brought into the open and resolved before something similar occurred again and left her reputation in tatters. As to the question of how successful he would be ... now, in this moment, while she was still euphoric over Guy's rescue, might be his best chance – or would be if he wasn't so tired he couldn't think clearly. Then again, the other side of *that* particular coin was that he didn't want her to say or do anything out of gratitude; he wanted ... well, it was abundantly clear what he wanted and the way she'd behaved in the hall suggested that it wasn't out of reach. She had seemed as relieved at his own safe return as she was at having her brother home. And she'd kissed him as if ... but best not to dwell on that.

He set his glass aside and, swivelling to face her, said cautiously, 'Perhaps tomorrow you and I could find an opportunity to speak privately.'

Her brows rose. 'Can't we do that now?'

'Not really.' He smiled wryly. 'I'm no good at graceful speeches at the best of times but right now I suspect even lucidity is beyond me.'

The silvery-green eyes searched his for what seemed a very long time before they darkened with suspicion and she said, 'What, exactly, has Rainham said to you?'

'What? Nothing. Nothing of any consequence, anyway.'

'So he *did* say something? Oh – why am I asking? Of *course* he did. He wouldn't be able to resist – well-meaning, interfering idiot that he is,' she muttered irritably. 'And then telling us to be grateful it was him and not Coombes? Well, I wish it *had* been Coombes. At least he'd just have melted quietly away instead of sticking his oar in. And I daresay Rainham didn't spare a second to think that perhaps you weren't the one to blame, did he? *Did* he?'

'No. But what has blame to do with it?' Adam hauled in a breath of pure desperation and shoved a hand through his hair. 'Can we please leave Rainham out of it? This isn't about him. It's about you and me. I've been saying for days that we'd talk when the time was right – and now we have Guy back, this is probably as good as it gets. But not right now. Tomorrow ... when my brain is functioning properly and before any fresh crisis rears its ugly head.' He paused and then added, 'If the rain has stopped, come riding with me. It's going to become progressively harder to find privacy here in the house, what with Rainham and Guy and the servants and the men in the cellar – and God knows who else turning up at the door. So ride with me. Please.'

It occurred to her that this rapid torrent contained more words than Adam usually strung together into one speech. Although she knew he was deadly serious, she couldn't help smiling a little. But he was right. It *was* time they talked – even though she was half eager and half terrified by the thought of what he might say. But for now there was only one answer so she gave it.

'Of course I'll ride with you. We'll slip away as soon as we have the chance.'

CHAPTER TWENTY-EIGHT

The morning mail brought a note from Sebastian saying that his men had reported no nocturnal activity at the four houses they'd been watching in Lydd. Adam and Rainham agreed that since it was possible Erasmus was the *only* such visitor and he was currently locked in Dragon Hall's cellar, Sebastian might as well end the surveillance.

The tiresome hour Rainham had spent the previous evening questioning Mr Reed had produced nothing that Camilla hadn't already told them other than a renewed mention of the *Woolpack* at Brookland.

'Virtually everything so far seems centred there,' observed Adam. 'Do you think a visit from Riding Officer Hindley along with two or three redcoats might prove instructive?'

Rainham nodded. 'Finch was going to collect the rest of our gear from the cottage this morning but putting Prentiss wise about the *Woolpack* connection is more important.'

'And while he's about it,' Adam suggested, 'he can deliver Reed to the redcoats. The fellow is no use to us, after all.'

'True. So ... are you ready for another session with Erasmus? With luck, the last thirty-six hours may have brought about a change of heart – though I'm not holding my breath.'

'Neither am I,' said Adam. And then, abruptly, 'One of us needs to question Guy. We've no idea how long and how deeply he's been involved with the smugglers but anything he knows could be useful.'

'Agreed. Perhaps Camilla could talk to him?'

'She could and she *would* – but she shouldn't have to. Also, quite aside from his recent captivity and rough handling, the young idiot needs to realise just how much *other* trouble he could be in. We may have kept his illicit doings from the squire and the Lord of the Level, but Levinson and Prentiss know perfectly well what he's been up to and have every right to arrest him.'

'Very well. You speak to Millie and I'll start putting pressure on Erasmus.'

'Take the cheese-grater,' advised Adam.

* * *

He found Camilla in the morning-room, consulting with the housekeeper on a suitable diet for their invalid. But when he hovered in the doorway, Camilla smiled, saying, 'Come in, Mr Brandon. I think we'd finished, hadn't we, Mrs Poole? All the things Doctor Quinn suggested plus your own special tonic for his chest.'

'Very good, Miss Millie.' The housekeeper bobbed a curtsy and withdrew.

'The doctor has been?' asked Adam.

'Yes. I sent Thomas for him first thing. He confirmed that Guy almost certainly has a cracked rib which will take time to heal, the only cure being rest.'

'How is he this morning?'

'Ned says he had a largely peaceful night although the cough woke him from time to time. And he was moderately cheerful when I visited him – though still weak and full of apologies for all the trouble he's caused.'

'I daresay he'll get over that fast enough.' He paused and added bluntly, 'As soon as you think he's fit enough, I need to talk with him.'

'Question him, you mean.'

'Yes. I'm sorry – but it has to be done.'

She sighed. 'I know. And deep down, Guy probably knows, too. But can it wait at least until tomorrow?'

'Of course. Harry is taking that fellow Reed to Lieutenant Prentiss and we'll --'

'The reward!' said Camilla suddenly. 'The lieutenant's troopers earned it, didn't they?'

'Two in particular did ... and four others tried their best.'

'So ... how much, do you think?'

'I'd suggest twenty pounds apiece for Fisher and Ellins. And a further forty to be shared between the four other fellows. Or is that too much?'

'No. I was prepared to part with a hundred and what they did is worth every penny. Tell Mr Finch to come to me for the money before he leaves.'

Adam nodded. 'If you want notes announcing Guy's safe recovery taking to the squire and Sir Cuthbert, Harry can deliver those at the same time.'

'That's probably unnecessary. I suspect that the news will be all over the Marsh by noon. Doctor Quinn's wife is a notorious gossip.' Her expression clouded as the consequences of this occurred to her. 'There will be *callers*. Damn.'

'Avoid them by not being here,' he shrugged. 'You have a prior engagement, after all.'

'Why, yes.' The sun came out as she beamed at him. 'So I do.'

* * *

Downstairs in the so-called visitors' parlour, Adam found Rainham looming over Erasmus and the pair of them seemingly locked in a silent battle of wills.

Leaning negligently against the door, he said, 'Have you broken the good news yet?'

Rainham straightened and scowled. 'No. You tell him, if you want to.'

Erasmus, hands still bound but no longer also tied to the chair, swivelled to look at Adam. 'What are you talking about?'

'Thanks to your tip about Denge Marsh, we recovered Mr Edgerton-Foxe last evening. Picking up the men guarding him was an added bonus.'

'I daresay,' muttered Erasmus sourly. 'Is that it?'

'By no means. We've also got a fellow named Reed who came here with an agenda involving Miss Edgerton-Foxe ... and let us not forget those of your friends taken during the run who are currently snug in Dover Castle. I imagine Major Levinson has his hands full.'

'Is that why I'm still here?'

'Not at all. You're here,' replied Rainham with laborious patience, 'and will *remain* here until you answer the question I asked before Mr Brandon joined us. Is some of the tea you bring in acquired directly from East India Company captains?'

Erasmus shrugged. 'Yes. But I have nothing to do with that side of the operation.'

'Somehow, I doubt that. But we'll return to that point later. For now ... let's try this instead. Is smuggling tea and abetting spies your sole occupation?'

Erasmus took his time thinking this over but finally said, 'No.'

'Then you have other employment?'

Silence.

'I'll take that as a yes – in which case your employer must be wondering where you've got to. Unless he's up to his neck in your other line of work. Is he?'

'No. And I've said as much as I'm going to.'

Adam strolled to a place where he could watch Erasmus's face and proceeded to speak of him as if he wasn't there. 'Here's what we know. He's educated, well-spoken, he doesn't work with his hands and his coat would have been quite smart before Harry roughed him up somewhat. So our earlier guess was probably right. He's a secretary or a valet ... or perhaps a clerk. Now, how hard can it be to find out who has been missing from his post recently?'

'Not very,' agreed Rainham. 'Time-consuming, of course – but not difficult.' And to Erasmus, 'So far as I can see, there is only one reason why you won't name your employer – and that is because he *is* complicit in your other business. If he isn't, you'd be wise to spare him the embarrassment of being arrested. For we *will* find him, you know.'

'Perhaps – or perhaps not. But you'll do it without my help,' came the stubborn reply. 'If I tell you what you want to know, I'll be dead long before you get me to trial. And I'd sooner take my chances in court, if it's all the same to you. So go and find out for yourselves if you think you can do it.'

'Don't you?' asked Rainham.

'No. I don't.'

* * *

Having spent most of the morning with her brother, Camilla joined the gentlemen for a simple luncheon of cold meats and game pie and, on learning what was required, said, 'Yes. I can make a list of gentlemen likely to have a secretary or a valet or both, and another one of local solicitors. But what makes Erasmus so sure you won't trace him that way? And why is he convinced someone will murder him if he talks? How would the man he works for even know he's *done* so?'

'Three very good questions,' replied Adam, 'none of which we can answer. But all of them suggest the wisdom of keeping him locked up here rather than sending him to Dover with the rest.'

'Agreed,' said Rainham. 'He's safer here than elsewhere – a fact of which I imagine he is well aware. For the rest, there's a small chance Guy may know something that might throw a glimmer of light. When will you speak to him?'

'As soon as Camilla feels he's up to it – tomorrow, hopefully.'

'The sooner the better,' muttered his lordship, clearly not very pleased. He pushed his plate aside, glanced around the table and added, 'The same applies to the list, if you've both finished eating.'

'Fine,' sighed Camilla, rising from her chair. 'The library, then.'

'I'm sorry if you find me importunate, Millie, but needs must. If you can give us the first few names that come to mind, we can start the rounds this afternoon.'

'*You* can,' said Adam, following him to the door. 'I'm promised elsewhere.'

'It had better be important.'

'It is.'

'Stop grouching, Rainham,' said Camilla over her shoulder. 'I haven't been through the door for two days and Adam has promised to take me riding. If I don't get some air soon, I'll either suffocate or kill someone.'

The first few names were obvious and came easily.

'Sir Cuthbert,' said Camilla, writing it down. 'Lord Blakely near Ashford, Sir Victor Amory at Hythe and Mr Harrington in Old Romney.'

'Squire Derring?' suggested Adam.

'No. He can't afford to pay someone to do what his son can do for nothing.' She tapped the tip of the quill against her lips. 'As for the Blane family ... I'd guess there are secretaries in both banking offices so it's unlikely there is a third at home. But at least one of the men in the family must have a valet.'

'Put them on the list,' said Rainham. 'What about solicitors?'

She nodded. 'Yes. Hartley, Hartley & Witherspoon in Tenterden; Bagshot & Soames in Hythe; and ... there's firm of lawyers in Lydd but I don't know the name of it.'

Rainham grinned at her. '*Forgotten* something, Millie?'

'No. Do not *know* it – as in *never* knew it,' she retorted, pushing the paper across the desk. 'Those are enough to start with – spread out all around the Marsh as they are.'

'Yes. I'd noticed that.' Rainham eyed the list with resignation. 'Hythe to begin with, I think – and Dymchurch on the way back to visit Sir Cuthbert. That will pick off three --'

He stopped as a tap at the door heralded Coombes who said, 'I beg your pardon, Miss Millie. Both the elder and the younger Mrs Blane are here, escorted by Mr Mark Blane and his brother. Are you at home?'

Camilla groaned. 'Do I have a choice?'

'Do you want one?' asked Adam.

'What do *you* think?'

'Very well, then. Where are they, Mr Coombes?'

The butler permitted himself a small smile.

'I took the liberty of placing them in the interrogation chamber, sir.'

Rainham gave a snort of laughter.

Adam said, 'Good choice. Tell them that Miss Edgerton-Foxe is unable to leave her brother at this time but has asked Viscount Rainham to receive them in her place.'

'Viscount ...?' echoed Coombes uncertainly, looking from Adam to Rainham and back again. 'Would that be ...?'

'Mr Gilbert, yes. One of us will explain later. Camilla; run upstairs and change into your habit. I doubt the Family Blane will stay long – in fact, we'll make sure they don't. *Go*!'

Not needing to be told twice, she fled with a whispered, 'Thank you!'

'Show the visitors in here, Mr Coombes – but take your time about it.'

'Certainly, sir.'

'This,' remarked Rainham when the butler had gone, 'could be useful.'

'My thoughts exactly. The Blane brothers will recognise me but I'll leave you to direct the conversation – as is only proper, you being a peer of the realm.'

'Due deference at last? How charming.'

'I thought you'd like it. Now, we *could* ask if they're missing a member of staff but, aside from wanting to be rid of them, I suggest we leave that for a more formal occasion – preferably one when Mr Blane senior is present.'

'Agreed.'

Mrs Blane the elder entered on Mark Blane's arm looking plump and grandmotherly. Her daughter-in-law, a pale, discontented-looking female, clung to Peter and almost tripped when he stopped dead on the threshold, his shocked gaze locked with Adam's faint smile.

'Good afternoon,' drawled Rainham, suddenly every inch the aristocrat. 'Miss Edgerton-Foxe regrets being unavailable just at present and has begged me to make you welcome in her place. I am Rainham.'

The ladies curtsied, Mark Blane bowed and, somewhat belatedly, Peter did the same.

Mark said, 'It is good of your lordship to receive us. My grandfather would be with us save that he is unwell today. However, may I present my grandmother, my mother and my younger brother?'

'A pleasure. How very good of all of you to call.' Rainham inclined his head and offered his arm to Grandmother Blane. 'Please sit, ma'am. Adam ...?'

'Certainly.' Adam handed the younger Mrs Blane into a chair and stepped back, the very picture of due deference.

'It's true then?' asked Grandmother Blane. 'Young Guy's safe home again?'

'Indeed he is,' replied Rainham gravely. And then, 'Good news has wings, does it not?'

'It does when Phyllis Quinn gets hold of it. But how *is* the poor boy?'

'Not at all well, I regret to say. His ordeal has taken its toll both physically and mentally – hence his sister's continued presence at his side.'

'I'm sorry to hear it,' said Mark gravely. 'Please tell Guy that I and the rest of my family will pray for his swift recovery.'

'How very kind.' Rainham paused. 'I trust you will forgive my not sending for refreshments but, as I am sure you will understand, the house has been in turmoil for some days. And at present, Mr Brandon and I are much occupied with the business of bringing the abductors to justice.'

'Of course.' The younger Mrs Blane stood up. 'We should not stay, Mama-in-law.'

'And we won't, Laura.' The old lady's shrewd gaze lingered on Adam for a moment before returning to Rainham. 'Has the young man been able to tell you anything about the villains who took him?'

'Sadly, not as yet. He has a severe chest infection and is extremely feverish. But we hope another few days will see him much improved.'

'Was it you who found him?' asked Peter abruptly.

'It was.'

'And where was he?'

'I'm afraid we are not sharing that information, at this time. Suffice it to say that all the relevant facts are in the possession of Major Levinson at Dover.'

'Best thing to do,' approved Grandmother Blane. 'And I'm sure Miss Edgerton-Foxe is very thankful to have you dealing with all this unpleasantness for her.'

'I certainly hope so, ma'am.'

'But how come you're here at Dragon Hall?' demanded Peter. 'Either you or *him*.' A jerk of his head indicated Adam. 'You ain't relatives, are you?'

'Peter!' snapped his brother. 'That is scarcely civil. Apologise to his lordship.'

'For what? It's a fair enough question, isn't it?'

Adam suspected that Rainham was wishing he had a quizzing glass to raise.

Since he didn't, he lifted supercilious brows and said, 'A fair question perhaps but, if I may be equally frank, none of your business. However ... since you ask, Mr Brandon and I are here at the behest of the Earl of Alveston. It goes without saying that his lordship is extremely concerned about the safety of his niece and nephew – and he wishes those responsible for Guy's abduction to face the gallows.' He paused, subjecting Peter to a long, chilly stare. 'Was there anything else?'

'Only to ask your pardon for my brother's manners,' began Mark. 'I fear he --'

'I don't need anybody apologising for me,' said Peter petulantly.

'You do if you can't govern your tongue,' said his grandmother tartly. And getting to her feet, 'Ignore my grandson, Lord Rainham. He was a sickly child but that don't explain how he somehow missed his share of the family brains. But we'll get out of your way directly. Thank you for receiving us and give Miss Edgerton-Foxe and her brother our best. If my husband's gout improves, we'll call again in a few days.'

'By which time I'm sure Miss Edgerton-Foxe will be happy to see you,' said Rainham, crossing to ring for Coombes. 'Meanwhile, I shall pass on your good wishes.'

'Please do. Come along now, Laura. And Mark – I'll want your arm for those stairs.'

While the rest of his family were taking a perfectly proper leave of Rainham, Peter hung back until he could say, 'Still sniffing round Millie, Brandon?'

'Still smarting because she showed you the door?' retorted Adam.

'She didn't mean it.'

'If you think that, you're even more stupid than I thought you were. Don't call again. You were only received today because your family was with you. Goodbye.'

Peter left scowling. A minute or two later Rainham strolled back in saying, 'Interesting.'

'Very. What did you make of them?'

'The younger grandson is lacking both brain cells and manners. The older one ... solid, a touch pompous and just what one expects of a banker. And I had the impression that their mother didn't want to be here at all.'

'And Grandmama?'

'Ah. Wits as sharp as her tongue and by no means decrepit. If there's a power behind the throne in that family, she is certainly it.'

Adam nodded. 'But how does any of that line up with the likelihood of one of them ruling a gang of smugglers and acting as a conduit for French spies?'

'It doesn't,' sighed Rainham. 'Unfortunately. So I shall take Millie's list and set off on my rounds in the hope of better luck. But first, I suppose I'd better clear up the matter of my identity with the staff. Never a dull moment, as they say.'

* * *

Adam met Camilla emerging from Guy's bedchamber. He said, 'How is he?'

'He's just fallen asleep again – but I think he's a little better. Have they gone?'

'Yes. Do you still want to ride?'

She gestured to her habit. 'What does it look like?'

'In that case, let's go – before any other visitors arrive and you have to spend the rest of the afternoon lurking up here. I sent word to the stables, so the horses should be ready.'

Outside, the previous day's rain had given way to fitful sunshine and a brisk breeze. At the end of the drive, Adam said, 'Which way would you like to go? The tide will be in so that rules out the beach but --'

'I'd like to go to the Wall anyway. I love it there at high tide when the waves are starting to splash over the top and the spray is flying. It's ... invigorating.'

He eyed her quizzically. 'If I'd known you find getting wet invigorating, you could have come out with Rainham and me yesterday.'

She merely shook her head, laughed and turned Sheba towards the sea. But after a few moments, she said, 'Did Peter Blane make an idiot of himself as usual?'

'Yes. But it was worth it to hear his grandmother calling him the fool of the family.'

'*Did* she? In front of you and Rainham?'

'Yes – though not in those exact words. And in front of us was rather the point.'

Camilla laughed again, that sultry, smoky ripple that never failed to draw a response from his body. He gritted his teeth and willed it away.

She said, 'I don't know her well – hardly at all, in fact – but I rather like her. I suspect she was a force of nature when she was my age.'

'I suspect she still is. Didn't you say that she gave you marriage advice?'

'Yes. She told me to find a man I fancy, catch his eye while I'm still young enough to do it and let him know he'd be lucky to have me.'

'If he needs to be told that, he doesn't deserve you.'

'Oh.' She blinked. 'Thank you. That's a – a very nice thing to say.'

Is that a blush, he thought, *or just the fresh air bringing some colour to her cheeks?* But he said merely, 'It's true.'

She didn't reply and, since they were approaching the narrow pathway that led to the track on top of the Wall, he drew back to let her precede him. Instead of doing so, she reined in and said, 'Sheba doesn't like the spray as much as I do. It makes her skittish. Can we leave the horses here for a few minutes and walk up?'

'Of course, if you wish.' He dismounted, tied Hector's reins to the railing, then reached up to grasp her waist and lift her from the saddle. Her eyes locked with his, she slid slowly down his body ... and this time he was sure about the blush. It made him forget to release her. Apparently, just for a moment it made her forget it, too. Then she stepped back and ran swiftly up the path.

At the top, the breeze became a stiff wind, whipping her skirts against her legs and making her hold on to her hat. The waves were slapping against the Wall and breaking over the top of it. The air was full of sea spray ... and Camilla was laughing again.

'Isn't this marvellous?' she cried, turning seawards to face the full blast. 'It doesn't just *blow* the cobwebs away. It *obliterates* them.'

'It's certainly obliterated my hat,' he replied ruefully, watching it roll away down towards the horses and having to shove back the hair that was already escaping its ribbon.

She didn't reply, merely took a couple of dance steps and attempted a twirl which, thanks to the trailing skirts of her habit, which she hadn't bothered to hook up, went awry. She stumbled, thus giving Adam an excuse to catch hold of her and draw her backwards into his chest, saying, 'You are quite mad, you know. And after these last days, it's a pleasure to watch.'

His breath was warm against her ear and the entire length of his body a solid wall of heat behind her. Camilla let her hat go the same way his had done and leaned back against him. Sounding amused and slightly puzzled, she said, 'You're very gallant today.'

'I'm trying. Is it working?'

'That depends on what you hope to achieve.'

'You don't know?'

'No.'

'Can't even make a guess?'

'Perhaps.' It was a mere whisper, almost borne away on the wind. 'But guessing involves making assumptions ... and they can be dangerous. So I avoid them.'

Because he suspected he knew where that had come from, the arm across her midriff that was holding her to him tightened reflexively. He said, 'Trust me, Camilla.'

'I do.' She turned her head to look at him. 'You know I do.'

I believe *you do*, he thought. *I just don't know if it will be enough*. But he said, 'Good. And now – if you're sufficiently invigorated – do you think we might go down? We can't hold a proper conversation here and my other coat hasn't dried out from yesterday yet.'

'Of course. I'm sorry.' She hugged his arm briefly, then turned back along the path. 'We can't hold a proper conversation on horseback either, can we? St Mary's, do you think?'

'Yes.' That church, the place where he'd first kissed her, had been his goal all along. 'With luck, we might have it to ourselves this time.'

She giggled. 'Do you think Mr Trot has got Izzy to the altar yet?'

'Not if her father has anything to do with it.' They'd reached the horses and, boosting her on to Sheba's back, Adam added, 'And probably not at all, ever.'

'Why not?'

He untied Hector's reins from the railing and climbed into the saddle.

'Because if she wanted him ... if she *loved* him ... she wouldn't let Pa stand in their way.'

'No,' said Camilla thoughtfully. 'No. I suppose she wouldn't. Poor Mr Trot.'

'Exactly.' Despite the roiling mess of nerves and emotion in his chest, Adam summoned a smile. 'Shall we go?'

They found the church of St Mary the Virgin as empty and peaceful as the first time they'd gone there. Camilla looked around and then, somewhat teasingly, up at Adam.

'Shall we sit in the same pew? Or will that tempt Fate and bring a family of six down on us?'

'I'll risk it if you will.' He unlatched the pew, handed her in and seated himself beside her. For a moment, he remained silent, staring down at his hands and scouring his brain for a better way to begin this than the one currently in his head. Then, failing dismally but knowing he had to say something, he opened his mouth on, 'I think we've become friends. More than that, perhaps – or I'd like to think so. And you can't have failed to notice that I ... want you. Quite ferociously, as it happens.'

Camilla's heart lurched and she felt her cheeks grow hot.

'Yes,' she agreed faintly. 'I – I had noticed that.'

Mentally girding his loins, he ploughed manfully onward. 'However, I'm not sure you realise that isn't *all* it is.' And in case he hadn't made himself clear, 'The wanting part, I mean.'

'It isn't?'

'No.'

'Oh.' And then, knowing this wasn't much of an answer, she hazarded, 'Good?'

'*Oh good*?' he echoed unwarily.

'Well ... yes.' He looked so ruffled and agitated, so unlike the wholly unflappable Adam Brandon she was used to that Camilla had to repress a desire to smooth his hair back from his face. Instead, she cleared her throat and said primly, 'Forgive me. Please go on.' And when he didn't immediately speak, added helpfully, 'You'd reached the bit where the wanting part wasn't everything.'

'I remember, thank you.' Since this was going from bad to worse, he decided the best thing was probably to get to the point quickly and in as few words as possible. 'When last we were here, I told you how I see you ... what I see *in* you. I won't repeat that because I'm sure you remember it perfectly.'

'I do, yes.'

He nodded. 'I meant every word then and I still mean it now. I will *always* mean it. But what it all boils down to is this. I love you – am *in* love with you. And I want – that is I'm *hoping* – that you might let me persuade you to consider marrying me.'

Then he shut his eyes, held his breath and prayed she wouldn't laugh.

CHAPTER TWENTY-NINE

Camilla didn't laugh. After only the briefest of pauses and somehow managing to sound a great deal calmer than she felt, she said, 'Yes. I will.'

At the same time, still desperately trying to think of something that might make his proposal irresistible, Adam said, 'I realise you'd decided against marrying at all but I promise you --' And there he stopped, his brain finally registering the fact that she'd answered him. '*What* did you say?'

'Yes. I said yes.'

The words had come out before she'd known she was going to say them, born of the sudden starburst of joy inside her. She'd forbidden herself to think of what her answer might be if he asked because he might *not* ask. But what she had *truly* never imagined was the feeling of *rightness* ... or guessed that sheer, blinding happiness could light up the entire world between one heartbeat and the next.

Adam, on the other hand, felt as if he'd been hit on the head with a brick and decided he'd better check for understanding before he made a fool of himself. What, exactly, had he asked her? He said cautiously, 'Yes, you'll let me try to persuade you – or yes, you'll consider it?'

'Neither. Yes, I'll marry you.'

He still couldn't believe he'd heard her correctly. 'You will?'

'Yes.'

'You mean it? You're ... sure?'

'I mean it and I'm quite, quite sure.' She smiled at him through the tears gathering on her lashes. And when he continued to stare at her, slack-jawed and apparently dumbstruck, she laid her palm against his cheek and said unsteadily, 'I love you and trust you and *want* you, Adam Brandon. So yes – of *course* I'll marry you. Why is that so hard to believe?'

'I don't know.' He trapped her hand with his. 'I thought ... I truly thought the very best I could hope for was that you would think about it.' He gave a shaken laugh. 'I hardly know what to say

... except that you are the most extraordinary woman in the world and that I love you with everything that is in me.'

'That's a good start,' she murmured, freeing the hand he held so she could slide both about his neck. 'But right now, a kiss would be enough.'

'No.' Adam shook his head. 'One will *never* be enough.'

And then they were in each other's arms and the world around them ceased to exist.

Eventually however, breathless and dishevelled, Adam settled her against his shoulder and said, 'This is all new, so you'll have to forgive me. Do I have to ask for permission to marry you? From Guy, perhaps ... or your uncle?'

'You certainly don't need Guy's permission – not that, after what you've done for him, he could possibly withhold it. And since I'm twenty-three years old, you don't really need Uncle Hugh's either – though you might ask for it purely as a courtesy.' She turned her head to look up at him and was promptly distracted by a need to kiss his throat, so it was some time before she voiced the question in her mind. 'Why did you think I'd say no?'

He sighed, not sure he wanted to venture into potentially risky territory.

'Do you really want to know?'

'Yes. I really do.'

'I thought a part of your heart still belonged elsewhere and I believed that you no longer had faith in either marriage or men generally. Also, although I knew you liked me, I knew that wouldn't be enough. Taking those things into account, my chances didn't look very promising.'

Camilla remained silent for a very long time whilst trying to decide what to say and what not to. Then she recognised that he'd never asked and never would ... and that, if he was going to be her husband, there were things he had a right to know.

Snuggling back against his shoulder and twining the fingers of one hand through his, she said, 'I didn't love him, Adam. Oh – I *thought* I did. I thought it until I began having feelings for you that were a world apart from any I'd ever had for him. And the more those feelings grew, the more I realised I'd never loved him at all. Not even a little bit. I'd just been blinded by the good looks and charm and the fact that, though he could have had any girl he wanted, I was the only one he looked at.' She made a small exasperated sound and added, 'I can't believe what a fool I was.'

Still holding her close, Adam said gently, 'You don't have to talk about this.'

'I do. I spent too long not talking – not even *thinking* – about it. And I want you to know. I was credulous and naïve and, above all, stupid because I never questioned any of it. I never wondered why *me*. No great beauty; in what, had my parents not died, would have been my fourth Season; and generally held to be the Least Charming Girl in London. I didn't question the whirlwind courtship or wonder why he never once tried to kiss me. And I not only convinced myself that I loved him – I also managed to convince myself that *he* loved *me*. Not just stupid, but *monumentally* stupid.'

'You don't think you're being a bit too hard on yourself?'

'No. It's how it was. It's why, even when I discovered that for years he'd been having an affair with a married lady he'd no intention of giving up and by whom he had two children, I let it *matter* so much.'

Adam swallowed the bad taste in his mouth. He said, 'It's not a question of *letting* it. It did matter,'

'Perhaps. But that's all over now. There is no question of any part of my heart being elsewhere because it never truly was. And I have the only faith I need. It's in the future ... and in you.'

He drew a long breath and loosed it, tilting her face up to his. 'Thank you. I'll try to live up to it.'

'Then why,' she asked, with a wicked smile, 'not start as you mean to go on?'

'Oh well ... if I must.'

His kissed her with tantalising languor ... slowly, sweetly, a kiss of endless promise. And then, no longer able to resist it, he did what he'd forbidden himself to do before and let his hands stray over her body. He traced the curve of waist and hip, discovered the contour of her breasts and managed to uncover a few inches of soft skin before the buttons of her riding jacket defeated his increasingly impatient fingers. Finally, he groaned into her hair and muttered, 'Please tell me you don't want a long engagement.'

Every bit as reluctant to stop as he but knowing they must – they were in a church, for heaven's sake! – Camilla pushed back her hair and, peering down at the buttons, made a clumsy attempt to re-fasten them. 'I don't. But if you're asking how soon we can be married ... I suppose that will depend.'

'On what?' Adam brushed her hands aside and, taking his time over it, set about doing the job himself.

'On how and where we marry. Here, with banns ... or London, with either banns or a special licence. Unless you want to elope?'

'I would dearly like to elope – but my mother would kill me.'

'She would?'

He nodded. 'Max and Frances deprived her of a wedding by tying the knot in Scotland. If we do something similar ... well, let's just say I wouldn't like to face the consequences.'

Camilla laughed and, while he struggled with her buttons, made an attempt to re-tie his hair. 'Is your mother really such a tyrant?'

'She's more terrifying than you can possibly imagine.'

Just for a moment, she almost believed him. Then she caught sight of the tell-tale quiver at the corner of his mouth and gave his queue a hard tug.

'Ouch! That hurt.'

'It serves you right. I know you adore her – so tell me the truth!'

He laughed, dropped a kiss on the tip of her nose and said, 'Mama only wants one thing for her children and that is for us to be happy. She'll love you just as she does Belle's husband and Max's wife. If she misses our wedding, she'll be disappointed but she'll put it aside for our sake and never say a word. I don't want her to have to do that.'

'In that case, neither do I,' she replied firmly. 'So how about a big society wedding at St George's, Hanover Square followed by an extravagant wedding breakfast at Alveston House, perhaps even concluding with a ball?' The look of utter horror on his face made it difficult not to laugh. 'Or would you prefer something a little less grand?'

'Yes,' agreed Adam chokingly. 'If you wouldn't mind.'

'I suppose,' she sighed, as if making a huge concession, 'we might do without the ball.'

'That would be a good start. Thank you.'

'And we don't *really* need to be married by a bishop.'

'I wouldn't think so, no.' His finger beneath her chin made it impossible to avoid the answering gleam in his eyes. 'What else?'

'I might manage without the twelve bridesmaids and – and the fanfare of bugles.'

There was a long silence. Then Adam said, 'You realise there will be retribution for giving me such a scare?'

'There will?' She smiled cheerfully at him. 'Oh. Good.'

* * *

They arrived back at Dragon Hall to find Rainham still absent.

Camilla went directly to her brother's bedchamber and found him arguing with Ned between bouts of coughing.

Rolling his eyes, the footman said, 'He wants to go downstairs for dinner, Miss Millie, but the doctor said he was to stay in bed for at least another day or two.'

She nodded. 'Leave him to me, Ned. Goodness knows, you've earned a break.'

'I can speak for myself,' croaked Guy crossly. 'And I want --'

'Want away, then. You're not getting up today and that is final.' As Ned slipped gratefully from the room, she sat on the side of the bed and took one of his hands in hers. 'Be patient. You've had a horrible time, you haven't been home for twenty-four hours yet and you *know* you're not well. Let's see what Doctor Quinn says in the morning.'

His free hand plucked fretfully at the bed covers and he avoided her eyes.

'They're going to want to talk to me, aren't they?'

'Rainham and Adam? Yes.'

'Nobody's explained anything.' He stopped, controlling a cough. 'I still don't know how come Viscount Rainham is involved in – in all this. I mean … *Rainham*, of all people.'

'Uncle Hugh sent him.'

'Yes. But why *him*? It doesn't make sense.'

Camilla sought a way of skirting the truth.

'Not to us, perhaps. I can only surmise that Rainham has hidden depths Uncle thought would be useful. As, indeed, they have been.' She grimaced slightly. 'I hate to say it … but I suspect this is one of those times when someone is going to say, *Ask no questions and you'll be told no lies* … which means we probably shouldn't. Now can we please stop this? There is something important that I need to tell you.'

Guy opened his mouth to answer but started coughing instead and was forced to lean back against the pillows, breathing hard and clutching his ribs.

'And that,' observed his sister flatly, 'is why you won't leave your bed today.'

It was a while before he could speak but finally he managed to say, 'Point made. Go on.'

It was Camilla's turn to draw a bracing breath. She and Adam had agreed that Guy must be told the news first but neither of them had been sure how he would react.

'Mr Brandon – Adam – has asked me to marry him. And I said yes.'

Guy stared at her, shock, disbelief and wariness chasing across his face in rapid succession. Finally he said, 'You aren't joking, are you.'

'No. Far from it.'

He frowned. 'But … why him, Millie? You hardly know him.'

'That's not true. We were already getting to know each other before you were abducted. But during the days Adam was moving heaven and earth to get you back, we grew very close. And now … well, it's very simple. I love him and he loves me and we are going to marry.' She paused, her gaze locked with that of her brother. 'It goes without saying that we would like you to be happy for us. And I think that if you allow yourself to know Adam better, you won't find it very difficult.'

There was a long silence. Finally Guy muttered, 'We didn't get off to the best start. I was ... I know I was rather rude to him.'

'You were. But does it look as if he's bearing a grudge?'

'No. And that doesn't make me feel any better.'

'If you want to clear the air and shake his hand before --'

'Before he interrogates me? Yes. I'll do that. But not until I'm in a chair, wearing more than a night-shirt. I'm at enough of a disadvantage already.'

* * *

Having changed into a becoming gown of aquamarine silk, Camilla found Adam awaiting her in the parlour, elegant in a coat of dark grey brocade over a rather flamboyant scarlet vest. With a sudden odd flicker of shyness, she said, 'You look very smart this evening.'

'Which, after the last few days, makes a pleasant change,' he replied, catching her in one arm to steal a kiss. 'You, of course, look as lovely as you always do.'

She laughed up at him. 'Is Rainham back?'

'Yes. He came in a little while ago and is making himself presentable. How is Guy?'

'The cough is still aggravating the damaged rib ... but he's fit enough to talk now.'

'Did you tell him about us?' And when she nodded, 'How did he take it?'

'He was surprised more than anything. I thought he'd ask to see you right away but he doesn't want to have to face you from his bed.'

'I can't blame him for that. But tomorrow, perhaps?'

'Yes. If this was just about you and me, I'd probably wait another day. But it isn't, is it?'

'No. And Rainham's losing patience. Speaking of which ... are we going to tell him?'

'Tell me what?' asked his lordship, sauntering through the open door in time to hear this. 'Good news, I hope?'

'The best.' Adam drew his love's hand through his arm. 'Camilla has done me the great honour of agreeing to be my wife.'

For a moment, Rainham merely looked from one to the other of them, a faint smile lurking in his eyes. Then, 'If you'll forgive me saying so, Millie, you missed an opportunity there.'

'I did?'

'Yes. You ought to have kept him in suspense for a little while.'

'Oh? Is that what Vivian did?'

'Lord, yes. She made me go through the whole down-on-one-knee rigmarole three times before she said she'd have me.' He grinned at them and held out his hand to Adam. 'But seriously – I'm delighted for you. My warmest felicitations to you both.' Having shaken Adam's hand and kissed Camilla's cheek, he added, 'For what it's worth, I think you'll find that Goddard will be equally pleased.'

'I hope so,' murmured Adam, not relishing the notion of opposition from that quarter.

'Uncle Hugh, like Grandmama, will simply be relieved to finally get me off the shelf,' declared Camilla firmly. 'And the sooner, the better.'

'I'm all in favour of that.' Adam accepted a glass of wine from Rainham and said, 'Did you have any luck this afternoon?'

'No. I visited Sir Victor Amory and the solicitors, Bagshott & Soames, in Hythe and was not only assured that their secretaries and valets were present and correct but was also introduced to them. The same was true in Dymchurch with the Lord of the Level – although naturally Sir Cuthbert wanted to know why I was asking.'

'Did you tell him?' asked Camilla.

Rainham shrugged. 'I didn't see any reason not to. Our parameters have changed since recovering Guy. Speaking of which ... is he both *compos mentis* and fit enough to talk?'

'Tomorrow,' said Adam firmly, 'as we have already agreed.'

'Fine. Still nothing from Goddard, Millie?'

She shook her head. 'I only wrote to him two days ago.'

'It seems longer.'

'Well, it isn't. He's probably only just received my letter – which means Vincent's barely had time to *look* at the despatch, never mind decode it.' She grinned at him. 'But if you want to try doing it yourself after dinner, you'll find Corbeau's original in the library. The brandy is there, too, if you recall. But don't ask Adam to help you. We have plans to make – so my need, as a newly betrothed lady, is greater.'

Rainham laughed. 'God, Adam. I hope you realise what you're getting.'

'Not entirely. But I look forward to finding out.'

* * *

Whether on account of the French despatch, the brandy or a fit of tact, Rainham did indeed withdraw to the library after they had eaten. Having gone to check on Guy and found him comfortable and sleepy thanks to the small dose of laudanum Ned had put in the one glass of wine the doctor had grudgingly agreed was permissible, Camilla returned to the parlour – and Adam's arms, which encircled her the instant she walked through the door.

The first passionate and extremely satisfying kiss soon led to her lying half on his lap and half leaning back against the sofa cushions while his hands and mouth roved about, teaching her and learning for himself other new and delicious pleasures. Eventually, however, a voice at the back of his mind told him that it was time to call a halt before things went too far so he said huskily, 'Sweetheart ... you have to tell me to stop.'

She trailed her lips along his jaw. 'But I don't want you to stop.'

'Neither do I. But I must. And I will if you tell me to.'

'But not,' she whispered hopefully, 'if I don't?'

Realisation that he wasn't going to win this argument and must therefore locate more will-power than was currently at his disposal arrived slowly but finally forced him to do what must be done. Hauling her off his lap and into a sitting position at his side, he took in the tumbled hair, smooth white shoulders and quite a lot of curving bosom ... and somewhat grimly told himself that he was a hero.

Camilla, meanwhile, toyed idly with a lock of thick, wheat-fair hair and murmured, 'You know ... I've been thinking.'

'What?' The bucket of cold water he'd needed five minutes ago arrived without warning. 'Thinking? Just now? While we were --?'

She laughed up at him. 'No. Of *course* not then. Earlier.'

'That's a relief,' he muttered. Then, 'All right. What were you thinking?'

'I was thinking that we're not going to be married as soon as we would like. As things stand, there's no saying when we'll be able to leave for London. And when we *do* finally get there, the banns must be read and --'

'The words 'special licence' were mentioned, as I recall it.'

'They were – and I'm sure Uncle Hugh could procure one of those for us. But there's still the matter of wedding arrangements and your family travelling from Yorkshire and ... well, it will all take *time*.'

Adam gently stayed the clever fingers currently making their way inside his shirt.

'I know. But, undesirable as it is, we are going to have to put up with it.'

Camilla said nothing for what seemed a very long time and during it, Adam began to suspect the direction in which her thoughts might have been travelling. He said, 'I'm going to risk being emasculated or otherwise maimed with a kitchen utensil ... but please tell me you aren't going to suggest that we anticipate our wedding vows.'

'Oh.' Stricken silvery-green eyes flew to his face. 'You don't want to.'

He knew he ought to simply agree but, with the part of his anatomy which had only just begun to settle responding enthusiastically, the best he could manage was, 'What I want isn't the point. It's just not --'

'So you *do* want to?'

'I'm a man, Camilla,' he ground out. 'And given what we were doing just now – what do *you* think? But that doesn't change anything. We can't.'

'I don't see why not. We're betrothed, after all.'

Even in the privacy of his head, Adam very, very rarely cursed but he wanted to curse right now. Didn't she *know* how tempting it was? How well-nigh impossible it was to say no? Worst of all, had she any idea just how easily she could make all his good intentions crumble into dust?

As gently as he could, he said, 'We're betrothed but, as you just pointed out, without any notion of when we'll be able to marry. I love you, sweetheart and of course I want to take you bed. But I won't do it yet.'

'Oh. And there's nothing I can say to change your mind?'

Nothing you can say. *But I'm only human, so for pity's sake, don't think of the something you could* do *or I'll be lost*, he thought. But said, in the most implacable tone he could find, 'No. Absolutely nothing.'

'And that's your last word?'

'Yes.'

Camilla sighed and curled into his shoulder. 'I knew you'd say that.'

He blinked. 'You did?'

'Yes. It's all honour and respect and doing the gentlemanly thing, isn't it? All the values you were brought up with. I know what you are and I wouldn't wish you any different so I knew you'd say no. But I couldn't resist trying.'

'You couldn't resist ... trying,' he echoed ominously, tilting her chin in order to trap her gaze with his own. 'Do you *enjoy* subjecting me to the torments of the damned?'

'I didn't,' she protested. And then, entranced by the possibility, 'Did I?'

'Yes – and it's the second time today. God knows the threat of a wedding resembling the Lord Mayor's show was bad enough. But *this*? This is just wanton cruelty.' He felt a tiny tremor ripple through her and gave her a shake. 'Stop that, you wretched girl. It isn't remotely funny.'

But suddenly, when she began to laugh in earnest, it was. And when she twined her arms about his neck to lay her cheek against his, Adam found himself laughing with her.

CHAPTER THIRTY

Belatedly joining the gentlemen at the breakfast table the following morning, Camilla said baldly, 'Guy is refusing to wait for the doctor and insisting Ned gets him up and into a chair, Adam. He'll be ready to receive you in about half an hour.'

'He's well enough?'

'He says so. And to be honest, I think he'll feel better when the ordeal of talking about what happened is behind him. So far, he's refused to say anything of it to either me or Ned – but he knows he has to tell you as much as he can.' She managed a crooked smile. 'As for our betrothal, he seems reconciled to that if not exactly overjoyed.'

'Good. For the rest, I promise not to agitate him unnecessarily and --'

'You don't need to tell me that. I know you'll be kind.' She set about buttering her toast and deliberately changed the subject. 'Did you make any progress with Corbeau's despatch, Rainham?'

'Possibly. I'm not sure. Why don't you take a look with me this morning?'

She sent him a brief, arid glance. 'You don't need to find ways to occupy me, you know. I've no intention of getting in Adam's way by hovering over Guy – or even listening outside the door. But I'll be happy to join you after I've gathered the servants together and announced my betrothal.'

'You don't want me there when you do that?' asked Adam.

'Better not. Unless you want to watch the maids cry?'

* * *

Adam found Guy sitting in an armchair by the window and swathed in a thick woollen robe that had seen better days but looked warm and comfortable. He was pale and a little gaunt, with dark shadows under his eyes, bruises lingering on cheekbone and jaw and lines of pain forming about his mouth. Although he looked a good deal better than when Adam had last seen him on the night of the rescue, he still appeared high-strung and fragile.

Deciding on a cautious approach, Adam said pleasantly, 'Thank you for agreeing to see me, Mr Edgerton-Foxe. I know you can't have been looking forward to it.'

'I haven't.' Guy waved him towards the chair opposite his own. 'But that's not your fault. And since we're to be related, you might as well drop the formalities.' He hesitated briefly and then added awkwardly, 'I owe you an apology. When we first met, I was … I wasn't very polite, though I can't recall why not. Anyway, I'm sorry for it.'

'Forget it, Guy. I have. It's of no consequence now.'

'Good of you to say so but not true.' He drew a slow, careful breath and then another. 'I know what you did for me – you and Lord Rainham. But for you, I'd still be rotting in some hovel or other. So along with the apology comes my gratitude. A great deal of it.'

Adam crossed one leg over the other and eyed the younger man thoughtfully. This wasn't the brash, bumptious idiot he'd met previously. His experience at the hands of the smugglers had clearly been a salutary one.

'Don't be too grateful. My motives weren't entirely unselfish. I had to do something half-way heroic – how else was I going to persuade your sister to look twice at me?'

Guy almost smiled but shook his head. 'I know what you did. I was there.'

'Yes. And I hope that only you, I and Rainham know how close my actions came to getting your throat cut. But at the time, it was either that or let his lordship blow the fellow's head off – in which case there was no predicting what might happen. So the risk seemed worth taking.'

'*Was* it a risk? It happened … it was so fast I couldn't … didn't …'

Guy lost his battle against the cough and gave way to it, arms tight across his ribs. Swiftly, Adam fetched a glass of water from the night-stand and put it in his hand, saying, 'Stop talking and just breathe. If you have a relapse Camilla will make me suffer for it and you have no idea how much trouble I'm in already – considering I only proposed yesterday.'

The awful coughing seemed to go on and on but eventually it ebbed, leaving Guy white with pain and breathing in short, uneven gasps. When he was finally able, he said, 'Don't ... please don't make me laugh. It bloody hurts.'

Adam nodded and said sympathetically, 'Gave you a kicking, did they?'

'More than one.'

Another nod. 'When you're ready, do you think you could tell me what happened – right from the first moment? I imagine it coincided with the arrival of the dragoons.'

'Yes. I was with Dan Clements – the fellow with the knife.'

'And who you'd thought was a friend?'

'Yes. And he had been, up until that night. He asked me if Millie knew I helped with the runs – if I'd told her. I said no. Then the dragoons came ... and the next thing I knew, I was tied up in a boat.'

The tale was delivered in short, staccato sentences, sometimes separated by pauses while Guy tried to control both his breathing and the cough. But bit by bit, Adam heard about the first forty-eight hours during which he had been beaten, repeatedly asked the same questions and kept in damp, reeking fishing huts; and then about the transfer to the lighthouse and seeing Clements for the first time since landing on Denge Marsh.

'You knew where you were?' asked Adam, frowning a little.

'Oh yes. Though not exactly till the lighthouse.'

'And the other men guarding you ... did you recognise any of them?'

'No. It wasn't always the same ones. They'd probably been chosen because they didn't know me. But I heard names from time to time and can remember some of them.'

'Good.' Adam didn't expect those names to yield much that was useful. They would almost certainly belong to men at the bottom of the pecking order – the ones who simply did as they were told. 'Write them down as they come to you. Meanwhile, does the name Seth Reed mean anything? No? What about Erasmus Wilson?'

'No. Should it?'

'I believe you'd know him as the Captain.'

'*What*? No. Are you sure? Nobody knows the Captain's name – *nobody*.'

'We do. Furthermore, if you ever feel a desire to meet him face to face, Rainham and I have him locked up below stairs.'

Guy gaped at him. 'When you told Dan that, I thought you were bluffing.'

'I wasn't.'

'How the hell did you manage it?'

'As with many other things … persistence mixed with the occasional stroke of luck,' replied Adam lightly. 'What do you know about him?'

'Personally? Nothing. He's the fellow who brings the orders about dates and times and where landfall's to be made. His word is law amongst the smugglers. I only saw him once … and he didn't seem like someone you'd argue with.'

'He's denying that part of his identity. It would be useful if you could confirm it for us. Can you?'

'Yes.' Guy was beginning to look and sound tired but he said, 'What else?'

'Tell me – very briefly – what your tasks were during a run.'

'Carrying cargo from the boats to the carts and ponies.'

'That's all?'

'It's enough to get me arrested, isn't it?'

'Yes. But we'll do our best to prevent that happening. Lord Alveston's name, a dose of chilly hauteur from Rainham and the fact that you're telling us what you know ought to persuade the authorities toward leniency. Unless …' Adam paused, frowning. 'Did you ever have dealings with a Frenchman by the name of Gaston Corbeau?'

'No. I've never heard of him.'

'Or any Frenchmen at *all*?'

'No. Never.'

'Thank God for that. Now … you've done well and I'm grateful but I think you've had enough for today.' He stood up, held out his hand and when Guy took it, 'If you think of anything else Rainham and I ought to know, send for one of us.'

'I can't imagine myself having the nerve to send for Lord Rainham,' muttered Guy.

'You haven't seen him in disguise,' grinned Adam, strolling to the door. 'It's quite an experience, believe me. I'll send Ned back to you. And if the mail has brought a reply from your uncle, I daresay Camilla will be up to share --'

'*Letters*!' croaked Guy. 'Damn! I forgot all about them.'

'Letters?' Adam froze, his hand already on the door latch. Then, turning slowly and speaking very, very gently, 'What letters?'

* * *

Five minutes later, Adam burst into the library and started talking very fast.

'Say that again,' demanded Rainham, after a moment. 'Guy did *what*?'

'After the previous run, he received orders to deliver a letter to a book-keeper in Dymchurch. He was asked to wait. Then he was given a second letter ... or quite possibly the *same* one in new wrapping,' said Adam as dispassionately as he was able. 'He took that one to a Mr Harker at the office of Meredith, Burridge & Harker, solicitors, in Lydd. We need to go there.'

'We do,' agreed Rainham, coming to his feet.

'Wait,' said Camilla. 'What else did Guy tell you?'

'Very little we didn't already know. One point of interest is that he wasn't normally charged with delivering paperwork. He said the Captain had a handful of trusted lieutenants who undertook that sort of thing – men like Thompson and Sedge. Another such was Brewster, the under-groom here at Dragon Hall – who disappeared the same night Guy was abducted.'

'And is therefore either dead, fled or in Dover Castle,' remarked Rainham. 'But we can find out which later. First, let's go and have a chat with Mr Harker.'

* * *

An hour after the gentlemen had ridden to Lydd, a smart travelling carriage drawn by four grey horses pulled up in the stable yard of Dragon Hall. Camilla, who was upstairs alleviating her brother's growing boredom with a sedate game of whist, knew nothing about it until Coombes appeared and said somewhat breathlessly, 'Sir - Miss Millie – my lord Alveston is here.'

Guy and Camilla stared, first at him and then at each other.

Camilla said, 'Good heavens! I expected him to write – not turn up on the doorstep.'

'Keep him away from me, will you?' muttered Guy miserably. 'I don't need a lecture.'

'Actually, you're due for one.' She threw down her cards and stood up. 'You've got off lightly so far – considering Adam and I both intended to rain coals of fire on your head once you were safe. And since you're not at death's door, I can't keep Uncle away indefinitely – or possibly even at all.'

She found the earl in the yellow parlour, stripping off his gloves and looking impatient.

'Uncle Hugh! This is a pleasant surprise.'

'A surprise, Millie? It shouldn't be.' But he took her hands in his and said, 'Coombes tells me you've got our idiot boy back.'

'The night before last,' she replied, rising on tiptoe to kiss his cheek. 'Not long after I wrote to you the first time. I sent another note yesterday but I suppose you left London before it arrived.'

'No doubt. How is he?'

'A little better than when they brought him back.' Very briefly, she described Guy's current sufferings and added, 'Doctor Quinn says the ribs will take time to heal and prescribes rest.'

His lordship nodded. 'I'll visit him later. For now, tell me exactly what has been going on here and what Brandon and Rainham are doing about it.'

'Aside from getting hold of a French despatch, you mean?' asked Camilla sweetly.

'Yes. Aside from that – and no, I am not dismissing its importance. But I want details.'

Smiling wryly, she sat down. 'It's … complicated.'

'Simplify it.' Alveston took the chair facing her. 'Where are they now, for example?'

'In Lydd,' she began, only to stop when Coombes arrived with tea. 'You'll be staying, Uncle?'

'For tonight at least – longer if it seems necessary.'

She nodded. 'Coombes, please see that a bedchamber is prepared for Lord Alveston and have his luggage taken up.'

'It is already in hand, Miss Millie. Mrs Poole is readying the chamber across the corridor from Viscount Rainham – unless his lordship would prefer your late father's rooms?'

His lordship shot a brief, hard glance at his niece and answered for himself. 'Thank you, Coombes – but any of the guest chambers will be perfectly adequate.'

The butler bowed and withdrew. Briskly, whilst pouring the tea, Camilla said, 'As I was saying, the gentlemen have gone to Lydd to interrogate a solicitor. But perhaps I'd better start at the beginning?'

'By all means, do.'

'Well, then ... I suppose it really started when Ad – when Mr Brandon persuaded Lord Wingham to host a meeting with three local Riding Officers.' With swift economy, Camilla listed all the subsequent events as they had happened, concluding with, 'And that brings us up to today when Guy spoke of a letter or letters he'd been sent to deliver after the run before last – which is what has taken Adam and Rainham to Lydd.'

Alveston nodded. 'In the matter of who is behind both the smuggling and the spying, it would appear that all they have so far is one small and completely inconclusive link to the Blane family. Or am I missing something?'

'If you are intent on avoiding all mention of Corbeau's despatch, yes. But Erasmus is still in the cellar if you want to get the thumbscrews out and question him yourself ... not that I think you'll get anything more out of him than we have already but you're welcome to try.'

'I believe I shall wait until the gentlemen return in the hope of hearing something encouraging.' Setting his tea aside, he said, 'So ... Rainham is staying here, is he?'

Knowing it couldn't be put off and inwardly groaning, Camilla nodded and said lightly, 'As is Mr Brandon. They were living in one of the estate cottages but that became less convenient as matters began to escalate.'

'Meaning what, precisely?' And with a hint of irascibility when she didn't immediately answer, 'How long have they been here, Millie?'

'As soon as Guy was abducted, Rainham suggested that, for the sake of security, Ad – Mr Brandon should move here and Coombes agreed that he would feel better knowing there was a gentleman on the premises. Rainham himself has been here since they brought Guy home two nights ago.'

His lordship subjected her to a long, level stare.

'Correct me if I'm wrong ... but this would mean that *Ad – Mr Brandon* has been in residence for some four or five days, would it not?'

'Yes.'

'And it didn't occur to you to send for your grandmother?' he snapped. 'No, of course it didn't. Indeed, you insisted she remain ignorant of the whole situation.'

'I didn't want her worrying about Guy,' muttered Camilla. 'And I didn't want her down here *fussing*. It would have hindered, not helped.'

'That may be so. But does the entire neighbourhood know that you are sharing this house unchaperoned with not one but *two* gentlemen?'

'Probably. But it hardly matters because --'

'Are you deranged? Of course it matters.'

'No. It doesn't – and please let me finish, Uncle Hugh. It doesn't matter because ... because Mr Brandon has asked me to marry him and I've said yes.' She watched him cautiously, waiting for him to say something and, when he didn't, added slowly, 'Rainham seems to think you would have no objection and might even be pleased.'

'If and when I want Rainham's opinion on this or any other matter, you and he may be sure that I will ask him,' retorted Alveston. And then, in a much softer tone, 'Are you quite certain about this, Millie? Is *he*? The two of you have known each other for little more than a month, after all. That isn't very long on which to base the rest of your life.'

'Not usually, perhaps. But the circumstances have been exceptional. I ... *know* him. And yes, I'm certain. I couldn't be more certain of anything.'

'Then I'll withhold judgement until I have spoken with him. After that, we shall see.' The earl came to his feet. 'And now, while we wait for the wanderers to return, I believe I will see what Guy has to say for himself.'

* * *

In Lydd, Adam and Rainham found the premises of Meredith, Burridge & Harker at the lower end of the High Street and, once inside, asked to see Mr Harker.

'He isn't here just at present, sirs,' said the very young clerk nervously. 'He's been called away on family business and we don't know when to expect him back.'

Rainham and Adam exchanged sardonic glances. Rainham said, 'I see. Then perhaps one of the other senior partners?'

'Both Mr Meredith and Mr Burridge are engaged with clients at present, sirs. You could wait, of course – or maybe old Mr Galton could help? He's been here longer than anybody.'

Seeing Rainham hesitate, Adam said, 'Worth a try, don't you think?'

Sighing in a very lordly way, Rainham said resignedly, 'Very well. Mr Galton it is.'

Visibly relieved, the clerk led them to a small rear-facing office, its walls lined floor to ceiling with wooden filing drawers. Behind his cluttered desk, a wrinkled old gentleman peered at them through pebble-thick lenses.

'Lord Rainham and Mr Brandon to see you, Mr Galton, sir,' announced the clerk loudly.

'Eh?'

'Gentlemen to see you,' bellowed the clerk again. And apologetically to Rainham, 'He's a bit deaf, m'lord, so you'll need to speak up.'

'For God's sake!' muttered Rainham irritably. 'This won't do. Let's go.'

But Adam had caught a gleam of something in the old man's eyes so he crossed to him, hand outstretched and shouted, 'Mr

Galton? Lord Rainham and I are looking for information and hoping that you may be able to help us.'

'Eh?' said Galton again. Then, to the clerk, 'Go away, boy – go away. Don't need you hovering, do I? Out. *Out*!'

The clerk slunk reluctantly from the room. As soon as the door closed, Galton gave a crack of laughter and said simply, 'He's new. I'm not.'

'And not deaf, either?' asked Adam, amused.

'No.' He waved his visitors to the chairs on the far side of his desk. 'So gentlemen ... why are you here and what do you want from me?'

'Whitehall has charged us with making certain enquiries in pursuit of which we need to speak with one of Mr Harker's clients,' said Rainham briskly. 'Unfortunately, we do not have a name and very few clues to go on. Long-shot though it is, we're hoping you may be able to help us identify this person.'

'I've worked here forty years and more, my lord. It's likely I know more about what goes on in these rooms than you think. Try me.'

'Very well. We believe that the gentleman we're looking for never visits Mr Harker in person, preferring to conduct his business through third parties. We know that correspondence for him comes to this office, roughly once a month but probably at irregular intervals. What we *don't* know but are trying to find out is what Mr Harker does next ... in particular, how he communicates with his client. If we knew *that*, we might --'

'Know who the client is,' finished Galton. He leaned back in his chair, looked at them over the top of his spectacles and smiled. 'It's your lucky day, gentlemen.'

'It is?' asked Adam. 'How so?'

'You're here looking for the truth – and you wouldn't have got it from Harker.'

'What makes you think that?'

'Because, Mr Brandon, you're talking about the Fordyce file.' Galton left his desk in favour of one of the banks of drawers. 'A lot of what's in these drawers ought to be in the partners' own rooms ... but they don't want their nice chambers cluttered up with ugly boxes of old paperwork. Dear me, no.' He pulled open a drawer and began leafing through it. 'I've been with this firm since it was Meredith, Burridge & Belcher. In that time, Meredith and Burridge senior both died and were replaced by their sons. Then, two years ago, Belcher sold his share in the partnership to Harker. Neither Meredith nor Burridge junior thought Fordyce important, so Harker got it … but to my knowledge he's never troubled to *read* the whole file. He merely puts the latest instalment on top of the rest.'

'But you *have* read it?' asked Rainham.

'Oh yes, my lord … and very interesting it is too. No mistaking what business H. Fordyce is in or how long he's been in it. High time somebody took an interest, if you ask me.' He pulled out a moderately thick dossier, walked back to his desk and set it down. 'I'm sure you would like tea, gentlemen. Please excuse me while I attempt to communicate that to young Collins. Also, my bladder is in need of relief so I may be gone for a few minutes.' Upon which note, he walked out.

The second the door closed behind him, Rainham whisked the file across the desk and opened it. 'That's *one* way to avoid breaching lawyer-client privilege.'

Adam grunted, already busy scanning lists of goods bought and sold; neat columns detailing costs versus profit, alongside the names and sailing dates of the ships on which these goods had travelled; and at the end of each quarter, entries showing amounts of capital either banked or withdrawn.

Rifling through a score of similar sheets, he said, 'Although they don't actually *say* as much, I think some checking would confirm that these pages record every smuggling run for the last five years. Damn. I wish we had Camilla with us.'

'Well, we haven't – so pocket a couple of the less recent ones,' returned Rainham absently as he continued to sift through a sheaf of brief letters. 'This is no time to worry about ethics – and if Harker never reads the file, he won't miss them.'

'Galton will.' But Adam folded two of the sheets and placed them inside the breast of his coat. 'What have you got? And best be quick. How long does it take to boil water?'

'A good many brief letters, all written in the same hand and all signed H. Fordyce. They contain instructions about deposits into and cash withdrawals from Deacon's bank in Rye. And this one dated four years ago, informing Mr Harker of a new go-between ... one Mr Garret. None of which,' concluded Rainham, moodily stuffing a couple of letters in his pocket and everything else back into the file, 'tells us who H. Fordyce actually *is*.'

'No,' agreed Adam, 'it doesn't. But I'll lay you five guineas that Galton can.'

They fell silent as Collins bustled in with the tea tray, followed a minute later by Mr Galton saying cheerfully, 'Apologies, gentlemen. Now ... where were we?'

Rainham pushed the file back across the desk.

'My colleague thinks you know who Fordyce is. Do you?'

'No. But his correspondence is collected from here by Arthur Garret. And I know whose pocket *he's* in.'

'Go on.'

'Garret is the local undertaker. He is also, thanks to the influence of one particularly prominent businessman, the district Coroner – a position of authority and standing in the community which he naturally wants to keep.'

'And one good turn deserves another?' suggested Adam.

'It does.' Galton nodded, smiled and poured himself a cup of tea.

Tired of this roundabout approach, Rainham snapped, 'And to whom does he owe these good turns?'

'The Blane family. In particular, Mr Blane the elder ... thanks to the influence he wields over most, if not all, of the committees of Romney Marsh.' The old man pulled a sheet of headed notepaper before him and began writing. He said, 'You won't find Garret today. It's Sir Edmund Morton's funeral. But when you do catch up with him, show him this.'

And he pushed the paper across for them to read.

If questioned, my advice is to tell the truth. They know.

A. Galton.

CHAPTER THIRTY-ONE

Since the day was well advanced and the ride back would take the best part of an hour, they abandoned any idea of calling on Sebastian. Instead, they discussed how best to use what they had learned and whether a visit to Mr Blane senior without first speaking to Mr Garret might be premature.

They arrived back at Dragon Hall to find a smart chaise in the yard and four perfectly matched horses in the stable.

'Goddard,' said Rainham immediately. 'I'd know those greys anywhere.' And to the head groom, 'How long has his lordship been here, Dawson?'

'Since early afternoon, my lord.'

'And has he brought anyone with him?'

'No, sir.'

Rainham nodded and, as he and Adam walked towards the house, said, 'He'll know everything by now – including your betrothal, I imagine. Better prepare yourself.'

'For what? He's hardly going to shoot me, is he?'

'No. If he wants you out of the picture, he'll find an assignment that will take you to the Outer Hebrides or some such. But my money is still on him being quietly pleased.'

'That's a relief. I might be quaking in my boots otherwise.'

Rainham laughed.

Inside the house, Coombes told them that they would find Lord Alveston and Miss Millie in the library and added that, being unable to put on a shirt as yet, Mr Guy had perforce to remain in his rooms.

'A welcome excuse, I daresay,' murmured Rainham. 'Doubtless he's already had a preliminary examination, coupled with the kind of dressing-down which has made him feel eight years old.'

'And which he thoroughly deserves but we've all been too soft-hearted to deliver,' responded Adam. 'Mr Coombes, please inform Miss Edgerton-Foxe and Lord Alveston that I'll join them directly I've washed and changed.'

'The same message from me,' added Rainham. And to Adam as they climbed the stairs, 'I wonder if Vincent has made any progress with Corbeau's despatch?'

'We'll soon find out,' shrugged Adam. 'Personally, I'm wondering who I'll be facing. Goddard, Section Chief or Uncle Alveston. Or both.'

In the library, his lordship frowned at the gentlemen's delay in presenting themselves.

Camilla, whose face had lit up at the news of Adam's return, said, 'Be reasonable, Uncle. They've ridden to Lydd and back so they'll be dusty and smelling of horse. Adam settles for being clean and tidy. But Rainham is obsessive about sartorial perfection.'

Lord Alveston merely grunted and said nothing. Camilla smoothed the folds of her skirt and watched the clock.

Either by luck or mutual consent, the gentlemen entered the library together. Rainham, extravagantly modish in sapphire watered silk and Adam, austerely dramatic in black but tactfully (or so Camilla thought) minus his sword.

'Gentlemen,' nodded her uncle.

'Sir,' they replied, politely and more or less in unison.

'Oh – sit down, the pair of you,' said Alveston in what they both recognised as Goddard mode despite the fact that he handed each of them a glass of wine. 'Millie has brought me up to date with progress so far, so you need not recapitulate. What news from today?'

With a minimum of explanation, the stolen pages from the Fordyce file were laid out before Alveston and Camilla. It took the earl less than a minute to evaluate the wealth of damning evidence contained in them and, looking up, he said irritably, 'You should have taken the entire file.'

'It crossed our minds,' sighed Rainham. 'But no one we saw had the authority to hand it over and forcible theft in front of witnesses is generally best avoided, I find.'

Alveston scowled at him. 'Very well. Who is H. Fordyce?'

'We can't be sure. But Fordyce's correspondence is collected from the solicitors' office and taken onward by the district coroner ... a fellow named Garret, who apparently owes his position to Mr Blane the elder.'

'Ah. No longer quite so tenuous and inconclusive now, is it, Uncle?' asked Camilla. And eagerly to Adam, 'Have you spoken to Mr Garret?'

'Not yet. His other role is that of undertaker and he was presiding at Sir Edmund Morton's funeral.'

'Oh. I'm sorry to hear that. The death was expected, of course but --'

'Yes, yes,' said Alveston impatiently. 'All very sad. But to resume ... the next step is obviously to learn where Garret takes the letters. And regardless of where that might be, I am sensing that you both feel a visit to Mr Blane is now justified?'

Rainham nodded. 'The connection may be coincidental or it may not. But we can't afford to ignore anything. Adam?'

'I agree. But not *just* Mr Blane. If he's at the heart of this business, it's possible the elder grandson is in it with him. Tomorrow is Sunday so the bank will be closed and, after church, all the Blane men are likely to be at home.'

'As will Coroner Garret,' Rainham pointed out. 'Him first, don't you think?'

Alveston nodded but before he could speak, Adam said abruptly, 'You should come with us, my lord ... to lend an aura of authority.'

'An excellent point,' observed Rainham, crossing to refill his glass. 'And prior to that, we might also have another word or two with Erasmus. A hint about our interest in the Blanes might encourage the spirit of cooperation.'

'Do it now, Rainham,' ordered Alveston just as the other man's fingers closed on the decanter. 'I'd like to meet him myself and will join you when I've had a word with Brandon. Camilla ... I'm sure you also can occupy yourself elsewhere for a while.'

'I *can*. But I don't see why I *should*,' she objected. 'If this is about --'

'What it may be about is not your concern. Rainham – take her away, please.'

Sending her what he hoped was a confident smile, Adam watched Rainham lead her gently but firmly from the room. Then, turning to the earl, he said, 'I had every intention of asking, if not for your permission then at least for your *acceptance* of my suit, sir.'

'Did you indeed?'

'Yes. But I didn't take it for granted that you would give it.'

'Well, that's something, I suppose.' Alveston eyed him enigmatically. 'I don't need to ask about your background and family connections. I learned all that before I recruited you to the Section. Your lineage, though not of the highest rank, is impeccable ... but you have only a younger son's portion. Correct?'

'Yes, my lord. But I plan to --'

'Open a *Salle d'Armes*. Yes, I recall. And there is no reason why you should not do so and make a success of it. But as a married man, what you can*not* do is ... live over the shop, as it were. Have you thought about that?'

Adam *had* thought of it and could see only one way around the problem, at least to begin with. He would have to accept help from Max; help that would be offered even before he asked for it. He said stiffly, 'My brother will help.'

'I can see,' remarked Alveston with arid amusement, 'that the prospect of that doesn't appeal. Tell me, Brandon ... has my niece mentioned her dowry at all?'

'No – and I haven't asked. I'm not interested in anything except --'

'Anything except Millie. Quite. But thanks to her mother's portion and her father's shrewd investments, she'll bring the man who marries her thirty thousand pounds.'

Adam winced inwardly and turned slightly pale. 'Ah. I see.'

'Yes. I thought you would.' The earl smiled suddenly. 'To your credit, you don't look as if you're inwardly cheering.'

'Did you expect me to be? Given that I'd prefer not to be indebted to my brother, I'm hardly likely to relish the prospect of living off my wife, am I?'

'No. But that is a battle you will have to fight with Millie. And I'm guessing you know her well enough by now not to assume you'll win. However ... tell me why I should give the two of you my blessing.'

This was unexpected but Adam wasn't sure he dared trust it. With all the natural awkwardness of a man with no alternative but to reveal his innermost feelings to another man, he said, 'I love her. Very much. And – incredible as it seems – she says that she loves me. That's it, really.'

'And a great deal more than I'd have dared hope for a couple of months ago when it seemed that she was going to let Staplehurst's perfidy blight the rest of her life. Has she told you about him? About what caused her to break the betrothal?'

'Yes. Not all of it, perhaps – but enough.'

Taking in the suddenly hard look in the younger man's face, Alveston nodded.

'Just so. I was abroad during their brief courtship so the rumours didn't reach me until I returned, barely in time for the wedding. And by then, Millie had given him his marching orders. But instead of being furious, she withdrew into a shell and stayed there ... until now, with you.' He rose, crossed to where Adam stood and held out his hand. 'So marry Millie with my good wishes. But don't disappoint me ... or her.'

'I won't, sir.' Thrown completely off-balance, Adam gripped the offered hand and smiled for the first time. 'You have my word.'

'Good. And now you'd better open the door – before her ear becomes numb from being pressed against it.'

Adam laughed, did as he'd been told ... and caught his love when she all but fell through it. He said, 'Did you manage to hear all that?'

'Enough,' she agreed, clinging to his arm and looking radiant rather than embarrassed. Then, releasing him in favour of hugging Alveston, she whispered, 'Be happy for me, Uncle Hugh. He's a good man. Honest, honourable and good.'

'And not too hard on the eye either?' he teased. Then, less flippantly, 'I know he's a good man, Millie. If I didn't, I'd be showing him the door – regardless. And now, I believe I will join Rainham and make the acquaintance of this fellow Erasmus. Where will I find them?'

'In the visitors' parlour on the ground floor. Coombes will show you.'

He nodded, tapped her cheek with his finger and stepped away from her. And very softly as he passed Adam, he said, 'Do I need to tell you to behave yourself?'

'No, sir. You don't.'

'Excellent.' And he was gone.

As soon as the door closed behind him, Camilla flung herself into Adam's arms and raised her face to his. For a handful of seconds, the kiss was slow and sweet before becoming increasingly heated. But when the explosion of passion threatened to get out of control, Adam drew her down beside him on a sofa and held her close against him, his lips resting on her hair. Eventually she said vaguely, 'I didn't really hear very much. What else did Uncle say?'

'He has understandable concerns about how I will support you.' Adam hesitated and then added reluctantly, 'And he took the ground from beneath my feet by breaking the news about your dowry.'

She looked up at him. 'That worries you? Why?'

'Do you really need to ask?'

'No. I suppose not.' She settled back comfortably against his shoulder. 'I won't start an argument about misplaced male pride. But --'

'You mean, you won't start one *now*.'

'No.' There was a smile in her voice and her fingers found and twined with his. 'I won't. I'll just say that we can work it out because we'll discuss it and *listen* to each other's point of view. And that being so, there's nothing we can't resolve. Ever.'

Adam's arm tightened about her and he said, 'I knew there was a reason I love you.'

She laughed. 'And I thought it was all purely physical.'

'Oh, it's that as well. Very much that as well.'

They fell silent for a while, both of them content simply to be together. But after a time, Adam sighed and said, 'Do you think Guy ought to be warned that current suspicion is pointing towards the Blane family?'

'Probably. He calls Mark and Peter friends, after all, so the betrayal will hurt.'

He rose and pulled her to her feet. 'Now, then. Let's get it over with.'

They entered Guy's room hand in hand and found him sitting by the window, wrapped in a chamber robe and looking bored.

'What did Uncle Hugh have to say to you?' asked Camilla, taking the chair opposite his. 'Rather a lot, I imagine.'

'Lord, yes. He asked me all the same questions you'd already asked,' said Guy, waving a hand in Adam's direction. 'Then he called me a bloody idiot, said I'd deserved everything I got and was lucky it hadn't been worse – only in a lot more words.'

'Nothing you didn't deserve, then,' murmured Adam.

To his surprise, the young man grinned. 'No. To be honest, I'd been counting myself lucky that *you* hadn't said it. I've an idea that your dressing-down might have been even more humiliating.'

'But briefer,' remarked Camilla. 'Adam doesn't waste words.'

'If you mean I don't use ten when one will do, I admit it.' The slate-blue gaze returned to Guy. 'This afternoon, Rainham and I paid a visit to the lawyers' office in Lydd where you took that letter. Mr Harker wasn't there but we spoke to an elderly man I took to be the senior clerk. He was very helpful.'

Guy frowned slightly. 'Go on.'

'He showed us a file that he should not have done containing the records of one H. Fordyce which clearly indicate the business of smuggling. And he told us that letters like the one you delivered are taken to what we believe to be their final destination by a fellow named Garret. Mr Garret is the district Coroner ... and he owes his position to old Mr Blane.'

'So?' shrugged Guy. And then, as the penny dropped, 'Oh. You think H. Fordyce is Grandpa Blane? Seriously? No. That can't be right.'

'It might be,' offered Camilla gently. 'We don't know. But Uncle Hugh and Rainham and Adam are going to visit the Blanes tomorrow in the hope of finding out one way or the other.' She hesitated briefly. 'Guy … I know Mark and Peter are friends of yours but --'

'Mark is a friend,' he interrupted. 'Peter is an idiot. If *he* had anything to do with any of this, he'd have been shooting his mouth off in all directions and somebody would have shut it for him before now. But Mark? No. I'll believe it when you have proof. But not until then.'

* * *

Alveston and Rainham re-joined the newly-betrothed pair an hour before dinner. Not bothering to rise from Camilla's side, Adam said, 'And how *is* Erasmus today? Happy to meet you, my lord?'

'Not noticeably.' Leaving Rainham to pour wine, the earl chose a chair near the hearth and frowned slightly. 'Although he tried not to show it, there were definitely signs of alarm when Rainham mentioned the solicitor, the coroner and our intention to visit the Blanes tomorrow. But he refuses either to confirm or add anything to what he's already said – which hasn't really been very much.'

'To be fair, he told us where to look for Guy,' objected Camilla. 'But for that, we might still be hunting for him and Guy would be even less well than he is.'

'And that is the only thing in his favour,' returned Rainham, handing round glasses of Chambertin. 'I'd be happier descending on the Blanes with better ammunition than is at our disposal – but I'm resigned to doing the best we can with what we have.'

'That decision has already been made and doesn't require further discussion,' said Alveston. 'That being so, I imagine you all want to hear about the Frenchman's report.'

'We're allowed to know, are we?' asked Rainham.

'Some of it, yes.'

'After all the work Adam and Rainham put in to get it and the hours I spent creating a nonsense version which, in the end, we didn't need,' muttered Camilla, 'I should think we're entitled to know *all* of it.'

'She has a point,' agreed Adam mildly.

Alveston eyed all three of them with faint exasperation. He said, 'Although Vincent broke the cypher fairly quickly, he was still in the process of decoding the last page of the report when I left London. Consequently, I don't yet know the entire contents – but what I *do* know is both important and classified.'

'He's saying he doesn't trust us,' remarked Rainham. 'That's just insulting.'

'I'm not saying any such thing,' snapped the earl. 'I am merely pointing out that there is a protocol to be observed here. However ... much of what Vincent has deciphered so far concerns one Edward Bancroft, a Connecticut doctor. He received his medical training in England and frequently travels here. Recently, he has been serving on the American Commission in Paris alongside Mr Benjamin Franklin with whom he has formed a friendship. But according to Corbeau's despatch, he is currently under suspicion of being an agent in the pay of the British government.'

'And *is* he?' asked Rainham.

'Yes.'

'Why?'

'I believe he claims to be opposed to Colonial independence. But whatever his reasons, a great many extremely useful documents have made their way into our hands through his agency over the last couple of years. For example, we knew every move Franklin made in his efforts to forge an alliance with France and had high hopes that knowledge would help us prevent it happening.'

'But it didn't,' said Camilla.

'Regrettably, no,' agreed Alveston. 'But to return to the matter of our agent, the Intelligence Service is naturally averse to losing such a valuable operative and, thanks to the despatch you got hold of, there may yet be time to make him safe.'

'How?' asked Rainham. 'By standing up and shouting, *"He's not one of ours!"*'

Camilla laughed, Adam grinned and Alveston said, 'Very funny. No. Most likely by arresting him on suspicion of spying for the Colonials – or some such ruse, none of which lies within M Section's scope.'

'One would think the gentleman is already beyond saving,' observed Adam. 'Won't Franklin have him arrested?'

'Perhaps, perhaps not. Franklin likes the man and may choose to trust him. For the rest, Vincent had reached mention of measures being taken to prevent our ships landing in the Chesapeake Bay area. If we're lucky, it might also discuss British activity in the region and tell us what General Washington may be doing to counter it. But, at this stage, that is pure speculation on my part and may be completely wrong. It is also the sum of what I am prepared to say on the matter – apart from the fact that the three of you have earned the thanks of a grateful government.'

CHAPTER THIRTY-TWO

Having calculated that families everywhere would be home from church by noon, the three gentlemen left Dragon Hall an hour or so earlier to ride the five miles to Lydd.

'What do we know about Mr Garret?' asked Alveston.

'Aside from his profession and his civic role?' said Rainham. 'Nothing. So far as we're aware, his only role is delivering the Fordyce letters.'

'Then let us hope he is more cooperative than Erasmus.'

'I suspect he may be,' offered Adam. 'If he's merely a go-between with no idea what is *in* the letters, he has little reason not to answer our questions. But if he's reluctant, there is always Galton's helpful note.'

Once in Lydd, discovering Coroner Garret's address was easily done and they were soon dismounting in front of a solid and unpretentious house in the centre of town. The door was answered by a trim housemaid who, after one glance at the Earl of Alveston's card, became extremely flustered but managed to show them into a small parlour before fleeing to summon her master.

Mr Garret, a bulky gentleman on the shady side of fifty, entered the room wearing an expression of concerned bafflement. 'Gentlemen?'

The earl held out his hand and received a brief, firm clasp in response.

'Thank you for seeing us, sir. I am Alveston and my companions are Viscount Rainham and Mr Brandon. Our apologies for disturbing you on the Sabbath ... but we are hoping you may be able shed light on something for us.'

'Well, I can't imagine what that might be, my lord, but I'll help if I can.'

'Thank you. I ought perhaps to mention that we are here in an official rather than a private capacity and that our enquiries pertain to something of major importance – though it may not seem so to you.'

'I take the point, my lord. What do you want to know?'

'We have been informed that, when required, you collect letters from Meredith, Burridge & Harker for delivery to one of their clients. Is that correct?'

The Coroner hesitated, looking uneasy. Finally, he said, 'Yes. What of it?'

'To whom do you deliver them?'

Uneasiness became alarm.

'I'm sorry, my lord, but telling you that would mean breaking my word.'

'I suspected that it might. But I'm afraid that, on this occasion, you must do so.'

'It isn't as simple as that.'

'Yes,' said Alveston flatly, 'it is. Adam ... the note, if you please.'

Drawing the paper from his pocket, Adam held it out to Garret. 'It's for you.'

'Me? How can --?' The rest of the question died unspoken when he unfolded the page and read the few words on it. 'Oh.'

'Indeed,' agreed Alveston. 'Shall we try again? To whom do you deliver the letters?'

'To ... to Henderson, the head gardener at ... at Blane House,' he muttered wretchedly. 'And that's as much as I know – as much as I've ever *wanted* to know.'

'Very wise. Thank you, Mr Garret. We need take up no more of your time.'

Garret gaped at him. 'That's *it*?'

'It is – and not too painful, I hope. May I suggest you speak of this to no one?'

'You don't need to tell me that. Will ... will you keep my name out of it?'

'If at all possible – though I cannot guarantee it.' Alveston smiled thinly. 'Look on the bright side, Mr Garret. Had you refused to help me, the result would have been a less cordial interview at Dover Castle.'

* * *

Outside and once more back in the saddle, Rainham said, 'Well, that's the extra bit of confirmation we needed. But the gardener? *Really*?'

'Yes. Ridiculous as it may sound, he wouldn't be such a bad choice. There's nothing odd about someone taking a stroll in the garden and perhaps exchanging a word or two with the gardener.' Alveston thought about it. 'I wonder if he's working today?'

'It's Sunday,' Adam reminded him.

'Ah yes. Pity. Now ... where is the Blane house?'

'Near the church,' said Rainham. 'This way.'

They navigated the streets in silence for a few moments until Alveston said, 'Mr Blane and his family are unlikely to take this well – so be careful what you say until we get some idea of what we're dealing with. Knowing that the Fordyce letters go to one of them strengthens our position but doesn't actually prove much. So we'll have no accusation and no confrontations, gentlemen. If we are barking up completely the wrong tree, it ought to become evident fairly quickly. And if we're not, we keep the heavy artillery in reserve until we need it. Clear?'

'Perfectly,' said Adam.

'You didn't bring us to talk,' responded Rainham dryly. 'Our role is simply to add silent gravitas to the proceedings – which I think we do rather well.' He drew his horse to a halt. 'That's the house – the one with the ugly stone vultures either side of the door.'

'Stables?' asked Adam.

'Presumably at the back.'

'Leave the horses here, tied to the railing,' said Alveston. 'If someone wants them moved, they can send a groom.'

This time the door was opened by an elderly butler who admitted them with a bow, placed the earl's card on a salver, saying, 'And your companions, my lord?'

'Viscount Rainham and Mr Brandon.'

'Very good, my lord. I will tell Mr Blane that you are here and ask if he can receive you.'

'You may also tell him that our business is a matter of some urgency but that it need not take long.'

The butler bowed again and set off up the stairs at a pace less sedate than funereal and eventually disappeared from sight. Then, reappearing, he made his way back down as slowly as he'd gone up and, gaining the hall, said, 'Mr Blane will see you now, my lords, sir. Please follow me.'

'Shall we give him a head start?' murmured Rainham.

Adam smiled but shook his head. 'Silent gravitas, remember?'

They were finally shown into a pleasant drawing-room overlooking the street. In it were four people; Mark and Peter Blane, their mother and a gentleman much of an age with the butler but apparently somewhat more spry. Crossing to them, hand outstretched, he said, 'I am Frederick Blane, gentlemen. I don't know what brings you here but if it is of a confidential nature or a matter of business, we can discuss it in my study away from my family.'

'That will not be necessary,' said Alveston, accepting the proffered hand and introducing himself. 'I believe your daughter-in-law and grandsons are already slightly acquainted with Lord Rainham and Mr Brandon.'

Adam and Rainham inclined their heads politely, Mark Blane and his mother did the same. Peter threw himself into a chair and drawled, 'We've met. But I can't say it was a pleasure.'

'Peter – *please*!' whispered his mother with an agonised glance at the visitors.

'That's enough from you, young man,' said his grandfather curtly. And to Alveston, 'Pardon me, my lord ... but you'll be the uncle of Guy Edgerton-Foxe and his sister?'

'I am.'

'I was glad to hear that the young man is back, safe and sound. Terrible business – shocking, in fact.' He indicated that his guests might be seated and looked a little surprised when all of them remained standing. 'Is that what brings you to the Marsh?'

'In part – but not entirely.' Alveston allowed a small pause to develop and then said, 'I will be frank with you, Mr Blane. There are concerns within the government about certain activities in this area; activities which Viscount Rainham and Mr Brandon have been looking into on my behalf for some weeks. Their findings thus far suggest that an official presence – namely, my own – would be advisable.'

Mr Blane's brows drew together.

'Are you *sure* we shouldn't be talking in private, my lord?'

'Perfectly sure. We think it possible that either you or one of your grandsons can help clear up a small mystery for us.'

'But my daughter-in-law needn't stay?'

'Not if she prefers not to.'

'Well then – off you go, Laura. Hester must be somewhere about and would doubtless be glad of your company, my dear.'

She rose instantly, setting her embroidery aside. And with a nervous jerk of a curtsy and murmuring, 'Thank you, Papa-in-law,' she made her escape.

'Now,' said Mr Blane. 'Let's have the gloves off, shall we? What's all this about?'

'I will come to that in a moment,' replied Alveston. 'First, I would like to talk about letters from Meredith, Burridge & Harker which are being delivered to your gardener.'

'Solicitors' letters for *Henderson*?' Mark Blane entered the conversation for the first time. 'That isn't possible. How could it be?'

'Indeed, sir. How could it? And yet it is. So naturally we're wondering on whose behalf Henderson takes receipt of this correspondence.'

'Not mine,' said Mark frigidly. 'Peter?'

'Don't be an ass. Who would *I* be getting secret letters from?'

'Exactly my question,' said Alveston gently. 'Or was that meant to be a "no"?'

'Of course it was a bloody no!'

'Moderate your language, boy,' snapped his grandfather. 'In fact, if you can't mind your manners, we can do without you altogether.'

'Suits me well enough,' muttered Peter, coming to his feet. 'I'll join Mama.'

'In a moment.' The slightest movement of the earl's head had Adam taking the couple of steps that would place him in front of the door. Meanwhile the cool grey gaze settled on Mr Blane senior. 'And you, sir? Might these letters be for you?'

'No. I've never had any dealings with with Meredith, Burridge & Harker. All our family and banking business is handled by Hartley, Hartley & Witherspoon in Tenterden.'

'All of it?'

'Yes. I just said so, didn't I?' Blane hauled in a calming breath and said, 'I've no wish to be as rude as my grandson, my lord ... but where is this going?'

Alveston took his time about answering. But finally he said coldly, 'It is going to smuggling, Mr Blane. And more to the point, to espionage.'

'*What*?'

'Yes. I'm afraid so.'

'Are you – are you accusing me or one of my grandsons of *spying*?'

'No. At present, I am merely clarifying the gravity of these enquiries. Are you acquainted with a man named Wilson?'

Mark and his grandfather exchanged startled glances. Peter opened his mouth to speak but for once thought better of it.

'He has been using the given name Erasmus,' continued the earl inexorably, 'though I doubt it is his true one.'

It was several moments before Mr Blane replied but finally he said slowly, 'My private secretary is Ernest Wilson. But I can't believe he is the man you're talking about. Wilson is a common enough name, after all.'

'True. And the matter may easily be resolved. Could you send for him, sir?'

'Now?' And when Alveston nodded, 'No. He's been absent these last few days. There was a note – something about a family crisis.'

'Lawyer Harker has one of those, too,' murmured Rainham. 'Perhaps there's an epidemic?'

'Indeed,' said Alveston with a quelling glance in his lordship's direction. 'Putting Mr Wilson aside for a moment, Mr Blane, perhaps you might tell me if the name Fordyce means anything to you.'

Uneven colour mottled the elderly gentleman's face and Mark was abruptly at his side, saying urgently, 'Sit down, Grandfather. There's no connection – merely coincidence.'

'What is?' asked the earl.

'Fordyce was my – my wife's maiden name,' said Blane faintly.

During the acute silence that followed this, Adam felt a cold sense of something like dread slither down his spine. He ignored it and concentrated on what Alveston was saying.

'I see. That is ... unexpected. And does Mrs Blane have any relatives?'

'Her younger brother is a vicar in Hastings,' replied Mark, clearly deciding to take charge. 'May we ask what interest the name has for you?'

'It is the name on the account at Meredith, Burridge & Harker from which the mysterious letters are generated. It may, of course, be an alias. Perhaps Mrs Blane might be asked to join us – purely in order to settle the matter?'

'Now wait just a minute!' began Peter hotly – only to be overruled by his grandfather who said, 'Yes. Pull the bell, Mark. Ask Witney to send your grandmother to us.'

Mark did so, his expression thunderous. He said, 'This is quite iniquitous, my lord. My grandfather is not in good health and subjecting him to accusations such as --'

'Forgive me, sir – but I have yet to accuse anyone of anything. I apologise for unintentionally upsetting Mr Blane and can promise to deal gently with his wife. But the seeming links to this house cannot be ignored. A few minutes ago we heard that Mr Wilson was not at his desk due to a family crisis. That isn't true. He has been absent from it because he is under arrest.'

'For what?' demanded Mark sharply.

'A number of things. For example, were you aware that the smugglers in these parts call him Captain?'

Peter's jaw dropped. 'Stick-in-the-mud Ernie? Involved in the *Trade*? You're joking!'

'Far from it. Furthermore, mistakenly believing my nephew had learned this, it was Wilson who ordered the abduction. He has admitted it. Indeed, he could scarcely do otherwise since, on the night he was arrested, he had been agreeing to return Guy in exchange for letters brought from France by one Gaston Corbeau.'

'With whom was Wilson negotiating this deal?' asked Mark.

'With me,' said Rainham, lazily. 'We have Corbeau's despatch, in case you were wondering. It's being decoded in London as we speak.'

'Thank you, Rainham. If you will be so good, we'll avoid indirect accusations as well as the other kind.'

A tap at the door heralded the butler. He said, 'I'm sorry, Mr Blane, sir – but it seems Mrs Blane has gone out.'

'Out?' asked Blane blankly. 'Why would she go out? We were barely back from church.'

'And according to her maid, she drove off again almost directly. But Price is unclear as to *why* she did unless it was because of the note.'

'Note?' Adam's voice cracked like a whip. The premonition of a few moments ago resolved itself into writhing snakes of as yet nameless anxiety in his stomach. 'What note? From whom?'

'Price doesn't know, sir. But she thinks the most likely explanation is that Mrs Blane has merely been summoned by a friend ...'

Adam had stopped listening. He thought, *Fordyce. Hester. H. Fordyce. It's her, isn't it? What if ... what if ...* But the thought remained incomplete, obliterated by a furious, mind-blistering curse that fortunately remained silent. Wheeling on his heel, he shoved the butler out of his way whilst shouting over his shoulder, 'She's going to Dragon Hall. To Camilla.'

And then he was gone, racing down the stairs and out of the house as if the hounds of hell were snapping at his heels.

* * *

At Dragon Hall, Camilla whiled away the gentlemen's absence writing a long overdue letter to her grandmother and keeping her brother company. Throughout it all, she wondered if the villain of the piece really *could* turn out to be either Mark Blane or his grandfather. In many ways, it all seemed ridiculously unlikely ...

but in others, it clearly merited investigation. She supposed that if it turned out to be a red herring, Adam and the others would be back quite quickly. If they weren't, it probably indicated that the reverse was true.

At just before one and still with no sign of them, she was about to order a light luncheon when Coombes informed her that Mrs Blane had called.

Camilla's brows rose. 'Mrs Blane? Here? On her own? On a *Sunday*?'

'Yes, Miss Millie.' He hesitated. 'I may be mistaken ... but she seems a trifle agitated.'

'Does she? Then I suppose you'd better show her up.'

Left alone for a moment, she frowned, trying to work out what might be going on. Mrs Blane shouldn't be here. She should be at home facing Uncle Hugh, Adam and Rainham with the rest of her family. So why wasn't she?

As ever, the elderly lady entered the drawing-room with the aid of her cane and, pausing inside the door as Coombes closed it behind her, said, 'Good afternoon, Millie. I hope I'm not disturbing you?'

'Not at all, ma'am. You are always welcome. Please take a seat and tell me what I may do for you. Shall I ring for tea?'

'No, no. I shan't stay so there's no need for that.' Mrs Blane chose a tall-backed chair and sat, placing the pocket which had been hanging from her wrist in her lap and propping her cane against the table beside her. 'How is your brother today?'

'Much improved, thank you. His cough is almost gone but the pain in his damaged ribs is still making dressing properly a too-painful process – much to his disgust.'

'Ah. Impatient to be up, is he? Well, that's young men for you.'

'Indeed,' nodded Camilla. And waited.

'I suppose having the other gentlemen here and not being able to get out and about with them doesn't help. Or are they upstairs keeping him company over a hand of cards?'

Not allowing her expression to change by a hairsbreadth, Camilla thought, *Does she* really *not know where they are? Surely she must do. Even if she left home before they arrived, she'd have met them on the road, wouldn't she? But neither explains why she's here. And if she* doesn't *know, I'm not about to tell her.*

'No – though I'm sure that is what Guy would prefer. But as it happens, our uncle arrived unexpectedly yesterday and --'

'The earl?' asked Mrs Blane rather too sharply.

'Yes.' Continuing to look the old lady in the eye, Camilla calmly lied. 'This morning they all rode off to call on Lord Wingham – some unpleasantness to do with the death of the late viscount's valet, I believe. You may perhaps have heard about it.'

'Not a word. Think it's murder, do they?'

'Apparently the possibility can't be discounted,' shrugged Camilla. 'Now, ma'am ... I'm sure you haven't given up part of the one day each week when you have your grandsons' company at home. So what brings you here?'

'A matter I'd much rather not have had to raise. But needs must, as they say.'

'And this matter is what?'

'Putting it bluntly, my dear, thanks to those meddlesome young men of yours – you've got a couple of things that belong to me.'

Warning bells sent prickles of alarm right down to Camilla's fingertips. But she merely shook her head slightly and said, 'I do? I wasn't aware of it.'

'I think you were. And if you'd gone with Reed when I sent him to fetch you, it would be water under the bridge by now. But that's neither here nor there, is it? All that matters is that you give them back without any fuss. Now.'

'You'll need to be more specific, ma'am. Precisely what is it you're asking for?'

Mrs Blane's face lost its habitual comfortable, motherly expression and grew surprisingly hard. She said, 'Don't play games, Miss.'

'I might say the same to you. What do you want?'

'Ernest Wilson, for a start. You'll know him as Erasmus. But since he ain't at Dover with the others, I reckon he must be somewhere in this house.'

'Then you reckon wrongly. And what is this man to you?'

'An employee who has likely come to the end of his usefulness.'

'Really? In that case, you can't have any great need of him, can you?'

'That's my business – not yours.'

'You made it my business when you came to my home making demands. However ... what is the other thing?'

'Raven's despatch. And don't pretend you don't know what *that* is. You've had it all along, haven't you? You or your fancy men.'

In a sense, Camilla found it heartening that the old lady was descending into rudeness. It suggested that she was less sure of herself than she wanted to appear. In fact, was it possible she might even be *frightened*? And if so, why?

Deciding to try buying time by continuing to cloud the issue, she said coolly, 'If by 'fancy men' you mean Viscount Rainham and Mr Brandon, you insult them as grossly as you do me. Indeed, Mrs Blane, I think it would be best if you took your leave.'

'Yes. I daresay you do. But I'm not going without Raven's letter. Get it.'

'You are clearly suffering from delusions, ma'am. I know of no one called Raven.'

'Don't lie to me – it won't wash. Just get me his *letter*!' Mrs Blane came smartly to her feet without the aid of her cane, one hand reaching into the pocket. 'Don't you understand, you stupid girl? *I have to have it!*'

Camilla also rose, but cautiously so as not to exacerbate the situation.

'I understand that you *believe* you do. But really, I can't give you what I don't--' She stopped abruptly as Mrs Blane's hand left the pocket to point a small, brass-mounted pistol directly at her. Drawing a harsh breath, Camilla said calmly, 'I don't know what you think to achieve by threatening me but --'

'I'll not say it again. I want Raven's letter. I'll shoot you if I have to.'

'No, you won't. You're bluffing.'

'Don't count on it. And don't be fooled by this only being a muff pistol. It's loaded and I know how to use it.'

'That's all very well. But if you fire, my entire household will come running.'

'That won't do *you* much good, will it?'

'Nor you either. How will shooting me give you what you want?'

For the first time, Mrs Blane looked uncertain. Then she said, 'Do you think I'd be doing this if I'd any choice? There's powerful men who want that despatch – and I *know* you have it.' Her fingers tightened on the pistol. 'You've got till I count to five. One … two …'

* * *

His chest roiling with the kind of fear he'd never before experienced, Adam rode hell for leather out of Lydd, leaving drivers and pedestrians shaking their fists in his wake. Once the town was behind them, he and Hector flew along the main road to the point where it intersected with the one to Brenzett, then set off cross-country. He knew the drainage ditches made it a risk but it was one he had to take. Something deep inside him was insisting there was no time to waste. He had no idea what he thought was going to happen to Camilla – only that she was in trouble and he had to get to her.

Later he would realise that he'd been exceptionally lucky. Hector had sailed over the only ditch that lay in their path as if it didn't exist. The turnings to Old and New Romney fell away behind them. Up ahead, he could see the tower of St Mary's church and, seconds later, he and Hector were swerving into the avenue leading to Dragon Hall.

By the time Adam flung himself from the saddle, both he and Hector were sweating – the horse from exertion and he himself mostly from renewed terror brought about by the sight of a smart, two-wheeled carriage. Shouting for Dawson to tend Hector but not waiting for him to appear, Adam raced into the house and, finding Thomas in the hall, said breathlessly, 'Where are they?'

'Drawing-room, sir. What --?'

'Send Harry up.' He was already running lightly up the stairs. 'He's to wait until I call.'

Moving silently along the upper hall until he stood outside the drawing-room door, he hesitated for a moment, unsure what he'd find inside. It was quiet so he tried telling himself he was over-reacting. It didn't work. Every instinct he had was screaming that Mrs Blane wouldn't have come here unless she was desperate … which meant he had to go into that room without provoking anything.

He hauled in a long, calming breath and put his hand on the latch. Then he opened the door an inch or two but checked on the threshold to say, as if over his shoulder, 'No hurry, Thomas. It can wait until the others are back.'

And summoning what he hoped was a convincing smile, he went in.

CHAPTER THIRTY-THREE

The scene in front of him was as motionless as a tableau and Adam froze along with it.

Camilla stood as if caught in some persuasive gesture, her face turned towards him with an expression of mingled relief and warning. And seven or eight feet from her, Hester Blane was pointing a small flintlock directly at her heart – although her head had jerked sharply in his own direction the instant he'd stepped into the room.

Slowly and quietly, leaving the door slightly ajar behind him, Adam took a small step in Camilla's direction, saying cheerfully, 'Why, Mrs Blane – here you are! When I left, your family was in a state of mild uproar, wondering where you'd got to.'

The tableau dissolved but not in the way he'd hoped. Shock quivered through the old lady but the pistol remained trained on Camilla. Somehow, he had to change that. It might be a ladies' toy but it was as potentially lethal as any of its larger brethren.

Mrs Blane said blankly, 'You've been at my home?'

'Yes. Lords Alveston and Rainham are probably still there.' He risked another step, saying reasonably, 'Why don't you put the pistol down, ma'am? Or give it to me? Whatever the problem is, I'm sure we can resolve it without anyone getting hurt.'

'She wants a letter from someone named Raven,' said Camilla remotely, 'and she is convinced that I have it. I can't persuade her otherwise – hence the gun.'

'Be quiet,' snapped Mrs Blane. And to Adam as he edged a fraction closer to, and slightly ahead of, Camilla, 'Stay where you are. What were you doing with my husband?'

'Talking. What else would we have been doing?'

'About what?'

'Put the pistol down and I'll tell you. You don't need it ... and I don't believe you really want to use it, do you?'

'I'll put it down when I get Raven's letter. Where is it? And no more lying!'

There was one possible way around this and Adam was sure Camilla would have already thought of it. They could hand over the nonsense version of Corbeau's original and hope it passed muster. So he sighed and said, 'Very well. You win. But it's in the library, so Miss Edgerton-Foxe will have to fetch it.'

'Not her. *You* get it.'

'And leave you pointing a gun at her? No. *She* will go. And if you first give me the pistol, she will do it quietly and without alerting the household.' Still holding Mrs Blane's gaze, Adam risked another step. 'If you do that, you have a chance of leaving here both free and in possession of the despatch. What do you say?'

For the first time, he could see her thinking about it. One more step, perhaps two ... that was all he needed. Keeping his tone pleasant and holding out his hand for the pistol, he said, 'They're threatening you, aren't they – the people who want the despatch? Lord Alveston can protect you from them ... but only if no one gets hurt.'

She hesitated and Camilla said quickly, 'You have only one shot, ma'am. In the circumstances, using it would be stupid. Mr Brandon is right. Let me fetch the despatch so you can go home.'

The pistol wavered indecisively and, seeing it, Adam prepared to take those last two vital steps – only to stop dead when the muzzle swung round to point at him instead.

Good, he thought. *Keep focussing on me*.

And to make sure she would do so, he stepped towards her, hand still outstretched and saying her name.

It was unfortunate that his movement coincided with the sound of loud voices and booted feet running up the stairs. The pistol fired with a deafening crack ... and Adam stumbled awkwardly into Camilla.

The door flew open and Harry Finch catapulted into the room, Rainham and Alveston hard on his heels.

'What the *hell*?'

In a single glance, Rainham took in the still-smoking gun in Mrs Blane's hand; Camilla trying to make Adam sit down; and Adam himself, white with shock and clutching his left arm, blood pouring over his fingers, muttering, 'Meet H. Fordyce.'

Shouting for someone to fetch the brandy and leaving Alveston to take charge of the pistol, Rainham moved past Camilla to shove Adam into a chair saying, 'Letting yourself get shot by an old woman, Adam? You're never going to live it down.'

'Not if you have anything to do with it, you mean,' gasped Adam on a grunt of pain.

'It's not *funny*!' snapped Camilla, pushing back her hair with shaking hands and leaving a smear of blood across one cheek. 'He was protecting *me*, you idiot – and he might not have been shot at *all* if you hadn't come charging up here like a herd of damned elephants!' She swung away towards the huddle of servants in the doorway. 'Hot water, cloths, towels and bandages – *now*, please.'

'Mrs Poole is on her way to get them, Miss Millie,' said Coombes. 'Shall I send Thomas for the doctor?'

'Yes. Everyone else can go but wait here yourself, please.'

'Should we not perhaps get Mr Brandon to his bedchamber?'

'No, we shouldn't.' Adam was aware that he was beginning to feel rather odd. 'But if somebody could just --'

He stopped as Rainham put a tumbler of brandy in his good hand, saying tersely, 'Drink that – and don't argue. You look as if you're about to pass out.'

'I'll be fine,' he protested, but took a swallow of brandy anyway and felt the light-headedness ebb a little. 'Can somebody please get me out of this coat?'

'Finch and I will do it. But finish the brandy first.'

Adam drained the glass and let Camilla take it from him. Then, as Rainham and Finch began gently easing him out of the ruined coat, he said distantly, 'I think the bullet went straight through but ...maybe not.'

Mrs Poole bustled in with scissors and an armful of linen, followed by Thomas carrying a large bowl of hot water. Camilla nodded her thanks and sent them away, saying she could do what needed doing.

On the other side of the room, Mrs Blane had resumed her role as a little old lady and sat rocking to and fro, moaning disjointedly to herself; a muddled litany about having done her best and it being an accident and nobody believing her.

'Whether you are believed or not, madam, will depend upon what Mr Brandon and my niece have to say,' Alveston told her. 'But the one thing you may be *sure* of is that you will not be going home. Unless you give me chapter and verse on your fellow conspirators in espionage, you are unlikely to see Blane House ever again. Coombes ... I require a reliable maid and a bedchamber with a stout lock. Take Mrs Blane away and see to it.'

'Certainly, my lord. This way, madam.'

No sooner had the butler led the old lady away than Guy appeared in the doorway, still wrapped in his chamber-robe and with his hair all on end. He said, 'I heard - oh God! Has Adam been *shot?*'

'Yes.' Kneeling on the floor at Adam's side, Camilla had cut away the sleeve of his shirt and was attempting to clean the ugly and still copiously bleeding wound.

'By Mrs Blane,' supplied Rainham helpfully.

Guy gaped at him. 'Grandmama Blane shot him? *Seriously*?'

'With a muff pistol,' added Rainham, grinning.

'Stop it, the pair of you,' shouted Camilla. 'It's not a joke, damn you! A few seconds earlier, she'd been pointing the pistol at me. So if Adam hadn't distracted her when he did, *I'd* be the one with a bullet in me.'

'Don't, sweetheart,' said Adam, attempting a smile. 'Let them have their fun. My brothers would be just as bad. Worse, probably.' Wincing as she touched a tender spot and looking past her to his tormentors, he added, 'Just so you know, bullets hurt every bit as much no matter what they're fired from. Or that's how it feels.' He peered down at his arm, '*Has* it gone through? I can't see.'

'Yes, it has,' she said unsteadily, busy applying pressure to both entry and exit wounds with warm, damp cloths. 'But you'll still need Doctor Quinn.'

'Not if it's just a flesh wound. I --'

'You'll let him look at it anyway.'

'She's right,' said Rainham, no longer with any hint of humour. 'If the bullet nicked the bone, there could be splinters so

Quinn will have to do a bit of ... poking about. And after that, you'll probably need stitches.'

'Is that supposed to comfort me?' grunted Adam.

Camilla discovered that she'd had enough. Placing Adam's good hand where hers had been to hold the cloths in place, she stood up and said, 'Uncle Hugh, Guy, Rainham and whoever is still clustered just outside the door ... will you all please just go *away*! I don't need any of you – and Adam certainly doesn't. So go!'

Alveston sauntered over and said quietly, 'You earned your spurs today, Adam. Well done. Back upstairs please, Guy. If you can manage a coat this evening – even if it's not one of your own – you can join us for dinner. And Rainham, it's Lydd again for you.'

'Yes. I was afraid it might be. You want me to break the bad news.'

'Yes. Tell the family that Mrs Blane is under arrest for shooting Adam – nothing more than that at this stage. And now, let us all give Adam a few minutes peace and allow Millie to continue with her ministrations.'

When the room was finally quiet and they were alone, Adam said, 'It's all right, you know. I'm going to be fine.'

'I know. I know you are.' She sank down at his side again and dashed the back of one wrist over her eyes. 'But you could have been *killed*. It – it's a miracle you weren't. The bullet could have – it could have --'

'But it didn't.' He touched her wet cheek with his fingers. 'Don't cry. It's almost worse than being shot.' And when she gave a watery chuckle, 'That's better. And might we also *not* think about what *might* have happened? That road leads to a particularly bad place for me. The one where I didn't get here in time.'

Pressing her lips together, Camilla nodded, took a bracing breath and resumed her work. The bleeding seemed finally to be slowing a bit. 'How did you guess she'd come here?'

'The Blane men had no idea what we were talking about. She wasn't in the house but had gone off to no one knew where in response to a note. And somewhere along the way, I realised that she was H. Fordyce. Hester Fordyce – or was before she married. Such a simple thing, really.' He paused. 'But that wasn't what sent me racing back here.'

'No? What then?'

'There was … I had a terrifying premonition. I can't describe it really. I just knew in every muscle and bone that I had to get to you. So I left Alveston and Rainham to it, fled more or less without a word and galloped here … *ventre à terre*, as Emile-Henri would say.'

'And did what you once told me you'd do but which I hoped you'd never have to,' she mumbled, shaking her head. 'I'd rather she had shot *me*.'

'Thank you – but I wouldn't. Firstly, if either of us has to acquire a scar, I'd prefer it to be me. Secondly, failing you would have hurt more than a bullet. And thirdly, Rainham wouldn't have been teasing me about being shot with a muff pistol. He'd be damning me for not protecting you.'

'Rainham,' said Camilla crossly, 'was lucky I was too busy to hit him. But he'd better take care or I still might. Guy, too. Be still now. The bleeding hasn't stopped but it's lessened enough for me to apply Mrs Poole's salve and bandage you up. Then I shall pour you another glass of brandy and after that --'

'After that I'll probably need to sleep it off.'

'Yes.' She sent him a wide, if fleeting, smile. 'That's the whole idea.'

* * *

When she'd seen Adam off to bed with Finch on hand to help him out of his clothes, Camilla washed her face and hands, changed into a clean gown and went to find her uncle.

He was in the library writing one of several letters but he laid down the pen when he saw her and said, 'How is the patient?'

'Sleeping, I hope. Martha tells me Mrs Blane is locked in the red room. How long are we supposed to keep her there?'

'As long as it takes me to prise everything she knows about French spies and their English helpers out of her head.'

'Ought you not to send her to Intelligence in London?'

'Yes, but I've sent an express to Sir Oswald, explaining that I believe I can move things forward more quickly *in situ* and offering him Erasmus – *Ernest* Wilson as an interim measure.' He sighed and rubbed the bridge of his nose. 'There's unlikely to be any speedy, clear-cut end to this, Millie. The arrests of Hester Blane and Wilson are a big step towards disabling the smuggling ring hereabouts but they are merely the first rung on the espionage ladder. And every rung thereafter will be just as hard to identify as this one was. But while France is still supporting the Colonies against us, finding out just how high the ladder goes is critical.'

'A lot of this is beyond the scope of your authority, isn't it?'

'There's always some leeway.' He shrugged and smiled at her. 'Let us speak of pleasanter things. Have you and Adam decided about your wedding yet?'

'Yes. In London and as soon as possible ... but with banns to give Adam's family plenty of time to arrive. I've written to Grandmama, sending her the glad tidings but haven't had a reply as yet.'

Lord Alveston nodded. 'Adam can stay in Berkeley Square, if he wishes – and his family as well once they arrive in town.'

'Thank you. I'm sure they'll appreciate it.'

'Am I to have the pleasure of hosting your wedding breakfast?'

'If you please,' said Camilla primly. 'I was hoping you might offer.'

He laughed. 'Minx. Does Adam know what a little schemer you are?'

'I think he may have his suspicions, yes.'

'And you? Do you know exactly what Adam is?'

'If I didn't a little while ago, I certainly do now, don't I?'

'Yes. There are many men who, in an extravagant moment, might *say* they'd die for their lady but not so many who'd actually *do* it. However, it's more than that with Adam, Millie. Have you realised yet how sharp his brain is?'

'Even *Rainham* couldn't help noticing that – much though he'd have liked not to,' she retorted. And then, 'What are you saying? You want to keep Adam in the Section?'

'If at all possible, yes. And you as well. You would make a formidable team.'

Perhaps fortunately, Coombes chose that moment to announce the arrival of Doctor Quinn. Camilla immediately stood up, saying, 'Show him to Mr Brandon's room, please. I'll be there directly.' And to her uncle, 'I'm sorry. I can't think about that now.'

'No.' He rose and gave her a swift hug. 'Just sowing the seed, my dear. That's all.'

* * *

Adam's journey from the drawing-room to his bedchamber had resembled a royal progress. Every servant in the house – even Dawson from the stables, together with a young fellow recently taken on to replace Brewster – had found an excuse to be somewhere along the route. And every single one of them hailed him as a hero. The men wanted to shake his hand; the female staff insisted on hugging him. By the time the door of his room was safely closed behind him, he was ready to die of embarrassment ... and aware that if Rainham had witnessed any of it, that might still happen later. But he said nothing, allowed Finch to help him out of the rest of his clothes and crawled gratefully into bed.

It seemed that, no sooner had he slid into an uneasy doze than Finch was gently prodding him awake. Groggily, he said, 'What? What's happened?'

'The doctor's here, sir.'

'Oh God.' An unwary attempt to sit up sent pain ricocheting through his arm and made him grit his teeth. 'All right. I suppose I'll have to see him.'

'Yes, sir,' agreed Finch firmly. 'You will.'

Although Doctor Quinn pronounced the wound clean, what followed during his thorough investigation of the place where the bullet had made its exit was unpleasant enough to leave Adam sweating and breathless. But finally, having inserted three stitches in both wounds and applying ointment and a fresh dressing, the doctor said, 'You've been lucky, sir.'

'Really? It doesn't feel like it.'

'I daresay. But splinters of bone would have made it much worse. Fortunately, I can find none so there's no reason it shouldn't heal well. Who did you say shot you?'

'I didn't. Are you finished?'

'Almost.' A few drops of something were added to the glass of water on the night-stand. 'Drink that.' And when Adam made no move to do so, 'It's merely a little laudanum for the pain, sir. You'll feel better for it.'

'I won't. I'll wake feeling my head's been stuffed with wet wool. Take it away, Harry.'

'Don't,' countermanded Camilla from the doorway.

Adam's head jerked around sending another lightning bolt up his arm. On a hiss of breath, he said, 'How long have you been there?'

'Not long.' The truth was that she'd been there throughout and watching what Doctor Quinn was doing to Adam with slender pointy instruments had left her feeling rather sick. She said, 'Take the laudanum, please. Then you can sleep for a few hours.'

'I don't want the laudanum and I don't want to sleep,' he muttered. 'I want to get up.'

'Later, perhaps. We'll see.' She smiled at the doctor, currently engaged in packing away the tools of his trade. 'He's not usually so difficult, I assure you.'

'I daresay he's never been shot before,' replied Quinn breezily. 'I shall call again in a couple of days but send for me if the wound becomes inflamed or there's any sign of fever. Good day to you, Mr Brandon ... and don't waste your breath arguing with this lady. You won't win.'

As Finch showed the doctor out, Adam became belatedly aware that the sheet was barely covering the essentials. Pulling it up a few inches, he said, 'He didn't need to tell me that. I already know you won't let me win.'

'Not over this.' She sat at his side, stroking back his loosened hair and wishing he'd left the sheet where it was. 'How badly does it hurt?'

'More than it did before Quinn set about prodding it … but I expect it will settle. What's happening downstairs?'

'Nothing. The excitement is over for the day so you can relax. Take the laudanum.'

He groaned. 'Do I have to?'

'Yes.' She held the glass out to him. 'If you take it and get some rest, you may be well enough to come down for dinner.'

'I have every *intention* of coming down for dinner. It's a flesh wound – not an amputation.' He drained the glass, grimacing. 'There. Do I get a lemon drop now?'

Shaking her head, Camilla leaned closer. 'Sorry. Will this do instead?'

And she kissed him, sweetly and simply, on the mouth.

* * *

Adam slept for over six hours and awoke in a brandy-and-laudanum induced thoroughly bad mood. Finch bore with this patiently and said as little as possible. Adam grumbled moodily about the time and Finch having allowed him to sleep too long. The news that Camilla had ordered a light meal to be served to him in bed produced a surly silence which lasted until he found himself staring at a tray bearing a bowl of broth, warm rolls wrapped in a napkin and a slice of something pale yellow and wobbly.

'What,' he asked with dangerous and glacial calm, 'is *that*?'

'Egg custard, sir.'

'God help me,' muttered Adam.

'Cook makes it regular,' continued Finch blithely. 'Old Dan who does the garden has trouble with his teeth.'

'I,' said Adam grittily, 'do *not* have trouble with my teeth. Neither am I an invalid – so I'd be grateful if you and Cam – and everyone *else* would stop treating me as such. Take this tray and put it on the table. I am not eating anything at *all* sitting up in bed without a stitch on. Bring me some breeches and a robe. I'm getting up.'

Although Finch did as he'd been told, he kept a careful eye on Adam as he swung his legs out of bed, stood up, swayed and then found his balance.

'Why did I let myself be talked into taking laudanum?' mumbled Adam, awkwardly struggling into a pair of breeches. 'I had it once, years ago – and once was enough. I loathe the stuff. Pain is preferable any day.'

'I suppose that would depend on the pain, wouldn't it?' Finch set a chair in front of the table and held out Adam's chamber robe so he could slip it on. 'Miss Camilla said I'm to tell her when you've eaten, sir – so best have the broth now while it's still hot.'

The immediate reaction to this was a silently fulminating glare. Then, muttering something else but this time under his breath, Adam sat and snatched up the spoon.

Harry Finch had known Adam Brandon since they were both eight. In the twenty years since then he had never seen him moody, ill-humoured or unreasonable. Now he was all three. Finch knew he shouldn't find this funny. He also knew this wouldn't be a good time to let Adam see that he did. So he kept his mouth shut and busied himself doing nothing on the far side of the room.

Although his head felt fuzzy and his arm ached, Adam discovered that he was hungry. The broth and bread quickly disappeared – as did the despised egg custard. Pushing the tray aside, he said, 'Take this away, Harry. And ask Cook to send me something solid to eat – it doesn't matter what.'

'Feeling better, are you, sir?' asked Finch cautiously, as he picked up the tray.

'Marginally, I suppose.'

Finch went out and Adam looked at the clock. A quarter before ten … so scarcely worth bothering to dress and go downstairs even if somebody didn't stop him doing it. From the passage outside his door he heard Finch speaking to someone. He couldn't hear the words but they were followed by Camilla's laugh; the smoky erotic ripple that had its usual effect. Adam told himself he should be pleased at least *one* part of his anatomy was working normally.

Then she was smiling at him from the doorway and saying, 'Rainham wants to know if you'd like company.'

'I would. Just not his.'

'That's what I thought.' She tilted her head and advanced a few steps. 'Finch says you're feeling better but that you're proving to be a very bad-tempered patient. Grumpy, was the actual word he used.'

'I ate the dratted egg custard. What more does he want?'

Camilla perched on the window seat in a pool of violet taffeta and eyed him thoughtfully. 'You really don't like being incapacitated, do you?'

'I'm not used to it.'

'At all? You must have been laid up sometime. Everyone is.'

He thought about it.

'I had the measles when I was nine but Max and Leo had them, too. And I wrenched an ankle falling from my horse when I was fourteen and couldn't walk for a few days.'

She stared at him. 'That can't be all, surely? You're addicted to lethal weapons. You must have been injured from time to time whilst playing with them.'

'I haven't.' Adam shrugged and then regretted it. 'I was disarmed often enough in the early years ... but since I became sufficiently advanced to fight with a naked blade, no one's touched me. Nor I them, for that matter – though there were times when I could have done. But to me, swordplay is the art of marrying strength to grace, speed to precision ... all of it in perfect balance. Blood would spoil that.' He watched her silently digesting this and then, with the first sign of a smile, added, 'The only scar I have is the one Mrs Blane's bullet is going to leave. I'll prove it, if you like.'

A mental image of Adam removing all of his clothes and letting her watch sent a tide of heat coursing through Camilla. Knowing that he was not only aware of it, but had done it deliberately, she refused to let embarrassment win. Instead, she laughed at him and said, 'Will you? When?'

CHAPTER THIRTY-FOUR

On the following morning with Finch's help, Adam was able to dress and join everyone for breakfast. The pain in his arm had retreated to a dull ache and only protested more vigorously when he required anything of it. He hoped Rainham had got over his Merry Jester mood and thought, *But if he hasn't, he may discover that my right arm is in good working order.*

Finding Camilla, Alveston and Rainham already at the table, he said, 'No Guy?'

'No.' Camilla rose and went to the sideboard. 'I think he over-did it last night. Sit down and have some coffee while I get you some breakfast.'

'I can do it myself. You don't know --'

'Unless, for the first morning since you've been here, you *don't* want scrambled egg, two slices of bacon and a sausage, yes – I do.'

Adam gave up and sat down. Rainham said, 'You look better. How is the arm?'

'It feels like lead … but otherwise not too bad. Have you ever been shot?'

'No.' Rainham grinned. 'My assignments regularly result in bruises and very occasionally in black eyes but, so far, fortunately no bullets. Vivian is remarkably tolerant of my 'other' life. But I suspect that going home with holes in me might change that.'

'And so it should,' declared Camilla, setting a plate in front of Adam and resuming her seat. 'What is the scenario for today, Uncle Hugh?'

'A formal interview with Mrs Blane,' he replied, reaching for the coffee pot. 'I need you there so that an accurate record can be made later.'

She grimaced. 'I'd rather not. Is it really necessary?'

'I'm afraid so. And while we do that, Rainham and Adam can write their reports.'

Adam looked up, a piece of sausage impaled on his fork. 'Pardon me?'

'A report on everything from start to finish in exhaustive detail,' groaned Rainham. 'Don't look so surprised. Everything has to be put down on paper and filed for the future.'

'Correct,' said Alveston. 'How fortunate that you are not left-handed, Adam.'

'Isn't it? You can't imagine how happy I am.'

There was a tap at the door and Coombes appeared.

'I beg your pardon, my lord ... but Mr Frederick Blane and Mr Mark Blane are here and asking to see Mrs Blane. What am I to say?'

'Nothing.' The earl rose, tossing aside his napkin. 'I'll speak to them myself.'

When he had left the room, Camilla said slowly, 'This is rather awkward, isn't it?'

'No. Failing to acknowledge a neighbour's supper invitation is *rather awkward,*' replied Rainham, preparing to quit the room himself. 'Having a neighbour locked in a bedchamber and pending arrest falls into another category entirely. Join me in the library when you're ready, Adam. We can collaborate on our thrice-blasted reports.'

Camilla watched Adam eating his breakfast mostly with only one hand. She said, 'Can't you use your left arm at all?'

'Yes. But I'm saving it for something worthwhile. And I think getting shot one day and being put back to work the next is deserving of a *little* sympathy. Don't you?'

'Not especially, no.'

'No? That's disappointing. Why not?'

'Well, let's just think, shall we?' She rose and gazed down at him over folded arms. 'All you and Rainham have to do is write down what you did, what you learned and when – making sure the two versions tally. *I* have to listen to Uncle Hugh's opening interrogation of an acquaintance who, until yesterday, I thought was a harmless old lady. *Then* I have to write down an entire conversation verbatim. And you really think *you're* hard done by?'

* * *

Lord Alveston permitted the Messrs Blane to satisfy themselves that Mrs Blane senior was being politely treated and well cared for but did not encourage them to linger.

'I will keep her here as long as I can,' he told them bluntly, 'but be aware that she will have to go to London eventually. It is unavoidable.'

A little later, Camilla sat in a corner while the head of M Section asked a courteous but frigidly implacable stream of questions. Mrs Blane refused to acknowledge her existence – for which she was grateful. Privately, she thought the old lady looked years older than she had yesterday, something that could only get worse as the days wore on.

At the end of an hour, Camilla had a headache and suspected that she wasn't the only one. But after a great many tears and protestations, Mrs Blane was finally persuaded to give up a few names, one of them possibly significant – but none of them the one the earl wanted; namely that of the next link in the espionage chain.

'Slow progress,' he sighed afterwards. 'She tires quickly and I will *not* be accused of bullying. However, I realise you have the task of transcribing it ... so perhaps an hour at a time is enough.'

'As always,' muttered Camilla, 'your consideration is legendary.'

'What was that?'

'My own convenience is secondary. I'll start work now, alongside the gentlemen.'

'One of them, anyway.' He opened the library door and stepped back to let her precede him. Then, 'Rainham ... you can finish that later. I need you to come with me.'

His lordship looked up from the pages he and Adam were perusing. 'Where?'

'We are going to speak with Mr Harold Deacon senior, of Deacon's Bank in Rye. It seems that he is, in some sense, Mrs Blane's partner in crime.'

'Excellent.' Rainham came smartly to his feet. 'We were more or less finished, anyway.'

'Actually, we were still arguing about Tranter and --'

'A minor point, Adam. Do what you think best,' said Rainham airily. And he followed Alveston from the room.

Adam and Camilla were left looking at each other. She said gloomily, 'This is the shape of things to come. You know that, don't you?'

'Not really.' Taking her hand, he drew her down beside him on a sofa. 'In what sense?'

'I was counting on catching Mrs Blane being the end of it. You and Rainham have accomplished what M Section was asked to do and everything ought now to be handed over to the Intelligence Service. Only it's not going to happen because Uncle Hugh has the bit between his teeth. He'll continue questioning Mrs Blane and then he'll move on to anyone she names. He won't send you or Rainham back to London because you're too useful – which means there is no point in *me* leaving either. We're all trapped. And you and I will lucky to be married before Christmas.'

Adam gathered her into his good arm and pressed a kiss to her temple. This inevitably led to another on her cheekbone and another, rather different one, at the corner of her mouth. Eventually he said, 'It can't be that bad, can it?'

'Yes. It can. Even when we're both finally free to leave here, it will take at least three more weeks for the banns to be read,' she replied distractedly. 'And it's all very well Uncle Hugh saying you and your family can stay with him in Berkeley Square but --'

'*Has* he said that?'

'Yes. But what use is it when he and you and I are all stuck here?' She pulled away and stood up. 'I want us to - to be *together*, Adam. And I don't want to wait weeks with no end in sight of it actually happening. But since the matter appears to be completely outside our control, I'll get on with Uncle's dratted transcription.'

Adam remained where he was, watching her sit down and pull writing materials in front of her. He didn't need to wonder what she meant when she said she wanted them to be together. He wanted the same thing. Last night was probably the only time since she'd said she would marry him that he hadn't tossed and turned, physically uncomfortable and unable to stop the refrain that continually crept past his conscience and which he had so far resisted.

He took a resolute breath, resisted it again and wandered to where she sat working. Then he distracted himself from the temptation to kiss her smooth, white nape by reading over her shoulder.

Record of Head of M Section's preliminary interview with Mrs Hester Blane of Blane House, Lydd, she had written in her easy, flowing script. *Interview held at Dragon Hall, Romney Marsh, first day of September, 1779.*

Q. *We have evidence pointing to your involvement in smuggling, ma'am – and will doubtless gather more. What I cannot comprehend is why you – a respectable matron – would do this, since I do not believe it can have been for the money.*

A. *Of course it wasn't for money.*

Q. *Then why?*

A. *Because I could.*

Q. *That is hardly sufficient reason.*

A. *And because, when my only son died, I didn't want what he'd created to go to waste. So I picked up the reins and carried on.*

Adam stopped reading, let out a startled breath and said, 'The *son* began it?'

'So she said.'

'How long ago?'

'She hasn't told us that yet but we know Henry died in 1776.' Camilla sighed and rubbed a hand over her brow. 'She delivered quite a diatribe at that point. She talked about her son as if he was some sort of genius. She ranted about what she called the *feeble little mouse* he'd married. She said Mark was as dull a stick as his grandfather and possessed of as little imagination; Peter wasn't worth wasting words on. Only her darling Henry had the Fordyce spark – and all she had left of him was the legacy she'd helped him build. It went on and on and on. And though I will write it all out, it doesn't belong in these pages. Oh – and she's adamant that she never meant to shoot anyone.'

'In which case, why was the pistol loaded?' asked Adam aridly.

'Yes. That's what Uncle Hugh said.' She paused, aware of his fingertips lightly stroking her neck. 'What are you doing?'

Adam's fingers froze and he stared down at them, faintly bemused.

'I'm sorry. Apparently, I couldn't ... resist. You don't like it?'

She stood up, turning into him and placing her palms either side of his face.

'If you honestly need to ask that --'

'I don't,' he said huskily. 'I really, really don't.'

Then she was in his arms and being pressed hard against him and his mouth and hers embarked on a different sort of conversation.

* * *

It took Camilla much longer than it should have done to finish transcribing Mrs Blane's first interview. Even though she'd sent Adam away, concentration proved impossible. Those hot, hungry kisses and the caresses that had accompanied them had left her fidgety and wanting. She was fairly sure they had left Adam feeling the same way. So throughout the rest of the day, she gave a great deal of thought to whether she should or indeed *could* give matters a little nudge.

By the time she went downstairs clad in pale grey tiffany, all the gentlemen were assembled in the library – even Guy, once more wearing a coat belonging to his uncle because it was easier to slip on than one of his own. They all rose when she walked in and then, with one exception, continued their conversation with scarcely a pause.

Adam, however, crossed to her side and brought her hands to his lips, his eyes holding her own. Then, drawing her with him while he poured her a glass of wine, he said softly, 'You were right. Lord Alveston is sending Rainham to ask Major Levinson for half a dozen redcoats on permanent loan so he can place Mr Deacon under house arrest.'

'Well, at least he seems to have realised that if he brings *all* his prisoners here, we'll run out of bedchambers. In my opinion, Mrs Blane is one too many but I realise that can't be helped. They can hardly put her in a cell, can they?'

'No. Even I couldn't vote for that.' He smiled at her, that sweet half-smile that lived mostly in his eyes and invariably caused everything inside her to dissolve. 'On another note entirely, I've an idea of how I might speed up our personal life.'

'You have?' A surge of hope shot through her and she thought, *Please let it be the same one I have.* 'How?'

'I could resign from the Section with immediate effect.'

Camilla's heart sank. 'That will only provoke hours of argument. Uncle Hugh wants to keep us both – particularly you.'

'He's said nothing of that to me.'

'He's biding his time. He told me an hour after you were shot – hardly the right moment to bring it up, which is why *I* didn't say anything either. I thought you and I could talk about it later. After we're married.'

Adam nodded and was about to answer when Guy turned to them saying, 'Millie ... do you suppose Mark *knew* his father was up to his neck in smuggling?'

'No. Not for a minute, nor his grandfather, either. And you can't tell them. So stay away from Mark, if you don't want to end up lying to him.'

Dinner passed pleasantly enough until dessert was on the table and Camilla said, 'Perhaps, Uncle, you might give Adam and me some indication of how much longer we'll be required here? Not unnaturally, we would quite like to schedule our wedding.'

'I realise that, Millie. But the situation is ... complicated.'

'Actually, it's not. Espionage is the business of the Intelligence Service – not M Section. And Adam and I have fulfilled our responsibilities there, have we not?'

Alveston looked back at her in what was clearly irritable silence. On the other side of the table, Rainham and Guy busied themselves with fruit and cheese, pretending to be deaf.

Eventually, Adam said quietly, 'Forgive me, sir – but Camilla is right. Not so very long ago you referred to proper protocol. Does not that apply here?'

'I expect a reply from Sir Oswald in the next day or two,' returned Alveston testily. 'Be patient. I will release both of you as soon as I am able.'

'Please do.' Camilla pushed back her chair and stood up – forcing the gentlemen to do the same. 'Adam and I would like our lives back.'

For the first time ever, she didn't join the gentlemen in the library but sent Coombes to tell them that she had retired. Then, once Martha had helped her undress and brushed out her hair, she curled up in a chair and remained there, deep in thought.

Surely it isn't unreasonable to ask Uncle to set a time limit? If he promised that we would be free in a week – or even two – I'd be content with that. But I doubt he will.

She knew what she *wanted* to do but was less sure how it would work out. She was also worried that if Adam resigned from the Section now, he might regret it later. So the sensible course of action was to wait a few more days – and tell Adam to do the same. She opened her door the tiniest bit so that, when he came up to his room, she would know.

* * *

Downstairs, Adam joined the others for a glass of brandy but refused to play cards and instead sat down with a book he didn't read. He suspected he could guess what was in Camilla's mind – or some of it, anyway. He'd been having the same thought himself and far too often for comfort. He wished she hadn't retired so precipitately. If she had remained downstairs, they might have found a moment for private conversation. Since she hadn't, he decided he might as well bid the others goodnight and go to bed himself.

He had his hand on the latch of his room when he noticed the narrow ribbon of light spilling from Camilla's door. Why was it open? It looked … it looked like an invitation. One he'd like to accept but must not. *Would* not. He pushed open his own door, stepped inside and discovered his feet wouldn't take him any further. He took a breath and then another ... and spun on his heel back into the hallway to find Camilla two steps away. Before his brain could process this, she put both palms against his chest and pushed, sending him stumbling back into the room. Then, following him, she closed the door and leaned against it.

CHAPTER THIRTY-FIVE

Everything in him froze. She was wearing a frothy blue thing over a lacy white thing with her hair tumbling over her shoulders and back in a glorious dark cloud. The edges of his mind turned fuzzy. She was speaking but he didn't hear the words. Finally, with a massive effort, he managed to croak, 'Love ... you shouldn't be here.'

'I know. But we need to talk.'

Talking was the last thing his body was thinking about – if, that was, it could be *called* thinking which clearly it couldn't. He said, 'Yes. But not here. Not now.' *And not with you wearing things that I could remove in an instant.* He managed to replace the last bit with, 'What did you want to say?'

'Don't resign. It won't work and you may be sorry later. Also ...'

She stopped so after a moment he prompted her. 'Also what?'

'You're too good at this. It would be a waste.'

Since merely looking at her was destroying his self-control, the easiest course was to simply agree. 'Very well. Is that all?'

'No.'

It *had* been all when she'd left her room. But now she was here it seemed foolish to leave without suggesting the other thing ... if only she could find the right words. To give herself a moment to think, she pulled the chamber robe closer around her and folded her arms across it beneath her breasts. She was concentrating too hard to notice that Adam had shut his eyes and was wearing an expression of something akin to pain.

Finally, drawing a deep breath and keeping her gaze fixed on his cravat, she said baldly, 'I could stay.'

His eyes flew open. 'What?'

'I could stay. Here. With you. Tonight.' She waited a moment and, when he didn't speak, raised her eyes to his. 'What do you think?'

Adam swallowed hard and waited for his brain to unscramble itself before the enthusiastic response generated elsewhere had him saying *Yes, please*. Finally he said, 'Did we not already discuss this?'

'We did. But ... since I'm here ... I wondered if you'd changed your mind.'

'I haven't. There can only be one first time – and I'd like our wedding night to be ours.' He suspected that she had no idea how hard that had been to say. Then he wondered if this was the moment to confess the *other* reason he wouldn't sleep with her yet. And without warning came the sudden notion of a compromise. It wasn't what either of them wanted ... and it wouldn't be easy. But since it wouldn't *actually* kill him even if it felt as if it might, he said slowly, 'However, if you wanted to stay and literally just *sleep* with me --'

'Yes.' Her glow returned, along with her smile. 'Yes. I'd like that.'

So would he – probably a bit too much. But that was his problem, not hers. He said, 'You do understand what I'm suggesting, don't you?'

'Yes. And cuddling will do very well for now ... though does that mean I'm going to have to wait a while to see you naked?'

He managed a tiny laugh. 'I'm afraid so. But we're agreed?'

'Yes.' She reached up to kiss his jaw. 'We are. Am I allowed to remove my robe?'

He nodded and stepped back from her, praying for restraint as she slipped the frothy thing from her shoulders and let it fall. Beneath it was a white lawn nightgown inset with strips of lace that skimmed the curves of bosom and hip. Adam forgot to breathe.

Camilla didn't. She said, 'Now you.'

Since thinking was beyond him, he did as he was told, quickly shedding both coat and vest. But when he'd pulled the shirt over his head and was about to draw her close ... he found that she was holding him at bay with both hands, her eyes riveted on the bandage around his arm.

She said, 'I forgot. I'm sorry. How could I forget?'

'It's of no consequence.' And then, his mouth muffled against her hair as he reached past her to lock the door, 'I told you I was saving it for something worthwhile. This is it.'

She made an odd little sound as their bodies met – for the first time without the impediments of corset and petticoats. Adam supposed she was enjoying the difference nearly as much as he was. With a chaste kiss on her brow, he murmured, 'Into bed and under the covers with you, you hussy – before I forget myself.'

She laughed, did as he asked and watched him shed his shoes and stockings before joining her. Then, turning her on to her side and sliding an arm beneath her, he moulded his body against her back and drew her close with his free arm.

'Comfortable?' he asked.

'Yes.' Her fingers closed over his. 'Are you really going to sleep in your breeches?'

'With the greatest possible reluctance, yes.' He gave a small, wry laugh. 'It's a ... necessary precaution.'

'It seems a shame ... but I suppose you know best.'

'Those are words I never expected to hear. Can I have them in writing?'

'Absolutely not.' She snuggled against him. 'You're so warm.'

'That's one way of describing it,' muttered Adam.

She yawned and said drowsily, 'This is nice. You feel lovely. I had no idea.'

'You feel lovely, too.' Unable to help himself, he placed a lingering kiss on her shoulder and said, 'Go to sleep. I'll wake you before the house starts to stir.'

'Mm. I love you.'

'And I, you. Goodnight.'

'Goodnight.'

* * *

Camilla had drifted into slumber fairly quickly. With her body warm and enticing against his and the scent of her hair teasing his nose, Adam didn't expect to sleep at all. So he told himself to enjoy what he had and not think about what he didn't have because it would be his soon enough. And gradually, without realising it, he fell sound asleep.

He awoke in broad daylight to the sound of shouting, running feet and someone hammering on the door. Suddenly fully alert and aware of Camilla opening sleepy eyes beside him, he catapulted out of bed, dragged his robe on and called, 'Yes? What is it?'

'Oh, sir! You have to come. Something terrible's happened!'

Camilla sat up, clutching the sheet to her chest. 'What on earth --?'

Adam signalled her to stay quiet, opened the door some four inches and peered around it. Outside was a small crowd. Two of the housemaids, Thomas and, at the head of the party, Camilla's maid. Adam began to get a seriously bad feeling. But before he could open his mouth, Martha wailed, 'Oh thank goodness, sir! It's Miss Millie – she's vanished. Her bed's not been slept in and we can't find her anywhere!'

Behind him, Camilla made a small, choking sound.

'Ah,' said Adam, literally unable to think of anything else to say. He suspected that there wasn't any way out of this but his brain still scurried around trying to find one. 'Give me a moment to dress. Have ... have you looked everywhere?'

Thomas and the housemaids assured him that they had.

Sounds from the bed attracted his attention. Instead of hiding under the covers overcome with embarrassment, Camilla was laughing herself silly and trying to muffle the sounds in a corner of the sheet. And the baleful scowl he sent her only succeeded in making her laugh harder. He was just concluding that he'd better contain the situation before somebody sent for the Militia when he became aware that Martha was staring past him, pointing at something on the floor.

Already knowing what it was, Adam realised the game was up even before the wretched maid exclaimed, 'Miss Millie's robe!' And promptly clapped her hand over her mouth, looking mortified.

'Quite,' said Adam dryly ... and opened the door wide so they could all see Miss Millie, drat her, flushed, bright-eyed and shoulders – one of them naked where her nightgown had slipped away – shaking with laughter. 'There she is. Safe and sound. So perhaps you might all now go about your business?'

Thomas turned scarlet and swiftly averted his eyes; the housemaids dropped giggling curtsies; and Martha muttered, 'Sorry. H-Hot water.' And fled.

Adam shut the door and locked it again. Then, regarding the love of his life over folded arms, he stalked towards her saying ominously, 'Thanks to all the noise they've made, there will be no keeping this quiet. In half an hour or less, your uncle, your brother and Rainham will all know where you spent last night. And you think it's *funny*?'

'Yes. D-Don't you?'

Actually, what he could only consider an insane part of him did ... but one of them had to take this seriously and clearly it wasn't going to be her. She just sat there, half-naked in his bed, pink-cheeked, happy and utterly irresistible. 'I might – were it not that the three of them will be drawing lots for who hits me first.'

That stopped her laughing. 'They'd better not.'

Adam raised a sardonically enquiring brow and said nothing.

Climbing unselfconsciously out of bed, Camilla discovered that one shoulder of her nightgown had become untied. Searching for the ribbons through a tangle of hair, she mumbled, 'An extra pair of hands would be helpful.'

'Mine wouldn't. They'd be taking advantage. So I'll stick to enjoying the view.'

Managing to tie the bow, she said, 'I don't care that they'll know. But if necessary, we could always tell them that you didn't ... we haven't ... that I'm still --'

'No,' said Adam, aghast at the idea of just how much sniggering Rainham could do over *that* little nugget. 'They'd never believe it. We'll just have to let them draw their own conclusions ... and be prepared to brazen it out.'

'Excellent,' said Camilla, advancing to pull his head down for a long, seductive kiss. 'My plan exactly. Give me half an hour and you can escort me to breakfast.'

* * *

One look at the three faces already at the table told Adam everything he needed to know. Guy appeared mildly uncomfortable; Rainham might or might not be holding a grin in check; and Alveston laid down his knife, looking frosty.

'Good,' said Camilla cheerfully, heading for the food. 'I see you've all heard?'

'We have heard *something*,' agreed the earl frigidly. 'Is it true?'

'You mean, did Martha find my room empty and start screeching before engaging her brain for a moment? Yes. If you also mean, did she and three other servants discover me in Adam's bed ... again yes.'

'I see.' Alveston's gaze travelled to Adam and stayed there. 'And you? Have you nothing you would like to add?'

'Not really. I think Camilla has covered everything quite neatly.'

Rainham choked on a piece of sausage. Guy thumped him helpfully on the back and continued watching the show.

Alveston rose. Adam squared his shoulders but kept his expression neutral.

Setting her plate down, Camilla said, 'Let me be quite clear, Uncle. Adam is not at fault in any way. And I won't have *anyone*,' she sent a brief, hard glance around the table, 'saying otherwise. We are betrothed and we will marry – soon, if we are given leave to go to London and start making arrangements.'

'And you think that excuses this – this *farce*? If it gets out --'

'It won't,' said Adam calmly. 'If there is one thing I've learned during my time here, it is that the Dragon Hall servants are unswervingly loyal and utterly discreet – as is my own man, Finch. So the only way for last night to 'get out', as you put it, is through one of you – which I think we can all agree is extremely unlikely. Guy?'

Guy started. 'Oh. Yes. *Extremely* unlikely.'

'Thank you. Rainham?'

The viscount regarded him pityingly. '*Now* who's being an ass?'

Adam shrugged. 'Just checking. Does no one want to take a swing at me?'

'Apparently not,' said Alveston. 'I shall see you in the library presently and we will speak of this privately.' And he walked out.

Camilla sat down and shook out her napkin.

'Well, that went better than expected. Have some breakfast, Adam. You shouldn't face Uncle on an empty stomach.'

'And you'll need to keep your strength up,' murmured Rainham. And grinned.

* * *

Although his interview with Lord Alveston was extremely chilly and by no means pleasant, Adam knew it could have been much worse.

As it was, his lordship mostly confined himself to expressions such as '*very disappointed*' and '*expected better of you*' ... finally concluding with, 'You're a bloody fool. And so is Millie. Didn't either of you have the sense to realise that if she was back where she should be by morning, no one need have been any the wiser?'

This, thought Adam, put an interesting complexion on Lord Alveston's attitude. However, since '*We fell asleep*' wasn't going to cut much ice as an excuse, he merely said, 'I know. And I'm very sorry about that.'

'I daresay you are. But there's to be no more of it – do you hear me?'

'Yes, sir.'

'And?' snapped Alveston.

'And you have my word that it won't happen again.'

'It better not. And regardless of what you *think*, you'd better speak with --' He stopped as the door opened on Coombes. 'Well? What is it?'

'An express courier has arrived with letters from London, my lord. Shall I --?'

'Send him in. I'll see him immediately.' And to Adam, 'As I was saying ... work your charm on the servants. It shouldn't be difficult. They already think you're a hero.'

'They don't know the half of it,' murmured Adam, not quite under his breath.

'What was that?'

'Nothing. Am I dismissed, sir?'

'Yes. Go away and keep out of mischief.'

* * *

Coombes having gathered the servants together in the kitchen, Adam said simply, 'Lord Alveston has told me to persuade you all to say nothing about what some of you witnessed this morning. I think it unnecessary because I don't believe any of you would ever say a single word to Miss Camilla's discredit. So may I do *all* of us the favour of saving my breath?'

There was a chorus of agreement and Thomas said, 'Not just Miss Millie, sir. I reckon I speak for us all when I say there's nobody here who'd speak harm of you either, Mr Brandon. Not after all you've done.'

This won a general murmur of agreement.

Feeling his neck grow hot, Adam said, 'Thank you. You're very kind and – and probably over-generous. But thank you.' And he beat a hasty retreat.

He eventually tracked Camilla to the garden. The day was a rare one of cloudless blue sky and only the merest suggestion of a breeze. Accepting his arm and leaning her head against his shoulder, she said, 'Uncle let you go quicker than I expected.'

'Thankfully, something came from London and reprieved me.'

'And before that? Did he make you feel as if you were back at school?'

'Worse. It felt like my father telling me I'd let him down.'

She winced. 'Oh. I'm sorry.'

'But then he inadvertently made it plain that he was less angry about what we'd been doing than about letting ourselves get caught doing it.'

She laughed and shook her head. 'Appearances are *everything*.'

'So I gather. He also ordered me to talk to the staff – just in case.'

'Totally unnecessary. But did you?'

'No. I told them to take it as read.' He hesitated and added, 'They think I'm a hero.'

'And so you are – in more ways than one.' She hesitated for a moment and then said quietly, 'I didn't thank you.'

'For what?'

'For last night.'

'Stop there, sweetheart. You have nothing to thank me for.'

'I think I do.'

'Not really. And the choice was mine.' He glanced around to make sure they were alone and said rapidly, 'I haven't been totally honest about my reasons for – for waiting until we're married. Everything I said was true ... but there's something I *didn't* say.'

'And you want to tell me now?'

'Not want – should.' He pushed aside a feeling of awkwardness and reminded himself that Camilla was the one lady in a million who wouldn't be shocked by plain speaking. 'I'm told that a woman's first experience of sex isn't entirely pleasurable; that, no matter how hard her partner tries to avoid it, there is inevitably some pain involved.'

'Yes,' agreed Camilla prosaically. 'It hurts. I know that. But only the first time.' Unexpected laughter lit her eyes. 'If it was like that *every* time, there would be fewer children in the world, wouldn't there?'

'Very possibly. But my point is that we can't embark on an ongoing affair here – so there wouldn't have been a *second* time until after the wedding. And I didn't want that for either of us. It wouldn't have been ... helpful.'

'No. I suppose not – though I hadn't thought of it that way.' She sighed. 'Ought I to thank you for that as well?'

'Not for that or anything else.' He leaned over to steal a quick kiss. 'On the other hand, if you wanted to reward my nobility in due course, I wouldn't say no.'

She blushed faintly but said, 'I'll look forward to doing so.'

'Not nearly as much as I will.' He lowered his voice and added, 'You won't mind me starting at your toes and taking an hour or so to kiss my way up, will you?'

'N-Not at all,' she managed. 'I always say that one can never be too thorough.'

'My thoughts exactly. Or rather, one of them.' Adam was tempted to find out if he could shock her but was forced to postpone doing so when he saw Lord Alveston striding towards them. 'Has something happened, sir?'

'Yes,' snapped the earl. 'I am bidden to take Mrs Blane to the Intelligence Office as soon as possible. Quite aside from other considerations, this means I must break the news to her family and discover if her personal maid is prepared to accompany her. Then, if she is not, I have to find a suitable replacement since, regardless of her guilt, it is out of the question for Mrs Blane to travel without a female companion. As for the question of where to house her in London, I would hope Sir Oswald is even now making suitable provision but doubt that it has yet crossed his mind.'

Aware that these complaints had more to do with Alveston's plans being upset than with travel arrangements and trying not to hope for too much on Adam's and her own account, Camilla said carefully, 'What a nuisance. Is there anything we can do to help?'

'Very little. And don't pretend you're not delighted, Millie. This gives the two of you what you've been asking for.'

Her fingers tightened on Adam's sleeve. 'It does?'

'Yes. If I'm to be in London, then so must you be,' said his lordship irritably. 'But here is how it is going to be. The courier will take my reply to Sir Oswald. He will also deliver a letter telling your grandmother to expect you, and another, instructing my butler at Alveston House to prepare rooms for Adam.'

'Thank you, sir.'

'Don't thank me, you young fool. I'm not finished. You may take my carriage and leave as soon as you're ready. *You,*' he stabbed a finger in Camilla's direction, 'will travel with your maid, have her share your room on the journey and go directly to Mount Street. *You,*' another stab, this time at Adam, 'will ride back on Hector and go directly to Berkeley Square. Between leaving here and arriving there, there will be no nocturnal wanderings in either direction. Do I make myself clear?'

'Yes, Uncle Hugh,' said Camilla.

'Abundantly clear,' said Adam.

'Good. Once in London, the pair of you may break the glad tidings to Lady Martindale and instruct her to start planning some sort of betrothal celebration. My secretary, Mr Worth, will put a notice of your betrothal in the *Morning Post* and have the first of the banns read at St. George's. You should also write to your family, Adam, inviting them to join you at Alveston House as soon as it may be convenient. I,' he concluded, 'shall be but a few days behind you. Any questions?'

'No, sir,' said Adam. 'As always, you've thought of everything.'

Alveston sent him a caustic look and said nothing. Camilla stood on tiptoe to kiss the earl's cheek whispering, 'Thank you, Uncle Hugh. We'll follow orders, I promise.'

'See that you do,' he growled whilst simultaneously giving her a quick hug. And then, setting her aside, 'One other thing, Adam. You've had Hector this last month and from what I've seen, you and he have formed a bond ... so you'd better keep him.'

Adam blinked. 'I ... sir, that is extraordinarily generous of you.'

'I know. We'll call him a betrothal gift. You can thank me by behaving yourself between now and the wedding and making Millie a good husband after it.'

'You have my word on both, sir. I'll do everything I can to make her happy – always.'

'Well, if you'd take a bullet for her there can't be much you won't do.' Alveston held out his hand and when Adam took it, added, 'Since I haven't yet done so, I suppose I'd better give you my blessing. Welcome to the family, young man.'

CHAPTER THIRTY-SIX

With so little time, Lady Martindale reluctantly agreed that a ball was out of the question and even more reluctantly yielded to Camilla's insistence that the guest list for the wedding be kept to moderate proportions. The eventual compromise was a decision to hold a dinner party for family and close friends at Alveston House a week before the happy day – by which time everyone should have arrived in town.

Lord Alveston followed the betrothed couple within three days, bringing Guy to reside under his eye in Berkeley Square. He also brought the latest news on the investigation with him.

'Mrs Blane has been placed in comfortable confinement in Whitehall, attended by her maid,' he told Adam. 'The older grandson has followed her, taken lodgings nearby and is trying to find lawyers to represent her. He's also hoping for permission to visit.'

'Is he likely to get it?'

'Not unless he undertakes to persuade her that her best hope lies in cooperation. As yet, she still refuses to accept quite how much trouble she is in and has convinced herself that her age and sex will protect her.'

'Which, of course, they are doing,' observed Adam dryly.

'Temporarily, yes. For the rest, news of her arrest has loosened Ernest Wilson's tongue. And while Sir Oswald's people dissect your and Rainham's reports, Millie's transcripts and the contents of the French despatch, the Fordyce bank account has been frozen and numerous new arrests are taking place. The Lydd solicitor who handled the Fordyce finances; Riding Officer Tranter; and Harold Deacon of Deacon's Bank. The general belief is that it is Hester Blane or Deacon who holds the key to the ongoing espionage trail and that one of them will eventually surrender it. Either way, Intelligence has taken over and the entire matter is now completely out of my hands.'

Adam wasn't sorry to hear this and neither, when he told her of it, was Camilla.

'Good,' she said, pulling him down for a kiss. 'When will your family arrive?'

'In a few days, weather permitting.'

'Including the Virtuoso Earl?'

'Yes. Why?'

'I want to hear him play, of course. And is there any news from Rainham?'

'He went to Wales to fetch his wife and is on his way.' He grinned at her. 'You know your adopted big brother won't let you get married without him.'

* * *

Adam's family managed to arrive on the same day. First, his mother, Max, Frances and Leo; and a few hours later, Arabella and Julian – for once, without the children.

Immediately drawn into the warmth of her new family, Camilla was soon shopping with Arabella and Frances, meeting Leo's incessant teasing with quips of her own and spending hours getting to know Adam's warm and lovely mother, listening to tales of his youth and going over final details of the wedding.

The Rainhams arrived the day before the dinner party, as did Lord and Lady Wingham. It wasn't until the evening itself that Adam learned that the Duke and Duchess of Rockliffe had also been invited due to the distant family connection ... as had Alveston's friend, the Marquis of Amberley and his Marchioness.

It was a large and merry party. Seated between Rockliffe and Viscount Wingham, Camilla was torn between the duke's dry wit and Sebastian's wicked one. Further along the table, she could see Adam laughing with Vivian Rainham over something which, judging by his pained expression, Rainham himself didn't find especially funny. But it was not until everyone repaired to the drawing room that talk became more general ... and Leo, who had spent most of dinner studying the marchioness, asked Amberley if he could paint her.

Several nearby conversations halted to listen.

'You're an artist?' asked Amberley, surprised.

'In an amateur way as yet – but yes,' said Leo. 'Just portraits, you know – and I'd like to try capturing that elusive expression in her ladyship's eyes.' Leo hesitated, baffled by the quality of the smile the marquis exchanged with his wife. Then, turning to where his soon-to-be new sister sat conversing with his mother, he said, 'Camilla? Can I drag you away for a few minutes?'

'Me?' she asked, baffled. 'Why?'

'Come and see.' And when Adam also rose, '*Just* Camilla, if you don't mind.'

'Not at all.' Adam sat down again. 'But if she sends for the cheese-grater – run.'

'Cheese-grater?' queried Leo, leading Camilla from the room while laughter and demands for an explanation broke out. 'Your weapon of choice, is it?'

'Don't laugh. It's been known to make men cry. Where are we going?'

'The small dining room. There's a bridal gift you haven't seen yet.'

Camilla was fairly certain she'd seen *all* of the gifts. Goodness only knew she'd been kept busy writing 'thank you' notes as each one arrived. 'How did that happen?'

'Because I only put it there a little while ago.'

Leo led her into the room which, at first glance, looked as it had the last time she'd seen it. Dinner services, crystal glassware and a good many porcelain ornaments ... amongst it all, several things she remembered returning last year. But Leo guided her to the far corner where a large rectangular shape hidden beneath a dust-cover reposed on a chair.

Gesturing towards it and sounding slightly tense, he said, 'You can look.'

Camilla lifted the sheet away ... and then froze, staring at the portrait. It was Adam, shown as she had never yet seen him but as his brothers must doubtless have done many times. He was in his shirt-sleeves, engaged in polishing a long, gleaming blade. The effect was immediate ... as if he had merely stilled briefly and might continue working at any moment. But it was the face that caught and held Camilla's gaze. It wasn't merely an uncannily accurate image of flesh and bone and the familiar half-smile lurking behind the cobalt eyes but something that spoke of what lay behind those things; the quiet but indomitable strength of character … and the innate integrity.

Something shifted inside her chest and she pressed both hands hard over her mouth for a moment before saying unevenly, 'This is for me?'

'Yes – and to embarrass Adam, of course. But yes, it's for you. If you like it?'

'*Like* it?' Camilla threw her arms around him. 'Oh Leo – it's wonderful! Thank you!'

He patted her shoulder and, to give her time to compose herself as she stepped back brushing fingers over wet lashes, 'I began it months ago but had put it aside, so I had to burn the midnight oil to get it finished.' He hesitated. 'I'd meant to show it to you tonight anyway … but do you mind if we also show it to Lord Amberley? I'm hoping it will help persuade him to let me paint his wife.'

She shook her head. 'Of course I don't mind. And you should show it to *everyone*. I wouldn't be surprised if you had half a dozen commissions by the end of the evening.'

He picked up the painting and grinned. 'I'm not that optimistic.'

As they re-entered the drawing-room, Max said, 'Just in time. Adam was about to organise a search party.'

Adam, who hadn't been about to do any such thing, raised a glass to his older brother and an eyebrow at his wife-to-be. 'Are the rest of us to be let into the secret?'

'Yes.' Camilla pointed to a bureau. 'There, Leo – where everyone can see.'

He set the portrait down, stepped away from it and folded his arms.

The room fell silent for a moment before a buzz of appreciation broke out and people rose and walked over to get a better look. But after a few minutes, Rosalind Amberley said, 'The only permission you need to paint me is mine, Mr Brandon. And you may have it … on condition that you paint my husband as well. Will you?'

'Certainly – if his lordship agrees,' said Leo, looking shy and a little stunned.

'You think I'll have a choice?' grinned Amberley, reaching out to shake Leo's hand. 'That is a remarkable piece of work. Where did you study?'

'Venice, mostly, but also in Florence for a time,' shrugged Leo. And then, finally meeting Adam's narrowed eyes and noting the hint of colour on his cheekbones, 'Yes, I know. Right now, you'd like to kill me. Fortunately, Camilla is on my side in this and won't let you.'

* * *

On the following afternoon, Camilla received a summons to join Adam, Rainham and her uncle at Alveston House. Adam met her in the hall and, after they had taken advantage of one of the few brief and, in the last week, rare moments they had alone to share an embrace, she said, 'Do *you* know what this is about?'

'No.' He tucked her hand in his arm and strolled unhurriedly towards the library. 'But since Rainham is here as well, I suspect we might hazard a guess.'

'Yes. And I sincerely hope Uncle realises you and I are on leave.'

'I daresay he does. But if not, I'm sure you'll remind him.'

The atmosphere in the library was that of Wilfred Street rather than Berkeley Square and the Earl of Alveston had become Goddard, Head of Section who, as soon as they were seated, came directly to the point.

'An unexpected development in the Blane affair has brought about swift and significant results to the whole enquiry. Sir Oswald, of course, would like to give the credit for this to the Intelligence Service. I have pointed out, in no uncertain terms, that it is thanks to M Section that Hester Blane is in custody – and that, had she *not* been, the events of the last three days could not have happened.'

'So?' demanded Camilla. 'What *did* happen?'

'An attempt was made to murder her.' He watched Rainham, Adam and Camilla exchange startled glances. 'You are thinking that, since she was under guard with two officers on duty at all times, this shouldn't have been possible? I entirely agree.'

'Heads will doubtless roll,' murmured Rainham. 'How embarrassing for Sir Oswald.'

Adam frowned slightly. 'You said an attempt, sir. It failed?'

'Purely by chance, yes. But perhaps I should start at the beginning – which is with Corbeau's despatch. You will recall that, when I arrived at Dragon Hall, Vincent had not finished decoding it – so I didn't learn the contents of the last page until I got back to town.'

'You got back two weeks ago,' observed Camilla acidly. 'And you didn't think *we* had any interest in learning it, too?'

'At the time, Rainham wasn't here and you and Adam were walking around in a haze of orange blossom – so no. I didn't,' returned Goddard irascibly. 'However, if I'm allowed to do so without interruption, I'll tell you now.'

'Certainly, sir,' said Adam blandly. 'We are all ears.'

Rainham raised a sardonic brow at him but said nothing.

'Well, then ... I expected the latter part to be about military matters in the Colonies. It wasn't. It concerned a plot against Lord North ... a scenario which those involved hoped would result in a change of government.'

'Ambitious,' remarked Rainham.

'The original intention was to achieve this by discrediting North personally. But the advice contained in Corbeau's despatch was that, character destruction being a lengthy and chancy business, a bullet would do the job quicker.'

Camilla sucked in a breath; Rainham swore quietly; and Adam said, 'That idea must have already occurred to them.'

'And been discarded? Yes. Certainly they are now vociferously repudiating it. However, I am getting ahead of myself. As soon as Vincent decoded that part of the despatch – and since I was absent – he took the matter to the Prime Minister's office. North was warned and all the necessary measures were put in place to ensure his safety. But there was little else that could be done because Corbeau's report refers to the English plotters by code names with nothing to tell us who they actually *are*.' Goddard leaned back, grimly smiling. 'That was true until they tried to poison Hester Blane.'

'How?' asked Camilla. 'No one outside Intelligence should have known about her – let alone where she was.'

'Quite. And yet, two nights ago, her dinner was accompanied by a box of sweetmeats – the sort made of coloured and fruit-flavoured marzipan. Fortunately for Mrs Blane, she dislikes marzipan ... so she gave the box to her maid who ate almost half of it. Within an hour, the poor woman was seized with violent cramps, vomiting and fits. Within two, she was dead. At that point, Sir Oswald's fellows did manage to get a couple of things right. They immediately summoned a doctor and, having established that the marzipan was the only thing the maid had eaten which Mrs Blane had not, started trying to trace its source. The errand boy was found and questioned but couldn't name the person who'd paid him to make the delivery. He was, however, able to furnish a description.'

The hint of satisfaction in the last words caused Camilla to say, 'Someone we know?'

'Yes ... but I'll come back to him in a moment. The death of the maid was a turning point. It finally made Hester Blane aware of her own peril. She realised that, if her former masters could get to her whilst under government protection, they could get to her anywhere and that her life was therefore hanging by a thread. So she started screaming that she'd talk – but only to me. Naturally, Sir Oswald did his damnedest to persuade her otherwise but she refused to budge ... and so, very reluctantly, I was sent for.'

Silence yawned about them until Rainham said impatiently, 'And?'

'And I spent a couple of exhausting but highly informative hours with the lady. To cut a long story short, in return for enhanced protection now and a more lenient sentence than she could otherwise expect, she gave me the names we needed. One of them was the gentleman described by the errand boy. A tall, skeletal man with white hair and spectacles.'

'Barrowby?' snapped Rainham. And when Goddard nodded, 'He's a boil on the backside of humanity. Vivian thinks he beats his wife. And the other fellow?'

'Humphrey Modiford; drowning in debt and barely keeping himself out of the Fleet. Both men were immediately arrested and I was happy to leave them to Sir Oswald's tender – or not so tender – mercies.' He paused and then added simply, 'Both of them also sit on the board of the East India Company.'

'Is *that* what all this has been about?' frowned Camilla. 'The East India Company?'

'Yes. The Company has been floundering ever since the debacle in Massachusetts six years ago. It has repeatedly lobbied Lord North to reduce the tax on tea but he hasn't done so – probably due, in varying degrees, to the war in the Colonies. According to their confessions, Barrowby and Modiford came to the conclusion that many, if not all, of the Company's problems could be solved by replacing Lord North's government. However, it became apparent to them quite early on that they wouldn't achieve this without outside help ... and fortunately they knew where to find it.'

'Christ,' muttered Rainham disgustedly. 'They went to the French.'

'Precisely. And the French, busy assisting their Colonial friends to throw off the yoke of Britain and only too eager for any opportunity to cause disruption on these shores were delighted to be offered a new channel of communication between their agents.'

'And the parts of Corbeau's despatch relating to Doctor Bancroft and the Chesapeake Bay area?' asked Adam. 'Where were they supposed to go?'

'According to Barrowby, they were destined for an under-secretary in the Foreign Office. He, too, is under arrest and busy protesting his innocence. Sir Oswald will doubtless get to the bottom of it in time. But happily, no real harm has been done. Perhaps it never would have been. But treason is never acceptable ... and it is thanks to all of you that we held the key to it in the person of Hester Blane. Had we not done so, the conspirators' identities would still be a mystery.' Goddard smiled. 'You've also successfully crippled – for the foreseeable future, at any rate – the largest smuggling operation Romney Marsh has seen for some years. And last but not least, the information in Corbeau's despatch enabled the Intelligence Service to preserve Doctor Bancroft's reputation with Mr Franklin. So, all in all ... well done.'

'Thank you,' drawled Rainham. 'But as usual no medals, I presume?'

'You presume correctly. Warm yourselves with the knowledge that your efficiency and tenacity continue to outweigh the intensely annoying qualities two of you possess in abundance ... and which the third, if he remains with us long enough, will also doubtless acquire far sooner than I would like.'

* * *

On the following evening, Rainham and Sebastian bore the Brandon brothers and a very reluctant Julian off to Sinclairs where they were joined by Amberley and Rockliffe. Then everyone settled in one of the upstairs dining salons under the personal supervision of Monsieur Delacroix.

After a convivial and leisurely dinner, some of them embarked on a game of basset while others chose to take their port to the comfortable armchairs by the fire. Being one of the latter, Adam joined Julian and was just about to speak to him when Rockliffe drifted over saying, 'Your younger brother is a very gifted artist. Has he told you that I have commissioned a portrait of Adeline and our children?'

'Only three or four times so far.'

'Ah.' The duke smiled. 'I understand from Max that your own talent lies in the sword – hence the subject matter of the portrait. I wonder if you might care to join me at Angelo's one morning? I fence there regularly but it is many years since I last used a sword. It would be interesting to discover if I retain any skill.'

Surprised, Adam rose and bowed. 'Thank you. It would be a pleasure.'

Rockliffe nodded. 'The day after tomorrow, then? Bring your brothers, by all means – perhaps also Sebastian? He is always amusing. And he fences rather well, too.'

When the duke moved away, Julian said, 'I hope Leo *wants* to be a famous artist.'

'Well, if he's going to be an artist at all, famous is probably better than starving in a garret.' And quickly before they could be interrupted, 'I want a favour, Julian – and I'm hoping you'll have some idea of how it can be managed.'

A smile touched the dark green eyes. 'Go on. I'm listening.'

* * *

While the bachelor party was in full swing at Sinclairs, the ladies had gathered in Mount Street. There were many failed attempts to persuade Camilla to give away details of her wedding gown … and much discussion about Leo's portraits – not merely the one of Adam but also those that Frances and Arabella said he had painted of Max and Julian.

'The only portrait of Sebastian was done when he was eight,' sighed Cassie. 'I would love to have one of him as he is now, in … in …' She stopped. 'How would one describe it?'

'The full flower of his manhood?' suggested Arabella innocently.

Three ladies choked over their wine and Frances said, 'If I were you, I wouldn't put it to Sebastian in *quite* that way, Cassie.'

'Oh – I don't know. It would be worth it just to see his face.'

In a far corner of the room, Camilla and Vivian Rainham sat in quiet conversation.

'I gather Mr Brandon was shot by this Blane female I've heard about whilst protecting you,' said Vivian. 'That says a great deal about him.'

'And all of it true,' nodded Camilla. And with a sudden smile, 'Rainham says you will put up with black eyes and so forth but not bullet-holes.'

'I'm glad he's registered that fact. One has to draw the line somewhere, after all.'

'One does.' Camilla stared at her hands for a moment and then said abruptly, 'Uncle Hugh wants both Adam and me to remain in the Section.'

'Of course he does. From what I've heard, Mr Brandon is exceptionally well-suited to the work.' A shrewd sideways glance. 'I take it you're not sure?'

'No. What *I* do for the Section is one thing. What may be asked of Adam is quite another. He took a bullet in the arm but he might just as easily have been killed. And it's all very well Uncle saying he's never yet lost an agent but …'

'There's a first time for everything?'

'Yes. And I don't want that first time to be Adam.' She sighed. 'He'd refuse Uncle if I asked him to … but I can't do it. Aside from it not being fair, he'd be wasting his talents. On the other hand, I'm going to be worried sick if he's sent away on Section business.'

'Assignments outside London are rare,' offered Vivian. 'This recent one is the first time Gil has been required to leave town. And until now, no one has ever been shot.'

'I know. But I'm not sure I can be as – as stoical about it as Rainham says you are.'

'Stoical? He says that, does he? How little he knows.' And when Camilla stared at her, 'If he believes I accept his other life easily … if he thinks me tolerant of it, he tells me the truth.' A slight shrug. 'I prefer that to being kept in the dark … as, I imagine, would you.'

CHAPTER THIRTY-SEVEN

The wedding day dawned bright but chilly.

At Alveston House and much to Finch's disgust, the earl's valet trimmed and brushed Adam's hair, before helping him into a new suit of midnight blue brocade, tastefully embroidered in pearl-grey. Then his brothers arrived to banish the slight queasiness in his stomach with a stream of cheerful insults and a good deal of unwanted advice.

In Mount Street, Arabella, Cassie and Frances were unanimous in voting the wedding gown a triumph. Made of silver-green shot silk the exact shade of Camilla's eyes and trimmed with intricately braided dark green and silver ribbons in places guaranteed to engage masculine attention, the colours of the gown shifted and changed with every movement. Elbow-length sleeves dripped cobweb-fine silver lace; and the décolletage was just low enough to reveal a shadowy hint of cleavage.

'Adam will be drooling,' declared Frances, as the three ladies watched Martha carefully setting a delicate pearl tiara in Camilla's dark hair. 'And I doubt he'll be the only one.'

'He won't,' agreed Cassie. 'That dress is truly *evil*, Camilla. I think I might hate you. However, to business. Martha – it's time for you to leave. Between three married ladies and a soon-to-be-bride, the conversation is about to become unsuitable for innocent ears.'

Martha giggled, bobbed a curtsy and fled.

'You might have told her something useful.' Arabella perched on the window seat, calmly spreading her dark rose skirts about her. 'Such as how to recognise when she's *really* not wanted, for example.'

'I think she already knows that,' muttered Camilla. 'But if you were planning on giving the kind of talk I had to suffer last night from Grandmama, you need not. I've known what goes where – that is to say, how the marital act is performed – for years.'

All three ladies stared at her open-mouthed.

'No! I don't mean *that*,' she said, belatedly realising what they were thinking and feeling her face get hot. 'I read a *book*, for heaven's sake! On *anatomy*.'

'A book,' said Cassie pityingly. And to the others, 'She doesn't know anything, really.'

Camilla kept her lips pressed together and, finding her fan, used it.

All three of them looked at her and then at each other.

'What do you suppose it is that she's not telling us?' asked Arabella.

'There's definitely something,' mused Frances.

'There isn't!' Camilla snapped the fan shut. 'Will you all please *stop*?'

'Very well,' said Cassie amenably. 'But just to be clear ... you and Adam haven't ...?'

'No. We haven't.' And then not quite under her breath, 'Not what you mean, anyway.'

For a few moments, three pairs of eyes examined her in thoughtful silence. Then Cassie said gently, 'How does she *know* what I mean?'

'You heard her,' grinned Arabella. 'She read a book.'

* * *

By the time Adam and Max arrived at St George's the church was already beginning to fill up with wedding guests and a procession of carriages was bringing others. A small group of gentlemen were chatting on the steps outside, from which Sir Vincent Clive broke away to shake Adam's hand, saying, 'So ... the hero returns. How is the arm?'

'As good as new, thank you,' replied Adam, wishing Vincent had kept his mouth shut.

Two steps inside the door, Max said, 'What's wrong with your arm?'

'Nothing.' Then, knowing that his brother wouldn't let it go, 'I was shot.'

Max's gaze snapped to his face. '*What*?'

'It was almost a month ago and the bullet went straight through so --'

'Oh *good*,' said Max sarcastically. 'And when were you going to mention this?'

'I wasn't – and I'm still not.' Adam continued walking down the aisle, smiling and nodding to people as he went. 'If you really want to know, ask Rainham. He'll give you the bare bones. In fact, he'll *enjoy* doing so.'

They reached the front and stood to exchange a few words with Louisa, Frances, Leo and Julian in the pew behind. Arabella, of course, was to arrive with Camilla.

As he and Adam took their seats, Max said quietly, 'One last question. How much of what you were doing on Romney Marsh can you talk about?'

'Very little. The matter is still under investigation at Whitehall.'

'Bloody hell,' muttered Max. 'Is Camilla involved in it as well?'

'Yes. And I thought you said *one* last question?'

Watching Adam lift a hand towards his throat and then restore it to his lap, knuckles glowing white, Max relented and grinned slightly. 'Cravat too tight, is it?'

Adam cast him a dirty look and declined to answer.

It was some ten minutes later when sounds from the back of the church had heads turning for a first glimpse of the bride. The organ burst into something loud and stately, everyone stood ... and Adam swivelled to gaze back down the aisle, aware that his heart was thundering as if he'd run a mile or so. Then Camilla was walking towards him wearing a gown that shimmered in the light, one hand resting on Alveston's arm and her face lit by a radiant smile. Adam took a half-step towards her only to be checked by a low chuckle and Max's restraining hand on his shoulder.

Throughout that seemingly endless walk, her eyes never left his. And when she finally reached his side, he was unable to resist taking her fingers in his and bowing to kiss them – which sent quiet laughter rippling through the congregation.

'Dearly beloved,' began the reverend reprovingly. 'We are gathered here together ...'

Afterwards, Camilla would wonder why the only things she remembered about the wedding ceremony were Adam's unconventional greeting at the altar and the expression in his eyes as they exchanged their vows. Everything else was muted, like quiet music played in the background. And almost before she knew it, she was walking back down the aisle between row upon row of smiling faces, her body pressed close against Adam's side.

Outside, a small crowd had gathered to gawk at the bride and groom. Someone began a ragged chorus of huzzahs and a couple of folk threw handfuls of rice; Adam laughed, kissed her hard on the mouth to a mixture of whistles and clapping, then grabbed her hand to run down the steps and into the safety of the carriage.

Camilla looked at him and, raising a hand to touch his cheek, said simply, 'I love you.'

'And I you, sweetheart – more than I can say.' And careless of their audience outside the windows, he pulled her into his arms for a longer, luxurious kiss … which was cut rudely short when the carriage began moving to the noisy accompaniment of the pots and pans someone had tied to the rear. He grinned and, for the first time, let his gaze stray below her face. One glimpse of the inviting décolletage of her gown caused his lungs to malfunction. He said unevenly, 'May I observe, *Mrs* Brandon, that you are looking particularly ravishable today?'

'The word,' she tutted, 'is ravishing.'

'It can't be. Clearly, since *I'll* be the one doing the ravishing, you must be ravishable,' he said reasonably. 'What do you think?'

'I think, *Mr* Brandon, that it's just as well it isn't far to Alveston House.'

* * *

The elaborate wedding breakfast had been laid out in the ballroom amidst huge tubs of flowers and greenery while, behind a latticed screen at the far end of the room, a small chamber orchestra played softly. One delicious dish followed another, glasses were filled and re-filled and the air was full of talk and laughter. But eventually it was time for the speeches. Lord Alveston formally welcomed Adam to the family and proposed a toast to the newly-wedded pair … and Max responded in a similar vein but managed to include several jokes at Adam's expense.

'Perhaps I really *will* kill him one day,' muttered Adam.

'Of course you will.' Camilla patted his hand. 'And between now and then, God help anyone who raises a hand to him. But if you feel like having your revenge, now is your chance.' She waved a hand at the room. 'Everybody is waiting with bated breath.'

Groaning inwardly, he rose, smiled and began by thanking Lord Alveston for his good wishes and for hosting such a magnificent wedding breakfast. Next, he thanked the guests for *'sharing this happy and very special day with my wife and I,'* ... which naturally won him a round of applause.

'I *would* thank my brother for standing up with me today if he hadn't made me want to hide under the table,' he went on. And when the inevitable laughter died away, voice and expression becoming utterly serious, 'Most of all, I want to thank this lovely and extraordinary lady for agreeing to be my wife. Quite frankly, I didn't think I stood a chance ... but she said yes and here we are.' He reached for Camilla's hand and smiled down at her. 'Always know that you have made me the happiest man alive – and the luckiest. But since words aren't exactly my *forte* ... and before my brothers start ribbing me for managing to utter more than two consecutive sentences ... I've enlisted help. This is for you, my love.'

And as the footmen began silently removing the screens, from behind them poured the sound of a harpsichord ... and the shining beauty of Mozart under the magic hands of the Virtuoso Earl.

* * *

Some hours later, alone in Mount Street except for the servants, Adam swept his bride up in his arms and carried her into the suite of rooms that had been prepared for them. Lady Martindale, he had been delighted to learn, would be spending the next three nights at Alveston House. Closing the door with his foot, he let Camilla slide slowly down until her feet touched the floor, then captured her mouth with his.

'At last,' he breathed gratefully.

'Yes,' she replied between kisses. 'At last.'

'Please tell me Martha won't be popping in here at any minute.'

'She won't come unless I ring.'

'Good. You won't need her.' He nipped playfully at her jaw, before lifting his head to smile at her. 'I can help you out of your clothes well enough.'

Disengaging herself, Camilla danced backwards into the room.

'And into them?'

'If necessary.' He took a couple of slow, lazy steps towards her. 'But it won't be.'

'Oh.' That predatory prowl, coupled with the heat in his eyes caused something deep inside her to coil and sizzle. She retreated a bit further. 'Why not?'

Adam followed, his gaze locked with hers. 'I want you all to myself for a time. So the only point of putting clothes on would be to give me the task of taking them off again.' He paused, watching her back across the sitting-room until she stood in the bedchamber doorway. Then, advancing again, his voice a little deeper and rougher than before, he added, 'Not that I'd mind. The gown you are wearing is an invitation to sin ... one I'm going to enjoy accepting.'

Tiny sparks pulsed in Camilla's veins and her breath had become light and shallow. She wasn't sure how he'd managed to make her want him with just a sultry look and a few words ... but it tempted her to prolong the moment. Three backward steps took her into the bedroom; three more of his had him leaning against the door jamb, watching her out of hungry dark eyes. Wanting to tease him a little, she said, 'And do *I* get an invitation?'

'No. You get a promise.' Suddenly he was inside the room with the door closed behind him. 'Whatever you want. *Everything* you want. But let's begin with this.'

And then his arm was about her waist, pulling her to him and his mouth was brushing hers. Camilla grasped his shoulders, wanting him closer ... but instead of staying to kiss her, his lips forged a leisurely trail across her cheek and jaw. Her head fell back exposing her throat, so he kissed that as well before taking her mouth again ... this time, deeply and with undisguised passion. She surrendered to him, all heat and sweetness and promise; and, distantly aware that his fingers were busy with the fastenings of her gown, she reciprocated by shoving blindly at his coat.

Adam released her for the seconds it took to shrug the coat off and toss it aside. Before it hit the floor, she was already at work on the buttons of his vest. On a shaky laugh, he said, 'Slow down, sweetheart. If you want me to strip for you --'

'I do. You promised.'

His heart gave a single heavy thud and his arousal spiralled.

'And I'll keep my promise. But all in good time.'

'You always say that,' she grumbled, still fumbling with the buttons. 'I want ... I want ...'

'I know. So do I.' Sweeping her hands aside, he finished the job and sent the vest in the wake of his coat. 'Now be still for a moment and let me.'

Entirely without haste, between random butterfly kisses and despite the slight unsteadiness of his hands, he finished unfastening and removing both gown and petticoats. Then he set about unlacing her stays.

Throughout all of this, Camilla somehow managed to explore the lines of his torso. He felt wonderful ... even more wonderful than she'd expected. But it wasn't enough so she tugged his shirt free of his breeches and slid her hands beneath it. Yes. *This* was what she'd wanted. Hot, firm skin over neatly-tailored muscles. She drew a sobbing breath and whispered, 'Take it off. Now. Please.'

Adam stepped back, shaking his head and simply staring at her, clad in nothing but her shift, stockings and pretty green slippers. All pearly-pink skin and luscious curves ... all of it even lovelier than the imaginings which had kept him awake at night. If there was a more erotic sight than this, he couldn't imagine it. He said unevenly, 'In a moment. In just a ... moment. First ... your hair.'

She made a small annoyed sound and nuzzled his throat while her fingers roved up and down his spine, sending a small tremor through him and causing him to send hairpins flying carelessly in all directions. And when her hair fell down around her shoulders, he plunged his hands into its soft, cool mass and possessed her mouth once more. Then, not waiting for her to ask again, he pulled the shirt over his head and let it fall.

'Satisfied?' he murmured.

'For now,' she replied, palms mapping his chest. 'I've wanted to do this since that day at Audley Court.'

'And I've wanted to do *this* …' One hand traced the downward curve of her back while the other cupped her breast over the thin lawn of her shift, both of which turned his last three words into a groan, '… for rather longer.'

Camilla pressed closer. Parts of her were melting. She wanted the rest of their clothing gone. She wanted something for which she had no name other than his. 'Adam …?'

'Yes, love.' In one smooth motion, he disposed of her shift and lifted her on to the bed. Then, taking his time about it, he knelt to roll down her stockings.

In some far off corner of Camilla's brain was the knowledge that she was naked and surprise that she wasn't embarrassed. But it was a *very* far off corner … and her body was drowning in powerful new sensations; and Adam … Adam was removing the rest of his own clothes to stand perfectly still for a moment so that she might look if she chose.

If she chose? Of *course* she did, absorbing lean hips and long, well-muscled legs. And …'My goodness! Those illustrations weren't *remotely* accurate!'

The unwary words were out before she could stop them.

Caught with one knee on the bed, Adam blinked and froze. 'Illustrations?'

A hand gestured vaguely towards the part of him that held her gaze transfixed.

'In the anatomy book. The p-proportions were all wrong.'

If Adam hadn't been aroused to a point very close to pain, he might have laughed. As it was, he moved onwards until his skin met hers and, when she gasped with the pleasure of it, managed to say, 'To the book's detriment rather than mine, I hope. But can we please talk about that later?'

She made a strangled sound that he took to mean 'yes'.

'Thank God.'

After that, there was no room for thought … no room for anything but the delicious slide of flesh against flesh. His mouth on her … her hands on him; every touch, every kiss … all fuelled by heat and hunger and instinct. His own desire held in an iron grip, Adam slowly unlocked the secrets of her body. He'd tortured himself imagining this in meticulous detail but the reality of it was beyond any dream. Everything felt new … as if he'd never touched a woman before. As if *her* first time was his, also.

With every new caress, the fires inside Camilla blazed ever higher until it seemed that her bones had been consumed, leaving only sensation behind. She couldn't stay still.

'Adam … oh. What … I … *oh*. D-Don't stop.'

He had no intention of stopping – wasn't sure he could have done so if the world had been coming to an end. There was only this; only *her*. He fed her arousal until every part of her was telling him that she wanted him as much as he wanted her. Only then did he finally and with infinite care join their bodies … and, summoning the last reserves of his control, ensured her pleasure before taking his own.

* * *

Camilla awoke still tangled in Adam's arms. Wondering if he was still asleep, she cautiously tilted her head to look at him but, before she got to his face, he said huskily, 'Ah. Awake at last?'

'Mm.' She stretched, relishing the feel of his body against her own. 'Is it very late?'

'No.'

She yawned and wriggled a little closer. 'So we needn't get up yet?'

'Not unless you're hungry. Are you?'

'Yes.'

The hand wandering down his torso suggested that she wasn't talking about breakfast.

Adam drew in a slow breath and said casually, 'Looking for something?'

'Mm,' she said again. And a few seconds later, 'I think I've found it.'

'So you have.' He knew what that teasing hand was telling her. He said, 'A bit more like those illustrations this morning, perhaps?'

'Ye-es. Except ...' Except that she could already feel his body changing. Fascinated, she continued her exploration and tried to read his face. 'Do you like this?'

'Somewhat. Can't you tell?'

Really, Adam thought, this wasn't a conversation he'd imagined having the morning after his wedding. And that clever little hand of hers was learning fast. Soon he'd either have to stop her or do something about it. He said, 'Tell me about the anatomy book.'

'Oh – *please*!' she groaned. 'I wish I'd never mentioned the wretched thing.'

'At that precise moment, so did I.'

With a tiny laugh, she propped herself on one elbow to look into his face. The sheet slipped, providing a view that inevitably went straight to his groin and she said delightedly, 'Oh! Did *I* do that?'

'In a manner of speaking.' Reluctantly trapping her roving hand in one of his and using the other to do a little teasing of his own, he said, 'That's enough for now, unless ...'

'Unless what?'

In one lithe movement, he rolled up on to his knees and sat back on his heels to look down on her. The silver-gilt hair was loose and tousled and his smile held a hint of wickedness. He seemed in no hurry to speak ... and Camilla was content to lie against the pillows admiring him and marvelling again how perfectly comfortable he was with his own nudity.

But finally he said slowly, 'Just before we left Dragon Hall, I described a small fantasy of mine. I'm sure you recall it.'

Her pulse accelerated and that now familiar coil of heat blossomed in her body. *You won't mind me starting at your toes and taking an hour or so to kiss my way up, will you?*

'Yes. But I thought you were joking.' And when he raised one eyebrow and continued to look at her, 'Oh. You weren't?' He shook his head. 'Not even about it taking an hour?'

'Not at all. I'll need time for the numerous places I plan to linger along the way. And didn't we agree that one can never be too thorough?'

'I ... yes. I believe we did.'

'Excellent.' He slithered down until he could lift one of her feet to his mouth and tease the arch with his tongue. Then, smiling, 'If you don't like it, tell me to stop and I will.'

The fires inside her were already spreading. Trying to sound reluctant, she said, 'Oh. Well, in *that* case I suppose I might allow you to ... to proceed.'

So he did.

It took quite a long time; and some of the places he chose to linger were, to say the least of it, a revelation.

But she didn't tell him to stop.

In fact, she liked it very much indeed.

As did he.

Thank you for reading ***Under A Dark Moon***. I hope you have enjoyed it.

Reviews are valuable to both authors and potential readers. If you could spare a few moments to leave your comments on the marketplace where you purchased the book, it would be greatly appreciated.

For questions or the latest news, drop in at my website,

https://stellarileybooks.co.uk

You'll always get a reply!

Stella Riley

Printed in Great Britain
by Amazon

59614583R00261